NEXT
IN
LINE

NEXT
IN
LINE

Jeffrey Archer is one of the world's bestselling authors, with sales of over 275 million copies in 97 countries.

Famous for his discipline as a writer who works on up to fourteen drafts of each book, Jeffrey also brings a vast amount of insider knowledge to his books. Whether it's his own career in politics, his passionate interest in art, or the wealth of fascinating background detail – inspired by the extraordinary network of friends he has built over a lifetime at the heart of Britain's establishment – his novels provide a fascinating glimpse into a range of closed worlds.

A member of the House of Lords, the author is married to Dame Mary Archer, and they have two sons, two granddaughters and three grandsons. He splits his time between London, Grantchester in Cambridge, and Mallorca, where he writes the first draft of each new novel.

Jeffrey Archer

NEXT IN LINE

HarperCollins*Publishers*

HarperCollins*Publishers* Ltd
1 London Bridge Street
London SE1 9GF

www.harpercollins.co.uk

HarperCollins*Publishers*
1st Floor, Watermarque Building, Ringsend Road
Dublin 4, Ireland

First published by HarperCollins*Publishers* 2022
1

A catalogue record for this book is available from the British Library

ISBN: 978-0-00-847432-4 (HB)
ISBN: 978-0-00-847433-1 (TPB)
ISBN: 978-0-00-852618-4 (US/CA)
ISBN: 978-0-00-852323-7 (IN)

Typeset in New Caledonia LT Std by
Palimpsest Book Production Ltd, Falkirk, Stirlingshire

Printed and bound in the UK using 100% Renewable Electricity
at CPI Group (UK) Ltd

To Janet

Is this a true story?

CHAPTER 1

AN OUTRIDER FROM THE SPECIAL Escort Group swept into Scotland Yard, closely followed by a green Jaguar and an unmarked Land Rover, while two police motorcycles brought up the rear, completing the royal convoy. They all came to a halt as Big Ben chimed eleven thirty.

A close protection officer leapt out of the front seat of the Jaguar and opened the back door. The Commissioner of the Metropolitan Police, Sir Peter Imbert, stepped forward and bowed. 'Welcome to Scotland Yard, Your Royal Highness,' he said, and was greeted with that warm, shy smile with which the public had become so familiar.

'Thank you, Sir Peter,' she replied as they shook hands. 'It was kind of you to agree to my unusual request.'

'My pleasure, ma'am,' said Sir Peter, before turning to the welcoming party of senior officers who were waiting in line. 'May I present the Deputy Commissioner . . .'

The Princess shook hands with each of the officers in turn until she reached the end of the line, when she was

1

introduced to the head of the Met's murder investigation teams.

'Commander Hawksby is known as "Murder One",' the Commissioner told her. 'And Chief Inspector William Warwick will act as your guide this morning,' he added as a little girl stepped forward, curtsied and offered the Princess a small bouquet of pink roses. She received the broadest smile of all.

The Princess bent down and said, 'Thank you, and what is your name?'

'Artemisia,' the bowed head whispered to the ground.

'What a pretty name,' said the Princess.

She was about to move on when Artemisia looked up and said, 'Why aren't you wearing a crown?'

William turned bright red, while his number two, Inspector Ross Hogan, stifled a laugh, causing Artemisia to burst into tears. The Princess leant down again, took the little girl in her arms and said, 'Because I'm not a Queen, Artemisia, just a Princess.'

'But you will be the Queen one day.'

'Then I'll wear a crown.'

This seemed to satisfy Artemisia, who smiled as her father led the Met's royal guest into the building.

The door was held open by a young cadet, who the Princess stopped to have a word with, before William guided her towards a waiting lift. A long discussion had taken place prior to the Princess's visit, as to whether she should walk up the stairs to the first floor or take the lift. The lift had won by five votes to four. An equally fraught decision was who should accompany her in the lift. The Commissioner, Commander Hawksby and William made the shortlist, while the Princess's lady-in-waiting would take the second lift, along with Inspector Ross Hogan and Detective Sergeant Roycroft.

William had his script well prepared, but was immediately thrown off course by HRH's first question.

'Is Artemisia your daughter, by any chance?'

'Yes, ma'am,' said William, remembering that the Hawk had told him that 'ma'am' had to rhyme with 'spam', not 'harm'. 'But what evidence do you have?' he asked, forgetting for a moment that he wasn't addressing one of his junior officers.

'If she hadn't been your daughter, you wouldn't have blushed,' came back the reply as they stepped into the lift.

'I did tell her not to speak to you,' said William, 'and certainly not to ask you any questions.'

'The fact she disobeyed you probably means she'll be the most interesting person I'll meet today,' whispered Diana as the lift doors closed. 'Why did you call her Artemisia?'

'She's named after Artemisia Gentileschi, the great Italian Baroque painter.'

'So, you must have a love of art?'

'A passion, ma'am. But it was my wife Beth, who's keeper of pictures at the Fitzmolean, who chose the name.'

'Then I'll have another chance to meet your daughter,' said the Princess, 'because if I remember correctly, I'm opening the Fitzmolean's Frans Hals exhibition next year. I'd better make sure I'm wearing at least a coronet if I'm not to be told off again,' she added as the lift doors opened on the first floor.

'The Crime Museum, ma'am,' began William, returning to his script, 'more commonly known as the Black Museum, was the brainchild of an Inspector Neame, who in 1869 felt it would assist his colleagues to solve and even prevent crimes if they could study well-known cases. He was assisted by a Constable Randall, who gathered together material from various notorious criminals and crime scenes, which made up the first exhibits in this rogues' gallery. The museum opened five years later, in April 1874, but it still remains closed to the public.'

William glanced back to see Ross Hogan, chatting to the Princess's lady-in-waiting. He led his guest down a long corridor towards room 101, where another door was being held open for the royal visitor. William found himself wondering if the Princess ever opened a door for herself, but quickly dismissed the thought and returned to his script.

'I hope you won't find the museum too disturbing, ma'am. The occasional visitor has been known to faint,' he said. They entered a room whose dim lighting only added to the macabre atmosphere.

'It can't be worse than four days at Ascot,' replied the Princess, 'when I regularly want to faint.'

William wanted to laugh, but managed to prevent himself. 'The first exhibit,' he said as they approached a large glass cabinet, 'includes the early pieces of memorabilia collected by Neame and Randall.'

The Princess looked closely at a collection of weapons used by seventeenth-century criminals to murder their victims, including a walking stick that, with a twist of its knob, became a sword, along with various flick knives, heavy wooden cudgels and knuckle-dusters. William quickly moved on to the next cabinet, which was dedicated to Jack the Ripper, and included a handwritten letter he'd sent to the London Central News Agency in 1888 at the height of his serial killings, taunting the police by predicting they would never catch him. But then, as William reminded his guest, that was before the Met had begun to use finger-printing to identify criminals, and more than a century before the discovery of DNA.

'I haven't fainted yet,' said the Princess as they moved on to the next cabinet, which contained a pair of antique binoculars. 'What's so special about them?' she asked.

'They weren't designed for Ascot, ma'am,' said William. 'They were a gift from a particularly unpleasant individual to his fiancée a few days after she had jilted him. When she held them up to her eyes and adjusted the focus, two nails shot out and blinded her. At his trial the accused was asked by prosecuting counsel why he'd done such an evil thing, and he simply replied, "I didn't want her to look at another man ever again."'

Diana covered her eyes and William quickly moved on.

'This next exhibit, ma'am, is particularly fascinating,' said William, pointing to a small, plain metal box. 'It provided the vital clue in the first case solved by the Met using fingerprints as evidence. In 1905 the brothers Alfred and Albert Stratton were arrested for the murder of a shop owner, Thomas Farrow, and his wife, Ann. They would have got away with it if Alfred hadn't left a single thumb print on the empty cash box. They were both found guilty and hanged.'

They moved on to the next cabinet, where the Princess glanced briefly at a photograph before turning to William and saying, 'Tell me about him.'

'On the eighteenth of February, 1949, John Haigh killed Olive Durand-Deacon, a wealthy widow, while she was visiting his engineering workshop in Crawley. After Haigh had removed everything of value she had with her, he dissolved her body in a drum of sulphuric acid, believing that if the police were unable to produce a body, he couldn't be charged with murder. However, he didn't take into account the expertise of a certain Dr Keith Simpson, a pathologist who discovered three gallstones and a couple of the victim's false teeth in a pile of rubble at the back of the workshop. Haigh was arrested, convicted and hanged.'

'You do like to take a girl somewhere romantic on a first date, don't you, Chief Inspector?' said the Princess, which caused William to relax and laugh for the first time.

'Another first,' he continued as they stopped in front of the next cabinet, 'was the arrest of Dr Hawley Harvey Crippen, an American homeopath who murdered his wife Cora in London before fleeing to Brussels accompanied by his lover Ethel Le Neve. From Brussels they went on to Antwerp, where Crippen purchased two tickets on the SS *Montrose*, a steamship bound for Canada. Ethel disguised herself as a young boy, so they could pose as father and son. The captain of the vessel had been shown a wanted poster before the ship set sail, and became suspicious when he saw Crippen and Le Neve holding hands and kissing. He telegraphed Scotland Yard, and Chief Inspector Walter Dew, who was in charge of the case, immediately travelled up to Liverpool and boarded the SS *Laurentic*, a much faster vessel, which reached Montreal some time before the *Montrose*. Dew, disguised as a pilot, boarded the ship as it sailed into the St Lawrence river, arrested Crippen and Ethel, and brought them back to England to face trial. The jury only took thirty minutes to find Crippen guilty of murder.'

'So he also went to the gallows,' said the Princess cheerfully. 'But what about Ethel?'

'She was acquitted of being an accessory after the fact. However, the jury did take considerably longer reaching their decision.'

'Interesting how it's so often the women who end up getting away with it,' said the Princess as they moved into the next room, which didn't look any more inviting than the previous one.

'You will now get to meet some well-known East End gang-sters,' declared William. 'I'll start with the most notorious of them all, the Kray brothers, Reggie and Ronnie.'

'Even I've heard of them,' said the Princess, standing in front of black and white mugshots of the notorious twins.

'Despite committing countless vicious crimes over many years, including murder, on more than one occasion, they proved almost impossible to charge, let alone convict, because no one was willing to come forward and testify against them, being too frightened of the consequences.'

'So how were they eventually caught?'

'The police finally arrested them after Reggie murdered a criminal associate called Jack the Hat McVitie in 1967. The Krays were both sentenced to life imprisonment.'

'And the person who gave evidence?' asked the Princess.

'Didn't celebrate his next birthday, ma'am.'

'I'm still standing, Chief Inspector,' teased the Princess as they moved into the next room, where she was greeted with a display of jute ropes of different lengths and thicknesses.

'Up until the nineteenth century, large crowds would gather at Tyburn to witness public hangings,' said the Commissioner, who was following close behind. 'This barbaric form of enter-tainment ceased in 1868, after which executions were carried out behind prison walls with no members of the public present.'

'As a young officer, Sir Peter, did you ever witness a hanging?' asked the Princess.

'Just one, ma'am, and thank God, never again.'

'Remind me,' said the Princess, turning back to William, 'who was the last woman to be hanged?'

'You're one step ahead of me, ma'am,' said William, moving on to the next cabinet. 'Ruth Ellis, a nightclub hostess, was hanged on the thirteenth of July, 1955, after she shot her lover with a Smith and Wesson .38 revolver, which you can see here.'

'And the last man?' asked the Princess, staring at the gun.

William racked his brain, as that hadn't been part of his prepared script. He turned to the Commissioner, but he didn't respond.

They were rescued by the museum's curator, who stepped forward and said, 'Gwynne Evans and Peter Allen, ma'am, were hanged for the murder of John Alan West on the thirteenth of August, 1964. The following year, a private member's bill to abolish hanging became law. However, it may interest you to know, ma'am, you can still be hanged for treason, or piracy with violence.'

'I think treason is more likely in my case,' said the Princess, which caused them all to laugh.

William guided his guest through to the last room on the tour, where she was introduced to a row of bottles containing various poisons. William explained that was a woman's preferred means of committing murder, particularly of their husbands. William regretted the words the moment he'd uttered them.

'And that, ma'am, brings us to the end of the tour. I hope you found it—' He hesitated, before replacing the word 'enjoyable' with 'interesting'.

'Fascinating, Chief Inspector, would be a better description of the past hour,' replied the Princess as William accompanied her out of the museum.

They walked back down the long corridor towards the lift, passing a lavatory that had been specially set aside for the royal visitor. Two young policewomen were in attendance, but they hadn't been required. They were disappointed. She sensed it, and stopped to chat to them, before moving on.

'I look forward to seeing you again, Chief Inspector, and to meeting your wife when I open the Frans Hals exhibition,' said the Princess as she stepped into the lift. 'That should at least prove a jollier occasion.'

William managed a smile.

When the lift doors opened on the ground floor, the Commissioner took over once again, accompanying his royal guest to the waiting car, where her close protection officer was holding the back door open. The Princess stopped to wave at the crowd that had gathered on the far side of the road.

'I noticed you didn't waste much time before chatting up her lady-in-waiting,' said William, when Inspector Hogan joined him.

'I think,' said Ross without missing a beat, 'I'm in with a chance.'

'Punching above your weight, I would have thought,' came back William.

'It never worried you,' said Ross with a grin.

'Touché,' said William, giving his friend a slight bow.

'The Lady Victoria told me that the Princess's close protection officer is retiring at the end of the year, and they haven't found a replacement yet. So, I was hoping you might put in a good word for me.'

'Which word did you have in mind?' asked William. 'Unreliable? Louche? Promiscuous?'

'I think that's pretty much what she's looking for,' said Ross, as the lady-in-waiting climbed into the back of the car ahead of the Princess.

'I'll think about it,' said William.

'Is that all you can say after all I've done for you over the years?'

William tried not to laugh when he recalled how their

most recent escapade had ended. He and Ross had only just got back from Spain, where they had been on the trail of Miles Faulkner. They had finally caught up with their old nemesis in Barcelona and dragged him back to Belmarsh prison – the same prison Faulkner had escaped from the year before. Triumphant as William and Ross felt, they were aware of the inevitable consequences they were certain to face, *after having broken every rule in the book*, to quote the commander. William reminded his boss that there *were* no rules in Miles Faulkner's book, and if they hadn't broken the odd rule, he would surely have escaped their clutches yet again.

Two wrongs don't make a right, the commander had reminded them.

But how long could they hope to keep Faulkner locked up, wondered William, when his corrupt lawyer was only too happy to bend those same rules to breaking point if it would guarantee his 'distinguished client' would get off all the charges and be released from prison without a stain on his character? They also accepted that Mr Booth Watson QC wouldn't be satisfied until William and Ross were made to face a disciplinary hearing, before being ignominiously dismissed from the force for unacceptable behaviour while serving as police officers. William had already warned his wife that the next few months weren't going to be plain sailing.

'What's new?' Beth had reminded him, before adding that she wouldn't be satisfied until Booth Watson was behind bars with his 'distinguished client', where they both belonged.

William snapped back into the present when HRH climbed into the back of the car and the police outriders revved up and led the royal cortège out of Scotland Yard and on to Victoria Street.

The Princess waved to the crowd from her car, and they all responded except for Ross, who was still smiling at her lady-in-waiting.

'Your trouble, Ross, is that your balls are bigger than your brain,' said William as the convoy made its way slowly out of New Scotland Yard.

'Makes for a far more interesting life,' responded Ross.

Once the Princess's convoy had disappeared from sight, the Commissioner and the Hawk walked across to join them.

'Good idea of yours,' said Sir Peter, 'to have two young officers showing our guests around the museum, rather than us old fogeys. Especially as one of them had so obviously done his homework.'

'Thank you, sir,' said Ross, which elicited a wry smile from the commander.

'In fact, I think Warwick's earned the rest of the day off,' suggested Sir Peter, before leaving them to return to his office.

'Not a hope,' murmured the Hawk, once the Commissioner was out of earshot. 'In fact, I want to see you both in my office along with the rest of the team, soonest – and soonest means now.'

CHAPTER 2

THE COMMANDER TOOK HIS PLACE at the top of the table, joining his inner team – a unit that had taken him five years to build, and was now acknowledged to be among the finest in the Yard. But their coup de grâce was surely catching up with Miles Faulkner in Spain after he'd escaped from custody and finally bringing him back to England to face trial.

However, the Hawk could only wonder how many of his team would be called on to give evidence in that particular case. William and Ross would have to face cross-examination from Faulkner's no-holds-barred counsel. Booth Watson wouldn't hesitate to let the jury know that two of the Met's most experienced officers had seized his client illegally during a trip to Barcelona. The Hawk still had one ace up his sleeve though – he knew something about Booth Watson that a leading QC wouldn't want the Bar Council to find out about – but it would still be a close-run thing.

The Hawk thought of the officers seated around that table more as family than colleagues, but then he had no children of his own. However, like all families, they had their problems and differences, and he wondered how they would react to what he was about to tell them.

Detective Chief Inspector Warwick may have been the youngest DCI in the Met, but no one referred to him as 'Choirboy' any longer, with the possible exception of DI Ross Hogan, who was sitting opposite him. Ross was undoubtedly the black sheep of the family, a maverick who was more interested in locking up criminals than filling in endless forms, and who had survived his frequent run-ins with superior officers only because the Hawk considered him the finest undercover operative he'd ever worked with.

On Hogan's right sat DS Roycroft, one of Ross's many former lovers, who was probably the bravest officer sitting around that table. As a junior PC just out of Hendon, Jackie had tackled a six-foot-six Algerian arms dealer and had him flat on the ground and handcuffed before the next officer arrived on the scene. But she was possibly better known among her colleagues for having knocked out an Inspector who had placed a hand on her leg while on duty. No one came to her defence when she reported the incident, as the Inspector in question was the only witness. And after that her career prospects had come to an abrupt halt, until the commander had spotted her potential and asked her to join his team.

Opposite her sat DS Adaja. Bright, resourceful and ambitious, he had handled any racial prejudice inside and outside the force with dignity and grace. The Hawk didn't doubt that Paul would be the first black man to make commander. And what amused him was that Paul didn't doubt it either.

Finally, DC Pankhurst, the youngest member of the team, who never mentioned her public-school upbringing, or first-class honours degree, and certainly not that one of her most famous ancestors had been to jail – more than once. Rebecca was possibly the cleverest officer sitting around that table, and the commander had already decided it wouldn't be too long before she was promoted, though he hadn't told her yet.

The trouble with commanding such a bright and energetic group was that you had to get up early – very early – in the morning if you hoped to stay a yard ahead of them. But on this occasion, the commander felt confident he was up and running before their alarms had gone off.

'Let me begin,' he said, 'by congratulating you all on the roles you played in solving the cold murder cases that the Assistant Commissioner asked us to deal with. However, that is now in the past, and we must look to the future.' He glanced up to find he had everyone's attention.

'The Commissioner, in his wisdom, has decided to take the unit off murder, and to present us with an even greater challenge.' He made them wait, but only for a moment. 'Royalty Protection Command,' he allowed the words to hang in the air, 'have become, in the Commissioner's opinion, a law unto themselves. Their commanding officer, one Superintendent Brian Milner, is under the illusion that his unit is untouchable, answerable to no one other than the Royal Family, and therefore no longer a part of the Metropolitan Police Service. We're about to disabuse them of that notion. For some time, Milner hasn't bothered to interview outside candidates whenever one of his officers moves on or retires. That way, he never loses control of the unit, which is a problem in itself, because following the recent terrorist attacks around the world, MI6 have been in touch to warn us that the next target could well be a member of the Royal Family, who they feel are all too often an easy target. And that includes the Queen.'

This silenced everyone for a few moments, before Paul

asked, 'And where do MI6 think such an attack would come from?'

'Probably the Middle East,' said the Hawk. 'Counter Terrorism are keeping a close eye on anyone coming into the country from Iran, Iraq or Libya, to name the three most obvious candidates. Assistant Commissioner Harry Holbrooke didn't leave me in any doubt what we're up against. He named the three terrorist organizations who are on his watchlist and pose an immediate threat.'

Everyone around the table continued to make notes.

'Holbrooke doesn't think they'll leave the safety of their own countries, but has no doubt all three of them will have placed several sleeper cells around the UK who can be ready to move at a moment's notice. He's already set up surveillance teams to keep a close eye on a dozen or more of the most obvious candidates, but admits he doesn't have enough foot soldiers to watch them all as his resources are stretched to the limit. With that in mind, he's asked us to share whatever intel we come across, however insignificant we might consider it at the time.'

'Cops and robbers are certainly a thing of the past,' said Ross with some feeling.

'The dim and distant past,' said the Hawk. 'And it doesn't help that Holbrooke, among others, has lost confidence in Superintendent Milner as head of Royalty Protection, and wants him replaced as quickly as possible.'

'For any particular reason?' asked Ross.

'Yes – when he phoned him at Buckingham Gate and left a message asking him to get in touch urgently, Milner didn't bother to respond until a week later. And after Holbrooke had fully briefed him on the latest terrorist threat, all Milner had to say on the subject was, and I quote, "Don't worry yourself, old chap, we've got it all under control."'

'Which prompts me to ask, sir,' said Jackie, looking up from her notebook, 'is the fact the Commissioner doesn't think Milner is up to the job the only reason we're all being assigned to Royalty Protection?'

Commander Hawksby remained silent for some time, before saying, 'No, it isn't. In fact, even Holbrooke doesn't know the full story, because I still consider it an internal matter.' He closed the file in front of him and added, 'Stop writing,' which they all obeyed without question. 'The Commissioner also has reason to believe that Milner and some of his inner circle are bent, not least because he appears to be living the life of a minor royal on the salary of a Superintendent. And if that turns out to be the case, we are going to need incontrovertible proof of what he's been up to for the past decade before we can even think about arresting him. Not least because, stating the obvious, he has friends in high places, some of whom he's worked with for several years. With that in mind, Milner will be getting four new recruits joining him in the near future, but they won't include Ross Hogan, who will be reporting directly back to me.'

'Am I going undercover again?' asked Ross.

'No,' said the Hawk. 'In fact you couldn't be more out in the open,' he added without explanation.

No one else asked the obvious question, or interrupted while the boss was in full flow.

'DCI Warwick will be joining Royalty Protection as Superintendent Milner's second-in-command, but not until the rest of you are all fully up to speed with the problems you'll be up against, which could take at least a couple of months. And remember, we don't want Milner to find out what we're up to. So make sure you don't express any opinions to other colleagues outside of this room. We can't afford to give that man the slightest opportunity to cover his tracks before we even turn up. DCI Warwick will be given considerable latitude to root out any other officers who consider themselves above the law, while at the same time trying to find out if they take the terrorist threat at all seriously.'

The commander turned to William. 'The first problem you may encounter will be Milner himself. If the biggest apple in the barrel is rotten, what hope is there for the seedlings? Don't forget that Milner has been in command of the unit for over a decade, and considers the only person he has to answer to is Her Majesty the Queen. You'll have to tread carefully if you're going to stick around long enough to find out how he's getting away with it,' the Hawk added, handing over the baton to the one person at the table who had already been fully briefed.

'During the next few weeks,' said William, 'I want you all to carry out some in-depth research on how the Royal Family go about their public duties, while at the same time assuming you've never heard of them. Start with a clean sheet and treat them as if they are all criminals who need to be investigated.'

'That should be fun,' said Jackie.

'You can start by booking a tour of Windsor Castle on an open day when no members of the Royal Family are in residence. Your single purpose is to get the lie of the land while at the same time checking security. I want you all to be a yard ahead, not a yard behind, by the time you report for your first day as Royalty Protection officers.'

'Any bets against me getting into the castle unnoticed?' said Ross.

'Don't even think about it,' said the Hawk. 'You're in enough trouble as it is. But if you should bump into any recently

17

retired protection officers, you're free to go on a fishing expedition. Just make sure you don't end up as the bait, because if you do, you can be certain their next call will be to Milner, and you'll have to be taken off the case.'

'However,' said William, 'when we do eventually report for duty, you can expect to be ignored, insulted, even ridiculed, by officers who don't realize they may not be there in a few months' time. But try to remember they won't all be corrupt; some may well feel the same way about Milner as the Commissioner does, while I fear others will be beyond redemption. Team meetings will continue to take place here at the Yard every morning between eight and ten, when we can share our latest findings, and hopefully find out exactly what we're up against, even before we turn up. Any questions?'

'You didn't mention what role I'd be playing,' said DI Hogan, trying to look offended.

'That will depend on whether she offers you the job.'

'She?' said Ross.

'Her Royal Highness, the Princess of Wales,' said William, turning to face his old friend, 'has requested we join her for tea at Kensington Palace at three o'clock tomorrow afternoon.'

Ross was silenced for a moment, unsure if this was William's idea of a joke.

'Sadly, I can't make it,' he ventured casually. 'I have a more pressing engagement tomorrow afternoon. I need to get my hair cut.'

The rest of the team waited for the Hawk's response.

'The only pressing engagement you'll have tomorrow afternoon, Inspector, should you fail to turn up at Kensington Palace on time, will be at the Tower of London, where you'll find I've put DCI Warwick in charge of torture. DS Roycroft will operate the rack, and DS Adaja the thumb screws, while DC Pankhurst will have the difficult task of finding a large enough block to put your head on. And you needn't ask who the executioner will be. Any more frivolous questions, DI Hogan?'

This time the laughter was supplanted by even louder banging on the table. After it had died down, William was the first to speak.

'You can all have the rest of the day off before we begin working on our new assignments. However, I'll expect you to be in my office by eight tomorrow morning for a full briefing on your individual roles. Just make sure you've read these carefully before then.' He passed each of them a thick file.

Paul glanced briefly at his file, before saying, 'Can I point out, chief, for the sake of evidential accuracy – something you've always felt strongly about – that if we all turn up at eight tomorrow morning, having read our files carefully, we won't actually have had any time off?'

'You're quite right,' said William not missing a beat. 'But should you fail to be on time and have not read all the documents, DS Adaja, we will have two Detective Constables in our ranks, and I may decide that one is surplus to—'

'I'll be on time, sir,' said Paul, picking up his file before William could complete the sentence.

'I'm glad to hear it,' said the Hawk, 'but for now, you, Jackie and Rebecca can leave us, while I have a word with DCI Warwick and DI Hogan.'

The Hawk didn't speak again until the door had closed. 'Now, as you both well know, we have an even more serious matter to discuss. Miles Faulkner is back in prison, resuming the sentence for fraud and deception he was serving before his escape, but there are going to be some very serious questions about how you got him back from Spain to Belmarsh. I assume,' he said, leaning forward and placing both elbows on the table, 'that you both have a credible explanation for the extra-curricular activities you got up to in Spain, which Mr Booth Watson will certainly describe to the jury as kidnapping and theft, not to mention a gross violation of his client's human rights?'

'Theft, sir, in legal terms, is when you take something which you have no intention of returning to its rightful owner,' said William. 'I admit to removing a Frans Hals portrait from Faulkner's home in Spain, but I immediately handed it over to its rightful owner in England. A fact that has been confirmed in writing by Faulkner's ex-wife, Christina,' he continued as he handed over a letter to the commander.

'So where is the painting now?' asked the Hawk, after he'd read the letter.

'At the Fitzmolean Museum where it will be displayed as part of their Frans Hals exhibition next year.'

'It doesn't help that your wife is the curator of that exhibition,' said the Hawk, looking directly at William.

'She and Christina have been friends for several years,' William reminded him. 'But then Beth always sees the best in people.'

'A fair-weather friend,' said the Hawk. 'Mrs Faulkner would switch sides faster than a spinning coin if it suited her purpose.' Neither officer commented. 'That doesn't alter the fact that we're still stuck with the kidnapping allegation. Would it be too much to hope you also have a credible explanation for that?'

'I saved Faulkner's life,' said Ross with some feeling. 'What more does the damn man want?'

'A get-out-of-jail-free card, I expect,' came back the Hawk's immediate reply. 'Whatever happens, the jury will want to know how and why you ended up saving Faulkner's life.'

'Faulkner somehow managed to lock himself into his own

safe, and I was the only other person who knew how to open it,' said Ross. 'In fact I got there just in time, otherwise Faulkner would sadly have died,' he added, not sounding at all sad.

'And as I'll remind the jury, Faulkner was unconscious when we opened the safe,' said William, checking his report. 'Lieutenant Sanchez of the Spanish police had to administer mouth-to-mouth resuscitation to revive him.'

The commander said, 'Booth Watson's next question will be, "Why didn't you immediately call for an ambulance?"'

Ross considered the question for a moment before he said, 'I was about to when Faulkner came around, and managed a few words. He was pretty incoherent, but he pleaded with me—'

'Insisted, would sound more convincing,' suggested the Hawk.

'He insisted on seeing his own doctor. I assumed they would be Spanish, but Faulkner told me his name was Dr Simon Redwood, and his practice was at 122 Harley Street.'

The Hawk turned to William. 'Then what happened?'

'We drove Faulkner to the airport, where his private jet was preparing for take-off.'

'How convenient,' suggested Hawksby. 'But surely the pilot asked you why you hadn't taken Faulkner to the nearest hospital? And before you answer, we should assume Booth Watson will put him in the witness box.'

'He did ask that question,' said Ross, sounding rather pleased with himself. 'And I told him I was simply carrying out Mr Faulkner's orders. I said he was welcome to express his opinion to his boss if he wanted to. But he didn't.'

'That was fortunate, wasn't it, Inspector?' said the Hawk, making no attempt to hide his sarcasm. 'However, you're still going to have to explain to the jury why, when you landed at Heathrow, you didn't take Faulkner straight to Harley Street, but had him driven to Belmarsh, London's highest security prison.'

'It was five o'clock in the morning,' said William. 'I did ring the Harley Street surgery from the car, but all I got was an answerphone saying the practice opened at nine o'clock.'

'Was the time of that call recorded?' demanded the Hawk.

'Yes, sir. At 5.07. I called back just after nine and told Dr Redwood he could visit his patient in the prison hospital at his convenience, and carry out a full examination. He did so later that morning.'

'Thank God one of you was thinking on his feet,' said the Hawk. 'However, I would suggest you both make sure you're singing from the same hymn sheet long before the case comes to court, as I can assure you that once Booth Watson returns from Spain, and has had a chance to consult his client, he'll quickly realize he has more than enough ammunition to drive a coach and horses through your evidence. You'll both have to pray that the jury accepts Ross's version of events rather than Faulkner's. Because if they find out that you seized Miles Faulkner illegally, and then dragged him back to England, you could both end up sharing a cell together.'

The phone on his desk began to ring. The Hawk grabbed it and almost shouted, 'I thought I said no calls, Angela.' He listened for a moment before saying, 'Put him through.'

CHAPTER 3

THE CAPTAIN OF FAULKNER'S YACHT felt something wasn't quite right when he double-checked their course. That same feeling had lingered ever since the beginning of the voyage, when he'd watched in disbelief as the staff from the villa had loaded all the paintings onto his yacht, before placing them in the hold. As there was no sign of the boss, he didn't lift a finger to assist them.

'Will Mr Faulkner be joining us?' he'd asked, when Booth Watson came onto the bridge.

'No,' said Booth Watson. 'He's been unexpectedly detained. But his instructions couldn't have been clearer.'

Captain Redmayne didn't believe him, as he'd never known Mr Faulkner to be parted from his art collection. He had been warned several times that if the boss wanted to leave in a hurry, he wouldn't risk going by car, or boarding his own plane, as long as there was the slightest chance of him being arrested. That was why the yacht always had to be ready to set sail at a moment's notice. So where was he? That was a question the captain didn't bother to ask Booth Watson, as he thought it unlikely he'd get an honest answer. 'So where is our next port of call?' had been his only question.

Booth Watson had already considered several alternatives, but accepted that he'd have to take the odd risk. He'd eventually said, 'Anywhere on the south coast of England where the customs officials aren't averse to receiving a bonus for not checking the cargo too carefully.'

Captain Redmayne looked uncertain, as that was not the destination Mr Faulkner had expressly told him would be their next port of call, should they have to make an unscheduled departure. He wanted to protest, but accepted he didn't have the authority to disobey the boss's representative on earth.

'I know the ideal port,' Captain Redmayne had eventually said, 'and can even give you a name. But be warned, you'll need a thousand pounds in cash if you expect a rubber stamp to land on all the right documents.'

Booth Watson had glanced at the Gladstone bag that rarely left his side. If you worked for Miles Faulkner long enough, you always carried enough cash to cover such eventualities. As they'd sailed out of the secreted inlet, he didn't once look back on the carnage he'd left behind.

When Booth Watson had arrived at Faulkner's villa the previous day, Collins the butler had told him anxiously that Miles was locked in his safe, and had been there for at least three hours. Booth Watson had concluded that Miles must surely be dead; it would be impossible to survive that long locked inside the safe, there simply wouldn't be enough air.

That was when the idea first crossed his mind. However, he had waited another hour, and only then given the order to pack up his client's legendary art collection, and store it in the yacht's hold.

He was confident that, if they could set sail before the Spanish police turned up at the villa, they would open the safe only to discover the man they had an arrest warrant for was dead. What must have been a long and painful death, thought Booth Watson, but he didn't shed a tear as he paced up and down Faulkner's study, his eyes rarely leaving the safe.

After yet another hour had crept by, he grew more confident that Miles couldn't possibly have survived. During the next hour he began to form a plan and, by the time the clock struck six, he was ready to move. He would return to England, store the paintings in a safe place, and, as he still had his client's – late client's – power of attorney, he would systematically transfer all the assets from his several banks to an off-shore account in Hong Kong that he'd set up years ago. Something else Miles had, by example, taught him.

Next, he would put all three of Miles's substantial properties up for sale and, as he wasn't in a hurry, could expect them to fetch a fair market price. He'd then get in touch with the Chinese collector who had recently approached him about buying the collection, only to be firmly rebuffed by Miles. But he would explain to Mr Lee that, due to his client's sad passing, his executor (him) would be willing to reconsider the sale of his works if the price was right. The only problem might turn out to be Miles's ex-wife Christina, who once she discovered what he'd been up to would undoubtedly demand her cut. Perhaps she would like to own a luxury yacht he would no longer have any use for?

He would then allow a few weeks to pass before letting it be known around the Inns of Court that he was thinking about retiring and, once the inquest was over, he would quietly leave the country without giving a forwarding address.

• • •

Miles Faulkner strolled into the prison canteen, unaware of what his lawyer was up to on the high seas. He was pleased to see Tulip, his old cellmate, sitting at their usual table.

'Morning, boss,' said Tulip as Miles took the seat opposite him.

A prison guard poured Miles his morning coffee, as if he'd never been away, and he took a sip before he began to read an article in the *Daily Telegraph*. The report was bad enough, but the accompanying photograph of his nemesis, DCI Warwick, sharing a joke with the Princess of Wales, only served to remind him who had been responsible for putting him back behind bars.

Tulip, Miles's eyes and ears in the jail, had tried to remove all the newspapers from the prison canteen before Miles came down to breakfast, as almost every one of them carried the same photograph on its front page.

To make matters worse, the *Telegraph*'s royal correspondent went on to describe Warwick as 'the outstanding young officer who had recently been responsible for putting the escaped felon Miles Faulkner back in prison'. The *Sun* – the most popular newspaper in every prison – had added 'where he belongs'. Miles tossed the paper aside, well aware that he was about to give the press an even bigger story. But all in good time.

'I could always arrange to have him snuffed out, boss,' said Tulip, pointing at the photo.

'No,' said Faulkner firmly. 'I intend my revenge to be more permanent.'

'What could be more permanent than death?'

'Being thrown out of the police force,' said Faulkner. 'Being charged with kidnap and theft, and having to spend the rest of your life in disgrace,' he added as a screw placed a plate of bacon and eggs in front of him. He paused. 'If we get lucky, he might even end up here.'

'Good one, boss. But how do you plan to pull that off?'

'When my trial comes up at the Bailey, I have a feeling the jury will be fascinated to learn the lengths Warwick and Hogan went to in order to smuggle me out of Spain without an extradition order. I can assure you, Booth Watson will repeat the words "bounty hunters" again and again during his opening and closing remarks.'

'Have you spoken to your brief since you were nabbed?' asked Tulip.

'No. I've phoned his office several times during the past week, but all his secretary said was he's abroad and she would let him know I'd called the moment he returns. That rather suggests he's still in Spain, wrapping up any loose ends. However, for the time being I've got an even more pressing problem to deal with.'

'What could be more pressing than preparing for your trial?'

'My ex-wife,' said Faulkner, almost spitting out the words as a guard refilled his coffee. 'God only knows what Christina will get up to now I'm out of the way.'

'My sources tell me she's spending your money like there's no tomorrow,' said Tulip. 'She regularly dines at the Ritz, shops on Bond Street while indulging a string of toyboys who keep taking her for a ride.' He looked furtively at Faulkner. 'She could end up having an unfortunate accident on her way to Bond Street?' he suggested. 'The traffic gets very busy during shopping hours, boss.'

'No,' said Faulkner firmly. 'At least not until the trial's over, if I'm going to convince the jury I'm a reformed character and was unlawfully arrested. So, for the next few months I need to be like Caesar's wife – "above suspicion".'

Tulip looked puzzled.

'However, I intend to make sure Christina ends up penniless long before the case comes to court, and Warwick will be lucky to get a job as a security guard at the Fitzmolean,' he added as he pushed his eggs and bacon to one side.

'What about Inspector Hogan?'

'You can dispose of him as and when you please. But be sure to make it memorable,' said Miles, once again looking at the front page of the *Telegraph*. 'As I plan to end up with more than a shelf in the Black Museum.'

• • •

'That was Lieutenant Sanchez of the Barcelona police,' said the Hawk as he put down the phone. 'He said Booth Watson boarded Faulkner's yacht soon after his men had turned up.'

'Interesting,' said William. 'Where's the yacht heading?'

'It was last seen rounding the Bay of Biscay – Interpol have kept a close eye on it.'

'So Booth Watson must be on his way back to England, under the illusion that his client was still locked up in the safe when he left, and couldn't possibly have survived.'

'You could be right, William, because Sanchez also said the only thing left hanging on the walls were the hooks, so he must have removed all the paintings.'

'In which case, sir, may I suggest we alert the coastguard to keep a look out for him, so we can be waiting on the dockside long before he enters territorial waters.'

'Good thinking,' said the Hawk as he picked up the phone.

• • •

'Mrs Christina Faulkner is on line one, Sir Julian,' said his secretary.

'Put her through,' her lawyer said reluctantly. Although he didn't care much for Mrs Faulkner, he always enjoyed their encounters. She'd made life difficult for his son over the years, and he knew William was concerned about Christina's friendship with his wife Beth, but she was like a good novel, and you could never be sure how it would end – the twists came when you least expected them.

'Good morning, Mrs Faulkner,' he said, 'how can I be of assistance?'

'My ex-husband is back in jail, Sir Julian, as I feel sure you already know.'

'I had heard as much.'

'What you may not know is that his yacht is heading for England with Mr Booth Watson aboard, as well as one hundred and ninety-one oil paintings of not unknown provenance.'

'How can you possibly know that?'

'Because Miles's butler rang me last night to tell me the yacht set sail from Barcelona over a week ago and asked me if I knew how to get in touch with Miles.'

'What else did he tell you?' asked Sir Julian as he picked up a pen and began to make notes.

'BW has not only removed all of Miles's paintings, but also ordered the butler to put his home in Spain on the market.'

'And has he?'

'No way. In fact, once he realized that Miles was still alive, and back in prison in England, he's been desperate to get in touch with him, which is why he ended up calling me.' She paused. 'And then who do you think called me in the middle of the night?'

Sir Julian didn't respond, well aware that Mrs Faulkner couldn't wait to tell him.

'None other than the yacht's captain.' Christina didn't give a reason, knowing he wouldn't be able to resist asking . . .

'And what did he have to say for himself?' enquired Sir Julian, finally giving up.

'They are on their way back to England, Christchurch to be precise, and anticipate docking imminently.'

'Once again I'm curious to know why he would call you, of all people?'

'I'm the lesser of two evils,' declared Christina. 'In fact, Captain Redmayne distrusts Booth Watson so much I think that, if he was given half a chance, he'd throw him overboard.'

That would solve all our problems, thought Sir Julian, but kept his counsel.

'So if you were able to contact the harbourmaster at Christchurch and find out when the yacht's due to dock,' suggested Christina, 'we could be standing on the quayside waiting to greet the eminent QC, leaving him little choice but to return my half of the paintings, as agreed in my divorce settlement – which you drafted.'

It always fascinated Sir Julian that Miles and Christina were two of the same kind, and he wasn't even sure which one of them was the more devious. However, he had to admit that sinking Booth Watson and Miles Faulkner at the same time was tempting to say the least.

'I think that might be possible, Mrs Faulkner,' said Sir Julian, still keeping her at arm's length.

'If you could let me know when the yacht has entered territorial waters, the captain assured me that would give us at least a couple of hours to make sure we can get there in time to give him a right royal welcome.'

It always amused Sir Julian that Mrs Faulkner assumed he would be available at the drop of a hat (her hat), but he had to admit she was far more interesting than the tax avoidance case he was currently prosecuting in the high court, which his daughter Grace was more than capable of handling. Although he would never admit it, he couldn't wait to find out how Booth Watson intended to explain to Faulkner – who had probably been trying to get in touch with him for the past ten days – why he had brought his pictures back to England and put his house in Spain on the market without consulting him.

However, Sir Julian was well aware he would have to be prepared for another surprise, as his old rival Booth Watson was every bit as cunning as Christina, and would happily play one against the other if it suited his cause.

'I'll be in touch,' he said, before putting down the phone.

CHAPTER 4

WILLIAM PICKED UP THE PHONE but didn't turn on the light as the digital clock on his bedside table turned from 5:17 to 5:18. He knew it could only be one person on the other end of the line.

'The harbourmaster has just called,' said a wide-awake voice. 'The yacht has been sighted, and he's predicting an ETA of around nine o'clock.'

William leapt out of bed, hit a chair, fell on the floor and woke Beth. Not a good start to the day.

• • •

The second call the harbourmaster made that morning was to Sir Julian Warwick, who turned on the bedside light before picking up the phone. He was already awake. He thanked the harbourmaster, put the phone down, threw on a dressing gown, and retreated to his study. He looked up a number, and it gave him considerable pleasure to dial it. The phone rang for some time before it was eventually answered.

'Who the hell is this?' a voice demanded.

'Sir Julian Warwick,' he said, without any hint of an apology for waking his client at what might have been for her the middle of the night. He relayed the harbourmaster's message, and to his surprise she said, 'My driver will be with you in twenty minutes.'

After putting the phone down, he rushed back upstairs to the bathroom, threw off his dressing gown and pyjamas, jumped into the shower, and swore out loud as the cold jets of water streamed down onto his bald head.

• • •

William arrived at Scotland Yard just after six and wasn't surprised to see Commander Hawksby sitting in the back of a squad car, impatiently tapping his fingers on the front seat. William jumped in beside him. Danny, his driver, set off even before he'd had time to close the door.

• • •

It wasn't twenty minutes but nearer forty by the time Mrs Faulkner's chauffeur entered the private domain of Lincoln's Inn Field, and pulled up outside Sir Julian's flat. Sir Julian, who had been pacing around for the past twenty minutes, quickly joined his client in the back seat.

'Good morning, Mrs Faulkner,' he said. Though looking at her attire, he wasn't altogether sure she'd been to bed the previous night.

'Good morning, Sir Julian,' replied Mrs Faulkner as the chauffeur closed the back door and returned to his seat before setting off for Christchurch.

• • •

The commander and William were the first to arrive at the port, and immediately checked in with the harbourmaster.

'The yacht will be docking at berth number fourteen, in about forty minutes,' he said as the two men shook hands. 'If you need any assistance, mental or physical, don't hesitate to ask.'

'Mr Booth Watson's only weapon will be his brain,' responded the commander, 'which won't need reloading.' The Hawk thanked the harbourmaster before returning to his car, and Danny drove slowly along the quayside, coming to a halt at berth fourteen.

The Hawk got out of the car, stared out at the open sea, and raised his binoculars. A few moments later he declared, 'Got you,' before passing the binoculars across to William.

William adjusted the focus and began scanning the horizon.

'It shouldn't be too long now,' said the Hawk as a dark blue Mercedes drew up beside them. 'Why am I not surprised?' he added when a chauffeur opened the back door to allow Mrs Faulkner and her legal representative to join them.

'Good morning, Sir Julian,' said the Hawk as if they had been expected.

'Good to see you, commander,' replied Sir Julian. William handed his father the binoculars. After he had settled on the approaching yacht and identified the rotund figure who was staring back at them, he announced, 'I've been looking forward to this moment for some considerable time.'

• • •

Captain Redmayne was focusing on the quay, where he saw Commander Hawksby, Chief Inspector Warwick, Christina Faulkner and Sir Julian Warwick all clearly waiting to welcome them with open arms.

'Looks as if we're expected,' said the captain, passing over his binoculars.

Booth Watson just about managed to get to his feet. He had not slept for more than a few hours at a time for the past ten days, continually rushing to the nearest rail, regretting his latest meal.

'Can we turn back?' were Booth Watson's first words once he'd spotted the commander.

'We could,' said Captain Redmayne, 'but I wouldn't advise it.'

'Why not?'

'If you look behind you, you'll see someone else has already considered that possibility.' Booth Watson steadied himself and turned around to see they were being followed into port by a border patrol vessel. 'And before you ask, yes, we are well inside UK territorial waters.'

'Slow down,' said Booth Watson. 'I need time to think.'

• • •

'What makes you think Booth Watson doesn't realize his client is still alive and back in jail?' asked William.

'Is it just possible,' responded Sir Julian, 'that I've worked out something my clever son hasn't?'

'And what might that be?' asked the Hawk, whose eyes remained focused on the yacht.

'I don't understand,' said William, genuinely puzzled. 'If Booth Watson doesn't realize Faulkner's back in Belmarsh, where does he think he is?'

'Locked up in a safe that no one other than Miles has a key for,' suggested Christina, speaking for the first time. 'And that's why they think he's dead. Suffocated.'

The Hawk lowered his binoculars and looked at William.

That would explain why Booth Watson hasn't been in touch with Scotland Yard and demanded his release.

'If he was aware that Miles had somehow managed to get out of the safe,' Christina continued, 'Booth Watson would have been on the next plane to London and not sailing back on Miles's yacht.'

'*Chapeau*,' said Sir Julian, bowing respectfully to his client. William didn't look convinced.

'We'll find out soon enough,' said Christina, 'because if I'm right there'll be something on board that Miles would never have considered bringing back to England.'

'And what might that be?' asked the commander.

'A hundred and ninety-one oil paintings I haven't seen for a very long time,' said Christina, 'but will be delighted to be reacquainted with, as half of them belong to me.'

• • •

'What am I missing?' asked Booth Watson of a passing seagull, which only squawked an unintelligible reply. Why are those four waiting on the dockside for me, he wondered. And how did they find out where the yacht was heading? 'Do they realize Miles is dead?' he asked finally, but the seagull was no more responsive.

'If they don't,' said Captain Redmayne, 'they'll assume he's on board, and I expect it's him they're waiting for.'

'If that was the case,' said Booth Watson, 'Sir Julian and Mrs Faulkner wouldn't be there. She must think the paintings are on board.' He continued to consider every possible alternative, but had to admit he ended up none the wiser. Eventually he repeated, 'What am I missing?' aware it wouldn't be too long before he found out.

• • •

None of them moved from their positions on the quayside until the yacht was finally tied up and the gangway had been lowered into place.

Sir Julian watched as his old adversary strode down the gangway with an air of confidence that made him realize he'd had more than enough time to prepare the case for the defence.

William greeted him with the words, 'My name is—'

'I'm well aware who you are, Chief Inspector,' said Booth Watson. 'The only thing I'm not sure about is why you're here.'

'I want to question you about Miles Faulkner, as we have reason to believe that—'

'Clearly you need reminding, Chief Inspector, that my distinguished client is dead.'

'Sadly not,' responded the commander, 'and I suspect *you* don't realize the escaped convict is back in Belmarsh where he belongs.'

Sir Julian looked carefully at his old rival, and had to admire the sphinx-like expression that settled on Booth Watson's face as he considered his options. He first looked at the commander, followed by William, and then Sir Julian. It wasn't until his eyes settled on Mrs Faulkner that he worked out the only reason she could possibly be there.

Sir Julian could almost see his mind ticking over, but even he was taken by surprise when Booth Watson turned to Christina and said, 'I have carried out your instructions to the letter, Mrs Faulkner, and brought back your husband's art collection from Spain. On our way to London, perhaps we should discuss where you would like the paintings delivered?'

A masterstroke, admitted Sir Julian, if only to himself.

They all turned to face Mrs Faulkner, not sure which way she would jump.

Christina also took her time considering the alternatives, before she finally turned to her legal adviser and said sweetly, 'I won't be needing your services any longer, Sir Julian.' And without another word, Christina walked over to her waiting car, where Booth Watson joined her on the back seat.

As the Mercedes moved slowly off, Sir Julian turned to the commander and said, 'Can you give me a lift back to London?'

CHAPTER 5

THE WALLS OF THE LEGAL consultation room at Belmarsh prison were made of glass. The table in the centre was fixed to the floor, and also made of glass. The white plastic chairs were screwed to the floor in order to ensure that the prisoner and his legal adviser remained at arm's length. The guards might not be able to hear what was being said inside, but they could watch every movement that took place during the designated hour, including any attempts to pass drugs, contraband or even weapons to an inmate.

Booth Watson turned up unusually early at the prison gates that morning, and not just because he hadn't slept for the past thirty-six hours. After he'd been searched and his Gladstone bag, crammed with legal papers, had been rifled through, he signed the inevitable release form before being escorted by a senior officer to the interview wing. Neither of them spoke. They despised each other.

As they approached the glass cage, Booth Watson could see that his client, dressed in regulation blue and white striped prison shirt and well-worn jeans, was already seated at the glass table waiting for him. He could read nothing from the sphinx-like expression on his face.

Miles stood up as Booth Watson entered the room and, although they were not allowed to shake hands, greeted him with the suggestion of a smile.

Booth Watson felt himself relaxing for the first time in days. 'As we only have an hour, Miles,' he said, taking off his Rolex watch and placing it on the table between them, 'we haven't a moment to waste.' Faulkner nodded as he sat down. 'I'll begin by bringing you up to date with everything that has taken place since I last saw you.' The QC bent down and took several files from his bag.

'I flew to Barcelona for our monthly consultation, only to discover you'd already been arrested and brought back to London against your will, on your own jet.'

'I presume it was Collins who told you?'

'No,' said Booth Watson, who had anticipated the question. 'It was your Spanish lawyer, Señora Martinez. She briefed me fully on what Warwick and Hogan had been up to before I arrived.'

Booth Watson removed a single document from one of the files in front of him before continuing. 'Señora Martinez has already filed an official complaint with the Spanish authorities, because depriving a citizen of their freedom without a trial is against the 1953 European Convention on Human Rights.'

'A fat lot of good that will do me,' said Miles.

'Normally I would agree with you,' replied Booth Watson, 'but this allows us to request that Lieutenant Sanchez of the Spanish national police attend any forthcoming trial and explain to the court why he didn't take charge of the case, but allowed DCI Warwick to assume command.'

'That shouldn't have taken you more than a few hours to find out, so why didn't you return to London the next day?'

Another question Booth Watson was fully prepared for.

'I made the decision to remain in Barcelona and gather as much information as possible to assist your case, before coming back to England.'

Faulkner didn't look convinced.

'Information that will not only make the possibility of an early release more likely, but also leave the police with little choice but to arrest both Warwick and Hogan, and charge them with kidnapping and theft.'

Faulkner smiled for the first time.

'Once I'd gathered all the information I needed, I flew back to London and immediately applied to the CPS for an emergency consultation with my client, which they rejected out of hand.'

'Why?' demanded Faulkner.

'I can't prove it, but I suspect that once they realized two of the Met's most senior officers were themselves in danger of being arrested, they did everything in their power to prevent me from seeing you. But I persisted, until they finally granted me a one-hour consultation this morning, so we can't afford to waste another minute.'

Booth Watson looked up at Miles, but had no way of knowing if he believed him. 'However, before I can proceed, I have to ask if you still wish me to continue as your legal representative?'

'Why do you ask?' said Faulkner, sounding even more suspicious.

'Because since your escape from Belmarsh two years ago, I haven't seen you – or at least that's what I told the CPS when they questioned me about our relationship earlier in the week.'

A few moments passed before Faulkner realized the significance of what Booth Watson had just told him. 'That must have taken a lot of shredding,' he said.

'Burning is more effective now the police have a machine that can put the pieces back together. However, if I am to remain your counsel, you will have to confirm that is the case,' said Booth Watson, extracting another sheet of paper from one of the files. 'I have prepared the necessary statement.'

Faulkner read the document carefully. 'And if I don't?' he asked, a touch of menace creeping into his voice.

'We'll both be looking for a legal representative.'

Faulkner waved a hand, accepted the proffered gold pen and signed on the dotted line.

'What about Christina?' he asked, slipping the pen into his pocket. 'She could blow both our stories apart.'

'I've already briefed her on the consequences of doing anything quite so foolish, and we've come to what I would describe as an understanding.'

'How much is this understanding going to cost me?'

'Ten million.'

'That sounds excessive,' growled Faulkner.

'Not if you read the sub-clauses attached to the contract that should ensure your present sentence isn't doubled.'

'How can you possibly prevent that?'

'Neither the police nor the CPS will want Warwick or Hogan to appear in the witness box and have to admit the extremes they went to to bring you back to England. It's far too much of a risk for them.'

'I'm all ears,' said Miles.

'Firstly, Warwick would have to explain, under oath, why

he abducted you from your home in Spain without the Spanish government's authority, then flew you back to London against your express wishes.'

'How can I prove I didn't come back to London of my own free will? After all, Warwick will point out it was my own plane.'

'Your pilot will confirm that when you arrived in London, Warwick and Hogan literally dragged you off the plane and threw you into the back of a waiting police car, despite his attempts to prevent them. It will become even more embarrassing for the police when I point out that no effort was made to have you held in Spain while they progressed through the official channels to obtain an extradition order, which ironically your Spanish lawyer, Señora Martinez, believes the authorities would have readily granted.'

A nod and a smile greeted this statement.

'Secondly, and equally damning, I shall ask Warwick to explain how a valuable self-portrait by a Dutch master disappeared from your home in Spain, only to turn up a few days later on the walls of the Fitzmolean Museum in London. I suspect it was also travelling on the same plane.'

'Christina will claim that the Hals belongs to her, and she's loaned it to the museum for their exhibition.'

'No, she won't,' said Booth Watson. 'Because that's one of the sub-clauses in her five-million-pound contract.' He produced another legal document, this one bearing a signature on the last page that Miles immediately recognized. His smile broadened after he'd read that particular clause.

'What about the rest of my collection? Is it still safely at my home in Spain?'

'Being looked after by Collins,' confirmed Booth Watson.

'A good man, Collins,' declared Faulkner. 'See that he gets a bonus. He's earned it.'

'Couldn't agree more,' said Booth Watson, writing a note with an identical gold pen.

'So, what happens next?'

'I will request a sub judice meeting with Sir Julian Warwick, who continues to represent the Crown in your case. I will make it clear to him that it would be unfortunate if the press were to get hold of the real story, which would be embarrassing for the police both here and in Spain, and that given the circumstances it might be wise for him to advise the CPS to drop the latest charges in exchange for you remaining silent.'

'How do you think the CPS will react to that suggestion?'

'I don't think they'll have a lot of choice, unless they want the story to end up on the front page of every paper with the headline, "Chief Inspector involved in kidnap and burglary".'

'And the odds?' said Miles, cutting to the quick.

'Better than fifty-fifty, in my opinion. Sir Julian may want to see your sentence doubled, but not at the expense of his only son being locked up in the cell next to you, rather than being promoted, which I hear—'

There was a sharp knock on the door, and a guard poked his head inside the room. 'Five minutes, sir.' Booth Watson couldn't be sure which one of them was being addressed as 'sir'.

'Anything else I need to think about before I see you again?' asked Miles.

'Yes – I've had an offer for your fifty-one per cent shareholding in the Malaysian tea company you purchased from another of my clients.'

'A drug dealer who's no longer with us. How much?'

'Sixteen million.'

'That must be an opening bid. An export and import company with Marcel and Neffe's turnover must be worth almost double that.'

'The shares have dipped since you changed address.'

'Ask for twenty-four million, and settle for twenty-two,' said Miles as there was a second rap on the door.

Booth Watson gathered up his papers and put them back in his Gladstone bag, feeling he'd achieved everything he could have hoped for. As he stood up, he said, 'You are entitled to a private consultation with your legal representative once a week. May I suggest we meet every Friday morning at ten?'

'Suits me,' said Miles. 'I'm not going anywhere for the foreseeable future.'

'I'm rather hoping to remove the word "foreseeable" and replace it with "near",' said Booth Watson, 'so that we can once again enjoy breakfast together at the Savoy.'

'Amen to that,' said Miles.

Booth Watson headed for the door. 'Thank you, officer,' he said, standing between them for a moment to allow Miles to pick up the Rolex watch and strap it on his wrist.

The guard accompanied prisoner 0249 back to his cell in A block, while Booth Watson went in the opposite direction and made his way to reception, feeling things couldn't have worked out much better. However, he knew he would still have to keep a close eye on Christina, to make sure she kept her part of the bargain.

CHAPTER 6

'I'VE NO IDEA WHERE WE are going,' admitted William to a guard carrying the inevitable clipboard.

'Then it must be your first visit, sir,' responded the guard as he checked William's warrant card, and placed a tick next to his name.

William nodded as he slipped the card back into his pocket.

'If you continue on up the road, you'll see a large white house on your right. I'll call ahead, to warn them you're on the way.'

'Thank you,' said William as the barrier rose, and Danny proceeded along a wide drive, never exceeding ten miles an hour. A speed he was unfamiliar with.

When the magnificent Wren mansion came into sight, Danny slowed down and circled a large rose garden before coming to a halt.

As if by magic, the front door opened just as William stepped out of the back of the car.

'Good morning, Chief Inspector,' said a man dressed in a

short black jacket, white shirt, grey tie and pinstriped trousers, with black shoes that shone like a guardsman's. 'Her Royal Highness is expecting you.'

William and Ross followed the butler into the house and up a wide sweeping staircase to the first floor. William was so nervous he didn't even glance at the paintings that adorned the walls. And then he saw her, standing by the entrance to the drawing room.

'How nice to see you again, William,' the Princess said as William bowed. He was taken by surprise when she called him by his Christian name, although the protocol officer at Scotland Yard had told him she often did so to put her guests at ease. However, the PO had reminded him firmly never to become overfamiliar and to always address her as 'Your Royal Highness' or 'ma'am'.

'May I introduce Inspector Hogan, ma'am.'

'We met at Scotland Yard, Inspector, but only briefly,' said Diana, 'when you accompanied my lady-in-waiting around the Black Museum. In fact, it was Victoria who suggested you might be suitable to take over as my personal protection officer.'

Ross didn't comment as the butler reappeared, carrying a heavily laden tea tray, which he placed on the table in front of them. William admired the Herend porcelain tea set decorated with insects and flowers, knowing that Beth would expect him, like a good detective, to recall every detail.

'Do sit down, both of you,' said Diana. 'I'll be mother. China or Indian, Inspector?'

The protocol officer had mentioned how to bow – from the neck, not the waist, like a cabaret artist – but she hadn't mentioned China or Indian.

'Indian,' said William, while Ross simply nodded.

'I read your service record with interest, Inspector,' Diana continued as she passed Ross a cup. 'Two Queen's Gallantry Medals and countless commendations. You sound like a cross between Sydney Carton and Raffles. Most impressive.'

'More Raffles, ma'am,' said William. 'We spared you the three official reprimands, not to mention a temporary suspension.' Diana laughed, while Ross remained silent. 'DI Hogan is the still waters type, ma'am,' added William, coming to his rescue.

'That's not what Victoria told me,' said Diana, placing a slice of plum cake on a plate in front of Ross, who didn't touch it. 'I also read about you, William, and your remarkably swift rise through the ranks,' she added as William picked up a pair of silver tongs and dropped a lump of sugar into his tea. 'But after my brief encounter with Artemisia, that hardly comes as a surprise.' She turned her attention back to Ross. 'I understand you also have a daughter?'

Over the years William had witnessed Ross chat up several women he hadn't even been introduced to, but this time he just sat there, bolt upright, his tea going cold and his cake still untouched.

'What a magnificent Frith,' said William, once again coming to Ross's rescue as he looked at a painting on the wall above the fireplace.

'Yes, one of my favourites,' said Diana, without glancing around. 'Ladies' Day at Ascot. Not part of the royal collection,' she whispered, 'but a gift from my late grandfather. Do tell me, William, how is my new best friend, Artemisia?'

'She tells everyone about meeting you, and the story becomes longer with each telling. She wanted me to let you know that she's looking forward to seeing you again when you open the Frans Hals exhibition at the Fitzmolean. I fear she'll be presenting you with another bunch of flowers.'

'Which reminds me,' said Diana, 'I have a little gift for her.' She leant forward and took a small box wrapped with a silk ribbon from the shelf below the table, handing it to William. 'And I haven't forgotten Jojo,' she added, retrieving a second gift which she gave to Ross.

'Thank you, ma'am,' spluttered Ross, pronouncing it incorrectly.

'Ah, you can speak!' teased Diana.

While William laughed, Ross turned a bright shade of red, something else William hadn't witnessed before.

'No doubt,' continued Diana, 'you've already been fully briefed on what the job as my protection officer entails. But my bet is they've only told you half the story, and not the better half.'

This was a statement that left even William wondering how to respond.

'There's never a dull moment,' she went on, 'but I fear you'll find the hours are unpredictable. I once had breakfast with Mother Teresa, lunch with Mikhail Gorbachev and dinner with Mick Jagger, all on the same day. No prizes for guessing which one I enjoyed the most.'

'Mick Jagger?' ventured Ross.

'I think we're going to get along just fine.'

Ross didn't respond.

'Can I pour you a fresh cup of tea, Inspector?' the Princess offered, glancing at his untouched cup.

'No, thank you, ma'am. But can I ask if you have any particular problems that you think I should know about?'

'Now you mention it, I'd like to be able to visit the gym, swim or even go shopping occasionally without being pursued by a dozen paps.'

'That might not always be easy, ma'am. After all, you're the most photographed person on earth,' Ross reminded her, 'but short of killing them, I'll do my best.'

Diana revealed that shy smile the public had become so familiar with, before saying, 'I also have friends who don't enjoy seeing their faces plastered across the front pages of every national newspaper: accompanied by articles about their past lives.'

Ross nodded, but didn't offer an opinion.

'And one or two of them might well visit me' – she paused – 'how shall I put it, outside of office hours.'

'Why would that prove a problem, ma'am,' said William, 'while you're safely ensconced in here? No one can get past the barrier unless you have given your express permission they can do so, as we've just experienced.'

'I can assure you, William, there are at least half a dozen photographers parked outside the front gate twenty-four/seven and they don't even take a break for lunch. Two in particular don't seem to appreciate that I have a private life and would like it to remain private whenever possible.'

'Understood, ma'am,' said Ross. 'You can be assured the only other woman in my life is two years old, and I won't be sharing your secrets with her.'

'I can't wait to meet her,' said Diana.

'We won't keep you any longer, ma'am,' said William, when the clock on the mantelpiece struck the half hour, 'remembering the important dinner you're attending this evening.' Something else the protocol officer had briefed him on.

'A state banquet in honour of the King of Saudi Arabia,' said Diana. 'I understand that the King speaks little English, while Her Majesty speaks no Arabic. So that should make for a jolly occasion. I, on the other hand, will be sitting next to the Saudi Arabian ambassador, who I'm told has four wives. So he won't be short of small talk.'

They both laughed dutifully.

'I do hope you will consider joining my team, Inspector,' she said, turning back to Ross. 'We have a lot more fun than the rest of the Royal Family' – she paused – 'put together.'

Ross managed a smile as the butler reappeared.

'Your next appointment has arrived, ma'am.'

'No, they haven't,' said Diana. Turning to William, she admitted, 'That's just a coded message to get rid of you two, whereas I'd much rather have tea with you than dinner with the King of Saudi Arabia. However . . .'

William immediately stood up. 'I think the time has come for us to leave, ma'am. Thank you so much for seeing us.'

'I do hope I'll be seeing you again, Inspector,' said Diana as she accompanied them both down the wide staircase to the hall. William was pleased to see Ross chatting to the Princess while he hung back to take a closer look at several paintings he might never have the opportunity of seeing again, including a seascape by the other Henry Moore. Beth would be certain to question him when he got home about which artists the Princess favoured. It would be an interesting challenge to see how many of them he could remember without being able to make a note.

As they walked back into the entrance hall, he paused to admire a Turner, a Millais and a Burne-Jones, only wishing he had longer to appreciate them. The Princess accompanied them out to the car, where she once again surprised William by having a long chat with Danny before they departed. She didn't go back inside until the car was out of sight.

William waited until they'd turned into Kensington High Street before saying, 'Well, do you want the job, chatterbox?'

'Of course I do,' said Ross, without hesitation. 'But I have a problem.'

• • •

'Will there be anything else, Mr Booth Watson?' asked his secretary as she closed her dictation pad.

Booth Watson sat back and considered the question of how to deal with the dual problems of Miles Faulkner and his ex-wife Christina. Although he'd seen both of them quite recently, he still wasn't sure if Miles had accepted his explanation of what had taken place in Spain, while Christina had certainly worked out what he'd been up to. He was aware she wouldn't hesitate to seek advice from Sir Julian if it were in her own best interests. But he also knew the ideal person to keep an eye on both of them, while only reporting back to him: a man who would have contacts in Belmarsh, both behind bars and on the landings, while at the same time keeping a close eye on Christina Faulkner, so he always knew who she was seeing, and what she was up to. Although Booth Watson detested the former Superintendent who'd left the Met under a cloud, he agreed with Lyndon Johnson who, after resigning himself to the difficulty of firing J. Edgar Hoover, had once commented, 'It's probably better to have him inside the tent pissing out, than outside pissing in.'

'Yes, Miss Plumstead,' he eventually managed. 'I want you to arrange an urgent meeting with ex-superintendent Lamont.'

'Of course, sir. But I should point out that your diary is back-to-back at the moment. You have two court appearances later in the week and—'

'In the next twenty-four hours,' Booth Watson said, interrupting her.

CHAPTER 7

WILLIAM QUICKLY TURNED THE KEY in the lock, hoping he was back in time to read a bedtime story to the children. He was delighted to hear cheerful young voices coming from the front room. He hung up his overcoat on the hallstand and extracted two boxes from the inside pockets before heading towards the boisterous noise.

No sooner had William opened the door than Artemisia charged across and threw her arms around his legs.

'Is it true,' she asked even before he could speak, 'that you had tea with Princess Di?'

'The Princess of Wales,' said Beth, correcting her.

'The answer is yes,' said William, 'and she said to say hi, and asked me to give you a present.'

Artemisia held out her hands, while Peter asked, 'Did she give me a present?'

'Yes, of course,' said William, producing the two boxes from behind his back. He handed them over, hoping the twins wouldn't notice that one of the gifts was far better wrapped than the other. He needn't have worried, because Peter ripped the wrapping off his present immediately, impatient to discover what was inside, while Artemisia took her time, undoing the silk ribbon and removing the pink paper, both of which would be given pride of place on her bedside table.

'Wow,' said Beth as Artemisia held up a small coronet made of shiny beads.

'Is it real?' she asked, clutching it tightly.

'If a Princess gave it to you, it must be,' said her mother, placing the coronet on her daughter's head.

Artemisia ran out of the room to take a look at herself in the hall mirror, while Peter began to unbutton his pyjama top.

'She even knows which team I support and that Kerry Dixon is my favourite player!' he proclaimed, pulling on a Chelsea shirt with the number nine on the back.

'And even more impressive,' whispered Beth, 'she knows what size he is.'

Artemisia reappeared, her head aloft as she began to stroll regally around the room, smiling and waving at the cat with the back of her hand. As she passed Peter, she said imperiously, 'You have to bow.'

'Chelsea supporters don't bow to anyone,' said Peter as he began to parade in the opposite direction, showing off his new kit to those seated in the stands.

Both parents somehow managed to keep straight faces.

'Can I wear it to bed?' pleaded Peter, after completing several circuits of the room.

'Yes, of course you can, darling,' said his mother, followed by a second 'Yes' to Artemisia even before she could ask. 'But you'll both have to write to the Princess in the morning and thank her.'

'Mine will be a long and interesting letter, because I have

a lot to say since I last saw her,' said Artemisia as their nanny joined them.

'Time for bed,' Sarah said firmly.

'I'm a Princess,' Artemisia replied. 'But you can call me Artemisia.'

'Thank you, ma'am,' said Sarah, giving her a slight curtsey, 'but even Princesses need their beauty sleep.'

Artemisia gave her father a hug before she and Peter left the room, both chatting away to Sarah at the same time.

'You're a good man, William Warwick,' said Beth as she bent down and kissed him on the forehead. 'The coronet I believe, but not the Chelsea shirt.' William smiled. 'But now I want to hear all about your visit to Kensington Palace. What was she wearing? What did you have for tea and, most important, which paintings were on display that I'll never have the chance to see?'

William was already regretting not lingering longer on the staircase while HRH was chatting to Ross.

'All in good time,' he said. 'But first, there's something more pressing we have to discuss.' He hesitated for a moment, before asking, 'How do you feel about having another child?'

Beth didn't respond immediately, but finally asked, 'What's changed? After all, we've discussed the subject ad infinitum, and always come to the same conclusion. We simply can't afford it.'

William settled back to listen to a speech he'd heard several times before.

'We're a typical modern couple,' Beth reminded him. 'We both have full time jobs, and wouldn't want it any other way. You're doing the job you've always wanted to do, and I don't have to remind you how lucky I feel to be working at the Fitzmolean. Not only that, but as a Chief Inspector you can't even claim overtime, despite the fact that your workload hasn't diminished. To make things worse, I'm paid a pittance compared to men who do the equivalent job. Such is the lot of women who work in the art world, publishing or the theatre. But that won't stop me pushing for change in the future,' she added with considerable feeling. 'Women will continue to be taken advantage of as long as there's a surplus of eager candidates vying for every job, especially when they daren't complain about the pay. And even then, a man far less qualified often ends up being appointed to the same job because he won't be taking time off to have a baby!'

William didn't interrupt her. He'd witnessed the same prejudice in the police force, where time and again women were passed over for promotion while less able men were advanced, often with the justification that 'He's got a wife and family to support.' He decided to let Beth continue to erupt, and then settle, before he posed his next question.

'And don't forget,' continued Beth, 'we have to employ a nanny, who's paid almost as much as I am. Don't get me wrong, Sarah's worth every penny, because she makes it possible for me to do the job I love. But whenever she takes a night off, we have to pay for a babysitter if we want to go to the theatre or eat out.'

The lava was still flowing steadily down the mountain towards him.

'It was different in our parents' day when it was assumed that women had been put on earth to raise children, clean the house, cook the meals and support their husbands in their careers. "Love, honour and *obey*",' she emphasized, 'just in case you've forgotten, caveman.'

William was once again reminded why he adored this woman.

'I swear my father doesn't know how many minutes it takes to boil an egg, while yours just about manages to carve the Christmas turkey.'

'He spends some considerable time sharpening the knife beforehand,' said William, trying to lighten the mood.

'The truth is,' continued Beth, ignoring the riposte, 'that both our mothers would have been well capable of holding down demanding jobs if only they'd been given the chance.'

'Your mother sat on the board of your father's company,' William reminded her.

'Ask her how much she was paid while she kept the books in apple pie order at the same time as raising me. Be warned, Detective Chief Inspector, a revolution is about to take place, in which *homo sapiens* will be replaced by *"femina sapiens"*. I predict it's going to happen in the not-too-distant future, even if most men can't see it coming.'

Her voice was now calmer, but no less determined. William didn't remind her that she'd left out the hunter-gatherer section of her speech.

'I admit,' continued Beth, 'that thanks to the generosity of my parents, we're fortunate enough to own our own home, but we still find it difficult to make ends meet, even though your father has set up a trust fund for the children's education. However, the colour of my bank balance has remained red since the day I left university and yours is only in credit on the day after you're paid. No, William, the simple answer to your question is we can't afford another child, however much we'd like one.'

'But if we could afford another one?'

'I'd have six,' said Beth. 'The twins are the joy of my life.'

'I'd settle for three,' said William. 'And I may have found a solution.'

'Have you won the pools, caveman? Or are we going to rob a bank like Bonnie and Clyde?' asked Beth, trying to imitate Warren Beatty.

'Neither will be necessary. We can have a third child at no extra expense, and you won't even have to take maternity leave.'

'I can't wait to hear how we're going to pull that one off,' said Beth with an exaggerated sigh.

'The Princess's personal protection officer will be retiring in the new year, and she's offered Ross the job.'

'So that's the reason she invited you both to tea?'

'Yes, but Ross doesn't feel he can take on the responsibility of trying to bring up Jojo at the same time. Single mothers somehow manage in similar circumstances, but single fathers are far less adaptable.'

'Especially single fathers who are workaholics,' said Beth. 'I can well believe if Ross took on the responsibility, his hours wouldn't exactly be sociable. Everybody knows Diana isn't someone who likes to stay quietly at home at night. But much as I'd like to help Ross, I don't see how it solves the problem of—'

'Our overdraft,' said William. 'Don't forget, Josephine left Ross enough money to ensure he'd never have to work again, which is somewhat ironic as Ross is happiest when he's working flat out, and the Princess has offered him a chance to put all the skills and experience he's acquired over the years to good use. Frankly, I don't know anyone who's better qualified for the job.'

'But being practical for a moment,' said Beth thoughtfully, 'how would it work?'

'Jojo would come and live with us as part of the family. Ross would visit her whenever possible and take her out on his days off. Of course, they'd go on holiday together when he takes his annual leave. In return, he'd pay Sarah's wages, and give us a hundred pounds a week to cover any other expenses. He'd also contribute one-third of the payments into the educational trust, so that Jojo would enjoy the same advantages as the twins.'

'On top of paying Sarah's wages? That's more than generous.'

'The downside is we'd have three children to take care of, not two.'

'That's the upside,' said Beth, unable to hide her excitement at the proposal. 'But how do you think the twins will react when we tell them?'

'Artemisia will mother Jojo to death, especially when she learns that it means Ross will be able to take care of the Princess. Peter will pretend not to notice, until she's old enough to play football.' William sat back and waited for Beth to reply before adding, 'I've already warned Ross that you may need a little time to think about it.'

'How about a nanosecond?' Beth replied.

• • •

Booth Watson peered across his desk at the former Superintendent – a man he loathed, and he suspected the feeling was mutual. Still, there was no one better qualified to do the job he had in mind. Lamont wore a suit which, although smart, was a little tight, indicating how much weight he'd put on since leaving the Met.

'I have a particularly sensitive assignment I need you to carry out on my behalf,' Booth Watson began. Lamont offered a curt nod. 'As you'll know, Miles Faulkner is back in prison, and I will be defending him when his case comes up at the

Old Bailey. Meanwhile, I have to be sure that my principal witness, Mrs Christina Faulkner, can be relied on should I decide to put her in the witness box.'

A further nod. Lamont knew when not to interrupt his primary source of income.

'You have had dealings with the lady in the past,' continued Booth Watson, 'so you'll be well aware she can't be trusted. It won't come as a surprise that I need someone to keep a close eye on her night and day.'

'Is there anything in particular I should be looking out for?'

'I need to know who she's in regular contact with, especially how often she sees Mrs Beth Warwick. Even more important, if she's ever in touch with that woman's husband.'

An expression crossed Lamont's face which suggested that, for him, DCI Warwick fell into the category of unfinished business. BW was well aware that Warwick had been responsible for Lamont having to leave the force only months before he would have qualified for a full pension. Nothing on the record of course, but no one was in any doubt why he'd had to resign and, perhaps more importantly, who was responsible for his sudden departure.

'Finally,' said Booth Watson, 'I know you have worked for Mrs Faulkner in the past. But from now on you'll *only* be working for me. If I were to discover that you're moonlighting, two things will happen. Firstly, your income will dry up that same day.'

And secondly, Lamont wanted to ask, but didn't need to.

'And secondly, I would have to inform my client of your treachery.' Booth Watson allowed the underlying threat to hang in the air before adding, 'Do I make myself clear?'

'Crystal.'

Booth Watson nodded, before opening the top drawer of

his desk and withdrawing a thick brown envelope. He pushed it slowly across the table to indicate the meeting was over.

'And don't even think about fiddling your expenses,' were Booth Watson's parting words, as Lamont stood and turned to leave. 'Because if you do, you'll end up with only your meagre pension to survive on. And yes, I do know about your wife's spending habits.'

The ex-superintendent was glad he had his back to Booth Watson so his paymaster couldn't see the expression on his face.

CHAPTER 8

ALTHOUGH WILLIAM COULDN'T WAIT TO get stuck into the Milner inquiry, the lengthy delay allowed him to get to know Jo Junior better while observing, a little apprehensively to begin with, how she was settling in with the rest of the family. He needn't have worried, because Artemisia, as Beth had predicted, quickly took her new little sister under her wing, even if Peter pretended to ignore Jojo, although he was always the first to stand up for her whenever she got into any trouble. The duo quickly became a trio, while anyone who saw them together assumed they were a family. As for the 'two indulgent grandfathers', in Beth's words, they were both infatuated with the new arrival, while the grandmothers doted on her.

William accepted that the transition was complete after a visiting colleague from the gallery told Beth, 'Jojo looks just like you.'

'I'm flattered,' Beth replied, recalling how beautiful Ross's wife Josephine had been.

Ross visited his daughter as often as he could, but as he'd had to go on an extensive training course before he could begin work as Princess Diana's personal protection officer, the visits were less frequent than he would have liked. But he did manage to escape for a few days over Christmas, and arrived at the house on Christmas morning loaded down with presents for the only other woman in his life.

Jojo gave her father a huge hug, before he handed three large boxes to three excited children, who didn't wait to ask if they could open them.

'Why haven't I seen you for such a long time, Papa?' asked Jojo as she tore the wrapping off her gift.

'Shall I tell her?' said Ross, turning to William.

'Yes, of course,' said Beth before William could reply. 'But you'd better have a good excuse, because young ladies don't like being stood up without an explanation.'

'I've been on an intensive close protection course,' said Ross as he sat cross-legged on the floor next to his daughter. 'Top secret,' he whispered.

'Details, details!' demanded Artemisia, imitating her grandfather.

'For the past six weeks, I've been learning how to drive backwards in the rain and perform a J-turn before taking off again at high speed.'

'What's a J-turn?' Peter asked as he took a model police car out of its box, wound it up and set it off, lights flashing, sirens blaring.

'You have to be able to turn a half circle while going backwards,' said Ross, 'so you're facing in exactly the opposite direction, and can move off quickly.'

'Is that where Princess Diana lives?' asked Jojo, staring at a picture of Buckingham Palace on her Lego box.

'Of course it isn't,' said Artemisia as Jojo tipped the contents out onto the floor. 'My friend lives at Kensington Palace with the Prince of Wales, and Ross, who takes care of her.'

'Do you have a gun?' asked Peter, pointing a forefinger at Ross.

'Yes, but my predecessor didn't once have to draw his weapon during the time he worked for the Princess.'

'And let's hope you don't have to,' said Beth.

'What does predecessor mean?' asked Artemisia as she fixed a large Lego cornerstone in place.

'The person who had the job before Ross,' explained Beth.

'Does the Princess have a police car like mine?' asked Peter, winding it up again.

'Sure does,' said Ross, 'and I sit in the front passenger seat, while the Princess sits in the back with her lady-in-waiting.'

'What's a lady-in-waiting?' asked Jojo as she picked up a window and checked the picture on the lid. It didn't help that the palace had seven hundred and sixty windows.

'Someone who accompanies the Princess whenever she attends an official function,' Ross explained. 'Usually a close friend.'

'I'd like to be a lady-in-waiting,' said Artemisia.

'What about protocol?' said Beth with a wry smile. 'Did they teach you how to behave in front of a member of the Royal Family?'

'You bow from the neck, not the waist, while making sure you always address them by their correct title,' said Ross looking up, 'and you must never ask a member of the Royal Family a question.'

'That must make for a one-sided conversation,' suggested Beth.

'How would I address the Queen if I met her in the street?' asked Jojo.

'You would curtsey, not bow, and address her as "Your Majesty",' said Ross as Artemisia fixed an archway into the front of the palace.

'What about Arti's friend, Princess Diana?'

'"Your Royal Highness", when you first meet her, then "ma'am" during any further conversation, and "Your Royal Highness" again when the conversation ends and she moves on.'

'Good morning, Your Royal Highness,' said Artemisia as she stood up and curtsied.

'But surely if you're a friend like Arti,' said Jojo, 'you can call her Diana?'

'Certainly not,' said Ross, with mock horror. 'Not even her lady-in-waiting addresses her by her Christian name.'

'Then who does?' asked Beth.

'Other members of the Royal Family and close friends, but then only in private.'

'And do the same rules apply for the Queen?' asked Beth. 'Does anyone call her Elizabeth?'

'I suspect only the Queen Mother, Princess Margaret and the Duke of Edinburgh, who all call her "Lilibet", but not in public.'

'Do they also bow and curtsey?'

'On state occasions, yes, and I'm told first thing in the morning and last thing at night.'

'I'll bet the Duke of Edinburgh doesn't bow before he climbs into bed,' said Beth.

'They have separate bedrooms,' said Ross, looking across at Artemisia and Jojo, who were continuing to build their palace. He was delighted to see how well his daughter had settled in, and that she was clearly now accepted as a member of the family.

Ross got up off the floor as Peter practised reversing his police car and turning a half circle before speeding away. 'I can't begin to thank you enough,' Ross said as Beth handed him a glass of mulled wine.

'We love her as if she were our own,' said Beth. 'So don't even think about taking her away.'

'Not much chance of that happening while I'm working for Diana,' said Ross.

'Princess Diana!' said Artemisia firmly.

Beth laughed. 'Why don't you two catch up,' she said, turning to William, 'while I go and check on the turkey, because it sure won't cook itself.'

Ross fell into the chair next to William and immediately asked, 'Has Booth Watson raised his head above the parapet while I've been away?'

'Not enough for me to take a potshot,' admitted William, while offering Ross a mock toast. 'However, we do know he's been holding legal meetings with his client at Belmarsh every Friday morning for the past few weeks. In fact, I'm beginning to wonder if he's decided not to take us on.'

'Why wouldn't he,' said Ross, 'when he's got nothing to lose?'

'Perhaps he has got something to lose,' came back William. 'Because I'm not altogether convinced Faulkner even knows his prized art collection is no longer hanging on the walls of his home in Spain, but is now stored in a warehouse near Gatwick airport.'

'Which would confirm,' suggested Ross, 'that Booth Watson didn't realize Faulkner was still alive when he set off for England in his yacht. Although that's hardly slam dunk.'

'Until you add the fact that Faulkner's home in Spain was put on the market at around that time, and has since been taken off.'

'What's he up to?' mused Ross.

'I suspect that, like us, he'd be quite happy to see his client remain in jail for a very long time. While the cat's away . . .'

'I can't make up my mind which one of them is the bigger crook.'

'A close-run thing,' suggested William, 'but we'll find out soon enough when the case comes to court.'

'Meanwhile, what has the home team been up to in my absence?'

'Preparing themselves for what I suspect will be a bruising encounter with Superintendent Milner and his cronies, once they discover what our real purpose is.'

'When's the opening round taking place?'

'Rebecca and I report to Buckingham Gate next Tuesday, while Jackie and Paul will be checking into Windsor Castle at the same time.'

'I can't believe either of you will receive a particularly warm welcome, and that may not be the least of your problems.' Ross lowered his voice, 'I received a private briefing last week about a possible terrorist attack on a member of the Royal Family.'

William nodded. 'Commander Holbrooke's been in regular touch with the Hawk and, following Lockerbie, I can assure you that anyone who lands at Heathrow in possession of a Libyan passport spends several hours being questioned before they reach the baggage hall, and the majority of them are sent back home on the first available flight.'

'That should please the Hawk, if not the liberal left,' commented Ross. 'And how is the old curmudgeon, dare I ask?' he said as Jojo slotted a double door into place, and began clapping.

'As feisty and cantankerous as ever, although recently he's been talking about retirement.'

'Now that he's found the right person to take his place?'

'That's assuming Booth Watson isn't planning to have us both locked up long before then,' said William as Beth walked back into the room.

She curtsied before announcing, 'Luncheon is served, my lords.'

'But we haven't finished building the palace!' said Artemisia.

'We'll finish it together after lunch,' promised Beth, 'while your father and Ross do the washing up.'

'I may have to go on another intensive training course before I can handle that,' said Ross as he stood up and took Jojo's hand.

'Can I go with you this time?' Jojo asked her father as Beth led them all out of the room and into the kitchen to find William sharpening the carving knife.

'I've got an even better idea,' whispered Ross as they sat down at the kitchen table. 'Why don't I take you to London Zoo tomorrow, and we can—'

'Only if Arti and Peter can come as well.'

That was when Ross finally accepted that Jojo truly was part of the family.

CHAPTER 9

WILLIAM AND REBECCA ARRIVED OUTSIDE Number 4 Buckingham Gate early on the Tuesday morning, unsure 'what they were about to receive'. They were, to quote Rebecca, bright-eyed, bushy-tailed and more than ready to begin their new assignment.

William knocked on the door, as he didn't have an entry code for the small keypad on the wall. He received no response. He banged a little harder, but still no response. He was about to try a third time when the door half opened and a man peered out at them over a chain. He looked as if he'd been woken from a deep sleep, and hadn't had time to shave.

'What do you want?' he asked gruffly.

'To come in,' replied William.

'Who are you?'

'Detective Chief Inspector Warwick,' said William, producing his warrant card. 'Who are you?'

'Sergeant Jennings. What can I do for you, Inspector?'

'Chief Inspector,' William snapped. 'You can start by opening the door and showing me to my office.'

Jennings took the chain off the hook and reluctantly opened the door to allow the two strangers to enter. He silently led them down a long dark corridor, switching on the lights as he went. They descended a staircase to a basement, the dank, putrid smell suggesting it was rarely visited. They stopped before a door at the far end, where Jennings took his time looking for the right key.

'Your office,' he announced, after he'd finally managed to open it. He'd clearly never been in the room before, and shivered before standing aside to allow them to enter.

A single light bulb hung from the ceiling. Below it was a small plywood desk that wobbled when touched, two plastic chairs and a few wooden shelves lined with last year's dust, along with a 1984 volume of the police yearbook.

'Is there anything else I can do for you?' asked Jennings, sounding as if they were keeping him from something more important.

'Should I presume you've been on night duty, Sergeant?'

'Yes,' came back the sheepish reply.

'Yes, sir,' corrected William.

'Yes, sir,' snapped Jennings, clicking his heels.

'The first thing you can do,' said William, 'is go and shave, put on a jacket and tie, and then report back to me.'

'I'm just about to go off duty.'

'*Were* just about to go off duty,' said William, correcting him. Jennings turned to leave, mumbling something incoherent under his breath.

'I've seen worse first thing in the morning,' said Rebecca once he'd closed the door behind him. 'But not since my student days.'

'Are you referring to the Sergeant or the room?'

'Both,' she said, looking around, 'but I'm confident I can improve at least one of them in the short term.'

'It's their way of letting us know how they feel about outsiders interfering with their entitled way of life. I think you can assume we'll be left in the basement until they find out we're not a bargain.'

'Don't worry, chief, I'll have a Renoir, a Picasso and a Matisse on the wall long before the Superintendent turns up.'

'I'd prefer a phone, a filing cabinet and a wastepaper basket,' said William as he began to open the desk drawers, only to discover the cupboard was bare.

Rebecca took a small notepad and a Biro out of her attaché case and handed them to William, as Jennings ambled back into the room.

'Go back out, Sergeant,' said William. 'Knock on the door and wait until you're asked to come in. And when you do, remember to bring your own chair.'

Rebecca would have liked to have captured the look on Jennings's face to remind her of their first day at work with Royalty Protection. This time he retreated without comment.

'I do believe you're enjoying yourself, chief,' ventured Rebecca.

'If Jennings is anything to go by, this is going to be more of a challenge than I'd originally thought.'

There was a knock on the door.

'Come in,' said William.

Jennings opened the door and walked back in, carrying a comfortable chair.

'You can sit down, Sergeant,' said William.

Jennings placed his chair in front of the desk and sat down. William remained standing, while Jennings leant forward, as

71

if perched on a stool in the corner of a boxing ring, waiting
for the bell to sound for the first round.

'Name and rank?'

'I've already told you,' retorted Jennings.

'One more piece of insubordination, Sergeant, and I'll be
getting my red pen out and asking for your pocket book.'

'Why, what have I done?'

'It's what you haven't done,' said William. 'You were on
night duty but, when you opened the front door, it was clear
I'd woken you, as you were unshaven and yawning.'

Jennings shifted uneasily in his chair.

'Name and rank?' repeated William.

'Sergeant Ray Jennings.'

'How long have you been a member of the police force,
Sergeant?'

'Six years.'

'Six years, *sir.*'

'Six years, sir.'

'What is your position?'

'I'm the third protection officer on the Prince of Wales's
personal team, sir.'

'Who are the other two officers on that team?' asked William,
making notes.

'Superintendent Milner, who's head of Royalty Protection
Command' – he stressed the word head – 'and Inspector
Reynolds, his number two.'

'When can I expect either of them to make an appearance?'

'Inspector Reynolds usually comes in around ten on a
Tuesday morning.'

'Around ten?'

'If he's been working over the weekend and HRH doesn't
have any engagements before midday, there doesn't seem

much point in coming in any earlier. In any case, he lives in the country.'

'And Superintendent Milner?'

'You can never be sure if he'll be at Buck House or Windsor Castle, but I'll let him know you're here the moment he arrives.'

'And you?'

'I'm on nights this week,' said Jennings, stifling another yawn. 'I was just about to go home.'

'Before you leave, I'd like a copy of your day sheet, and the name of the officer who signs you off. If I ever see you incorrectly dressed and unshaven again, Sergeant, you'll be back on the beat with the rank of Constable.' Jennings immediately sat bolt upright, the surly look disappearing from his face. 'You can go off duty now, Sergeant.'

Jennings rose, picked up the chair and headed for the door.

'You can leave the chair, Jennings.'

• • •

Jackie and Paul had met up outside Windsor station earlier that morning, and joined a small group of commuters, none of whom was heading for the castle. Paul was unusually silent, displaying a slight nervousness both of them felt. They arrived outside the castle gates a few minutes before eight to be challenged by a guardsman who clearly wasn't expecting them.

When Jackie produced her warrant card, he reluctantly opened the gates and let them both in. They made their way across to the protection officers' quarters, which Jackie had identified on one of her tourist outings.

Jackie walked straight into the main office to find a smartly dressed young woman seated at a desk poring over some figures in a ledger. She looked even more surprised to see them than the guardsman.

'Can I help you?' she asked.

Once again Jackie produced her warrant card, pleased to find they were not expected.

'I'm Constable Smart,' the young woman said, immediately standing up, but clearly still unsure what they were both doing there.

'Are you the only officer on duty this morning, Constable?' Jackie asked.

'Yes,' she replied defensively. 'The others don't usually turn up much before lunch on a Tuesday unless one of the royals has an early appointment,' she added, trying to cover her indiscretion.

Jackie couldn't miss the hint of disapproval in her voice, and wondered if Constable Smart might, given time, turn out to be a useful ally.

'Can I get you a coffee, Sergeant?' the Constable asked politely.

'Thank you,' said Jackie as she sat down beside her and turned her back on Paul.

Paul took the hint and went off in search of an office they might occupy, only to end up finding a spare desk and a broom cupboard. However, when he returned, he was pleased to find Jackie enjoying a second cup of coffee with Constable Smart.

●　●　●

DI Hogan rang the front doorbell at ten minutes to eight. It was opened a few moments later by someone who was clean-shaven, smartly dressed and clearly expecting him.

'Welcome to Kensington Palace, Inspector,' said the butler.

'Please come in. The Princess is having breakfast in her room. I don't expect to see her much before nine, so why don't I show you around while we've got the chance? Let's start with your living quarters, which are on the top floor.'

'Where I come from,' said Ross, 'that's called the attic.'

Burrows laughed as he accompanied the Inspector upstairs. 'I admit your quarters are a little cramped, but you can always join me in the kitchen if you're at a loose end.' He opened a door to reveal a room that was larger than any in Ross's flat. A single bed was tucked away in one corner. 'In case you arrive back late and have an early appointment the following morning,' Burrows explained, 'which isn't unusual. You'll soon learn that HRH is more of an owl than a lark.'

Ross nodded as he looked around the room, surprised by how well equipped it was. He picked up a handwritten card on the desk which read simply, *Welcome*.

'How do I address you?' Burrows asked politely.

'Ross is fine,' he said, opening a wardrobe to find a dozen coat hangers on the rail.

'No, I meant Inspector or sir?'

'I meant Ross.'

'Thank you, Ross. I'm Paul. But not in front of the Princess. You'll find a copy of her engagements for the next week on your desk. She's attending a heart charity lunch at the Dorchester today. The venue's already been checked by an advance team. That will be one of your responsibilities in the future. But whenever you're stuck indoors, as she calls it, you can take a break.' He opened one of the desk drawers and handed over a thick file. 'Here's your prep, Ross. I'll try to answer any questions you might have, but not until you've done your homework. Could I just say you're unusually well-dressed for a policeman?'

'You can blame my late wife for that,' said Ross. 'Jo was French, and didn't have a high opinion of the Brits' dress sense, even less about our lack of appreciation of haute cuisine or fine wine, and gave up completely when it came to how to treat a lady.'

'No wonder the Princess took a liking to you.'

They both laughed. The laughter of two men getting to know each other.

'You'll need to keep a couple of changes of clothes to hand,' continued Burrows. 'A suit for formal occasions, morning dress for weddings or funerals, and a dinner jacket in the evening. Sometimes you'll need all three on the same day.'

'Help,' said Ross.

'Fear not. The cupboard may be bare, but I can guide you in the right direction. If you report to Cassidy and Cassidy in Savile Row, Mr Francis Cassidy will kit you out. He also knows where to send the bill.'

'Will that really be necessary?' asked Ross. 'I've already got a couple of decent suits and a DJ—'

'Not appropriate, I'm afraid. Can't afford to have you looking out of place. You must blend in, so no one gives you a second look. We don't want it to be too obvious that you're her protection officer.'

Ross sat down at his new desk and opened a file marked 'CONFIDENTIAL'.

'Time for me to collect the breakfast tray and help HRH decide what she should wear for her first outing. She always likes a second opinion. I'll let her know you've arrived.'

'Is the Prince of Wales up there with her?'

'You'll soon learn, Ross, there are some questions you just don't ask.'

• • •

The phone on William's desk began to ring, and he picked it up to hear a voice bark, 'Report to my office, immediately.'

William didn't need to be told who was on the other end of the line. He had a feeling Superintendent Milner's office wouldn't be in the basement.

After a couple of enquiries on the way, William ended up outside a door on the second floor where he was greeted with a sign that read in large gold letters:

SUPERINTENDENT BRIAN MILNER

Head of Royalty Protection

He knocked and waited until he heard the command, 'Enter,' before he walked into a large, comfortably furnished room that wouldn't have looked out of place in Buckingham Palace, rather than Buckingham Gate. The walls were lined with photographs of Milner with various members of the Royal Family, leaving the impression they were close friends.

'Sit down, Warwick,' said the Superintendent, without any suggestion of a welcome. William hadn't even sat down before he added, 'I understand you bawled out one of my officers when he was off duty.'

'If you're referring to Sergeant Jennings, sir, when I arrived this morning at sixteen minutes to eight, he was unshaven and incorrectly dressed, despite still being on duty. I didn't bawl him out. But I did leave him in no doubt how I felt about his attitude and appearance while serving as a police officer.'

The look on Milner's face rather suggested he wasn't in the

habit of being addressed in this manner by a junior officer. 'Try to remember, Warwick, they still report to me and not you.' He stared long and hard at William, before adding, 'That is of course, Chief Inspector, unless it's my job you're after.'

'I have no interest in your job, Superintendent. Only doing mine.'

'Frankly, Warwick,' he said, 'I'm at a loss to work out what your job is.'

'I've been asked by the Commissioner to make a comprehensive report on the workings of this unit, to see if any improvements can be made.' William took an envelope from his inside pocket and handed it across to the Superintendent.

'I'm confident, Chief Inspector,' said Milner after he'd read the enclosed instructions, 'that you'll find everything in this outfit is running smoothly and above board.' William wondered why he'd unnecessarily added the words 'above board'. Always wait for a sentence the suspect will later regret, the Hawk had taught him. 'Be assured that if I can assist you in any way, I'll be only too happy to do so,' continued Milner. 'But frankly, I think you're wasting your time.'

'Let's hope you're right, sir,' said William. 'However, would it be possible for DC Pankhurst and me to have an office that doesn't suggest we're the janitors?'

'I don't have any spare rooms at the moment.'

'Perhaps one of your Constables could—'

'And perhaps they couldn't,' snapped Milner.

'I'll also need a secretary,' came back William, 'who can spell as well as type, before we begin to interview all sixty-three members of your staff at Buckingham Gate, as well as those based at Windsor.'

'Is that really necessary?' asked Milner, his voice softening. 'After all, my lads have demanding schedules, and I'm sure I don't have to remind you that the Royal Family don't exactly keep office hours.'

'I'll try not to interfere with their daily duties,' William assured him, 'but if I'm to complete a meaningful report for the Commissioner—'

'I'll want to see that report before you hand it in,' interrupted Milner.

'Of course, sir. I'll keep you informed of my progress at all times, and I feel sure your staff will do the same.'

'Anything else, Warwick, before I'm allowed to get on with my job?' asked the Superintendent curtly.

'Yes, sir. Two members of my team, DS Adaja and DS Roycroft, will be based at Windsor Castle during our inquiry. Can I hope they received a warmer welcome this morning than I did?'

'If you'd let us know when you were coming, Chief Inspector, I would have been here to welcome you myself,' said Milner, not attempting to hide his irritation.

'That would have rather defeated the purpose, sir,' said William, not flinching.

'And what might that purpose be?'

'Simply to prove that your section is, to quote the Commissioner's instructions, fit for purpose.'

'I'm confident you'll find that is the case. However, you need to understand right from the start that Royalty Protection Command is a unique outfit, to which the normal rules don't apply. Try not to forget, Warwick, we are only answerable to the Royal Family, no one else.'

'We are all servants of the Crown, Superintendent. However, I'm also answerable to Commander Hawksby, who in turn will be reporting to the Commissioner.'

The look on the Superintendent's face suggested he was well aware of the Hawk's reputation.

'I feel sure we'll be able to rub along together,' said Milner, the bully suddenly replaced by the sycophant. 'William, isn't it?'

'Chief Inspector Warwick, sir.'

'You have to try and understand, Warwick, the challenges I have to face on a daily basis.'

'I'll do my best to ensure that everyone is given the chance to explain those challenges in great detail, sir.'

'If that's your attitude, Warwick, you might do well to remember that my boss outranks Commander Hawksby,' said Milner, barely able to keep his temper.

'Not to mention the Commissioner, sir,' said William. 'I'll be sure to let my boss know your thoughts on the subject.'

'I think it's time for you to leave, Warwick.' Milner picked up the phone on his desk. 'I'm about to have a word with your commander, so don't bother to settle in. I have a feeling you'll be heading back to Scotland Yard later today. Get me Commander Hawksby at the Yard,' he barked down the phone while waving a dismissive hand in William's direction.

'Thank you, sir,' said William, before leaving the room and closing the door quietly behind him. He returned to the room in the basement to find that Rebecca had somehow managed to commandeer several boxes of paper, a typewriter and even a filing cabinet.

'How did it go?' she asked.

'It could have been worse,' said William, after relaying their conversation, 'but I can't imagine how.'

'Does that mean we'll be back at the Yard in time for lunch?'

'You know very well the Hawk doesn't approve of lunch breaks,' said William as he sat down at his desk and waited for the phone to ring.

CHAPTER 10

'IN THEORY, THIS ONE SHOULD be an open-and-shut case,'
declared Sir Julian as he paced around his office clutching the
lapels of his jacket as if addressing a jury. 'However, in practice,' he paused before continuing, 'there are one or two
anomalies the Crown is unable to ignore.'

Neither Grace nor Clare interrupted their leader while they
took notes.

'Let's begin with the facts of the case. The defendant, Miles
Faulkner, escaped from police custody while attending his
mother's funeral and, some months later, staged his own funeral
to convince the police he was dead.'

'Mrs Faulkner even offered to supply his ashes,' said Clare,
'but I explained to her that we haven't yet mastered how to
identify someone's DNA from their ashes.'

'Faulkner would have been well aware of that – otherwise
he wouldn't have offered them on a silver platter,' said Sir
Julian. 'However, what he couldn't have anticipated was a
vigilant policewoman' – he paused and looked down at the

notes on his desk to check her name – 'Detective Constable Rebecca Pankhurst,' he continued, 'who spotted Faulkner's lawyer, Mr Booth Watson, in a departure lounge at Heathrow, waiting to board a flight for Barcelona. DC Pankhurst interrupted her own holiday so she could join him on that flight without him being aware of her presence. Thanks to the cooperation of the Spanish police,' said Sir Julian, still perambulating, 'Scotland Yard were able to track down Faulkner, who was living in a large, secluded country house a few miles outside the Catalan capital.

'He might have evaded the police yet again had it not been for an equally resourceful Detective Inspector, who ironically ended up saving Faulkner's life. However, that's the point at which it stops being an open-and-shut case. I'll leave you to bring us up to date, Clare,' he said, before turning to his daughter, 'while you, Grace, as my junior, can act as devil's advocate and try to think like Booth Watson.'

'I presume by that you mean devious and amoral, while exuding oily charm when it comes to addressing the jury.'

'Couldn't have put it better myself,' said Sir Julian.

'I have already interviewed both DCI Warwick,' began Clare, avoiding saying 'your son', 'and DI Hogan. Hogan claims that while Faulkner was attempting to escape, he locked himself into his own safe and would have suffocated if he hadn't come to his rescue.'

'That much I believe,' said Sir Julian. 'But I fear the rest of Hogan's story sounds less credible. However, please continue.'

'DI Hogan went on to report that Faulkner was still alive but unconscious when he pulled him out of the safe. With the help of a Lieutenant Sanchez of the Spanish national police, who performed mouth-to-mouth resuscitation, Faulkner regained consciousness and asked to be taken back to London so he could consult his own doctor. He then fainted.'

'That's the bit I find less convincing,' said Sir Julian, 'and I'm sure Booth Watson will find several holes in DI Hogan's evidence once he gets him in the witness box – and will then grandstand when it comes to how it was possible for Hogan to commandeer Faulkner's private jet, and then fly him back to London without his express permission.'

'But Inspector Hogan was able to supply us with the name of Faulkner's physician in Harley Street,' said Grace.

'I suspect that Hogan is a risk-taker, who took a punt on Harley Street and got lucky.'

'Unfortunately, neither Lieutenant Sanchez nor DCI Warwick were able to confirm the exchange between Faulkner and Hogan,' continued Clare, 'and, at the time, they took Hogan at his word. It wasn't until they'd got Faulkner back to England, and he was locked up once again, that DCI Warwick began to consider the consequences of their actions.'

'We should remember,' said Grace, 'that Faulkner was responsible for the tragic death of the Inspector's wife, so Hogan's judgement might well have been, to use a legal term, temporarily impaired.'

'Booth Watson won't be bothering with *temporarily*, once he gets Hogan into the witness box,' said Sir Julian. 'He'll start by raising the subject of kidnapping, which I don't think you'll find is recommended procedure in the Metropolitan Police handbook.'

'And that will be before he turns his attention to the theft of a Frans Hals self-portrait, worth at least half a million,' added Grace, 'that the general public will have the chance to view at an exhibition to be opened by the Princess of Wales.'

'An exhibition that will take place at the Fitzmolean

Museum,' said Clare, 'where coincidentally DCI Warwick's wife just happens to be the keeper of pictures.'

'Booth Watson won't consider it a coincidence, and you can be sure that "the keeper of pictures" will be words he repeats *ad nauseam* while addressing the jury,' said Sir Julian. 'Is there any good news?'

'That problem could well resolve itself as the trial doesn't begin until after the exhibition has closed,' said Clare, 'and the painting will have been returned to its rightful owner.'

'Whoever that might be,' said Sir Julian, the lines on his forehead creasing to reveal deep furrows. 'But how does that help our cause?'

'Mrs Christina Faulkner has signed an affidavit stating that the painting belongs to her,' replied Clare, 'and she therefore has the right to loan it to whomever she pleases.'

'Unfortunately, we won't find out which side that woman is on,' said Grace, 'until she enters the witness box, and that's not a risk I'd be willing to take while BW has more to offer her than we do. And in any case, by then it may be too late.'

'I fear you're right,' said Sir Julian. 'And we're already on shaky ground when it comes to defending our position, as Booth Watson will undoubtedly point out when he joins us for a preliminary consultation' – he checked his watch – 'in about twenty minutes' time.'

'I have a feeling,' said Grace, 'that he'll be only too happy to make a deal that will allow him to get Faulkner off the hook, remembering that he stayed in contact with him after his escape from prison, and even played the conductor at his orchestrated funeral.'

'Let's hope you're right,' added Sir Julian. 'But will it be enough to stop him raising the subjects of kidnap and theft?' He paused for a moment before he picked up a sheet of paper from his desk. 'I've already made a wish list for us to consider,' he declared, 'were we in his shoes.'

'So have I,' said Clare, extracting a sheet of lined yellow paper from the agreed bundle.

'Good, then let's compare notes,' said Grace.

'One,' began Sir Julian, 'BW will demand that the case be heard in open court so all the damning evidence concerning Chief Inspector Warwick will be in the public domain. And by that, I mean on the front pages of every tabloid newspaper, because if there's one thing the press enjoy more than being responsible for putting a criminal behind bars, it's having a go at the police.'

'Judges aren't influenced by the red-tops,' said Grace.

'But juries are,' countered Sir Julian. 'And don't forget not many of them read the *Guardian*.'

'But—' began Grace.

'Therefore,' he continued, taking over from his daughter before she could offer an opinion. 'Don't be surprised if BW advises Faulkner to plead guilty to a lesser offence in exchange for a suspended sentence.'

'Unlikely,' said Grace. 'If that were to happen, the press would want to know the reason why he'd got off so lightly.'

'Two,' said Sir Julian, 'for not raising the subject of a stolen painting, he will demand his client's current sentence be halved to four years, which would mean with good behaviour he'd be released in about a year's time.'

'Hogan should have left him in the safe,' muttered Clare, before putting another tick on her list.

Sir Julian ignored the comment before summing up. 'So, what we're looking at is the Crown calling for the judge to double Faulkner's sentence to sixteen years for absconding from prison, while the defence will be pushing for us to drop the latest charges in exchange for not raising the subject of kidnap and theft, while at the same time halving Faulkner's present sentence if he's willing to plead guilty, thus ensuring nothing gets into the press. So what have we got to offer,' he continued, 'to prevent that from happening? Because at the moment, frankly I can't come up with a whole lot.'

'As I mentioned,' said Grace, 'Booth Watson has one or two of his own problems that he certainly won't want raised in open court.'

'Rehearse your argument as if you were addressing the jury,' instructed Sir Julian, gripping the lapels of his jacket before setting off on another circuit.

'If Booth Watson attended Faulkner's staged funeral in Geneva, as DCI Warwick will confirm he did, and later flew to Barcelona to see him, as witnessed by DC Pankhurst, he must have known all along that Faulkner was still alive, which means, under the 1967 Criminal Law Act, he was aiding and abetting a fugitive. If we can prove that, the police would have no choice but to open a preliminary investigation into his conduct, the results of which they'd pass on to the CPS and the Bar Council. That could result in Booth Watson being struck off, and even arrested for criminal conspiracy, which would make him ineligible to defend Faulkner, or anyone else for that matter.'

Sir Julian considered this for a few moments before saying, 'Much as I dislike the man, let's hope we don't have to stoop that low.'

'Even if we did,' said Clare, 'I feel confident BW will stoop even lower.'

• • •

Ross sat silently in the front passenger seat of the Jaguar while the Princess and Lady Victoria Campbell chatted happily in the back. He tried not to show how nervous he was, remembering this was his first official outing with the Princess.

He had already visited the Dorchester earlier that morning to liaise with the forward recce officer. Together they'd walked the course, so HRH couldn't take a single step in any direction he hadn't anticipated, and after that the sniffer dogs carried out their own form of surveillance.

The FRO briefed the hotel's manager to expect a VIP visitor without naming them, while warning everyone that if any details were to leak, the event would be cancelled or moved to another venue at a moment's notice. That usually ensured everyone involved kept their mouth shut.

Ross had joined them when they'd checked HRH's designated route in and out of the building, while at the same time considering if any alternative was available, should an emergency arise. He'd also requested a private room be put aside with a landline, in case HRH wanted to make a personal call, as well as a rest room for her use only.

Once everything had been covered to his satisfaction, he'd asked the manager if anyone had been sacked recently, someone who might have a grievance they'd want to air in public in the hope it would ruin their day. The last thing Ross double-checked was to confirm there would be an escape vehicle hovering at the rear of the building, with a doctor on board and a driver who enjoyed cutting corners, just in case they needed to leave sharpish.

A second advance team would have gone over everything again after Ross had left, and would have already arrived earlier that morning – not that you'd have noticed them keeping a jaundiced eye on anyone or anything that looked out of place, while a member of the public couldn't have got past the front door without an invitation card, plus personal ID with an up-to-date photograph – which, Ross had been reliably informed, had once stopped Billy Connolly joining HRH for lunch.

And despite all the preparation, they still knew there was always the possibility that something might arise they hadn't considered, which would mean standard procedure would be thrown out of the window. If that were to happen, Ross would be expected to make what the pros called a thinking-on-your-feet decision. It was a protection officer's worst nightmare, because on that one decision alone, your whole career might be judged. Princess Anne's PPO had made an instant decision when the royal car was attacked in the Mall by terrorists – but luckily for him, and for her, he got it right. He was awarded the George Cross, promoted and ended up being the Queen's personal protection officer. But Ross was still hoping something like that would never occur on his watch.

As the car approached the Dorchester, Ross could see a large crowd had gathered on the pavement outside, keenly awaiting the arrival of the Princess. When they drew up at the ballroom entrance, Ross jumped out and opened the back door for his charge. As Diana stepped out she was greeted with cheers and popping flashbulbs.

Ross had been warned by his predecessor that the next few minutes, when she would stop and chat to members of the public, were always the most fraught for any protection officer. He scanned the crowd. Ninety-nine per cent of them would be harmless, but he was only interested in the other one per cent: someone who wasn't waving or cheering; someone he recognized from the mugshots back at the Yard which were indelibly etched on his memory; someone hoping to make it onto tomorrow's front pages. That handful of people who were classified as 'fixated individuals' – the fanatics, the deluded, or even a passionate republican who wanted to express their opinion to a captive audience.

The Princess was met on the pavement by Sir Magdi Yacoub, the eminent Professor of Cardiothoracic Surgery at Imperial College, whose work she'd supported for many years.

After welcoming the Princess, Sir Magdi guided her into the hotel, where a long line of carefully selected supporters and volunteers had been patiently waiting for the past half hour. Diana took her time chatting to each one of them as she progressed slowly down the line, finally to be presented with the obligatory bouquet of flowers by a young nurse. She accepted them with a gracious smile before handing them to her lady-in-waiting. She spent the next twenty minutes mingling with some of those who hadn't been chosen to stand in line.

Ross continued to watch carefully for anyone who stepped into her path or clung on to her hand for a little too long. Despite having carried out a recce of the site earlier that morning, he knew he couldn't afford to relax even for a second.

A gong sounded just before one o'clock. The toastmaster stepped forward and, with a booming voice worthy of a sergeant major, invited the guests to make their way through to the dining room as luncheon was about to be served.

The Princess hung back until everyone had left the room except Sir Magdi, who was waiting for the toastmaster to make a further announcement.

'Please be upstanding for Her Royal Highness the Princess of Wales, accompanied by your chairman, Sir Magdi Yacoub.'

Four hundred guests rose and applauded the Princess all the way to the top table, and no one sat down until she had taken her place. Not for the first time Ross thought how difficult it must be not to allow such unbridled adoration to go to one's head.

His eyes continued to move restlessly around the crowded room of chattering guests who couldn't hide their excitement at being there. He was asked a couple of times if he'd like to sit down and have some lunch, but politely declined, preferring to remain in the wings, just a few steps away from his charge. He hoped he would never have to walk out onto the centre of the stage and play a leading role.

While Diana enjoyed her smoked salmon and chatted to her neighbours on the top table, Ross watched the waiters vigilantly. In Russia, they would be considered the biggest threat.

Once the last plate had been cleared away and coffee served, the speeches began with the chairman's introduction about the charity's work, before he welcomed the guest of honour. The toastmaster placed a small lectern on the table in front of the Princess, and her lady-in-waiting handed her the speech, which she'd seen for the first time that morning; just enough time to add one or two personal comments.

The guests listened to Diana's words with rapt attention, laughed at her jokes and, when she sat down, they rose as one to give her a standing ovation few politicians would ever experience. Not for the first time, Ross wondered if she ever thought about how different her life would have been if she hadn't married the Prince of Wales.

It was finally the turn of the charity's auctioneer to coax money out of the guests. He offered them everything from a box at the Royal Albert Hall for the Last Night of the Proms, to a couple of debenture seats for the women's semi-finals at Wimbledon. After the last item had come under the hammer, he announced that the auction had raised £160,000 for the charity, which was greeted with further loud applause. The Princess leant across and whispered something in the auctioneer's ear.

'Ladies and gentlemen,' he said, returning to the micro-phone. 'Her Royal Highness has agreed to sign your tablecloths for any generous person who will donate one thousand pounds to the charity.'

Several hands immediately shot up, and Ross accompanied the Princess as she moved from table to table, signing the white linen cloths, and a number of napkins – for £500 – using a black felt-tip pen supplied by her lady-in-waiting.

When she finally returned to the top table, the auctioneer announced that the charity had benefited by a further £42,000, making a grand total of £202,000 which would benefit disad-vantaged children in need of heart surgery.

Once again, the audience rose to their feet, the sign it was time for the Princess to leave. Ross stepped forward and cleared a path to ensure she had an uninterrupted journey back to the main entrance. As she passed the auctioneer she whispered, 'Thank you, Jeffrey, it never fails.' The auctioneer bowed, but didn't comment. During his time in the Met, Ross had often witnessed blatant deception, but never at a royal level. As the Princess stepped outside, the flashbulbs once again began to pop, while Ross continued to scan the crowd, some members of which had hung around for hours, hoping for a second glance.

Ross then witnessed one of those personal touches that made Diana so popular with the public. She spotted someone she recognized as having been there when she'd first arrived, and stopped to chat to them. Ross didn't relax until she finally climbed into the back of the car, where Victoria was waiting for her.

The Jaguar moved slowly off, allowing Diana to continue waving until the last well-wisher was out of sight, when she breathed a deep sigh of relief.

'Two hundred and two thousand, ma'am. Not bad,' said Victoria as the car speeded up and two police outriders, their lights flashing and shrill whistles blasting at every junction, cleared the path for her smooth return to Kensington Palace.

'What next?' Diana asked.

'Nothing else today, ma'am,' said Victoria. 'You can relax this evening and enjoy *Blind Date* with Cilla Black.'

'Perhaps I should enter?' she said wistfully.

Ross had quickly come to realize that Diana never wanted to relax. The rush of adrenaline she experienced at these public functions was what kept her going. He still hadn't told William that he'd yet to meet the Prince of Wales.

• • •

'It's good of you to join us, BW,' said Sir Julian, after Booth Watson arrived a few minutes late for their meeting, which didn't surprise the home team. 'I think you already know my junior, who assisted me when you and I crossed swords during Faulkner's first trial.'

'You needn't look forward to the same result this time, young lady,' said Booth Watson, giving Grace a patronizing smile and receiving a curt nod in return.

'And my instructing solicitor for this case,' Sir Julian continued, ignoring the barb, 'will be Clare Sutton.' Booth Watson barely acknowledged her before taking his seat on the other side of the table. 'I thought it might be useful to have a preliminary discussion now that the trial date has been set.'

'Couldn't agree more,' said Booth Watson, taking the Crown by surprise. 'That's assuming you have something worthwhile to offer that I can take back to my client for his consideration.'

'Not a great deal,' admitted Sir Julian, unwilling to reveal his hand. 'We will be recommending that the judge doubles Mr Faulkner's present sentence to sixteen years, which I doubt will come as a surprise to you. However,' he continued before Booth Watson could respond, 'Mr Justice Cummings has agreed to knock two years off the sentence if your client pleads guilty, which would save the court considerable time and expense.'

The three of them waited for the volcano to erupt, but no lava appeared.

'I will put your offer to my client,' said Booth Watson, 'and let you know his response.'

'Are there any mitigating circumstances that you would like us to consider at this juncture?' asked Grace, delivering a well-prepared line.

'None that I can think of, Ms Warwick,' came back the immediate reply. 'But should anything arise following my consultation with Mr Faulkner, you'll be the first to hear.'

Once again, Sir Julian was taken by surprise, and it was a few moments before he responded. 'Well, if there's nothing more to discuss, BW, we'll wait to hear back from you in the fullness of time.'

'That's good of you, Julian,' said Booth Watson, rising from his seat. 'I'll be seeing my client towards the end of the week, and will be back in touch as soon as I've received my instructions.'

Sir Julian reluctantly stood and shook hands with his rival as if they were old friends before accompanying him to the door, where he said, 'I look forward to hearing from you, BW.'

Clare waited until after the door had been closed before she said, 'What's he up to?'

'One of two things,' said Sir Julian. 'He's either keeping his powder dry until after he's consulted Faulkner, which seems to me the most likely explanation, unless—' The two of them waited for him to complete the sentence. 'No,' he said eventually. 'I'm unwilling to believe that even BW would sink that low . . .'

CHAPTER 11

WILLIAM WAS THE SECOND PERSON to arrive at the meeting that morning, and wondered if the commander ever went to bed.

The rest of the team were all seated around the table long before the appointed hour and, as each one of them had placed a thick file on the table, it was clear no one had been keeping office hours.

'Welcome back,' said the Hawk. 'As I've not been on the ground for this particular operation, I'll ask DCI Warwick to bring us up to date.'

William outlined in detail the reception he'd received when he and Rebecca had first arrived at Buckingham Gate, before he turned to Jackie and Paul to find out if they'd fared any better at Windsor.

No one was surprised that Paul was the first to offer an opinion.

'You wouldn't think we were all serving in the same outfit,' he told them. 'Milner addressed me as Detective Sergeant

Sambo when he first met me the other day, so heaven knows what he calls me behind my back.'

'I wish I could say I'm surprised,' said William, unable to hide his anger.

'That lot are sexist as well as racist,' said Rebecca. 'Women are only good for two things in Milner's opinion, and one of them isn't being a Royalty Protection officer.'

'At least you've got an office,' said Jackie. 'They've put me in an outbuilding that must have been a garden shed before I turned up. I don't have a desk, just a wheelbarrow and a flower pot.'

Nobody laughed.

'That's good to hear,' said the Hawk, taking them all by surprise. 'Because it only confirms my feeling that they've got something to hide. Our job is to find out what that something is.'

'Check with Admin for a start,' said Ross. 'I took a taxi from my home to Kensington Palace last Thursday, and claimed it on expenses, despite the fact that the number fifty-two bus would have dropped me outside the palace gates. Milner didn't even query it.'

'We're lucky to have you on the inside,' said William, 'because the rest of us are still on the starting line.'

'And I'm fed up with being told that if I've got a complaint, I should have a word with the Prince of Wales,' said Paul.

'I suspect,' said the commander, 'that the Royal Family have no idea what's going on in their names.'

'And worse,' said William, 'when I was given the one chance to discuss a possible terrorist threat with Milner, he dismissed it out of hand. Told me I was overreacting and, in time, I'd realize he had everything under control.'

'Until the one time something does go wrong,' came back

the commander, 'when he'll realize it's too late to do anything about it.'

'Meanwhile,' said William, 'we're just banging our heads against a brick wall.'

'It's just possible, sir,' said Jackie, 'that I may have found a loose brick in that wall, and if I could remove it, the whole edifice could come tumbling down.' She paused for a moment, clearly enjoying herself.

'Take your time, Detective Sergeant,' teased William.

'There's a Constable Jenny Smart who currently works in admin, who's considering applying for reassignment.'

'Why?' asked the Hawk.

'I think that Milner has promised her once too often that she'll be next in line to join a Royalty Protection team, and be allocated to her own principal,' said Jackie. 'But the last three officers to retire have all been replaced by men, one of them a young Constable only three years into the job, who just happens to be the son of a recently retired officer. Constable Smart remains stuck on the bench while less experienced colleagues are invited onto the field of play. If Milner passes her over one more time, he may end up shooting himself in the foot.'

'The foot's far too good for him,' said Paul. 'He'd take early retirement and claim a full disability pension.'

'Patience,' said Jackie once the laughter had died down. 'We may not have too long to wait before the odds change in our favour.'

'How come?' asked William.

'Princess Anne's personal protection officer retires at the end of the month, and Constable Smart is the obvious person to take his place.'

'If Constable Smart doesn't get the job,' said William, 'that might be our chance to turn her into a whistleblower.'

'I've no doubt she knows where all the bodies are buried,' said Jackie. 'So I'll keep working on her.'

'Drop regular hints as to why she's the obvious choice to be the next Royalty Protection officer,' suggested the commander, 'sprinkled with how well she'd do the job. Just keep sowing the seeds of doubt in her mind, and she'll begin to feel she's at last got someone on her side.'

'But reel her in slowly,' said William, 'because it won't be easy for her to break ranks after all these years. Meanwhile, let's all get back to our desks, or our wheelbarrows, and work on gathering as much muck as we can, so that it won't be possible for Milner to find a loophole, a credible explanation, or any other way of getting off the hook.'

'But keep in mind,' said Ross, 'that Milner has the ear of the Prince of Wales, who he's taken care of since he left the navy, which may make him almost impossible to remove.'

'That sort always think they're above the law,' said the commander. 'But Ross has already identified his Achilles heel.'

'Cash,' said William.

'In one,' said the Hawk. 'So, let's stick to the old maxim when chasing a criminal. Follow the money.'

'But be sure to tread carefully,' said William, 'because that lot won't hesitate to leave landmines in your path. Step on one, and we'll all be blown to smithereens.'

After a long pause, the commander said, 'Perhaps the time has come for a change of tactics.' He hesitated for a moment while he weighed up the consequences of what he was about to say. 'Why don't you all play along for now and, like Ross, make it look as if you've climbed aboard their gravy train. And Ross, see how much you can get away with before Milner queries your expenses.'

'I was thinking of inviting the Princess's lady-in-waiting out for dinner this weekend,' said Ross. They all laughed, except William.

'She'll be used to the finest food and wine,' the commander chipped in, 'so you can run up a hefty bill and then see if Milner questions it. But we'll need other examples of blatant disregard of normal police practice before we can make a move. Be cautious, and act dumb, which shouldn't be too difficult for Paul.'

The gentle ribbing caused more laughter, which William knew would only spur Paul on to outdo them all.

'And, Jackie,' said the commander, 'keep working on your new best friend' – he glanced down at his notebook – 'Constable Smart, because she could turn out to be our best bet. Good hunting.'

• • •

Jackie followed the commander's advice, and over the weekend she and Jenny Smart went clubbing in the West End. Although William had warned her to be patient – not a virtue Jackie had in abundance – a dimly lit basement and one too many vodkas had loosened Constable Smart's tongue enough for Jackie to come away with all the ammunition she needed.

When Jackie got home just after two a.m., she spent the next hour writing up copious notes. She may have told Jenny how much she expected her to get the job (richly deserved) as Princess Anne's PPO, but she secretly hoped she'd be passed over once again, because she felt confident that would be the last straw for Constable Smart, and it wouldn't take a dark basement in a nightclub for her to reveal everything she knew about Milner and his extra-curricular activities.

Jackie was getting off the bus on her way back to work the

following morning when she spotted DI Reynolds and Sergeant Jennings entering 'Pride of Plaice', which she'd been assured by Jennings was the best fish and chip shop in Windsor.

She was about to cross the road and join them when she saw Reynolds take the owner to one side, clearly having a quiet word. She slipped into a shop doorway and remained out of sight. The two officers reappeared a few moments later and began to eat their lunch out of a newspaper as they headed back in the direction of the castle. Jackie waited until they'd turned the corner, before she crossed the road and strolled into the fish and chip shop.

'A portion of cod and chips,' Jackie said when she reached the front of the queue.

'Coming up, my dear,' Jackie the assistant.

'They must be good,' remarked Jackie. 'I saw you serving a couple of my colleagues a moment ago.'

'You work for Royalty Protection?' he said, giving her a closer look.

'Sure do,' Jackie replied as he took his time selecting her fish.

'Then I hope you'll become a regular, like the rest of the lads from the castle. Salt and vinegar?'

'Yes, please.'

He wrapped up the order and placed it in a bag before handing it to her. 'That'll be three quid.'

Jackie handed him a five-pound note and waited for the change.

'Will you be wanting a receipt?'

'Yes, please.'

He nodded to the girl on the till, who handed back two pounds in change along with a receipt, which Jackie slipped into her handbag. Once she was out on the pavement, she unwrapped her unexpected meal and took a bite from a succulent piece of cod as she walked slowly towards the castle. The Plaice's reputation turned out to be well-deserved, although she could hear her mother saying, 'Nothing wrong with fish and chips, my dear, but you should never eat them out of a newspaper on the street.' Not for the first time, Jackie was glad her mother was more than a hundred miles away.

She'd devoured the last morsel by the time she was back at her desk, where she dropped the front page of last week's *News of the World* into a wastepaper basket, before washing her hands. She placed her handbag on the desk, took out the receipt and looked at it for the first time: £9.50.

• • •

The prisoner was seated in the glass cube waiting for his lawyer long before Booth Watson appeared. It used to be the other way around.

When Booth Watson entered the inner sanctum, he sat down opposite his client. 'Good morning, Miles,' he said as if it were a private consultation in his chambers, and not in a glass cage being spied on by a couple of prison guards. 'I'm sorry I haven't seen you for some time,' he continued, placing his Gladstone bag on the floor by his side, 'but I wanted to wait until I had something worthwhile to report. To that end, I've already had meetings with Sir Julian, who continues to represent the Crown in this case, as well as your ex-wife. Remembering that we only have an hour, let's get Christina out of the way before I move on to my consultation with Sir Julian.'

'How much is she expecting to get to keep her trap shut?'

'Thirty million,' said Booth Watson without batting an eyelid.

'She must be joking,' said Miles at the top of his voice, which caused the guards to look more closely.

'Christina is not known for her sense of humour,' Booth Watson reminded him. 'And don't forget that she was married to you for ten years, so is well aware what your art collection is worth. While she may not know how much you've got stashed away in your Swiss bank accounts, just the mention of Switzerland to her friend Beth Warwick will be more than enough for her husband to ask the tax authorities to instigate a full inquiry. Not something you need at the moment.'

Miles was about to respond when Booth Watson raised a hand. 'However, I'm convinced I can get her to settle for twenty,' he paused, 'in cash, explaining that way she would avoid capital gains tax, which has the added advantage of ensuring she can't risk letting anyone know about any of your other activities.'

'How much do I have in my safe-deposit boxes at the bank?'

'Just over twenty-two million,' said Booth Watson, who had anticipated the question.

'So that would just about clean me out.'

'If you were to offer her the apartment in Mayfair as well as the villa in Monte Carlo, you might end up only having to part with ten million in cash.'

'And there's nothing to stop me mortgaging both properties up to the hilt and leaving her with the repayments,' said Miles. 'Do you think you can pull that off, BW?'

'It would present somewhat of a challenge,' admitted Booth Watson, 'but it's not impossible.'

'Then get the agreement signed as quickly as possible.'

'We've agreed to meet at the bank next Friday afternoon, when I'll be bringing along two large empty suitcases. I have a feeling that when she sees ten million in cash, it will prove very persuasive.'

'Perhaps the suitcases could be reclaimed before they reach her bank?' said Miles, allowing his words to hang in the air.

Booth Watson didn't make any notes while his client explained what, with the help of ex-superintendent Lamont, he expected to happen not long after Christina had left the bank.

'And if you pull that one off, BW,' he said, 'you can keep a million for yourself.' That wasn't the figure Booth Watson had in mind. 'But none of this is going to make a blind bit of difference,' continued Miles, 'if you can't get me out of here to enjoy the proceeds. So tell me, how did your meeting with Sir Julian Warwick go?'

'I don't think it could have gone much better. But I'll leave you to be the judge of that.'

Miles sat back, folded his arms and listened.

'I reminded Sir Julian that kidnapping is a serious crime, and also pointed out that stealing a painting worth over a million pounds might just whet the press's appetite, especially if it were to result in his son ending up in the dock. It didn't take him a great deal of time to decide which was more important: extending your stay in prison or saving his son from the same fate.'

A flicker of a smile appeared on Faulkner's face.

'However, he still wanted his pound of flesh.'

'Without spilling any blood, I hope,' said Faulkner.

'A scratch at most,' promised Booth Watson. 'That's assuming you are willing to plead guilty to the charge of escaping while in police custody.'

'You must be joking.'

'I've never gone in for jokes, Miles, as you well know.

However, if you did plead guilty, Sir Julian would recommend to the CPS that you receive a suspended sentence.'

'Why would they agree to that?' asked Miles incredulously.

'The last thing the CPS would want is for the whole unfortunate episode in Spain to be made public. The Met have enough problems of their own at the moment, and if the trial were to collapse, Sir Julian could end up having to defend his son rather than prosecuting you. No, I'm fairly confident they'll want to keep this case out of court. So, if you were to instruct me to inform the other side that we might agree to their terms, subject to a written agreement' – he paused – 'written by me, I will brief Sir Julian accordingly.'

'How long will that take?'

'I've already prepared a preliminary draft, so a few days at most. Once you've signed the agreement, I would start work on your early release, which means you'll have to be a model prisoner for the next few months. And, Miles, I mean model.' Booth Watson bent down and placed the file back in his Gladstone bag. 'What's the first thing you'll do once you've been released?'

'Treat you to a slap-up meal at the Savoy, with a good bottle of wine, as I won't be ending the evening back in my cell.'

'I'll look forward to that,' said Booth Watson, knowing that if he could get Miles to sign the agreement, he needn't bother to book their usual table at the Savoy – for the next fourteen years.

CHAPTER 12

FAULKNER USED THE DAILY EXERCISE break productively.

Tulip had fixed a meeting with the one person who could make it happen. Reggie the pimp, sentenced to five years for importuning young boys for personal gain.

'How can I be of assistance, Mr Faulkner?' Reggie asked as they strolled around the exercise yard together. Two heavily built prisoners in front of them, and a couple more a few paces behind, ensured that the boss wasn't interrupted.

'I need a male prostitute for Friday evening,' said Faulkner. 'He has to be all things bright and beautiful.'

'It will be quite difficult to smuggle one into the prison, Mr Faulkner, even with your contacts.'

'Not for me, moron. It's for my wife.'

'Sorry, guv, misunderstood you. So what will my boy be expected to do?'

'My wife always goes to Tramp on Friday evening, hoping to pick up someone she can later take home. I need one of your more experienced lotharios to oblige, and make sure he gets invited back for the night.'

'I know someone she won't be able to resist,' said Reggie. 'Goes by the name of Sebastian.'

'That's the beautiful part,' said Miles. 'Now for the bright bit, which could prove more of a challenge. If he's done the first part of his job properly, he'll have to stay put until she falls asleep. That's when he'll really start to earn his money. Somewhere in my wife's apartment will be two black Tumi suitcases. They'll be fairly large, so they shouldn't be difficult to locate. Once he's got them, he'll find a man waiting outside the apartment to pick them up. So, what's the damage?'

'Shall we say a couple of grand, Mr Faulkner?'

Faulkner nodded and the two men shook hands – the only way of closing a deal in prison, and heaven help anyone who even thought about breaking the unwritten contract.

'Consider it done,' said Reggie as the five-minute hooter blasted, the sign that the prisoners should return to their cells. 'Dare I ask what's in them suitcases?' he asked, as they left the yard.

'No,' said Faulkner. 'But if your boy fails to hand them over, don't even think about going into a shower on your own.'

• • •

Booth Watson waited for his secretary to leave the room before he looked up the private number and began dialling.

'Warwick,' said a voice on the other end of the line.

'It's Booth Watson, Julian. Just wanted to let you know I've consulted my client and, to my surprise, he has agreed to your terms.'

'He's willing to plead guilty to all the charges in exchange for two years being knocked off his sentence?' said Sir Julian, but didn't add, I don't believe you.

'I advised him against it, of course, which won't surprise you.'

Sir Julian was surprised, but kept his counsel.

'I did everything in my power to dissuade him, but he'd already made up his mind.' One sentence too many – that only convinced Sir Julian that Booth Watson wasn't telling the truth. 'So, if you'll go ahead and draw up an agreement, I'll arrange for him to sign it. Pity,' Booth Watson added. 'I was looking forward to crossing swords with you again.'

That much Sir Julian did believe.

'I'll come back to you,' he said, 'as soon as the CPS have given their seal of approval.'

'I look forward to hearing from you, Julian. We must have lunch sometime. The Savoy, perhaps.'

Another unnecessary sentence that gave the game away, thought Sir Julian as his secretary entered the room.

'Tell me, Miss Weeden, am I dreaming?' he asked as he put the phone down.

'I don't think so, Sir Julian,' said his secretary, looking puzzled.

'In which case, please ask Ms Warwick and Ms Sutton to join me immediately for an urgent consultation.'

• • •

'Mrs Faulkner and I will be coming out of the bank at around five o'clock,' said Booth Watson. 'She'll have two large suitcases with her, which no doubt her chauffeur will place in the boot of the car, a dark blue Mercedes J423 ABN.' Lamont made a note. 'As all the banks will have closed for the day, she's likely to be driven straight home.'

'What if the chauffeur just drops her off, and she leaves the bags in the boot of the car for him to take care of?'

'Unlikely. I don't think Mrs Faulkner will be willing to let the money out of her sight. She won't feel safe until it's inside her apartment.'

'Why don't I grab the bags as they're being taken out of the car boot?' asked Lamont.

'Can't risk it. We'll have to be more subtle than that. The chauffeur will probably carry the bags into her apartment block, and don't forget the porter will be standing by the door. And I've checked, he's six foot two, and has a broken nose, so I don't think so.'

'So how do I get my hands on the two cases?'

'Mrs Faulkner will probably return to the flat around midnight, after spending the evening at Tramp. She will be accompanied by what she imagines to be her latest conquest, a plant called Sebastian, who will in fact be our man. You will be waiting outside in your car until he comes out in the early hours with the suitcases, which he'll hand over in exchange for this.' Booth Watson pushed a thick brown envelope across the desk.

'What do I do with the suitcases?'

'Bring them straight back here to my chambers.'

'But it might be three or four o'clock in the morning,' said Lamont.

'I don't give a damn what time it is. Just get them here as quickly as you can. *Your* payment will be strictly cash on delivery.'

Lamont picked up the package and rose to leave, assuming the meeting was over.

'And don't think about looking inside those suitcases,' Booth Watson warned him. 'Or even consider short-changing the man who hands them over, because three of us know exactly how much is in that envelope, and one of them is Miles Faulkner.'

• • •

'I think I've worked out what BW is up to,' said Sir Julian, once his daughter and Clare had settled.

'Which is more than I have,' said Grace.

'First, you have to ask yourself why Faulkner would be willing to go along with our proposal that if he pleads guilty all he will get in return is two years knocked off a sixteen-year sentence. Have either of you worked that one out?'

Clare raised a hand like a swot at the front of the class. Sir Julian nodded.

'Booth Watson knows if the case comes to court, the judge might ask him a question that would not only get him disbarred, but could cause him to end up in jail himself.'

'And what is that question?'

'When did you first realize that Mr Miles Faulkner was still alive?'

'He'd bluff and prevaricate,' said Sir Julian, 'and claim he didn't know until after Faulkner had been arrested, and he was as surprised as any of us.'

'BW's well capable of ditching Faulkner,' said Grace, 'if it means saving his own skin.'

'But how will he explain what he was doing at Faulkner's home outside Barcelona on the day he was arrested?' asked Claire.

'Representing the interests of his client, Mrs Faulkner, by making an inventory of her late husband's possessions,' suggested Sir Julian.

'But what if the court requested to see Booth Watson's diary as evidence?' came back Clare.

'You can be sure that BW keeps at least two diaries,' said Sir Julian. 'But if you're so clever, perhaps you can tell me how Booth Watson is going to get Faulkner to sign an agreement that ensures his client spends the next fourteen years in jail?'

'That's been puzzling both of us,' admitted Clare. 'I'd certainly like to be a fly on the wall when BW next visits Faulkner in prison.'

'There's another question that's even more intriguing,' said Grace. 'Why does Booth Watson want Faulkner to spend the next fourteen years in jail?'

'Because he knows where the bodies are buried, would be my guess,' said Sir Julian.

'The bodies?'

'Rembrandt, Vermeer, Monet, Manet, Picasso, Hockney . . .'

CHAPTER 13

BOOTH WATSON KNEW IT WOULD be a question of careful timing if he hoped to pull it off. He'd have to keep one eye on the clock to make sure it was 10.56 before he made his move.

He entered the lawyer's glass domain at one minute past ten, sat down opposite his client and smiled, before placing his Gladstone bag on the floor next to his chair.

'Good morning, Miles. Shall we start with the good news?' He bent down, took out the first contract and pushed it across the table for his client to consider. 'I'm confident this agreement will ensure that Christina won't cause you any trouble in future. But you should still go over it carefully, and don't hesitate to query anything you're not sure about.'

Faulkner put his glasses on and began to read the document line by line. The occasional nod or smile, while Booth Watson kept his eye on the clock. But he couldn't make the minute hand move any faster.

When Faulkner turned to the last page, a smile of satisfaction appeared on his face.

'I couldn't have asked for much more,' he said. 'That's assuming Lamont has been fully briefed on what's expected of him when our toyboy reappears with the suitcases?'

'The moment they've been handed over to Lamont, he'll bring them straight to my chambers.'

'What if Lamont decides not to show up? He could then live the rest of his life in luxury, while I'd have to spend a fortune trying to track him down.'

'I already have a back-up following him to cover that eventuality.'

'You can't trust anyone nowadays,' commented Miles. 'Least of all a bent ex-copper with a history of backing losers, whether they're nags or fillies.' He quickly changed tack. 'What about the more important contract, which will determine if I'll get to enjoy the before life again?'

Booth Watson glanced at the clock on the wall: 10.25. He'd hoped there would be several more questions before he had to move on.

'It's important,' he emphasized, replacing the first contract with another, 'that you read this contract even more carefully, as the rest of your life depends on it.'

Faulkner looked at a document that had been typed up on Crown Prosecution headed paper, which Booth Watson had slipped into his bag during a visit to their offices on Petty France earlier in the week.

'I can't believe the CPS has agreed to such favourable terms,' he said long before he reached the last page.

'I allowed the director to read my opening speech to the jury,' said Booth Watson. 'It helped to concentrate his mind on the alternatives.'

'You seem to have covered everything, BW,' said Faulkner, checking the last paragraph once again.

Let's hope so, thought Booth Watson. 'Do you have any questions before you sign?'

'Just one. Can you explain the significance of the non-disclosure clause, and the repercussions should I break it?'

'Put simply, if at any time in the future you were to mention what took place at your home in Spain last September, the deal would be off and you'd be arrested, returned to prison, have to complete your original sentence, and possibly face new charges. So whatever you do, Miles, don't say a word to anyone other than me until the judge passes sentence.' He paused to make sure the threat had sunk in. 'Anything else?' he asked, stealing another glance at the clock: 10.51. Still time to kill.

'I had a word with my parole officer on Monday,' said Faulkner, 'and he made no mention of an early release.'

'He won't be put in the picture until after you've signed the agreement. Once you've done that, he'll simply carry out orders from above.'

'Where do I sign?'

'You don't. That's just a copy for you to hold on to. I'd advise you to keep it away from prying eyes.'

There was a firm rap on the door, and they turned to see the duty officer standing there. 'Five minutes, sir.'

'Mr Harris,' said Booth Watson, 'I wonder if I might call upon your services. My client is about to sign an important legal document, and I need someone to witness his signature.'

'Happy to oblige,' said Harris.

Booth Watson took three new agreements from his Gladstone bag and placed them on the table in front of him. He then turned to the last page of each one. Faulkner was pleased to see that Sir Julian had already signed all three of them. The duty officer waited for Faulkner to add his signature, before scribbling his name and occupation on the dotted line below.

Once both of them had signed all three documents, Booth Watson didn't wait for the ink to dry before he dropped them back into his bag.

'Thank you, Mr Harris,' he said to the innocent bystander. Turning back to Faulkner, he added, 'That completes our business for today.' Booth Watson picked up his bag then stood aside to allow the guard to accompany his prisoner back to the cells while he left in the opposite direction.

'Good luck!' shouted Faulkner as he was led away. Booth Watson turned nervously, unsure what his client was referring to. 'Be sure to give my love to Christina when you see her this afternoon.'

• • •

When Christina was dropped off at the bank later that afternoon, she found Booth Watson already waiting by the entrance. His Gladstone bag had been replaced by two large black empty suitcases.

After a brief salutation, he led her towards the lifts on the other side of the foyer. It was clear he knew exactly where he was going. They didn't speak to each other during the short journey to the basement. When the lift doors opened, they were greeted with the words, 'Good morning, Mr Booth Watson. My name is Bradshaw. I'm the bank's security officer. Please allow me to accompany you to the safe-deposit vault.'

Without another word, he led them along a well-lit corridor to the entrance of the bank's vault. Bradshaw entered an eight-digit code on a panel in the wall, and waited for a moment before pulling open the vast circular steel door to allow his two customers to enter the private domain. A large wooden table dominated the centre of the room, and as far as Christina could see the walls were lined from floor to ceiling with numbered boxes: a bank's library.

Bradshaw checked his clipboard before selecting a key from a large ring, knelt down in front of two of the largest boxes in the room, and turned his key in the bank's lock. Booth Watson then produced his key and opened the customer's lock. Bradshaw pulled out the two heavy boxes, heaved them up onto the table, and said, 'I'll leave you now, sir. Once you've completed your business, just press the green button by the door and it will automatically open. I'll be waiting on the other side.'

Booth Watson waited until Bradshaw had left, and the vast door had been slammed shut behind him, before he lifted the lids of the boxes to reveal row upon row of freshly minted fifty-pound notes neatly sealed in bundles of five thousand pounds. Twenty minutes later they had completed the task of transferring the cash from the strongboxes into the two suitcases.

After double-checking that Christina hadn't been overpaid, Booth Watson took an envelope from an inside pocket and produced a contract she thought she'd read the day before. Christina signed all three copies of the agreement without a second thought.

Booth Watson pocketed the contracts, but not before he said, 'You now own the flat in London and the villa in Monte Carlo.' He made no mention of the substantial mortgages he'd recently obtained on behalf of his client, and were now her responsibility. 'However, I must warn you,' he added, 'should you fail to honour your side of the bargain, I will not hesitate to inform the tax authorities about your unexpected windfall.'

'You assured me I wouldn't have to pay a penny in tax,' Christina reminded him.

'And you won't, just as long as no one else learns about our little arrangement.' Without another word, Booth Watson pressed the green button on the wall and the door swung slowly open. Once they'd stepped back outside, Bradshaw closed the door behind them and led them back down the corridor towards the lift, Booth Watson pulling one of the heavy suitcases, with Christina following in his wake tugging the other.

When they reached the ground floor, Booth Watson handed the second case to Christina, who dragged both of them slowly towards the entrance. She'd had no idea how heavy ten million pounds would be.

Booth Watson stood aside and watched as a dark blue Mercedes pulled up outside the bank's entrance. A chauffeur got out, opened the boot and stowed the two suitcases inside before returning to his place behind the wheel. At the same time, Christina opened the rear door of the car and climbed in the back. Once she'd pulled the door shut, the Mercedes drove off and joined the early-evening traffic. The whole process had taken less than a minute, and had clearly been carefully planned, probably even rehearsed. Booth Watson smiled to himself: it wasn't the only plan that had been well-rehearsed.

He strolled out of the bank as a black Volvo tucked in behind the Mercedes, an ex-superintendent at the wheel. Booth Watson crossed the road, hailed a cab, and headed in the opposite direction.

As the Mercedes came to a halt outside Christina's

apartment in Eaton Square, Lamont pulled into a residents' parking bay a few yards away on the opposite side of the road. The chauffeur opened the boot, lifted out the two suitcases and accompanied Mrs Faulkner to the front door, which a liveried porter held open for them.

Lamont only had to wait for a few minutes before the chauffeur reappeared and drove off. Job done. Well, not quite.

CHAPTER 14

DURING HIS UNDERCOVER DAYS AT the Yard, Lamont had become used to waiting for hours on end for his quarry to appear. This evening he sat through the six o'clock news, a comedy game show, an episode of *The Archers* and a current affairs programme about the Falklands, before Christina reappeared in what he would have described as her glad rags. A bomber jacket covered in studs, a loose-fitting blouse with one button too many undone, faded jeans, ripped in all the right places, and a pair of high-heeled shoes completed an outfit she no doubt hoped made her look ten years younger.

She hailed a passing taxi and Lamont followed, making sure he kept his distance. But then, he already knew where she was going. When the cabbie turned into Jermyn Street, he parked across the road from his mark, knowing he couldn't afford to nod off, as that would surely be the one moment when she reappeared. He settled down to listen to *The World Tonight*, while Christina made her way down the metal steps to one of London's most fashionable nightclubs.

The maître d' welcomed her with open arms, before accompanying his customer to her favourite alcove table. She didn't need to peruse the cocktail menu, as a glass of champagne appeared moments later. Christina began to look around the room, her eyes settling on several young men, each with an even younger woman seated beside them.

Christina was sipping her second glass when she spotted him at the bar. He could have had any woman in the room, but they both knew she had something they didn't. Their eyes met, and she raised her glass in a mock toast. He returned the compliment, slipped off his stool and strolled across to join her.

• • •

Ross watched Diana from a discreet distance, tucked behind a pillar at his usual table. She was sipping champagne with a man he didn't know, but whose life story he'd have after one phone call in the morning. The man couldn't have known her that long or he'd have realized she was teetotal, and only raised her glass whenever a toast was called. Ross couldn't deny he was a good-looking guy, though he didn't care for the ponytail. He also had to admit he'd never seen HRH looking so relaxed and happy, but he could hear his old Irish mother saying, 'Mark my words, it will end in tears.' Between courses the couple spent some time on the dance floor, and Ross recalled HRH once telling him she would rather have been a professional dancer than a Princess. But her dance instructor had told her she had a problem, 'You're too tall! You could work the cruises,' he assured her, 'but not the west end.' She now worked both.

Ross glanced around the room and spotted Christina Faulkner seated on the other side of the dance floor. It wasn't difficult to work out what her young companion was hoping to get in exchange for spending the night with a lonely, middle-aged woman. Ross wondered what the going rate was.

His gaze returned to his charge and her dancing partner, who were now holding hands below the table, while Mrs Faulkner's latest already had his hand on her thigh. As Ross ate a house salad, and sipped a glass of water – very expensive water – he couldn't help thinking about Jojo, who he'd promised to spend the weekend with. When the DJ changed the mood from pop to a ballad, Diana and her partner returned to the dance floor, where Ross didn't like what he saw. He looked away, to see Christina's head resting on her conqueror's shoulder, while his hand moved lower and lower down her back.

Ross drank a black coffee and thought he'd much rather be sharing a chocolate nut sundae with Jojo at the zoo. His eyes returned to another zoo, where the animals had only one thing on their minds, while he thought about Jojo's mother, the only woman he'd ever loved, and didn't envy either Diana or Christina.

Lamont couldn't miss the Princess of Wales as she left the nightclub just after midnight surrounded by a throng of photographers, with DI Hogan holding them back as he open-ed the car door to allow her to escape. God, how he hated the paparazzi.

Ross slipped into the front passenger seat, relieved that the Princess's dinner companion was nowhere to be seen. The photographers continued flashing until the car had turned the corner, when they all headed back to Fleet Street hoping to catch the second edition.

It was another hour before Christina appeared with her young man, one hand having moved onto her denim-clad bottom, while he hailed a taxi with the other. Lamont kept his distance as he followed them back to her apartment and, after they'd disappeared inside, he settled down for another long wait. Long enough to contemplate what he might do when he got his hands on those two suitcases. He had no idea what was inside them, but Booth Watson's threat suggested it might just be worth the risk.

• • •

DI Hogan dropped the Princess back at Kensington Palace, before leaving her to walk home. He wanted to clear his head while he considered the implications of what he'd witnessed that night.

As he was passing the Albert Hall he spotted a pink Porsche coming in the opposite direction. He was just thinking how tasteless it was when he caught sight of the driver, who was clearly heading in the direction of the palace. He made a note of the number plate. Was it his responsibility to report everything he'd seen to the commander, or should he mind his own business?

By the time he'd reached his little flat – Jo's little flat – he'd made up his mind to tell William everything he'd seen, and let him decide whether or not to pass it on to the Hawk. It was, after all, way above his pay grade. He took a cold shower before going to bed, and fell asleep within minutes.

• • •

Sebastian pulled the sheet slowly back, slipped out of bed and placed both feet silently on the floor. After checking the steady breathing coming from the other side of the bed, he got dressed in the dark, something he was used to.

121

It hadn't been difficult to spot the two large black suitcases, which were not very well hidden under the bed. He lowered himself to his knees and slowly pulled them out, pausing briefly to make sure he hadn't disturbed her. He waited a few moments before gently dragging them across the carpet, his eyes never leaving the bed. They were far heavier than he had anticipated, which made him wonder what was inside. He stood up and tentatively opened the bedroom door – no creaks, no bedside light switched on. He didn't even risk a sigh of relief.

Once he'd got the two bags out of the bedroom, he closed the door quietly behind him. He avoided switching on a light, and as he moved slowly across the room, he banged his shin on the corner of a low glass table. He collapsed onto a sofa, somehow managing not to cry out. No light appeared below the bedroom door, but he still didn't move for some time. The only noise to accompany his breathing was the relentless ticking of a grandfather clock. He set off again, making his way even more cautiously as he pulled the two cases towards the front door. He removed the security chain, slowly turned the latch and poked his head out into the dimly lit corridor. After checking both ways, he pushed the suitcases out into the corridor and quietly pulled the door closed behind him, the only sound a sharp click.

He wheeled the two suitcases towards the lift, not daring to breathe that deep sigh of relief until the doors slid closed. When they opened again on the ground floor, he already had a well-rehearsed line should the night porter question him – Mrs Faulkner will be down in a few minutes. We're off to her home in Surrey.

Lamont had told him where her country home was.

Sebastian crossed the hall to see the porter was beyond

asking questions, slumped at his desk and quietly snoring. A copy of the *Racing Post* was open by his side. When he stepped out onto the pavement, a car's headlights flashed a couple of times before the driver got out, and walked to the back of the car. He pulled the two heavy suitcases across the empty street, and Lamont helped him lift them up into the boot.

Lamont slammed the boot shut, took a thick envelope from his jacket pocket and handed it to Sebastian. Moments later he was back behind the wheel, and took off before he'd even fastened his seatbelt.

It was some time before the young man was able to hail a passing cab. But he couldn't complain – it wasn't often he got paid twice for a night's work. As the taxi pulled away, he glanced up at the bedroom window, which was still shrouded in darkness, and thought he would have enjoyed having breakfast with Christina.

• • •

Lamont was speculating about what might be in the two suitcases now safely locked in his boot. He gave it a second thought, but not a third when he noticed another car was following him.

Twenty minutes later the barrier outside Middle Temple was raised, but not before the guard had checked the registration number against the one Mr Booth Watson had given him. As Lamont drove slowly across the square, bump after bump, he could see a light shining from the head of chambers' office. He brought the car to a halt, and checked in his rearview mirror to make sure he was no longer being followed. Satisfied, he got out, opened the boot and lifted the cases onto the pavement, before entering the building and humping them slowly up the stone staircase, one step at a time. When he finally reached the second floor, he found Booth Watson waiting for him on the landing.

Lamont wheeled the two cases into his office but, before he could ask, Booth Watson handed him a thick brown envelope and said, 'Goodnight, Superintendent.' He didn't add, I won't be needing your services again.

After Lamont had closed the door behind him, Booth Watson locked it, walked over to the window and watched as the black Volvo made its way back across the square. He didn't move until the barrier had gone down and the car was out of sight.

He sat down in his chair and licked his lips as he stared at the two suitcases. He'd already decided what he was going to do with the ten million, and his disappearance had been planned like a military operation. Miles Faulkner had taught him a great deal over the years.

A taxi had been booked to take him to Heathrow at six o'clock that morning. He checked his watch. Just over an hour's time. At the airport, he would board a private jet for Hong Kong. That hadn't come cheap, but it would cut down the chances of bumping into anyone he knew while carrying luggage that he couldn't let out of his sight. Once he touched down in the protectorate, he would be met by a senior executive of a private bank that didn't pick up clients after midnight. Well, not for less than ten million. A security van would deliver the two cases to the bank, while the senior executive would drop Booth Watson off at an unfashionable hotel.

After the money had been deposited, he would fly South African Airways, business class, to Cape Town, where he would stay overnight in an airport hotel, but only overnight. The following morning American Airways would take him to San Francisco, where he would board a shuttle bus to Seattle, his final destination. No one would find him there, least of all a man who was going to spend the next fourteen years in jail.

He glanced across the square to see a taxi coming to a halt by the barrier. He'd have just one look before asking the driver to carry the two cases downstairs. He unzipped one of the bags, and could feel his heart hammering in his chest as he stared down at the neatly stacked contents. Row upon row of paperback books were crammed next to each other. He clumsily unzipped the second case, to discover it was full of hardbacks. An envelope marked 'Personal' addressed to 'Miles Faulkner, prisoner No.0249' had been placed on top of them. He tore it open and read the short, handwritten note.

> Dearest Miles,
> You should have more than enough time to read these. I particularly enjoyed The Great Escape, a pageturner. By the way, the young man you set me up with was very good, worth every penny.
> Don't hope to see you soon – I won't be visiting you in prison. Not part of my long-term plan.
> Love,
> Christina x

Booth Watson fell on his knees and threw up as the taxi drew up outside number 5 Fetter Chambers. The cabbie turned off the engine and waited for his passenger.

• • •

'What time did you turn up at the bank?' asked Grace.

'A few minutes after five,' said Sir Julian, his eyes lighting up as Clare placed a plate of eggs, bacon, tomatoes, mushrooms and sausage in front of him on the kitchen table.

'I thought banks closed at four on a Friday afternoon.'

'They do,' said Sir Julian, unscrewing the top of a bottle of HP sauce. 'But as I've been with Barclays for over forty years, and have never once been overdrawn' – neither of them doubted it – 'they were only too happy to make an exception.'

'What did they do,' asked Clare, 'when you presented them with two suitcases?'

'Locked them in a strongroom for the weekend, and gave me a receipt in the name of Mrs Christina Faulkner.'

'Weren't you tempted to take a quick peek inside?' asked Clare.

'Certainly not,' said Sir Julian as he tucked into his breakfast. 'That wasn't part of my brief.'

'I can't quite visualize you in a chauffeur's uniform, Dad,' said Grace.

'Including the peaked cap!' volunteered Clare.

'It gets worse,' said Sir Julian. 'I had to park on a double yellow line outside the bank, and ended up with a parking ticket.'

'I'm sure Mrs Faulkner will be happy to reimburse you,' said Clare, making a note under expenses.

'You have to promise me not to tell your mother what I've been up to.'

'Do you mean the day job?' said Grace, grinning.

'No, I mean what I had for breakfast.'

CHAPTER 15

'So for the past few weeks,' said William, 'Jackie has been reeling Constable Smart in, and if she does decide to cooperate with us, we'll have more than enough evidence to throw the book at Milner and his cohorts for fraud on a gigantic scale.'

'And DS Adaja?' the Hawk asked. 'What's he been up to in Windsor?'

'He's gathered more than enough proof of racial prejudice, but nothing Milner won't dismiss as barrack-room humour.'

Hawksby frowned. 'It's a problem the force is going to have to deal with in time if we hope to attract people as able as Paul in the future.'

'He also thinks he may be on to something Milner won't be able to dismiss out of hand,' William added. 'But doesn't want to say anything until he has sufficient evidence to leave a jury in no doubt of his guilt.'

'The idea of a young immigrant from Ghana bringing down

127

the head of Royalty Protection has a certain irony about it,' said the commander with a wry smile.

'That's the problem with racial prejudice,' said William. 'It won't have crossed Milner's mind that Paul just might be as clever as he is.'

'How about you?' asked the Hawk. 'Are you as clever as Milner?'

'I've managed to collect a ton of circumstantial evidence, but nothing that would stand up in a court of law.'

'Just remember you'll need a ton of indisputable evidence to bring down Milner, because that man has brought a new meaning to the words "friends in high places". Who do you think the Palace will instinctively believe – a man who's served the Royal Family for more than a decade, or a DCI they've never heard of? So it sounds to me as if Jackie and Paul have the best chance of derailing the Milner gravy train.'

'Especially as he's rarely in Windsor. While—'

'—the cat's away,' said the Hawk. 'But what about Ross? Has he carried out my instructions?'

'To the letter,' replied William.

'Details,' demanded the Hawk.

'He took his daughter to London Zoo quite recently, and claimed it on expenses, including a chocolate nut sundae, and when he presented the claim, Milner didn't question it.'

'Which only makes me wonder what can possibly be his chocolate nut sundae. Has Ross come up with anything else we ought to know about?'

'It would appear that Princess Diana is conducting a relationship with a young—'

'Gigolo,' said the Hawk. 'Yes, I read the details in Dempster. So we can only hope that she eventually comes to her senses.'

'Ross tells me it's getting quite serious.'

'In which case the problem will be taken out of his hands, but it might be wise in future for him to put everything on the record, because if it does get out of control, they'll be looking for someone to blame, and he'll be the obvious scapegoat,' said the Hawk just as the phone on his desk began to ring.

'I'll let him know, sir,' said William.

'I've got Geoff Duffield on the line,' said his secretary when he picked up the receiver. 'He's calling from Heathrow – says it's an emergency.'

'With Duffield, everything's an emergency,' said the Hawk. 'Put him through.' He touched the speaker button so William could listen to the conversation.

'Good morning, Superintendent,' Hawksby said. 'Last time you called me it was a hijacking. What have you got for me this time?'

'Worse, I'm afraid,' said Duffield. 'A private jet has made an unscheduled landing at Heathrow to refuel and change crews before going on to Moscow. We think it's possible Mansour Khalifah is on board.'

'If he is,' said the Hawk, 'that certainly qualifies as an emergency.' He tapped away on his computer to find that Khalifah had twenty-six outstanding arrest warrants in almost as many countries, and was near the top of Interpol's 'Most Wanted' list.

'We'll have to be sure it's him before we can make a move. The last thing we need is a major diplomatic incident when we're accused of arresting an innocent man. Start by questioning the incoming crew.'

'I already have, sir. All they were able to tell me was that the plane flew in from Libya, and there are only three passengers on board.'

'Libya might be considered a clue,' suggested William.

'But not conclusive,' replied the commander.

'How much time do we have before the flight's cleared for take-off?' William asked.

'An hour at the most,' said Duffield. 'But we haven't allocated them a departure slot yet. The replacement crew are waiting to board.'

'Stop them in their tracks,' said William. 'Lock them up if necessary.'

'I'm not sure I have the authority to do that,' said Duffield.

'You do now,' said the Hawk.

'Have you got an emergency SO19 team in place?' asked William.

'Yes, under the command of an Inspector Roach. They're on standby.'

'Get them kitted out as the replacement crew, and tell them we'll supply the stewardess,' said William. 'We should be with you in about forty minutes.'

'Who have you got in mind as the stewardess?' asked the Hawk after he'd put the phone down.

• • •

'Please take me through the programme one more time, Victoria,' said the Princess as her car drove into Prince's Gardens.

'It's a lunch with a difference, ma'am. Only a hundred guests, but every one of them has paid a thousand pounds to be there, so the charity has already benefited by a hundred thousand.'

'Before expenses?'

'That won't be a problem. Asprey's are hosting the event, and are picking up all the costs as a way of celebrating their hundred and thirtieth anniversary of being granted a royal warrant by Queen Victoria. In fact, David Carmichael, their chairman – who'll be sitting on your right – told me they would be displaying their unique silver collection in your honour, including a statue of Queen Victoria which is the pride of the collection.'

'How very generous of Mr Carmichael,' said Diana as the car drove past Harvey Nichols, a place she'd once told Ross was her favourite store. 'I must remember to thank him.' She added a sentence about the silver collection to her speech.

Ross sat silently in the front, thinking about the crowd that would be waiting to greet the Princess. It wouldn't be large when they arrived, as the guest of honour's name had been left off the invitation card for security reasons. But the red carpet and the smartly dressed guests all heading in one direction would inevitably attract a group of curious onlookers. By the time they left, there would be people hanging out of windows, clinging onto lampposts, and spilling onto the road just to get a glimpse of her. That was when he would need three pairs of eyes.

HRH interrupted his thoughts. 'Are you expecting any problems, Ross?'

'We've got a nutter who's turned up for the last three of your events, and claims he's married to you.'

'Is that a crime?' asked Diana.

'It is while you're still married to the Prince of Wales,' said Ross, immediately regretting his words.

'What about the guest list?' said Victoria, trying to get him off the hook.

'Mainly the great and the good, with one or two exceptions.'

'Even more nutters?' asked Diana.

'No, ma'am, but two of the guests do have criminal records.'

'Tell all,' said Victoria.

'Burglary and fraud. I'm going to have to make sure, ma'am,

that you're not photographed with either of them, because you can be sure that would be the one picture on all of tomorrow's front pages.'

As the car swung into Bond Street, a dozen photographers leapt out into the middle of the road, while someone in the crowd shouted, 'It's Diana!'

· · ·

'Mansour Khalifah,' said William, 'is, without question, among the most wanted terrorists on earth. We don't even know how many people he's killed, or been responsible for killing. If he is on that plane, and we let him get away, the Americans, not to mention the Israelis, might have a word or two to say on the subject. However, as we're still not certain it's him on board, we'll have to tread carefully.' He passed Jackie another photograph of Khalifah, which she studied carefully as their unmarked car, a single blue light flashing, touched 100 mph as it sped down the motorway.

'Does he have any distinguishing marks?' Jackie asked.

'A birthmark on the side of his neck, just below his left ear. He claims, and his followers believe, it's a scar inflicted by an American sniper. But it will be well hidden if he's wearing a traditional robe and headdress.'

'How am I going to get on the plane?' asked Jackie as she studied the front cover of an old *Newsweek* showing Mansour Khalifah was holding a scimitar high in the air, moments before he beheaded a captured American soldier.

'You'll be joining a group from the anti-terrorist squad who will be replacing the crew that was meant to be flying him to Moscow. As the stewardess, you'll have the best chance of identifying him. But leave SO19 to take him out, because this man,' said William, tapping the cover of the magazine, 'would kill his mother without a second thought.'

Danny slowed down as they came off the motorway and headed for an unmarked gate that would take them directly onto the main runway.

The officer on the gate was clearly expecting them, because he spent only a moment checking William's warrant card before pointing him in the direction of an isolated building on the far side of the runway. Danny didn't slow down again until he spotted Superintendent Duffield standing alone. Not a uniformed officer in sight.

• • •

Ross hovered a few paces behind the Princess, who was chatting to the chairman of Asprey as the guests were served their first course. His eyes swept the room once again. That was when he saw her.

She was seated near the back of the room, sprinkling a little too much salt on her food. Then she glanced around furtively before dropping a silver salt cellar into the open handbag on her lap. She clicked the bag shut and went on eating. In normal circumstances Ross would have approached her discreetly and suggested she put the salt cellar back on the table, to avoid any further embarrassment. But these were not normal circumstances, and his instructions were set in stone. Never allow anything to distract you from the primary responsibility of protecting your principal. But he did find himself becoming distracted a second time, when he spotted a man on the centre table slipping a silver napkin ring into his handkerchief while pretending to blow his nose. It then disappeared into a trouser pocket.

By the time HRH rose to make her speech at the end of the meal, six salt cellars, four pepper pots, three napkin rings and a mustard pot – full of mustard – had gone AWOL, and there was nothing Ross could do about it. Among a hundred of the wealthiest people in the land were at least a dozen petty thieves Fagin would have been happy to employ.

The chairman of Asprey listened to the Princess's speech, a smile of satisfaction never leaving his face. Ross wasn't going to be the person to tell him his unique Asprey silver collection would be missing several pieces by the time it was returned to the vaults.

The standing ovation that followed the Princess's speech allowed two or three more guests a chance to take their pick: a silver teaspoon and another pepper pot were among the spoils. Easy for Ross to spot the thieves – they were the ones who weren't clapping.

After the Princess had signed several menu cards, the chairman accompanied his guest of honour back to her car. On the way she stopped to chat to a few members of the waiting crowd, including an old woman in a wheelchair who told her she had once shaken hands with the Queen Mother. Diana gave her a hug and she burst into tears.

'How many did you spot, Mr Hogan?' said a voice behind him.

Ross turned to see a man he remembered arresting for burglary when he was a young Constable.

'A dozen, possibly more,' admitted Ross. 'I was glad to see you weren't among them, Ron.'

'I'm not a souvenir hunter, Inspector. In any case, the only thing worth stealing was the statue of Queen Victoria, and to pull that off I would have had to cause a diversion.' Ross wanted to laugh. 'Mind you, Mr Hogan, if I'd known you were going to be in the room, I wouldn't have bothered.'

Ross allowed himself a smile before stepping forward and opening the car door to allow HRH to join Victoria in the back seat.

'Give my best wishes to the commander,' said Ron as Ross closed the door and joined the driver in the front.

• • •

While the team were changing into their Russian aircrew uniforms – a nice touch, thought William – Inspector Roach continued to brief them. Time wasn't on their side.

'Right, chaps,' said Roach, revealing his military background. 'Try not to forget we're up against three ruthless terrorists whose job description doesn't include taking prisoners. However, we have a secret weapon,' he said, before introducing them to Detective Sergeant Jackie Roycroft. 'While DS Roycroft will be handing out magazines, and serving coffee, we'll be on the flight deck, ready to go into action the moment she gives us the heads-up.'

'Won't they be suspicious when we go on board and they don't recognize any of us?' asked Jackie.

'Unlikely,' said Roach. 'The plane's not registered in Khalifah's name and it was chartered by a third party. In any case, when they see Tiny, they'll think he couldn't snuff out a candle, but they'll soon learn how he became the police lightweight boxing champion, as well as why Sergeant Pascoe's nickname is "One Blow".'

'So, once Jackie says the word "seatbelts",' said Pascoe, 'that's our sign to move in. It should be all over in a matter of seconds.'

'I hope so,' said Tiny, 'because it's my night for giving the kids a bath.'

Everyone laughed except William and Jackie, who weren't accustomed to SO19's humour before an operation.

'Right, chaps,' said Roach, after he'd double-checked the Russian uniforms, 'let's get moving.'

William watched from inside the building as Roach led his little gang across the runway towards the waiting jet. None of them could have missed a pair of eyes that was peering out of one of the cabin windows following their every move.

Roach and his two companions climbed the short flight of steps that led up to the plane, and disappeared onto the flight deck without glancing in the direction of the passengers.

Jackie followed close behind. On entering the plane she placed her handbag on the little fold-down table at the front of the cabin. She turned her back on the passengers, opened her bag, took out her lipstick and checked her make-up in a compact mirror. Her eyes settled on a man dressed in a long white thawb with a gold cord around his keffiyeh, who was reading the *Financial Times*. No one could have looked less like a terrorist. She adjusted her mirror slightly and focused on the two younger men seated behind him. One of them was resting his right hand on a gun, while the other didn't take his eyes off her. She put the lipstick back in her compact and took out a small can of hairspray, before once again checking in her mirror. She still couldn't be completely sure it was Khalifah who appeared so relaxed as he turned a page of his *FT*.

Jackie slipped the hairspray into a jacket pocket and turned around, to find the second bodyguard was still staring at her. She took a risk and gave him a smile, which to her surprise he returned. She kept to the plan and began to straighten the magazines in the rack, the agreed signal that One Blow should join her in the cabin. She was surprised to spot three copies of the out-of-date *Newsweek* with Mansour Khalifah's photograph on the cover. Vanity had got the better of him. One Blow strolled past her, and she waited a few seconds before following him down the aisle.

'Good morning, sir,' said One Blow as he came to a halt by Khalifah's side. The first bodyguard didn't take his eyes off him, while the other was still looking at Jackie, although Khalifah barely gave either of them a glance.

'Flight control have given us permission to take off, sir,' said One Blow, 'if that's convenient for you?'

Khalifah lowered his newspaper and managed a nod.

'Thank you, sir,' said One Blow.

Jackie stepped forward and said, 'Gentlemen, would you please fasten your seatbelts,' just as Tiny appeared carrying a bottle of champagne on a silver tray.

Two of them reached for their seatbelts, giving One Blow the split-second he needed to take out Khalifah with a single sharp blow to the neck, while Jackie sprayed the first bodyguard in the eyes with her hairspray and then delivered a blow he couldn't have expected. But the second guard had spotted the champagne and, long before Tiny had the chance to raise the bottle above his head, he'd leapt up and grabbed Jackie's arm, twisting it sharply behind her back while thrusting the barrel of his gun firmly against the side of her head.

Tiny immediately realized his mistake.

'One false move,' said Khalifah's bodyguard, 'and I'll blow her brains out.'

Tiny didn't doubt it and slowly lowered the bottle of champagne while One Blow took a pace back.

'You two,' said the bodyguard, nodding at Tiny and One

Blow, 'will get off the plane immediately.' They hesitated for a moment, but when the bodyguard forced the barrel of his gun into Jackie's mouth, they reluctantly retreated back down the aisle and down the steps onto the runway.

The gunman ordered Jackie to pull up the airstairs and close the plane's door. On the runway she could see William, standing there looking helpless, while One Blow and Tiny stared up at her. She knew a long-range rifle would be focused on the plane's doorway from the roof of the terminal, but the officer with his finger on the trigger wouldn't risk squeezing it while she was still in his line of fire. Once Jackie had closed the door, the bodyguard pushed her forward towards the cockpit, where DI Roach was sitting in the captain's seat; all part of Plan B, should Plan A go wrong. It had gone spectacularly wrong.

'Let's get moving!' the bodyguard yelled at Roach, the barrel of his gun now lodged painfully in the nape of Jackie's neck.

Roach didn't think this was the moment to let him know he was a SO19 and had never flown a plane in his life. He put on his headset and began to pray. A voice from above answered his prayer.

'Follow my instructions carefully,' said the real pilot. 'Turn on the engines by pressing the start switches in the centre of the overhead panel.'

Roach obeyed the command. He rotated the two switches and the engines spooled up, reaching idle within moments.

'Now you need to arm the autobrake. The switch is in the centre front panel. Rotate it to RTO. Now push the two thrust levers next to your right leg forward, to about half-way, and the plane will start to accelerate. Steer with your feet – you'll have to ease the pedals gently if you hope to remain in a straight line.'

Roach looked left and right before tentatively easing the thrust levers forward a few inches. The plane started to move forward.

'Everything on the runway in front of you has been cleared, Inspector,' said the voice. 'Now I want you to push the levers a little further forward but not suddenly. The plane will speed up, until you're doing about ninety miles an hour.'

What then, Roach wanted to ask. The gunman placed a hand on the side of the cockpit door to steady himself as the plane began to gather speed.

'Now, get ready to shut down the thrust levers in one movement, Inspector. When you do that, the brakes will automatically be applied violently. It will feel like hitting a brick wall. The gunman is certain to be thrown off balance, and that will be your one chance to disarm him.'

'Understood,' said Roach, who could see the runway ahead of him was coming to an abrupt end.

'Now,' said the voice firmly.

Roach slammed both thrust levers closed, and as the brakes came on, the gun went off. Roach watched as a body slumped to the ground.

• • •

'They did what?' said the Princess as the Jaguar turned right out of Bond Street onto Piccadilly, a pair of outriders making sure the traffic was held up until the car had safely crossed the junction.

Ross told HRH what he'd witnessed during lunch as the car continued on its uninterrupted journey, and why he hadn't been able to do anything about it.

'Poor Mr Carmichael,' said Diana. 'Surely there must be something I can do to help?'

'Nothing short of searching every guest as they leave,' said Ross. 'That would only embarrass some of Asprey's best customers, which wouldn't exactly please Mr Carmichael.'

'But he was such a nice man, and took so much trouble to make it a memorable event. Now he'll only have bad memories of the occasion. Perhaps I could try to make it up to him by ordering a hundred silver frames from Asprey's, and giving one to anyone I send a photograph to after an official function.'

'That would only make the situation worse,' suggested Victoria. 'The last time you did that, ma'am, Asprey's didn't send you a bill.'

The Princess remained silent for some time before saying, 'I know something that will put a smile back on Mr Carmichael's face. I'll ask Her Majesty to award him the MVO.'

'But that's only usually given to people who've served the Royal Family for several years,' Victoria reminded her.

'Precisely,' said Diana. 'Don't forget that Asprey's have served the monarchy for over a hundred years.'

'Forgive me for asking, ma'am,' said Ross, 'but what is an MVO?'

'A Member of the Royal Victorian Order,' replied Victoria. 'The equivalent of an MBE, but rarer because it's in the personal gift of Her Majesty.'

'So, if you take care of me for the next twenty years, Ross, you might even get one,' said Diana.

That's something to look forward to, thought Ross as the car drew up outside Kensington Palace, but he didn't express an opinion.

• • •

William watched as four paramedics carried two stretchers down the steps of the plane and onto the runway. They walked slowly towards a waiting ambulance everyone had hoped wouldn't be required, and gently placed the two stretchers next to each other. One figure had a sheet over its head.

Moments later, two men in handcuffs were bundled off the aircraft and led unceremoniously to separate police cars, the back doors of which were already open.

'Brave girl,' said Inspector Roach as the ambulance drove off. 'She would have made a damn fine member of our unit.'

William didn't comment, but if he'd been carrying a gun at the time he would have shot Khalifah there and then, and it would have taken a lot more than Inspector Roach to restrain him.

CHAPTER 16

BOOTH WATSON RECOVERED FAIRLY QUICKLY from what he tried to convince himself was no more than a temporary set-back, but was now resigned to putting off his trip to Seattle for a few months. While Faulkner was still in prison, with no chance of an early release, he would simply have to bide his time. And time was on his side.

He would need to arrange an early consultation with Miles, at which he would show him the handwritten letter Christina had left in the suitcase. That should ensure Miles's anger was directed elsewhere, and prevent him from suspecting what his lawyer had been up to in his absence. He would recommend to Miles that an anonymous source should tip off the taxman about Christina's windfall, thus killing two birds with one stone.

Despite Christina's sleight of hand, Booth Watson felt all was not lost. There was still twelve million in cash lodged in the bank's vault, and he was the only person Miles had entrusted with a key to the strongbox. He would just have to make a few more visits to the bank during the coming weeks. He would also carry out Miles's instructions to the letter, and accept a bid of twenty-six million pounds for his fifty-one per cent holding in Marcel and Neffe, which he would then deposit in his client account for safekeeping, where it would remain until sentence had been pronounced, when the money would be transferred to Hong Kong the moment Miles was safely ensconced in Belmarsh – for the next fourteen years.

But that was a mere bagatelle compared with the amount Booth Watson would make when he sold Miles's art collection, along with the Raphael, the Rembrandt and the Frans Hals he'd be claiming back from the Fitzmolean once their forthcoming exhibition had closed. That wouldn't please Warwick's wife, which he considered a bonus.

So, other than having to pay a redundant taxi driver who'd been booked to take him to Heathrow, and the deposit on a jet that never took off, it hadn't been a complete disaster. He would just have to wait a little longer before he took early retirement. However, there was still one mystery he hadn't yet solved: who was it who had been wearing the chauffeur's uniform? And then he remembered that whoever it was hadn't opened the car door for Christina when she left the bank, so it couldn't have been his day job.

• • •

'Why did Sir Julian Warwick roll over quite so easily?' said Miles, when he sat down opposite Tulip and a guard handed him a steaming cup of black coffee and a copy of *The Times*.

'Because if he hadn't,' suggested Tulip, 'that precious son of his might well have ended up joining us for breakfast, rather than hobnobbing with Princesses.'

Miles scowled. 'I'm missing something,' he said as an inmate placed a plate of eggs and bacon in front of him.

'But BW gave you a copy of the agreement, and you even witnessed Sir Julian's signature on the original.'

'On the original,' repeated Miles, 'but his signature isn't on my copy.'

'You can't be suggesting that BW would double-cross you? He's been your lawyer for as long as I've known you. In any case, what's in it for him?'

'About two hundred million pounds,' said Miles as his coffee went cold. 'I suspect even you'd double-cross me for that amount, especially if you knew I was safely locked up in jail.'

Tulip was silent for some time before he said, 'But just think about how much he would have to lose when you found out.'

'Just think about how much he'd have to gain if I didn't,' said Miles.

'But how could you ever be sure while you're banged up in here?'

'Perhaps the time's come for me to take out an insurance policy with ex-superintendent Lamont as the beneficiary.'

'But he's a man you've never trusted,' said Tulip. 'And in any case, he's probably already working for BW.'

'Then we'll have to double his salary and make it clear exactly what would happen to him if he decides to double-cross me.'

Miles pushed his untouched breakfast to one side and glanced at a photograph of Mansour Khalifah on the front page of *The Times*.

'Now there's a man I would happily kill,' said Tulip, pointing to the photograph.

'It might be in our best interests to keep him alive,' said Miles as a guard poured him a second cup of coffee.

'Why, boss? What would be in it for us?'

'Khalifah will have information that the police, not to mention the Foreign Office, would be delighted to learn about. Information that might persuade a judge to knock even more time off my sentence.'

'But Khalifah would never share that information with infidels like us, boss.'

'Possibly not. So we need to convert a True Believer to our cause. How many of them are there in Belmarsh?'

'A dozen? Possibly more. But they all look on Khalifah as a hero, and they wouldn't consider crossing him.'

'Do any of them drink or have a drug problem?'

'Not one of them,' said Tulip, who knew his customers. 'That won't be the way to make contact with him.'

'A dozen, you say. Then we need to find the Judas among them, because I'd be happy to supply him with a damn sight more than thirty pieces of silver.'

'None of them will betray him for money,' said Tulip. 'However much you offered.'

'Find out what they *will* betray him for, and then I'll have two insurance policies.'

• • •

Miles Faulkner read Christina's note a third time before he spoke. 'I should have killed the bitch years ago,' he said, banging a clenched fist on the table.

'Don't say that even in jest until the trial is over,' said Booth Watson. 'We wouldn't want to harm your chances of an early release.'

He waited for his client to calm down before carrying on with the rest of his agenda. 'There are one or two more papers that require your signature if we're to have everything in place by the time you're released.'

Miles nodded.

'First, I have, as instructed, sold your fifty-one per cent shareholding in Marcel and Neffe.'

'How much did you get?'

'Twenty-six million – four million more than you asked for.'

'Where have you deposited the money?'

'It's currently in your client account, but I can transfer it to any bank you choose. Just give me the name and account number.'

'Put the full amount into my numbered account at the Bank of Zurich. I have no intention of remaining in England once I get out of this place, and I certainly don't intend to pay forty per cent in tax to the people who put me in here.'

Booth Watson made a note of his client's instructions, even though he had no intention of carrying them out.

'You can deduct one per cent for yourself,' said Miles before adding, 'of the four million.'

Booth Watson didn't remind Miles that he'd originally promised him a million – why bother, when he was going to take it in any case?

'Thank you, Miles,' said Booth Watson as he passed across two more documents for him to sign. He didn't realize that the entire amount would eventually be transferred to a private account, not in Zurich, but Hong Kong. Booth Watson didn't bother to mention that his client's prized art collection was in storage in a warehouse near Gatwick airport and he'd already arranged a meeting with a prospective buyer who'd shown an interest in purchasing the entire collection.

'Anything else?' asked Miles after glancing at his watch to see they had only fifteen minutes left.

'One more thing. The Frans Hals exhibition opens at the

Fitzmolean in a few weeks' time and, with your permission, when it closes, I'll collect the self-portrait.'

'On the same day. And you can inform the Fitzmolean that I expect my Raphael and Rembrandt to be returned as well, since they were only ever on loan to them in the first place.'

'On permanent loan,' Booth Watson reminded him. 'But I'm confident I've found a loophole in the contract they won't have considered, that will turn permanent to temporary.'

'Then you can ship all three of them back to Spain to join the rest of the collection.'

Booth Watson had every intention of making sure the paintings joined the rest of the collection, but not in Spain.

'What's the latest on the trial?'

'The CPS have finally fixed a date, September fourteenth. So as long as you're still willing to plead guilty, we should have you out of here by Christmas.'

'Or possibly earlier.'

'You're planning to escape again?' asked Booth Watson, who didn't like being taken by surprise.

'No. What I have in mind requires me to remain inside,' said Miles. But he had no intention of letting BW know what he had planned for Khalifah.

'Dare I ask?' said Booth Watson, trying to remain calm.

'Not until I've got Hawksby by the balls and he's begging me to "enlighten" him.'

Booth Watson was about to ask . . . when there was a loud rap on the door.

'Time's up,' said the duty officer, who remained standing in the doorway.

Booth Watson was lost for words, and even forgot to ask Mr Harris to witness Miles's signature on the three documents that would have made it possible for him to book a one-way ticket to Hong Kong.

Miles rose from his place on the other side of the table and left without another word. He stepped out of the glass chamber, where Harris was waiting to escort him back to his cell. 'Damn,' Miles said after he'd walked a few paces. He turned around but BW had already disappeared.

'Anything wrong, Mr Faulkner?' said SO Harris, as a double-barred gate was locked behind him.

'Nothing that can't wait until next week.'

CHAPTER 17

WILLIAM GAVE HIMSELF THIRTY MINUTES to make the short journey.

It hadn't come as a surprise to receive a summons to the palace to attend the ceremony. The commander had already fully briefed him on the role he would be expected to play. When it came to an award for bravery, he'd told him that Her Majesty would not allow any other member of the Royal Family to take her place for the presentation. After all, the medal bore her name.

He drove out of Scotland Yard and headed in the direction of Whitehall. He turned left at Trafalgar Square, passed under Admiralty Arch and onto the Mall. When the lights at the end of the Mall turned green he circled the statue of Queen Victoria, before coming to a halt outside the North Centre Gate of Buckingham Palace.

A guard checked his name on a clipboard, then directed him through the left-hand archway into a large quadrangle. Following his instructions, William parked his Mini next to the commander's Jaguar. Once again, the Hawk had beaten him to it.

He got out of the car, unsure where to go until he spotted the Commissioner of the Metropolitan Police in full dress uniform, striding out ahead of him; a man who clearly knew where he was going.

When William reached the vast double doors that heralded the state entrance to the palace, his name was taken once again before a page, bedecked in gold – who could have stepped out of an earlier century – led him silently up a wide, red-carpeted staircase, to the first floor.

'If you go through the Long Gallery, sir,' said the page, 'the Throne Room is on your right.'

William glanced at his watch; there were still twelve minutes before the ceremony was due to begin, so he walked very slowly down the centre of the Long Gallery. The room was as wide as a country road, and the walls that towered high above him were littered with pictures. He stopped to admire so many paintings that until then, he'd only seen in *The Queen's Pictures*, a book his father had given him when he was a boy. He came to a halt when he reached Van Dyck's *Charles I* and *Henrietta Maria*. He had to take a step back to fully appreciate the large portrait, almost colliding with another guest.

'Good morning, sir,' said DS Adaja.

'Morning, Paul,' said William without turning round. 'Beth's going to be so envious,' he added, unable to hide a smirk.

'I doubt she'd even have made it to the Throne Room,' said Paul. 'And neither will we if we don't get a move on.'

William reluctantly followed him, trying to take in a Canaletto and a Van Dyck before he finally entered the Throne Room. Once again, the phrase, 'took your breath away', seemed inadequate for what he saw in front of him. He stood for a moment and admired the vast crystal chandelier suspended from the high ceiling in the centre of the room, but then his eyes were drawn to the two high-backed red thrones perched on a raised dais at the far end of the room, on which only two people were entitled to sit. The huge room was filled with long lines of gold chairs that he guessed could seat a couple of hundred guests, but on this occasion, only those in the front row would be occupied. He walked slowly down the red-carpeted aisle towards the thrones. Once he had reached the front row, he spotted the Commissioner and the Hawk deep in conversation. He took his allotted seat at the far end of the row, next to Rebecca. Another 'Good morning, sir,' before he smiled at Ross, who was seated on her right. William was about to ask him a question, when everyone fell silent, and rose from their places. He glanced to his left, to watch his boss make her entrance.

So tiny, was his immediate thought, as the Queen walked past them. He wondered if she would sit on her throne, but she came to a halt on the step leading up to the dais, and turned to face her audience.

A gentleman usher indicated with a slight wave of the hand that they should all be seated, while another handed the Queen her speech. William remained standing.

'First, may I welcome you, and say how glad we are you were all able to join me for this special occasion.'

William couldn't help wondering who would have a more pressing engagement.

'We have all gathered today to acknowledge the service given by a remarkable individual, who can surely be described as no ordinary woman.' She paused to turn a page of her script. 'When she was called upon to do her duty, she did not

151

hesitate to put her life on the line. As a result of her extraordinary courage a ruthless terrorist was brought to justice.' The Queen looked up and smiled. 'So, it gives me considerable pleasure to award Detective Sergeant Jacqueline Michelle Roycroft the Queen's Gallantry Medal, allowing her to join that select group of police officers who have received the honour and, in her case, the first woman.'

The gentleman usher handed Her Majesty a blue leather box which she opened as William pushed Jackie's wheelchair forward, coming to a halt in front of the Queen.

Jackie's colleagues burst into spontaneous applause as the Queen bent down and pinned the medal on her uniform. Until that moment, Jackie had remained reasonably composed, firmly gripping the arms of her wheelchair, determined not to show how nervous she was. Facing an armed terrorist was one thing; facing the monarch was quite another. Despite the fact Jackie had known about the award for several weeks, it didn't help.

It later became legend among the team that the Hawk had shed a tear, although he denied it to everyone, except his wife.

During the reception that followed, the Queen spent some time chatting to Jackie, although it was William who told her about the bullet that had torn through her chest as the plane screeched to a halt, missing her heart by millimetres.

Her Majesty's final words were: 'We are lucky to have officers of your calibre serving in the police force.'

When HM moved on to chat to other members of the team, William took Inspector Roach to one side and thanked him for the role his unit had played in capturing the three terrorists. 'Although I must confess,' William added, 'you misled me when you said Jackie would have made a damn fine member of the anti-terrorist squad, because I assumed—'

'So sorry, old chap,' said Roach, clearly unrepentant. 'I simply meant to point out that we don't have any women in our branch of the service. But after working with Jackie, I'm bound to say more's the pity, because I'd like to sign her up.'

'You can forget that,' said William. 'Once she's back on her feet Jackie's got an equally challenging task to deal with, and what makes it worse is that this time the suspect is one of our own.'

'Anything I can do to help?'

'I'm afraid not. We're going to have to be a little more subtle than you lot. All I can tell you is that my next meeting with a member of the Royal Family may not be quite as pleasant.'

. . .

'Do you want to hear the good news or the bad news?' Beth asked when William arrived home later that evening.

'Why don't you start with the bad news?' said William, closing the door behind him.

'Tim Knox is leaving the Fitzmolean. He's been offered the position as Surveyor of the Queen's Pictures.'

'I'm sorry to hear that. He'll be difficult to replace. What's the good news?'

'He's suggested I apply for the position,' said Beth as they walked into the kitchen, where the twins and Jojo were tucking into a large pizza under Sarah's watchful eye.

'Do they ever stop eating?' asked William, joining them at the table.

'He thinks I have a fair chance of being offered the job as director, as several members of the board have made it clear they'd support me, and he'd certainly back me if it came to a vote.'

'They'd be lucky to get you,' said William, eyeing the last slice of pizza, but he wasn't fast enough on the draw.

'The board will have to advertise the post, so I'd be facing some stiff opposition.'

'God help the person who dares to stand against you.'

'Naughty Daddy,' said Artemisia between mouthfuls. 'My Sunday School teacher says you should never take the Lord's name in vain.'

'Never,' said Peter.

'Never,' repeated Jojo.

'Quite right. What I meant to say was, heaven help anyone who dares to stand against your mother.'

'Bath time, children,' said Sarah firmly.

'Will you read to us before we go to sleep, Daddy?' asked Peter as he got down from the table.

'Of course. Is it still *The Wind in the Willows*?'

'No, we finished that ages ago,' said Artemisia. 'We're now reading *Alice's Adventures in Wonderland*.' William felt guilty about how many times he'd failed to get home before the children fell asleep. His father had warned him often enough how quickly these years would slip by.

'I may be able to pull off a little coup,' said Beth as Sarah took the children up for their bath, 'which wouldn't do my chances of getting the job any harm.'

'You're planning to bribe the selection committee.'

'I don't have enough money to do that,' said Beth. 'However, I've spotted a painting by Jan Steen that's coming up for sale at an auction in Pittsburgh, which I might be able to pick up for a reasonable price, although it's quite possible we'll be outbid, as it's on the cover of the catalogue.'

'How would that help you land the job?'

'It won't. But in the same catalogue I came across a pencil drawing by an unknown artist that I'm convinced is a preliminary sketch for the lamp in *The Night Watch*.'

'What's the estimate?'

'Two hundred dollars. It may be a copy by one of Rembrandt's contemporaries but, at that price, it's a risk worth taking.'

'And if it's actually by Rembrandt?'

'It could be worth as much as forty thousand pounds.'

'So selling it would make a welcome contribution to the museum's impoverished coffers.'

'Not a chance. The board would never agree to sell a Rembrandt drawing. They'd put it on permanent display, even though it would cover the cost of the director's salary for a year.'

'I'm sure you'll find a subtle way of letting them know that.'

'Only if I turn out to be right.'

'Having been the only one who spotted it,' said William, before pointing upstairs. 'But now for higher things. Time for me to go and join the Mad Hatter and find out why he's having tea with the Queen of Hearts.'

'What would you like for supper?' Beth asked as he got up from the table.

'Any chance of a pizza?' he said, staring down at the empty plate.

'You got lucky, caveman. I've accepted for some time that there are four children in this family, so I ordered an extra one. When you come back down, you can tell me all about your day.'

'Just another day at the office,' said William. 'Though I did have an interesting chat to the Queen . . .'

· · ·

William turned up late for work at Buckingham Gate the following morning, and was back home in time to read the next chapter before the children fell asleep. By the end of the month, they'd finished *Alice's Adventures in Wonderland*, and had reached Chapter 5 of *Through the Looking Glass*, only because his more relaxed attitude to timekeeping fitted in with the team's long-term plan to convince Milner they were only too happy to climb on board his gravy train as first-class passengers.

For the past six weeks, they had been keeping to a strict timetable. They would turn up late every morning, enjoy long lunch breaks, which they then claimed on expenses, before leaving early, all part of a well-orchestrated performance, conducted by William.

When Milner began calling him Bill, he knew Operation Overcharge was falling neatly into place. The Superintendent would have done well to remember that Constable William Warwick hadn't been nicknamed 'Choirboy' by chance when he first joined the force.

The eight o'clock team meetings at the Yard became more regular as they approached the window of opportunity – that ten days when Prince Charles and Diana would be carrying out an overseas tour. Superintendent Milner, DI Reynolds and Sergeant Jennings, who had recently been promoted as a personal protection officer ahead of Constable Jenny Smart, would be with them on the far side of the Atlantic, while DI Ross Hogan would be able to keep a close eye on all of them.

• • •

'How did you manage to pull that off?' Faulkner asked Tulip as the two men strolled around the exercise yard together.

'I found a Judas who didn't even want thirty pieces of silver to betray him,' replied Tulip. 'His name is Tareq Omar.'

'And why is he willing to take such a risk?'

'Khalifah was responsible for his brother's death during the recent coup in Algeria, so for him, revenge will be a sufficient reward in itself.'

'How do we bring the two of them together?'

'I've arranged for Omar to be transferred to cleaning duties on Khalifah's wing, so their paths will cross regularly, when he'll pose as a devoted follower of the cause. My only fear is he might kill him.'

'We want to keep him alive while there's the slightest chance Khalifah could be my passport out of here.'

'I thought that was all under control.'

'So did I,' said Miles, 'until BW turned up for our weekly meeting and told me he'd been to see Sir Julian Warwick to confirm our agreement.'

'What makes you think he didn't?' asked Tulip.

'Lamont says they haven't seen each other since they met in his chambers soon after he returned from Spain.'

'Which one of them do you believe?'

'Lamont, because if he'd been working solely for BW, he would have confirmed his story. So I may need to cash in one of my insurance policies if I'm to have any hope of getting out of this place.' Tulip knew when not to interrupt the boss. 'One thing's for certain,' continued Miles, 'I can't risk meeting Omar myself, so how will he get any worthwhile information he picks up to you, without attracting yard gossip?'

'My cell's on the same landing as his, so he can drop in from time to time without anyone becoming suspicious. But it could still be some time before Khalifah trusts him enough to confide in him.'

'I haven't got a lot of time left,' said Miles, not elaborating. 'If Omar does come up with anything worthwhile, let me know immediately, as I've already made an appointment to see Commander Hawksby.'

Tulip couldn't believe what he'd just heard.

• • •

William arrived at Buckingham Gate just before eight o'clock the following morning, to find Rebecca waiting for him on the doorstep. Once the night watch officer had gone home, he locked the front door, aware they couldn't afford to be disturbed, while Milner and the away team were abroad, watching over their principals.

Paul had left home just before seven a.m., and made only one stop on his way to Windsor, to pick up Jackie. She was entitled to six months' sick leave, but had soon realized that Rebecca dropping in from time to time to bring her up to date wasn't that exciting, besides which, she'd already become bored with afternoon television.

The vital piece of the jigsaw had fallen neatly into place when Constable Jenny Smart had decided to resign from the unit and applied to be transferred to another section, having been passed over for promotion once too often.

Paul and Jackie hadn't needed to break into the administration block, because Jenny had left the door wide open.

They spent night and day during the week poring through file after file that provided them with more than enough of the evidence they needed to convince the Hawk about the lifestyle Milner and his cohorts had been enjoying for the past ten years at the taxpayers' expense.

As they had only got half-way through the damning evidence

by Friday night, they didn't go home, but, despite sleeping on camp beds during the weekend, they still had two more filing cabinets to go through by the time Milner accompanied the Prince and Princess back on the plane to Heathrow.

Back at Buckingham Gate, William used a pass key to enter Milner's office, while Rebecca found that DI Reynolds's door hadn't been locked. He obviously thought no one would dare to enter his sanctuary while he was away. Sergeant Jennings's office was locked; that would have to wait, but then he'd only recently been promoted, so his sins wouldn't be quite as damning.

The four of them worked around the clock for the next ten days, and by the time the royal flight landed back in England, they had gathered enough evidence to ensure that Milner would not be retiring to the country in a couple of years with a KCVO as he'd promised his wife (who never hid the fact she was looking forward to being Lady Milner) but would be summarily dismissed from the force without a pension.

Milner turned up at Buckingham Gate in time for lunch the following Monday and was unconcerned to learn that DCI Warwick was on annual leave, DS Adaja was attending a training course in Manchester, that DC Pankhurst was at her grandmother's funeral in Cornwall, and DS Roycroft wasn't expected back at work for at least another three months. He was equally unconcerned to find Constable Smart's letter of resignation waiting for him on his desk.

If Milner hadn't been so convinced he was untouchable, he would have discovered that all four of them were in fact holed up in Scotland Yard, putting the final touches to a report they would be presenting to Commander Hawksby by the end of the week.

CHAPTER 18

'I WON'T BE TAKING ANY calls for the rest of the morning, Angela,' said the commander. 'Only interrupt me if the building is on fire,' he added before putting down the phone.

He looked around the table at his team. 'Why don't you open the batting, William?'

'As you all know, sir,' began William, 'for the past ten days we've taken advantage of the fact that Superintendent Milner, DI Reynolds and Sergeant Jennings have been on the other side of the world with their principals.'

'As opposed to their principles,' interrupted the Hawk.

'We've also been able to make good use of Constable Jenny Smart's imminent departure from the unit,' continued William. 'Without her assistance, it could have taken us months to follow the paper trail.'

'She must have felt some loyalty to the people she'd worked with for the past six years,' said the commander. 'Why was she willing to throw in her lot with a bunch of intruders she hardly knew?'

'She agrees with the intruders that a bent copper is every bit as bad as any other criminal, if not worse,' said Jackie. 'And Milner, Reynolds and Jennings are among the worst I've ever come across. I was finally able to convince her that most of her colleagues would applaud the stand she's taken.'

'I have a feeling,' said William, 'that your winning the Queen's Gallantry Medal couldn't have come at a better time.'

'She was certainly more cooperative after I returned to work,' said Jackie.

'What else did you discover while the cats were away, DS Roycroft?' asked the Hawk, cutting to the chase.

'I began by checking every PPO's expenses for the past five years, when I came across claims I would never have thought possible.'

'Give me an example.'

'Milner spent three nights at the Ritz in Paris while on a recce for the Queen's state visit next year. He was so blatant about it that he even took his wife and daughter with him, claiming the adjoining room was occupied by his secretary, who was at home in Potters Bar at the time. I must say,' Jackie added, 'when he dines out, he doesn't start at the top of the list when selecting his wines.'

'Do you have a ballpark figure for the three of them over the past five years, with all the accompanying receipts to back it up?' demanded the Hawk.

'£442,712,' said Jackie, who had obviously anticipated the question.

'Made up of?'

'Mainly travel expenses, dinners, clothes allowance, and overtime, despite the fact that, as senior officers, they're not entitled to claim it.'

'Details?'

'When the Royal Family go to Balmoral for their summer break, Milner spends most of his time on the grouse moors – I'm told he bagged more pheasants than the Duke of Edinburgh last year – while Reynolds prefers fishing on the Dee. Virtually their only duties are to accompany the Queen to the Highland Games. But when they return to London they put in claims for "unsocial hours" allowance as well as an "away from home" expenses, not to mention overtime.'

'If I'm to instigate a full inquiry,' said the Hawk, 'how much wriggle room do they have? And as important, how much do you think you can make stick?'

'About half,' said Jackie. 'But I've already gathered more than enough evidence to fill my wheelbarrow.' She continued when the laughter had died down. 'My favourite claim is for a Burberry raincoat and umbrella Milner bought in Bermuda during a heatwave. The receipt shows that the raincoat just happened to be a perfect fit for his wife.'

'This can't be allowed to get out,' said the Hawk. 'The press would have a field day.'

'Reynolds and Jennings are every bit as bad,' chipped in William. 'But it was Milner who made sure they got away with it by never questioning their expense claims, which suggests they were acting in unison.'

'What will their defence be?' the commander said, almost to himself.

'Milner will claim that the Prince of Wales knew exactly what he was doing, and approved of it. But I'm convinced HRH had no idea what they were getting up to in his name.'

'Do you agree with that, Ross?'

'I do, sir. Princess Diana has no way of knowing what claims I make on my expenses, and the subject has never arisen. Milner approves every one of my claims without checking them and, once he's scribbled his initials on the bottom of the chit, the accounts department pays up without question. It's a gravy train that has no red flags and doesn't bother to stop at any station.'

'It might also amuse you to know,' said Jackie, 'that during his years as head of Royalty Protection Milner has accumulated over a million airmiles in his own name. All legal and above board.'

'He may end up having to live in mid-air once he realizes we're on to him,' said the commander. He paused for a moment before adding, 'This evidence you've gathered, Jackie, is compelling to say the least. But if we're going to bring down the head of Royalty Protection, I'll need a damn sight more than that. So, Rebecca, it's your turn to tell us what you've been up to for the past few months.'

'Superintendent Milner never travels on public transport while he's on duty,' said Rebecca, 'despite having an authorized travel card which entitles him to do so.'

'He probably uses his own car and claims a petrol allowance,' said the Hawk, playing devil's advocate.

'He never drives his own car. Always takes a taxi and puts it on expenses.'

'Then the only person who benefits is the taxi driver, and no doubt Milner has the receipts to prove it.'

'But why take a cab to Buckingham Palace or York House,' asked Rebecca, 'when both are within walking distance of his office in Buckingham Gate?'

'He would claim he can't risk being followed while carrying confidential documents,' said the Hawk.

'He also takes taxis to Windsor and back, which doesn't come cheap, when he could take the train from Victoria, a few hundred yards from the office.'

This silenced the Hawk for a moment, which Rebecca took advantage of.

'If you then check his expenses claims carefully,' she said, opening a file and running a finger down some figures before continuing. 'Last year alone, Milner made a hundred and seventy-one such taxi journeys at a cost to the taxpayer of just over £33,000.'

'And if you dig a little deeper, as we did, with the help of Constable Smart,' chipped in Paul, not needing to check the figures, 'you'll find that over the past eleven years, Superintendent Milner has claimed £434,720 on taxis alone, which I think even the BBC might describe as excessive.'

'However,' said Rebecca, 'the truth is that Milner never takes a taxi when he's on duty.'

'You'd better be able to back up that statement with hard facts, DC Pankhurst,' said the Hawk. 'Otherwise it will be your word against his.'

'I had a feeling you might say that, sir,' said Rebecca, 'so with DCI Warwick's permission I took a week off my normal duties and went undercover.'

'For what purpose?'

'To follow a week in the life of our most senior royalty protection officer.'

William allowed himself a smile as Rebecca opened an even thicker file in front of her. 'Every morning at around eight, eight fifteen, Milner leaves his home in Barnes and takes the train to Victoria using his police permit.'

'As he's entitled to do,' said the Hawk.

'On arrival at Victoria,' continued Rebecca, unperturbed, 'he then walks the half mile to Buckingham Gate. If he has an appointment with HRH, he walks across to York House, often accompanied by DI Reynolds, the Prince's PPO. Once

HRH leaves York House, Milner hot foots it back to Buckingham Gate. On two separate occasions during that week he took the train from Paddington to Windsor using his authorized travel card. On arrival, he walked from the station to the castle and disappeared into his office, not to be seen again until he left at around four thirty, when he took the train back to Barnes. During that week, he didn't once take a taxi, but it didn't stop him claiming £529 in expenses,' said Rebecca, handing over fourteen expenses claims for the Hawk to consider. 'They're not only claiming expenses for journeys that never took place, but along with his cohorts, they're coining in around quarter of a million a year, with no one else to check on them.'

The commander studied the claim dockets for some time before he said, 'Excellent work, DC Pankhurst. But it's still not enough. What else do you have to offer me?'

'Nothing else, sir. However, the chief came up with something that needs explaining.'

Everyone around the table turned to face William.

'I found this locked in the top drawer of Milner's desk,' said William, placing an expenses docket in front of the commander.

'What does this prove?' asked the Hawk, after carefully checking several expenses claims.

'It's not the claims Milner did make that we should be looking at,' said William, 'but the half-empty expenses book with his signature already on every page, only waiting for the details to be filled in. He's like a man at the roulette table who knows which number the ball will land on. He's perfected a system that always pays out, even when it lands on zero.'

'Believe me,' said the Hawk, 'that man could still bluff his way out of that. No, I need a silver bullet that Milner won't be able to put back in the chamber.' The commander noticed a grin appearing on DS Adaja's face. 'You've been unusually silent, Paul. Can I assume you're about to produce that bullet?'

'And the gun to fire it with,' said Paul. 'However, you're never going to believe what I'm about to tell you, sir, despite the fact that you've dealt with some of the sharpest criminal minds in the game.'

'Stop wasting my time,' said the Hawk.

'For the past month, I've been taking a particular interest in a certain Sergeant Nigel Hicks.'

'And what's so special about Sergeant Hicks?'

'He's been the Royalty Protection forward liaison officer for the past eleven years.'

'How fascinating,' said the commander, stifling a yawn.

'It would be, sir, if only Sergeant Hicks existed.'

The look on the Hawk's face didn't suggest that of a seasoned poker player. 'Details,' he demanded, sitting bolt upright in his chair.

'Sergeant Hicks retired eleven years ago – and died a couple of years later. He was buried at his local church in Sevenoaks.'

'You have proof, of course?'

Paul produced a photograph of Hicks's headstone and handed it over to the commander.

NIGEL HICKS

1918–1981

'You're not going to tell me that—'

'He still receives his full salary, and last year somehow managed to claim over £70,000 in expenses, without actually turning up at the office.'

'But did they get away with it?'

'It's possible Hicks was involved,' suggested William.

'But he died.'

'Not according to the record book.'

'But surely someone—' began the Hawk.

'That's the point, sir,' came back William. 'Milner, Jennings and Reynolds were all in on the scam, and were only too happy to take their cut. In fact, Hicks still has his own office in Windsor, with his name on the door.'

'And how did Milner explain why no one else ever saw him?'

'He was the forward liaison officer, sir, so he was always abroad, checking out venues on behalf of minor members of the Royal Family who were due to visit that country at some time in the future. He claimed travel expenses for cities he never visited, an accommodation allowance for hotels he never stayed in, as well as regular claims for unsocial hours and overtime. In fact, during the past eleven years, the phantom sergeant has been paid over £270,000 in wages, supplemented with another £700,000 in expenses. Not to mention claiming a million airmiles without ever getting on a plane.'

'What happened to the tickets for those flights he never took?'

'Some were cashed in, others were used whenever one of the three of them went on holiday. They've all visited some fairly exotic places during the past eleven years: Rio, Cape Town, Mexico, St Petersburg . . .'

'How did you find out?' barked the Hawk, barely able to control his temper.

'I finally broke into the missing sergeant's office, sir, only to discover that the cupboard was bare.'

'The dog that didn't bark in the night,' said the commander. 'Bravo, Paul. However, I still require icing on my cake before I report to the Commissioner. Tell me how they disposed of their ill-gotten gains, because it's always how a criminal spends the money that catches them out in the end.'

'Pull the trigger, Jackie,' said William.

'Once Paul and Rebecca had produced enough evidence to prove exactly what Milner was up to,' said Jackie, 'I took your advice and followed the money.'

'And what did you come up with?' asked the Hawk.

'Milner does have a car, a Mercedes SI, latest model, which he paid for with cash, because there's no sign of any entries other than his salary as a Superintendent, going into his bank account. So someone might be tempted to ask how he can possibly own a three-storey house on the common in Barnes, a country home in Berkshire with five acres, and a substantial property in Ibiza that could only be described as front line.'

An even longer silence followed before the Hawk said, 'How did he get away with it for so long?'

'That was the easy part,' said William. 'Because there was no one to question him until we turned up, and if Constable Jenny Smart hadn't felt it was her duty to point Jackie in the right direction, it might have taken us years to nail him. But with her assistance,' continued William, 'the team have been able to gather enough evidence, along with Paul's silver bullet to ensure that Milner will not be spending his retirement in Ibiza, but as a resident of Belmarsh prison at Her Majesty's pleasure.'

'A different form of royal protection,' suggested Paul.

The commander smiled for the first time that morning. 'Once you've handed in your report, DCI Warwick,' he said, 'I'll brief the Commissioner so he has all the ammunition he needs when he has his audience with the Prince of Wales. Meanwhile, I congratulate you all on a job well done. But if it should blow up in our faces, I fear DS Adaja will have to carry the can.'

'And if I'm proved right?' asked Paul, after the laughter had died down.

'I will personally sack Milner and his two partners in crime,' said the Hawk, 'take all the credit, promote DCI Warwick to Superintendent, and put him in charge of Royalty Protection, and will allow DS Adaja to keep reminding us all that he was the brains behind Operation Overcharge.'

The rest of the team rose and warmly applauded Paul, as the phone on the commander's desk began to ring. The Hawk picked it up. 'Angela, I said no calls unless the building is on fire.'

'It's Superintendent Milner on the line, sir. Says he needs to speak to you urgently.'

'Tell him his pants are on fire,' said the Hawk, before putting down the phone. He looked round at William. 'I think he may have noticed his expense book is missing.'

CHAPTER 19

'IT'S MY GREAT PLEASURE,' ANNOUNCED the new director of the Fitzmolean, 'to welcome you all to this remarkable collection of Frans Hals' work. I would now like to invite Her Royal Highness, the Princess of Wales, to open the exhibition.'

The Princess stepped up to the microphone. The applause continued as she glanced down at the opening paragraph of her speech.

'Can I begin by saying how delighted I was to be invited to open this much-anticipated exhibition, which has already received glowing reviews. *The Times's* critic reminded us this morning that great art transcends all prejudice and social barriers. When we look at a painting, we are unaware of the artist's colour, religious beliefs or political views. Until I read that review, I hadn't realized that Frans Hals is considered by many art historians to be in the same league as Rembrandt and Vermeer, or that although he was never short of commissions during his long life, he died almost penniless. Perhaps because he had eleven children.' The Princess waited for the laughter to die down before she continued.

'However, he left a legacy we can all admire and that will surely last for many generations to come. A Dutch master of the Golden Age would surely have been delighted that this museum has honoured his memory with such a comprehensive display of his work, which is thanks to Beth Warwick, the curator of this exhibition. Her energy, endeavour and scholarship are clear for all to see.'

A warm round of applause followed, and Beth bowed her head.

DI Ross Hogan would have liked to join in the applause, but not while he was on duty. His eyes swept the room as HRH continued her speech. He noticed his boss, Commander Hawksby, standing at the back of the assembled guests, observing proceedings; even at a gathering like this, he was clearly unable to stop being a policeman.

A few paces in front of the Hawk stood DCI Warwick. Next to him was his father, Sir Julian Warwick QC, whom Ross had previously seen only at a distance when appearing in the witness box at the Old Bailey. Ross assumed the woman on his left must be William's mother.

His eyes moved on to William's sister Grace, and her partner Clare. The formidable couple were holding hands, unafraid of making a public statement about their feelings for each other. Ross couldn't help wondering what Sir Julian thought about that. To their right were Beth Warwick's proud parents, Mr and Mrs Rainsford, to whom he would be eternally grateful for the way they had also welcomed Jojo into the family as their second granddaughter.

Ross suppressed a smile when he caught the eye of Victoria Campbell, who was standing to one side, carrying out her anonymous role as a lady-in-waiting. He had to admit that he still fancied her, but he didn't need anyone to remind him: in your dreams.

At the very front of the gathering stood Christina Faulkner, who was holding hands with the young man Ross had last seen at Tramp. He had assumed Sebastian had been a one-night stand, but clearly he was not. His attention was then drawn to another man he hadn't expected to see at the opening. He didn't appear to be listening to the speech, his eyes remaining fixed on one particular painting.

With Miles Faulkner's trial now only a few weeks away, it puzzled Ross why no one had yet questioned him about the painting Booth Watson was staring at, and how it had ended up being part of the exhibition. Even more surprising, Faulkner's lawyer hadn't made an official complaint about his client being forcibly removed from his home in Spain and dragged back to England to face a second trial.

Equally puzzling was Faulkner's decision to plead guilty in exchange for two years being knocked off his sentence. It didn't make any sense. Faulkner had the reputation of being a sharp deal-maker, and that certainly wasn't a good deal. There had to be something neither he nor William was aware of. Ross wondered if he'd ever find out. He glanced back at Booth Watson, whom he assumed must know the answer to all of those questions.

The Princess turned to her final card.

'I have no doubt that, like us, the public will derive great enjoyment from this remarkable exhibition,' she said. 'And I'm delighted to declare it open.'

Another round of applause followed. The Princess left the stage, accompanied by the museum's director, and headed straight for the keeper of pictures to congratulate her.

Artemisia, her little coronet wedged firmly in place, somehow managed to squeeze in between them.

When Diana and the new director moved on to chat with some of the other guests, Beth had to hold firmly on to Artemisia's hand to stop her becoming a supernumerary lady-in-waiting. The commander chose that moment to come out of the shadows and have a quiet word with William.

'Look over there,' he whispered.

'I've already seen him,' said William.

'Why's he so interested in that particular painting?'

'Caravaggio's *Christ Descending from the Cross*,' said William not turning his head, 'was loaned permanently to the gallery by Miles Faulkner, in exchange for a suspended sentence following his first trial.'

'I'm bound to say Booth Watson doesn't appear to have a permanent look on his face, more temporary,' mused the Hawk.

'I wonder what Faulkner would be willing to offer in exchange for a suspended sentence this time,' said William.

'Even if he were to offer us his entire collection, I can't see the judge being swayed.'

'Unless Beth was the judge,' responded William.

'Even Faulkner couldn't fix that. But that wasn't the reason I wanted to speak to you. I had a call from the Commissioner just before I left the Yard this evening. He told me he has an appointment to see the Prince of Wales on Monday morning at twelve o'clock, when he intends to fully brief him on Superintendent Milner's extra-curricular activities.'

'Milner spent this afternoon with the Prince of Wales, sir,' said William, 'while he was on a visit to the Royal Geographical Society. He'll have had more than enough time to put his side of the story long before the Commissioner turns up.'

'I fear a quiet resignation due to ill health may be the best we can hope for.'

'The damn man should be hung, drawn and quartered,' said William, 'and his head left on a spike on Tower Bridge, while Reynolds is put in the stocks on Ludgate Hill and pelted with rotten tomatoes.'

'It's so refreshing, William, to find that, after all your years in the force, the heart of a choirboy still beats within your breast,' said the Hawk as he glanced across the room to where Sir Julian Warwick was deep in conversation with Beth Warwick.

'Were you very disappointed not to get the job as Director?' Julian asked his daughter-in-law.

'I was,' admitted Beth. 'And it didn't help when Tim Knox told me the board voted seven to five in favour of Gerald Sloane. To make it even worse, the chairman told Tim that if it had been six all, he would have given his casting vote to me.'

'What can you tell me about Sloane?' asked Julian, glancing across at the museum's new director.

'He's been director of the Manchester Municipal Gallery for the past seven years, and I'm told he looks upon the Fitzmolean as a stepping stone to greater things, whereas I wanted to build the museum's reputation so that no one would ever consider it to be a stepping stone.'

'Bide your time, young lady, would be my advice,' said Julian. 'You just might find yourself getting the job sooner than you think. But at the same time, keep your eyes wide open, because Sloane will look upon you as a rival. He'll either befriend you, or try to undermine you. Possibly both.'

'You think like a criminal, Julian,' said Beth.

'That's what I'm paid to do,' was his response.

'I know I shouldn't listen to gossip,' whispered Beth, 'but I have it on good authority that only half the staff turned up for his leaving party in Manchester.'

'All the more reason for you to be cautious. It's no secret that if the Fitzmolean staff had been able to vote, you'd have won by a country mile.'

Beth nodded. 'I know this isn't the appropriate occasion,' she said, 'but I need your advice on a private matter.'

'Why don't you all come down to Nettleford for lunch on Sunday? That should give us more than enough time to talk it through,' said Julian as his wife joined them.

'I'm surprised to see Mr Booth Watson here,' said Lady Warwick.

'Perhaps he's an admirer of Frans Hals,' suggested Beth, knowing only too well why he was there.

'Mr Booth Watson isn't an admirer of anyone,' said Julian, 'unless there's a chance they could turn out to be a potential client. And Frans Hals certainly doesn't fall into that category. Although he wouldn't be the first dead client BW has represented.'

'You're such an old cynic, Julian,' said his wife.

'You don't have much choice when you have to spend your professional life crossing swords with the Booth Watsons of this world,' he replied. At that moment Artemisia let go of her mother's hand and shot off across the room.

'What's the little minx up to?' asked Julian.

'Wants to say goodbye to her friend, would be my bet,' said Beth as Artemisia grabbed Ross by the hand.

The last person the Princess said goodbye to, after admiring her coronet and giving her a kiss, was Artemisia, which didn't please the new director.

CHAPTER 20

ROSS CLIMBED INTO THE FRONT of the Jaguar after the Princess had taken her seat in the back. He checked in his personal rear-view mirror, and saw that Victoria hadn't joined them, so she must have gone home. Although Victoria would never have raised the subject in front of him, it was clear she didn't approve of Diana's other life.

Only one member of the paparazzi was waiting for them when they drove into Jermyn Street. He jumped out into the middle of the road the moment he spotted the car. Ross wondered if he was just there on the off chance, or if someone had tipped him off. Given half a chance, he'd have run him over.

The Princess used her handbag to shield her face as she ran down the steps into the nightclub. The maître d' accompanied her to her usual table – heads turning as she crossed the dance floor – where she found Jamil standing waiting for her. He kissed her on both cheeks and, once they'd sat down, they held hands openly across the table, no longer even attempting to conceal their relationship.

Ross retired to his usual discreet table behind a pillar. When the two of them strolled out onto the dance floor shortly afterwards, it would have been obvious to any casual observer they were lovers. The bobbing ponytail still irritated Ross. He wrote nothing down, but would make a full report to William in the morning. He knew William was keeping the commander up to date so that no one was left out of the loop.

Once again, Diana left the club just after midnight. As she stepped out onto the pavement, she found several photographers waiting to greet her.

Ross did his best to protect her from the more persistent of them as she scrambled into the back of the car, but they still pursued her, cameras flashing, until the Jaguar turned the corner into St James's only to find one of them waiting by the traffic lights as they slowed down at the top of Piccadilly. Ross clocked that it was the same one who'd been waiting outside Tramp when she'd arrived there earlier that evening.

'Do you know the name of that photographer, Ross?'

'Yes, ma'am. Alan Young.'

'Poor man, standing out there just in case I turn up.'

'I wouldn't waste your sympathy on him, ma'am. He's the best-paid snapper in Fleet Street, and he only takes photos of you.'

They travelled on in silence for some time before the Princess eventually said, 'I'll be spending the weekend with Jamil at his home in Sussex. It's not on the official schedule, of course, but I hope you'll be kind enough to make the usual arrangements.'

'Of course, ma'am,' said Ross without hesitation, although he'd been looking forward to spending a weekend with Jojo. He'd planned a trip to the cinema to see *The Little Mermaid*

– ending up at her favourite ice cream shop. Thank God for William and Beth, he thought as the car swung into Kensington Palace Gardens.

• • •

'I thought Jojo was meant to be spending the weekend with Ross,' said Beth as she strapped the three children into their car seats.

William climbed behind the wheel. 'Change of plan. Seems the Princess needs him for a special assignment.'

'What could be more special than Jojo?' asked Beth, not letting him off the hook.

'Well, she won't be spending the weekend with Prince Charles,' was all William had to say on the subject.

'Are you telling me Diana's having an affair?' whispered Beth as they set off for Nettleford.

'I'm not telling you anything,' said William.

Beth was about to protest when Artemisia said, 'What's an affair?'

William and Beth remained silent, but were rescued by Peter asking, 'How long before we get there?' even before they'd reached the first set of traffic lights.

'About an hour,' said William. 'But you always enjoy spending the day with your grandparents.'

'Why doesn't Grandpops have a TV?' asked Peter.

Beth and William were trying to come up with a suitable response, when Jojo asked plaintively, 'Will Daddy be there?'

'No, he won't,' said Artemisia. 'He's spending the weekend with my friend, the Princess of Wales.'

'But I know he's got next weekend off,' said William, 'when he still intends to take you to see *The Little Mermaid*, and if

178

you're very good, you may even get your favourite double chocolate sundae.'

Jojo clapped her hands.

'What are you up to next week,' asked Beth, 'other than spying on the Princess?'

'Don't even ask,' replied William, lowering his voice. 'The Commissioner has an appointment with the Prince of Wales tomorrow morning, and none of us has any idea how he'll react when he hears what his senior protection officer has been up to for the past eleven years.'

'They'll want to make sure nothing gets into the press that will embarrass the Queen. Although I have a feeling the Prince of Wales will know only too well that Diana's playing away from home.'

'Princess Diana,' said Artemisia, correcting her mother.

'Well, at least you must be looking forward to next week,' said William. 'The museum should be packing them in after all those five-star reviews for the Frans Hals exhibition in this morning's papers.'

'I would be, if the new director didn't spend so much of his time trying to undermine me in front of the rest of the staff.'

'Don't worry, I'm sure he'll come round, given time.'

'I doubt it. We've barely exchanged a civil word since the day he took over, and there doesn't seem to be anything I can do to appease him.'

'What does appease mean?' asked Artemisia.

'Falling in with someone else's views to please them,' said Beth, looking around to see that Peter and Jojo had fallen asleep.

'I sympathize,' said William. 'Especially remembering how well you got on with Tim Knox.'

'Don't remind me. And it doesn't help that Sloane's asked to see me first thing tomorrow morning, leaving me to stew over the weekend wondering what he's annoyed about this time.'

'Perhaps he wants to congratulate you on the successful opening of the Frans Hals exhibition?'

'Don't bet on it. Much more likely he's found something new to grumble about.'

'You mustn't become paranoid about him,' said William. 'He's not worth it.'

'What does paranoid mean?' asked Artemisia.

• • •

This was one meeting Booth Watson wasn't going to be late for. He'd never visited the Connaught Hotel before, but was well aware of its reputation. Old-world, luxurious, the finest cuisine, and always fully booked for months in advance. Americans, they'd discovered, were happy to be parted from their money as long as it was masked in the cloak of tradition, especially as the hotel was almost as old as their country.

Miles had once complained to Booth Watson that he hadn't been able to make a booking in the hotel's restaurant despite several attempts. His lawyer didn't explain why they wouldn't have offered him a table even if they'd been empty.

Booth Watson gave his name to the receptionist who, without bothering to check, said, 'Mr Lee is expecting you, sir. If you'll take the lift to the top floor, someone will meet you.'

'What's his room number?'

'There is only one suite on the top floor, sir,' the receptionist said, the courteous smile never leaving her face.

Booth Watson crossed the lobby to the lift, now even more convinced that he'd found the right man. A profile in *Forbes* magazine had described Lee as a successful Chinese businessman with banking and real estate interests, whose hobbies included collecting art and fine wines. He had outbid Miles at Bonhams for a Blue Period Picasso a few years before.

Booth Watson stepped into a lift that had only one button, and proceeded without interruption to the top floor. When the doors opened, he was greeted by a young woman dressed in a red silk cheongsam. She bowed low and said, 'Please follow me, Mr Booth Watson.'

Without another word she led him along a thickly carpeted corridor towards an oak-panelled door, which she opened before standing aside.

Booth Watson entered a large, ornately furnished room, bedecked with a fresh flower arrangement on almost every available surface. But what struck him most were the superb paintings that adorned every wall. Miles would have both admired and envied the collection. It was obvious why no one else was permitted to book this particular suite.

'Can I offer you some tea while you're waiting?' asked the young woman.

'Thank you,' said Booth Watson, just as a door on the far side of the room opened and a tall, grey-haired man dressed in a double-breasted suit, white shirt and silk tie walked across to welcome his guest. A typical Hong Kong businessman, who knew no international borders, was Booth Watson's first impression.

'Forgive me for keeping you waiting, Mr Booth Watson,' Lee said as they shook hands. 'The phone always seems to ring just as a guest is about to appear.'

'What a magnificent art collection you have,' said Booth

Watson as the young woman reappeared carrying a laden tea tray which she placed on the table, before lowering herself to her knees and serving the two men.

'How kind of you to say so,' said Lee. 'I confess that what began as a hobby has over the years become something of an obsession.'

'Milk and sugar?' asked the young woman.

'Yes, thank you,' said Booth Watson.

'I have never mastered the English tradition of small talk,' said Lee. 'So I'll put this as delicately as I can. Would I be right in thinking that due to his present circumstances, Mr Miles Faulkner is considering parting with his fabled art collection?'

'That is correct. But I would stress,' said Booth Watson, 'he is only considering.'

'I once spent a couple of years in such an establishment,' said Lee, taking Booth Watson by surprise, 'as a rebellious student during the revolution.'

'What happened?'

'I was released, but only because my side won.' Both men laughed as the young woman returned carrying a plate of salmon and cucumber sandwiches, which she placed on the table between them.

'I confess,' Lee continued, 'to have learnt almost as much in prison as I did at the Harvard Business School. And indeed, the contacts I made there proved every bit as useful.'

Booth Watson helped himself to a sandwich before returning to the subject they both wanted to discuss. 'Are you familiar with Mr Faulkner's collection?' he asked.

'Indeed I am. When he put his villa in Monte Carlo on the market several years ago, I viewed the house as a prospective buyer. I took photographs of all one hundred and seventy-three paintings, as well as the twenty-one sculptures in the garden, every one of which I was later able to verify in the relevant catalogues raisonnés. I particularly admired the reclining nude by Henry Moore.'

'There are actually a hundred and ninety-one paintings and twenty-six sculptures in the collection,' said Booth Watson after selecting another sandwich.

'Then eighteen of the paintings and five of the sculptures must have been acquired after he moved into his most recent home just outside Barcelona,' Lee said casually, once again taking Booth Watson by surprise. 'In any case,' continued Lee, 'I'm sure Mr Faulkner has a view on what his collection is worth.'

'According to the experts,' said Booth Watson, 'somewhere in the region of three hundred million.'

'We all have experts to advise us, Mr Booth Watson, and they usually know if their client is a buyer or a seller. Mine consider one hundred million is nearer the mark.'

'I believe Mr Faulkner would consider two hundred million a fair price, given his present circumstances,' said Booth Watson, picking up Lee's earlier expression.

'Then I won't waste any more of your time,' said Lee standing up. 'No doubt you have other interested parties, who would be only too willing to write a cheque for two hundred million without asking too many questions.'

'If my client were to consider your offer of one hundred million,' said Booth Watson, trying to recover his composure, 'would it be possible for the money to be deposited with a bank in Hong Kong?'

'I have a controlling interest in two banks in the protectorate,' said Lee as the young woman reappeared and cleared the table.

'And could you give a guarantee that no items from Mr Faulkner's collection would come on the market in the near future? Because that could cause him considerable embarrassment.'

'Look around you, Mr Booth Watson,' said Lee as he sat back down, 'and you will see I am a collector, not a dealer. I can assure you none of the works will come up for sale during my lifetime.'

'Before I consult my client, Mr Lee, can I also confirm that one hundred million pounds is your final offer?'

'Dollars, Mr Booth Watson. I don't deal in pounds. It's not a currency I feel safe with.'

'I'll let you know my client's answer as soon as I have consulted him,' said Booth Watson, heaving himself up out of his chair.

'As I'll be in London for the next few weeks, please feel free to call me at any time,' said Lee. 'A simple yes or no will suffice, as I wouldn't want to waste your time.' He rose from his seat and once again the young woman reappeared as if he'd waved a wand. Lee bowed low, but not as low as the woman, who accompanied Booth Watson out of the room and back to the lift.

As the doors slid closed, she bowed once more before returning to the suite.

'What did you think of our guest, Mai Ling?' Lee asked as she re-entered the room.

'Not a man I would trust.'

'I agree with you. In fact, I'm not convinced Mr Faulkner is even aware that the meeting was taking place.'

'What would convince you either way?'

'If Booth Watson accepts my offer of one hundred million dollars, you can be fairly sure he isn't representing his client, but himself, because I don't think Mr Faulkner would consider parting with a collection it's taken him a lifetime to put together for such a paltry sum.'

'I can think of another way you can find out if he's telling the truth, Father,' said Mai Ling.

• • •

'Audrey's such an excellent cook,' said Beth, 'that, whenever we visit you, I always feel guilty about my feeble efforts in the kitchen. Not that William ever complains.'

'You have other gifts,' said Julian, 'which I can assure you Audrey greatly admires. Not least how well you're doing at the museum.'

'That may not be the case for much longer.'

'I'm sorry to hear that. Is that the reason you wanted to see me?'

Beth nodded. 'I'm afraid so. I can't pretend I'm enjoying working under the new director, and although I don't think he'd consider sacking me, unless he found me with my hand in the till, I'm seriously considering resigning.'

'Would you be able to find an equivalent position in another gallery?' asked Julian.

'Not easily. They don't come up that often. The irony is the Tate approached me a few months ago to ask if I'd be interested in the post of deputy director. I would definitely have considered the offer if Tim Knox hadn't told me he'd already recommended me to the board as his replacement.'

'Is the job at the Tate still available?'

'No. It was filled by an outstanding candidate from the V&A, who I'm told is doing an excellent job.'

'Then my advice would be to stay put until another

opportunity arises. You won't enjoy being unemployed, not to mention the loss of income.'

'That's the real reason I needed to seek your advice, Julian. I'd like to take advantage of an opportunity that's arisen, but it poses a bit of a moral dilemma for me.'

'Details, details,' demanded Julian as if dealing with one of his clients.

'I may have come across a pencil drawing by Rembrandt, which is coming up for sale at a small auction house in Pittsburgh.'

'So, where's the moral dilemma?'

'The drawing isn't listed as a Rembrandt, but by an unknown artist. The truth is, I'm not altogether certain about it myself. But if I'm right, it could be worth up to forty thousand pounds while the auction house's estimate is only two hundred dollars.'

'That's called experience and scholarship, while at the same time being willing to take a punt,' said Julian. 'It's not your fault the auction house hasn't done its homework.'

'I couldn't agree more,' said Beth. 'But should I tell Sloane about my possible discovery, or should I risk two hundred dollars of my own money, in the hope of making a killing myself?'

'What would you have done if Tim Knox was still director?'

'Told him immediately,' said Beth without hesitation, 'so the Fitzmolean could benefit.'

'Then you've answered your own question. Your first responsibility is to the museum, not its director, whoever that might be. Museums are permanent, directors are temporary.'

'Even if Sloane were to tell the board it was his discovery, and take the credit for it?'

'You really don't like him, do you?'

'No, I don't,' said Beth not attempting to hide her feelings.

'Disliking the man is not a good enough reason to allow it to cloud your judgement, or lower yourself to his level.'

'Of course you're right. I'll tell him about the drawing first thing in the morning.'

'I think that would be wise,' said Julian. 'If nothing else, it might improve your relationship with him.'

'Don't count on it.'

'Let's rejoin the others before William starts wondering what we're up to,' said Julian.

'I have no secrets from William,' said Beth. 'I've already discussed the problem with him, so you won't be surprised to learn he agrees with you.'

'He's a lucky man,' said Julian as he got up from his chair, opened the study door, and stood aside to allow Beth to make her way back to the drawing room.

'Artemisia has been telling us about her most recent conversation with the Princess of Wales,' said Audrey, when they reappeared.

'Verbatim,' said William.

'Yes, I was,' said Artemisia. 'I can't wait to see her again, because I have an important question to ask her.'

'And what might that be?' enquired Julian.

'In the car Mummy told Daddy that Diana was playing away from home, and I wondered which sport she was playing.'

Sir Julian didn't answer his granddaughter's question, as he wasn't altogether sure how to advise his youngest client.

CHAPTER 21

RADIANT WAS THE WORD THAT came to Ross's mind when he saw her for the first time that morning.

'Good morning, your Royal Highness,' he said, holding open the back door of the car.

'Good morning, Ross,' she replied as she climbed in. 'It was kind of you to give up your weekend. I do hope Jojo isn't too cross with me.'

'She understood, ma'am.'

Both of them knew that wasn't true.

Making their way out of London on a Saturday morning with no police escort was an unusual experience for both of them. Having to stop at traffic lights that didn't instantly turn green, waiting to give way at roundabouts, and being overtaken by other cars, allowed Diana a rare glimpse of the real world.

Ross glanced in his rear-view mirror to see her chatting on the phone. She was clearly looking forward to a weekend in the country with her . . . he couldn't find the appropriate word.

Not for the first time, Ross was grateful that the back windows were tinted. Otherwise, there would have been a steady stream of gawpers in other cars trying to take photos on the move, some even while they were driving.

Although he wasn't looking forward to spending a weekend in the country with 'His Royal Upstart', as William referred to him, he was interested to see what Jamil Chalabi's home was like. Glitzy and vulgar, he assumed. His thoughts were interrupted when Diana asked, 'When do you think we'll get there, Ross?'

He checked his watch. 'About another forty minutes, ma'am. So we might be a few minutes late.'

She then blindsided him by asking, 'You don't like Jamil, do you?' Ross couldn't think of a suitable reply. 'Just as I thought,' she said as they drove into Guildford.

As they proceeded slowly along the high street, she delivered the single word he most dreaded.

'Stop,' she said firmly – more of a command than a request. Her former protection officer had warned Ross that it always happened when you least expected it.

He slowed down and parked on a single yellow line. He unbuckled his seatbelt, but she'd escaped before he could reach the back door. One look, and he knew exactly where she was heading. He quickly followed her into the shop to find her gazing around, her eyes lit up like a drunk who's found the only bar in town.

Wherever you looked, there were handbags of every shape, size and colour, that had found their way from all over the world to a boutique in Guildford. HRH was clearly in paradise.

To Ross's relief there was no one else inside the shop, other than a young woman behind the counter, whose mouth was wide open, though no words were coming out. HRH was enjoying the feast that surrounded her, still unsure which would be her first course.

Ross quickly switched the open sign to closed and stood with his back to the door – though within minutes, he accepted that everyone in Guildford would know who had just ridden into town.

HRH was taking her time, closely examining various bags that particularly appealed to her, looking inside to make sure they would cater for the needs of a princess, which often included somewhere to put 'today's speech'.

She'd just about completed her preliminary search when an older man appeared from an office at the back of the shop. After a second take, he stammered, 'Good morning, Your Majesty,' and bowed low from the waist. 'Is there anything I can help you with?'

'Thank you. I'm finding it hard to choose between these,' said Diana, placing two handbags on the counter.

'This one,' he said, picking up the first bag, 'is a classic French model made by Le Tanneur, who have been established for almost a hundred years. And this one is a Burberry. Your Majesty will be familiar with the brand, as I know it's one of your favourites.'

Diana turned to Ross. 'If you had to choose one of these for Josephine, which do you think she would have preferred?'

Ross deserted his post by the door and joined HRH at the counter. He took a closer look at the bags before saying, 'You have to remember, ma'am, that Jo was French, and when it came to style, she considered the British were still on a learning curve, so there's no doubt which one she would have selected.'

'I agree with her,' said Diana, after taking a third look at both bags. 'I'll have this one,' she said, handing the Le Tanneur to the young woman, who still hadn't spoken.

'An excellent choice, Your Majesty, if I may say so,' said the owner as he began to wrap up the chosen bag.

HRH's next request didn't take Ross by surprise.

'I don't have any money on me, Ross, so could you possibly . . . ?'

'Not a problem, ma'am.' Ross took out his wallet and not for the first time, handed over his credit card.

Once the owner had finished wrapping up the bag, he rushed across to the door, opened it, and said, 'We look forward to seeing you again, Your Majesty,' followed by an even lower bow.

When Ross stepped out of the shop, he wasn't surprised to find that a large crowd had gathered on the pavement outside. They began clapping and taking photos the moment she appeared; one particularly enterprising mother had bought a bunch of flowers from the shop next door, which her young daughter held up as she passed. Diana bent down, accepted the bouquet, and gave the girl a hug. The mother got her photo opportunity.

As Ross shepherded HRH back to the car, he made a request of a young constable who'd assessed the situation.

Diana waved as the car moved off and made its way slowly through the enthusiastic crowd that had spilled out onto the road. When Ross was finally able to speed up, he checked the rear-view mirror and satisfied himself that the young policeman had followed his instructions. He was holding up the traffic to make sure no one could chase after them – a protection officer's worst nightmare.

As they drove out of town, Ross was beginning to feel grateful that they appeared to have escaped unscathed, when a cry came from the back seat.

'Oh, help!' said Diana. 'We're going to have to go back.'

'Why, ma'am?' asked Ross, who had no intention of returning, even if it was a royal command.

'He's given me both bags.'

'Hardly a surprise, ma'am,' said Ross.

'How much was the bill?' she asked.

'There was no bill, ma'am.'

'Then how am I going to pay them?'

'You already have, ma'am.'

'You're not making any sense, Ross.'

'When Frank Sinatra visited Naples last year, he dropped into a pizza parlour along with his bodyguards and ordered a Margarita they've now called Sinatra. I'm told there's been a queue outside the shop ever since. I predict that by the time the shop you've just visited closes tonight, there won't be a bag on the shelves, and the owner won't need to advertise for the rest of his life.'

'We should drop into shops like that more often.'

'No, thank you, ma'am.'

'The least I can do is send him a note to thank him. Did you find out his name, by any chance?'

'I did. Aloysius.'

'You're kidding me.'

'No, ma'am. Apparently his friends call him Al.'

'And the young woman behind the counter?' asked Diana, making a note.

'His daughter, Susan.'

'How did you find that out?'

'I served undercover for twelve years, ma'am.'

'How lucky I am to have you serving me now, Ross,' she said coyly as she placed her diary back into her handbag.

Ross was no different from any other man. Despite trying to remain cool, he melted.

As they turned off the main road, Ross checked once again to make sure no one was following them. No one was. They had only travelled about another couple of miles when they entered the picturesque hamlet of Chalfordbury, and moments later they approached two ornate iron gates heralding the entrance to a large estate. The gates began to swing slowly open when the car was still a hundred yards away. A guard saluted as they passed by.

A winding drive led through a dense forest and past a large lake, before a grand Lutyens mansion loomed up in front of them that wouldn't have failed to impress even a Princess. They finally circled a rose garden in full bloom before coming to a halt in front of the house.

Jamil Chalabi was standing on the top step waiting to greet them. As they were over an hour late, Ross wondered how long he'd been standing there. Chalabi walked down to greet his royal guest as she stepped out of the car.

'I'm so sorry,' Diana said as he kissed her on both cheeks.

'Not a problem,' he replied, leading her up the steps and into the house. 'I'm just delighted you made it.'

As Ross entered the house, he was surprised to find it was anything but glitzy and vulgar. Beth and William would certainly have admired an art collection that would have graced a gallery. Was it possible he'd misjudged the man?

An under-butler peeled Ross off from the main party and guided him on a long circuitous route to the west wing, before dumping him in a room that was cramped and cold and could only have been described as staff quarters. Ross accepted that that was exactly how Chalabi thought of him.

Once he'd unpacked, he carried out an inspection of the grounds. He began by walking around the perimeter of the property, which took him almost forty minutes. The ten-foot flint stone wall that surrounded the entire estate would have put off the most determined professional burglar, let alone a trainee.

Ross introduced himself to the guard on the front gate, whom he thought he recognized. He was assured that during the weekend there would never be fewer than three guards on duty twenty-four/seven; one on the gate, with two more patrolling the grounds. After confirming there was no other entrance to the estate, Ross made his way back to the house, stopping only to admire the vast oval lake which was stocked with asagi carp. He'd once read that asagi were so highly prized, they cost as much as a thousand pounds each. Ross tried not to think how many of them it would take to fill a lake that size; another way of Chalabi subtly reminding his guests how wealthy he was.

When he returned to the house, there was no sign of HRH or her host, although so many staff were rushing about, they might have been preparing for a banquet, rather than what he had been led to believe would be a cosy *tête-à-tête* supper.

Ross entered the dining room to find a long oak table had been set for twenty-four, with the finest Wedgwood china, an array of Baccarat wine glasses and a silver cutlery service that took up almost every available space. A tall vase of white orchids dominated the centre of the table.

He checked the place cards and recognized a few well-known names, and some others that were vaguely familiar, but mostly they were unknown to him. He suspected they all had one thing in common; they were there to be impressed by the presence at Chalabi's table of HRH, so they could be made use of at a later date. Not for the first time, he reflected ruefully that Diana was so sophisticated at some levels, while being so naïve at others. However, he accepted that there was little he could do about it.

Ross spent the rest of the afternoon carrying out a thorough examination of the house's layout, identifying all its entrances and exits. When the hall clock struck six, he returned to his room, took a shower and changed into a dinner jacket. He was standing discreetly in a corner of the hall twenty minutes before the first guest arrived, and he remained at a distance throughout the evening. The finest wines and dish after dish of mouth-watering food passed him every few minutes, and from the exuberant noise and banter that flowed during dinner it was clear that everyone was enjoying themselves, although he wasn't convinced it was HRH's idea of a Saturday night on the tiles. He didn't return to his room in the west wing until the last guest had departed.

Ross left the curtains in his room open and his window ajar so the dawn chorus would ensure he was among the first to wake.

He climbed into bed just before one o'clock and quickly fell asleep.

• • •

Ross had showered and shaved, and was just about to go down for breakfast, when a discreet red light began flashing on the telephone next to his bed. He picked up the phone, surprised HRH was already awake, but before he could say a word he recognized Chalabi's voice, and remained silent.

'They've been told to expect you at the gate, but once you're on the estate, make yourself scarce, because Diana's protection officer will be hanging around. Nothing would give him greater pleasure than to kick you out, and I wouldn't be able to prevent it.'

'I know that bastard only too well,' said a second voice that Ross immediately recognized. 'He kneed me in the balls once, and if he came across me again, he'd happily throw me over the wall.'

'Do you think we'll make the front pages tomorrow?' Chalabi asked.

'Along with several inside pages,' promised the second voice. 'But I wouldn't recommend you letting Di read them over breakfast, or you'll be toast.'

'Don't worry, she'll have gone long before then.'

'When are you seeing her next?'

'Thursday, at Harry's Bar, eight o'clock. Make sure you're there,' said Chalabi, before hanging up.

When the light went off, Ross suddenly had a purpose – to make sure no photographs from the weekend appeared in any morning papers.

Ross went down the back stairs and had a quick breakfast in the kitchen. Although he was met with the occasional questioning look, no one asked him why he was wearing a black tracksuit and black trainers.

After downing his orange juice, he slipped out of the back door and made his way quickly to the edge of the forest. From his concealed position he could see HRH enjoying breakfast with her host on the veranda. It wasn't difficult to work out where the line of fire would be for a hit man or a paparazzi photographer, but it would still require all his skills to take this particular snapper by surprise now he'd been warned to be on the lookout for him.

Ross crept stealthily across the lawn to an ancient oak tree on the far side of the lake and climbed its branches like a schoolboy until he reached one that was large enough to perch on. He took out his monocular and scanned the arc of fire. It was some time before he spotted the snapper, as his camouflage was good, and his chosen spot was well hidden. Although he'd blackened his face and hands and wore a green and brown woollen hat, a glint of sunlight caught the long lens that poked out from below a bush and gave him away.

'Got you,' muttered Ross. He pocketed the monocular, climbed back down the tree and inched his way cautiously towards the wall, making sure he remained out of sight. Every one of his senses was on the highest alert as he skirted the perimeter until finally he saw a foot sticking out from beneath a bush.

Ross crouched down and advanced more slowly, careful not to make the slightest noise. A breaking twig would sound like a gunshot. When he was about thirty feet away, he lay flat on his stomach and, like a predator that's spotted its next meal, advanced even more slowly towards him, his eyes never leaving the target.

He stopped when he heard the click of a shutter. *Click, click, click*. Another couple of feet, *click, click*, and then the final few inches, *click*, before he raised himself onto his hands and knees. He took a deep breath, leapt forward and grabbed his prey by the ankles, before yanking him unceremoniously from his hiding place.

When the man saw who it was, he said, 'Fuck off, Inspector. I was invited, unlike you.'

'Shall we go and find out if that's true?' said Ross, twisting an arm half-way up his back. 'If, as you claim, Chalabi invited you to take photos of him with the princess, which you'll then sell to the papers without her permission, I have a feeling that, like St Peter, he'll deny you at least three times. But then it's possible you know Chalabi far better than I do, so I'll leave the choice up to you: the front door or the main gate?'

Ross gave the man a few moments to consider his options before he grabbed the other arm and started frog-marching him towards the gates.

'What about my equipment?' the snapper demanded.

'What about it?'

'It's worth thousands of pounds.'

'Then you were foolish to leave it lying about, weren't you?'

'I'll sue you.'

'If I were to kill you right now,' said Ross as they reached the gates, 'there isn't a jury in the land that would convict me.' The snapper groaned as an arm was shoved further up his back.

'He's leaving,' Ross said firmly to the guard on duty, who reluctantly opened one of the gates, allowing Ross to hurl the intruder out onto the road. 'Make sure he doesn't come back, unless you want your references checked more carefully.'

The guard looked suitably contrite.

Ross returned to the outskirts of the forest and picked up the camera, but left the rest of the snapper's equipment where he'd found it. On his way up to the house, he paused by the lake, where several asagi carp were poking their heads out of the water, mouths wide open, clearly hoping to be fed. Ross sat down and examined the expensive Leica camera for a few minutes, even took some photos of the carp, before it slipped through his fingers and fell into the water, causing the carp to scatter in every direction, while it sank below the surface.

'What a pity,' he said as it disappeared out of sight.

Before he got back to the house, Ross put a call through to the local police, gave the duty sergeant the name of the photographer and the registration number of his Porsche. He asked him to make sure he didn't come within five miles of the estate for the rest of the day.

'My pleasure,' was all the sergeant had to say.

After keeping watch for the rest of the morning to make sure the photographer didn't reappear, Ross returned to the kitchen and enjoyed what his mother would have called a slap-up Sunday lunch. He thanked the cook before preparing to accompany HRH back to London.

When the car set off on its return journey, Ross noticed that Chalabi didn't have the same self-satisfied grin on his face that he'd displayed when they'd arrived the previous day.

'I do hope the weekend wasn't quite as bad as you feared it might be,' said Diana as they drove out of the gates and headed back towards London.

'Thank you, ma'am,' said Ross. 'It turned out to be far more agreeable than I would have thought possible.'

CHAPTER 22

WILLIAM WAS SURPRISED TO SEE DI Reynolds standing by the entrance to Number 4 Buckingham Gate when he turned up the following morning, not least because it wasn't yet eight a.m., an hour William didn't normally associate with Reynolds. But he quickly discovered why he was there.

'Superintendent Milner wants to see you in his office now,' said Reynolds, emphasizing the word 'now'.

'Thank you, Inspector,' said William, walking straight past him. 'I was rather hoping to have a word with him myself, so you've saved me the trouble of having to make an appointment.'

When he reached the Superintendent's office on the second floor, he knocked and waited for the command, 'Come,' before entering. Milner waved William to a chair on the other side of his desk without any suggestion of a greeting.

'Warwick,' he barked, even before he had sat down. 'It has come to my attention that, while I was accompanying Their Royal Highnesses the Prince and Princess of Wales on their official tour, you broke into my office, rifled through my files, and removed several items, including my diary, without my knowledge or permission. Is that correct?'

'Yes, sir,' said William, not flinching.

'Who gave you the authority to carry out this unwarranted intrusion?'

'Commander Hawksby, sir.'

'Hawksby has no authority over Royalty Protection. I report only to the Prince of Wales.'

'And to the Commissioner of the Metropolitan Police, who will be seeing His Royal Highness at twelve o'clock today.'

'At which time he will be told in no uncertain terms who is in charge of this department.'

'If you say so, sir.'

'I do say so, Warwick, and what's more, I will be recommending to the Commissioner, who is not only a colleague but an old friend, that you should be suspended with immediate effect, pending a full inquiry into your disgraceful and unprofessional behaviour. That recommendation will also include your accomplices, DS Adaja, DS Roycroft and DC Pankhurst.'

'They were simply carrying out my orders.' William paused before adding, 'Sir.'

'Don't get cocky with me, Warwick,' Milner said, staring directly at William. 'You're in quite enough trouble as it is. I'm also told by Inspector Reynolds that his office was broken into by DC Pankhurst, despite her claiming she was attending her grandmother's funeral in Cornwall at the time.'

'She didn't need to break into Reynolds's office, sir – it wasn't locked.'

'She still had no right to enter the room without his permission,' snapped back Milner. 'And I'm told DS Roycroft was also involved in your clandestine behaviour, despite being on sick leave.'

'Yes, sir. I admit it was out of order for her to return to work when she should have been convalescing, having risked her life to arrest one of the world's most dangerous terrorists, for which she was awarded the Queen's Gallantry Medal. But no such courage was required for her to unlock a dozen filing cabinets and inspect your expenses claims over the past eleven years.'

'I'm glad you mentioned expenses, Warwick, because your colleague DS Adaja will be facing a full inquiry for submitting false claims to the tune of £4,332.' He threw down a thick wad of claims on the table in triumph.

'He paid back every penny of those expenses, which you yourself authorized without questioning him.'

'Don't bother to try and get him off the hook, because it's no more than you can expect when that sort join the force.'

'What sort might that be, sir?'

'Well, let's face it, Warwick. He's not one of us, if you catch my drift?'

'That's possibly why he got on so well with your Royalty Protection forward liaison officer, the late lamented Sergeant Nigel Hicks.'

Milner turned chalk white.

'Who I understand the Commissioner is keen to have a word with before he visits the Prince of Wales later this morning.'

Milner's whole body began to shake.

'If I might be allowed to give you one piece of advice,' said William, 'I would write your letter of resignation now, and make sure it's delivered to the Commissioner's office before midday. That way, he'll be able to cancel his appointment with the Prince of Wales, and avoid having to tell HRH the real reason you had to resign.'

Milner was now breathing heavily, large beads of sweat appearing on his forehead.

'I would also suggest you advise DI Reynolds and Sergeant Jennings to take the same course of action – unless of course they are willing to face a full inquiry, that would undoubtedly result in them also being dismissed from the service. I have a feeling they wouldn't hesitate to drag you down with them if they thought it might save their own skins.'

'Yes, I've always suspected those two were fiddling their expenses,' said Milner calmly, 'and I was about to make a full report on what they've been up to. I'll have it ready for you by midday, Bill. Then perhaps you could have a word with your friend, the commander?'

'What word did you have in mind, sir?' said William. 'Crook? Embezzler? Thief? I don't think so. In fact, if I were the Commissioner, I'd instigate a full public inquiry, confident you'd be spending your retirement in a cell in Belmarsh, rather than a cottage in the Cotswolds. However, I suspect Commander Hawksby will do everything in his power to avoid that, as he no doubt considers the Met's reputation as rather more important than yours.'

William glanced at the photographs on the office walls and added, 'Not to mention the reputation of your close friend, the Prince of Wales. So I'm sorry to say you'll probably get away with it, unless of course you decide to dispute the allegations. I confess I hope you do – not least because it will allow DS Adaja to receive the praise he richly deserves for identifying the gravestone of the late Sergeant Nigel Hicks – if you catch my drift.'

• • •

'How did your meeting with Milner go?' Rebecca asked as they left Buckingham Gate and set off for the Yard.

'I have to admit the damn man riled me, and I may have gone over the top,' said William as they crossed Victoria Street. 'If he decides to wait until the Commissioner's seen the Prince of Wales, heaven knows which one of us will be out on our necks.'

'But you were doing no more than the Hawk instructed you to do.'

'I'm afraid not,' said William. 'I didn't follow the commander's advice, and simply deliver the facts while remaining calm.'

'I have a feeling you'll be all right, sir,' said Rebecca.

'What makes you say that?' asked William as they crossed Victoria Street.

'DI Reynolds and Sergeant Jennings were standing outside in the corridor listening to every word and, when you came out, they didn't rush in to join their paymaster, but disappeared into their own offices. So I think you'll find all three of them are writing their letters of resignation right now, and will hand them in before midday.'

'How can you possibly know that?'

'Bullies are invariably cowards,' Rebecca replied.

· · ·

Beth knocked on the director's door just before nine o'clock, and waited for the word 'Enter.'

When she did, Sloane waved her into the chair on the other side of his desk, as if she were a junior member of staff.

'I thought you'd like to know, Gerald—'

'I think, Mrs Warwick, it would be more appropriate if you addressed me as director or sir, during working hours.'

'As you wish, sir, but I thought you'd be pleased to hear—'

'Later,' insisted Sloane. 'I have more pressing matters to discuss with you at the moment.' Beth fell silent. 'In this morning's post I received a letter from a Mr Booth Watson QC, who informs me that once the Hals exhibition is over, he will be collecting the self-portrait, which he claims belongs to his client, Mr Miles Faulkner, and was removed from his home without his permission.' He peered across at Beth as if she was in the witness box.

'Faulkner doesn't own it,' protested Beth. 'It belongs to his wife, Christina.'

'It would seem that is not the case,' said Sloane. 'Mr Booth Watson assures me that your friend Mrs Faulkner returned the picture to her ex-husband as part of their recent divorce settlement.'

Beth would have protested, but realized that once again Christina hadn't told her the whole story.

'Our lawyers have advised me it would be pointless to dispute the claim. And as if that wasn't enough,' said Sloane once again returning to the letter, 'Mr Booth Watson goes on to say that his client will also be reclaiming his Raphael and Rembrandt, which you led me to believe were on permanent loan.'

'They are,' protested Beth. 'We should not hesitate to dispute his claim—'

'On this, the lawyers suggest we are on firmer ground,' admitted Sloane. 'However, if Mr Faulkner were to sue, as Booth Watson threatens he will, we might well win the case, but only at considerable cost both financially and to our reputation. Should we lose, and I'm advised it's a fifty-fifty call, it would drain the museum's resources to breaking point.' Sloane paused, before adding, 'I'm sure you wouldn't want to be responsible for that.'

'Of course not,' said Beth. 'But I may have found a way to cover the cost—'

'Frankly, Mrs Warwick, I think you should have read the contract more carefully before you misled the board into believing we owned the painting.'

'But we can still hold on to it if—'

'Given the circumstances, I wonder if you should consider your position as Keeper of Pictures, because clearly that is the one job you are not doing, Mrs Warwick.'

Beth had to grip the arms of the chair to stop herself telling Sloane what she really thought of him. Knowing that William would have advised her to remain calm and bide her time, she delivered a sentence she felt confident even Sir Julian would have approved of. 'I'm sure you're right, director.'

Sloane was taken by surprise, having assumed this was only the first round in what would be a long skirmish. But he recovered quickly, and said, 'I think that's a wise decision, Mrs Warwick.' He gave her a warm smile before adding, 'I believe there was something else you wanted to discuss?'

'No, it wasn't important, director. Especially as I won't be around to see it through.'

Beth returned to her office, sat down and wrote out her letter of resignation, and was surprised how relieved she felt when she handed it to the director's secretary an hour later. She spent the afternoon saying goodbye to old friends and colleagues who she'd worked with for many years, before clearing her desk and packing eight years of memorabilia into three large cardboard boxes.

At one minute past five, Beth left the museum, hailed a taxi and, after giving the driver her address, sat in the back surrounded by boxes and unashamedly shed a tear.

The moment Beth arrived home she went straight to her

study, looked up a number and rang a small auction house in Pittsburgh. She registered her interest in Lot 71, and told them five hundred dollars was her upper limit. She didn't mention that if her bid was successful, it would clean out her account.

William got back in time to help bath the children. Before she had a chance to tell him her news, he said, 'Milner, Reynolds and Jennings have all handed in their resignations. The Commissioner was relieved he wouldn't have to tell the Prince of Wales the real reason he'd had to let them go.'

'I resigned today too,' said Beth. She paused before adding, 'Sloane couldn't hide his delight.'

William took her in his arms. 'I'm so sorry, my darling, I didn't realize . . .'

Artemisia threw her soap out of the bath, clearly feeling she wasn't getting enough attention.

'Not only have I lost my job,' said Beth as she picked up the soap, 'but I've risked every penny I have on a drawing that might turn out to be worthless. So please tell me some good news!' she added as William scooped Artemisia out of the bath.

'Paul Adaja has been made up to Inspector, and Constable Smart will finally—'

'—become a Royalty Protection officer?'

'Not much gets past you,' smiled William.

'Christina did. When will I realize you can't believe a word that woman says?'

The phone on the landing began to ring. William dropped the towel on the floor and went to answer it, while Beth tucked the children up in bed. She was about to read to them when William returned.

'It's for you. Long distance. Lot seventy-one will be coming up in a few minutes' time,' he said, before settling down on the end of the bed. 'What page are you on?'

'A hundred and forty-three,' said Artemisia. 'Peter and the Lost Boys are surrounded by bloodthirsty pirates!'

'I know the feeling!' said William as Beth quickly left the room.

Fifteen minutes later, William closed the book, having decided he rather liked Captain Hook, whom he considered a great improvement on both Milner and Sloane. He switched off the light and joined Beth on the landing.

'No, don't send it to the Fitzmolean,' she said, before giving the auction house her home address. She put the phone down and turned to William. 'I've just spent four hundred and twenty dollars I don't have.'

'Not a problem,' said William. 'I've been temporarily made up to Superintendent on full salary, while Milner goes on gardening leave – and he has a large garden.'

'Trouble is, I will need even more if I'm going to make a go of my new business.'

'Then I'll just have to open a taxi service . . . in Windsor.'

CHAPTER 23

THE ONLY QUALIFICATION FOR THE job of librarian in any prison was the ability to read and write. You worked in a large warm room all day, weren't bothered by too many inmates, and if you didn't look out of the window, you wouldn't even know you were in a prison.

Most inmates preferred to work in the kitchen, some in the gym, and a few as wing cleaners. However, the position of chief librarian suited all of Miles Faulkner's immediate requirements.

He was also able to select his deputy, and he chose someone whose reading and writing skills wouldn't have made him an obvious candidate for the job.

Faulkner was reading Lex in the *Financial Times* when Tulip returned from his morning round collecting overdue books from the cells. This gave him the opportunity to drop in on any prisoner Faulkner needed to do business with, and ensured he remained the best-informed person in the jail, including the governor.

Mansour Khalifah never visited the library, so Tulip had to rely on Tareq Omar, his wing cleaner, to pass on any information that might prove useful. Until now, nothing worthwhile had come his way, other than that Khalifah was planning something big, but Tulip still had no idea what. But that morning he rushed back to the library to report a breakthrough to his boss.

Faulkner put down his paper, switched on the kettle and settled back in the most comfortable chair in the prison to listen to Tulip's news. He didn't press his deputy to get to the point, as neither of them had a great deal to do for the rest of the day.

'It may have been a long wait, boss,' began Tulip, 'but Omar's finally come up with the goods.' The kettle whistled, and Tulip got up from the second-most comfortable chair in the prison and poured two mugs of coffee. Faulkner added one lump of sugar but no milk to his, and extracted a single biscuit from a packet of shortbread. Not because they were in short supply, but because he was hoping to lose a stone before he was released.

'Omar,' Tulip continued after taking a sip, 'has managed to convince Khalifah he's a True Believer.'

Faulkner leant back and closed his eyes, storing every detail in his notebook mind.

'You were right, boss, Khalifah is planning something big.' Tulip took another sip of coffee. It was still too hot. 'The Albert Hall,' he announced triumphantly.

'What about the Albert Hall?'

'It seems that every year there's a series of concerts held there called the Proms—'

'Tell me something I don't know.'

'The Last Night of the Proms is always sold out months in advance.'

'Get on with it,' said Miles, sounding irritated for the first time.

'But did you know they remove all the stalls seats for a group of fans known as the promenaders, who stand throughout the entire concert?' Faulkner nodded, waiting for Tulip to turn the page. 'One of Khalifah's contacts on the outside has got hold of a scalper's ticket, and paid way over the top.'

'Shit,' said Miles, who'd already skipped to the last chapter. 'You mean he's planning to send in a suicide bomber and blow the place apart?'

'While the promenaders are singing "Land of Hope and Glory", just to rub it in.'

'Guaranteeing headlines on the front page of every paper across the world.'

'But if you could warn the police about what Khalifah's got in mind . . .'

'Even the Home Secretary would be kissing my arse.'

'And you'd be out of here faster than shit off a shovel.'

'I'll need to see Hawksby as soon as possible,' said Miles as there was a knock on the door. 'Who's that?' he growled.

The door opened, and the visitors' warder appeared.

'Sorry to bother you, Mr Faulkner, but someone's made an appointment to see you on Saturday.'

'That would be a first,' said Tulip.

'Probably Christina wanting her pictures back. Tell her to bugger off.'

'That's not the name on the application form,' said the warder. 'It's someone called Miss Mai Ling Lee.'

'I don't know anyone by that name, so she can bugger off as well.'

'It would get you out of your cell for an hour,' Tulip said, 'plus tea and biscuits . . .'

'I'm hardly ever in my cell, in case you haven't noticed, Tulip. And you're eating my biscuits.'

'She might be good-looking.'

'She could also be old and ugly.'

'She's twenty-six,' said the warder. 'And as regulations demand, she's supplied a photograph.'

After one look Tulip said, 'I could take your place, boss.'

But Miles was already signing the form, though not for the reason Tulip had in mind.

• • •

Christina asked Beth to join her in the Palm Court tea room at the Ritz, which was just about enough to tempt Beth to see her again.

'It's kind of you to come,' said Christina after they'd ordered.

'I was fascinated to find out what excuse you'd come up with this time,' said Beth, not attempting to hide her anger.

'I don't have any excuse,' replied Christina. 'I just wanted to say how sorry I was to hear you'd been sacked.'

'I resigned,' said Beth firmly as a pot of tea and a three-tier silver stand loaded with cakes, scones and wafer-thin sandwiches was placed in front of them.

'That's not what the director told me when I visited the museum last week.'

'Why would you want to see Sloane?'

'To tell him why I will be cancelling my annual donation of ten thousand pounds. He grovelled of course, but I also insisted my name be removed from the patrons' list. I didn't leave him in any doubt that you were the only reason I supported the Fitzmolean in the first place.'

Beth found herself beginning to thaw, but couldn't help wondering if Christina had even seen the director.

'I also told him,' she continued while pouring Beth a cup of tea, 'that I would double my annual donation if he offered you your job back.'

'I don't want my job back. Well, not as long as Sloane's the director.'

'But you have to earn a living, Beth. And I know you're not the begging type.'

'I've had a bit of a triumph on that front,' said Beth, desperate to tell someone. 'I picked up a sketch at a sale in Pittsburgh for four hundred and twenty dollars. Christie's Old Masters expert has authenticated it as a Rembrandt, and valued it at twenty to thirty thousand pounds. So I could make more in one day as a dealer than I did in a year as Keeper of Pictures at the Fitzmolean. And that's only for starters,' she added, after selecting a smoked salmon sandwich from a lower tier.

'What do you mean?' asked Christina.

'Although that kind of opportunity doesn't arise too often, with so many small auction houses all over the world, important works are occasionally overlooked. For example, a painting by an artist who's well-known in one country may sell well below its market value in another. Have you ever heard of Hercules Brabazon Brabazon?'

'Can't say I have.'

'He was a nineteenth-century English watercolourist, and one of his landscapes is coming up for sale in Frankfurt next week with an estimate of twenty-five thousand marks. I know several galleries in London that would pay double that, without a second thought.'

'So you'd double your money?'

'No, it's never that straightforward. After deducting the auction house's commission of around twenty per cent, and the gallery's profit margin, I'd be lucky to end up with twenty-five or thirty per cent, and that's assuming no one else has spotted the picture, which would probably put it out of my price range.' Beth's gaze settled on a tiny chocolate éclair, but she resisted the temptation.

'Why don't I become your backer?' said Christina. 'That would allow you to deal at a higher level, and help me to assuage my guilt.'

Beth was silent for a few moments, still staring at the éclair, while Christina continued. 'If you spotted something you knew was underpriced and could make a decent profit on, I'd be happy to put up the capital. With your expertise and my resources, we could both end up making a killing.'

'That's generous of you, Christina, but auction houses require you to put down ten per cent of the hammer price on the day of the sale, and to pay the balance within fourteen days. If I failed to do so, not only would I lose the picture but they wouldn't deal with me again.'

'Why should that be a problem?'

'You haven't exactly proved reliable in the past,' Beth reminded her sharply.

Christina looked suitably chastened before saying quietly, 'Would it help if I were to give you a hundred thousand in advance?'

Beth refused to believe the offer was real, but somehow managed, 'What would you expect in return?'

'Twenty-five per cent of the profits.'

'There has to be a catch,' said Beth, still not convinced.

'There is,' replied Christina, opening her handbag. She took out her cheque book and wrote a cheque for £100,000, made out to Beth Warwick. 'You'll give me a third chance – or is it a fourth? – to prove whose side I'm on.'

Beth stared at the noughts, but was distracted when Christina began to remove the cakes from the stand, before wrapping them up in her napkin one by one.

'What are you doing?' said Beth, horrified.

'You can share these with the children when you get home,' said Christina, handing her the napkin.

'But how do the management feel about that?'

'They've got used to it,' said Christina as she signalled to a waiter for the bill.

• • •

The prisoner didn't take his eyes off the young woman who was heading slowly towards him.

It wasn't until Miles had seen a photo of Mai Ling that he'd considered the possibility she might be the daughter of his rival art collector, Mr Lee, a man who had outbid him several times in the past. He had therefore agreed to see her.

Mai Ling took the seat on the other side of the table. 'Good afternoon, Mr Faulkner,' she said as if she was joining him for tea at the Savoy rather than visiting him in a category A prison, with guards, not waiters scattered around the tables.

Faulkner nodded.

'My father has been offered your art collection for one hundred million dollars, and wanted to be sure the seller had your blessing,' said Mai Ling. Like her father, she didn't deal in small talk.

It was some time before Miles recovered enough to reply. 'Blessing isn't the word I would have chosen. As I know your father to be a man of few words, you can tell him,

215

never. But I would like to know who it was claiming to represent me?'

'My father thought you might ask that question and, if you did, instructed me not to answer it.'

Miles accepted that bribery wouldn't work with this young woman, and even the suggestion of a threat would have been counter-productive. He simply said, 'Was it Booth Watson, or my ex-wife?'

Mai Ling rose from her place, turned her back on him and walked away without once looking back.

The duty officer looked surprised when Mr Faulkner's guest left the visitors' room only a few minutes after she'd booked in, and the lip-readers on the balcony were even more puzzled.

Faulkner had only one thought on his mind as he made his way back to his cell. His next visitor would have to be ex-superintendent Lamont.

• • •

When Beth walked in the front door of their home, having had tea with Christina, she heard the phone ringing in the hall. She grabbed it, and was surprised to be greeted by a familiar voice she hadn't heard for some time.

'James,' said Beth, 'how lovely to hear from you.'

Beth happily recalled first meeting James aboard the SS *Alden* when they were on holiday. They had both liked the precocious and bright young American who had helped William to solve the murder of his grandfather. She assumed he would want to have a word with William.

'I'm afraid William's not at home,' Beth said. 'But I'm expecting him—'

'It's not William I wanted to speak to,' said James. 'I've got a problem I'm not sure how to deal with, and I think you'd be the ideal person to advise me.'

'I'm flattered.'

'In William's latest letter,' said James, 'he wrote to explain why you'd left the Fitzmolean, which I was sad to hear, but he also told me you'd started your own business.'

'Which is still in its infancy and I'm afraid works on a limited budget,' said Beth. 'But if I can help in any way, I'd be delighted to do so.'

'Do you specialize in anything in particular?'

'We represent buyers and sellers of fine art, and I occasionally buy works myself if I spot something I think I can turn quickly. But I repeat, my budget is limited.'

'But your brain isn't, and that's what I need.'

'It's clear you've inherited your grandfather's charm,' teased Beth.

'That's not the only thing I've inherited,' said James, 'which is why I need to seek your advice.'

'Sounds intriguing,' said Beth.

'You're right about that,' said James. 'But it's also a little too sensitive to discuss over the phone, so I was thinking of coming to London so I could brief you in person.'

'Then you must stay with us,' said Beth. 'Though I have to warn you the spare room is about the size of a below-deck cabin on a Buchanan cruise liner.'

'Couldn't be better because it's a deckhand you're dealing with.'

'When were you thinking of coming?'

'Next Monday.'

'Then that's something else you've inherited from your grandfather, James. You don't hang about.'

CHAPTER 24

'WHY ARE YOU LOOKING SO pleased with yourself?' asked Beth as William parked the car on the far side of the cricket ground.

'To start with, there isn't a cloud in the sky, so there must be a fair chance we'll get in a full day's play.'

'I can't think of a more exciting way of spending a Sunday afternoon than having to watch a cricket match for five hours.'

'Be thankful it's not a test match that can last for five days,' said William. He got out of the car and opened the back door, releasing three caged children.

'Daddy,' said Artemisia, grabbing his trouser leg. 'Can we have an ice cream?'

'Certainly not,' said Beth firmly. 'You've only just had lunch. So you'll have to wait until the tea interval.'

'I told you Mum would say that,' said Peter, who left them and ran off to watch the players warming up in the nets.

'Ah, I spot a cloud,' said William as they walked around the boundary.

Beth was puzzled, because the sky was clear with the sun beating down on a contented crowd. Then she saw Christina, sitting on her own.

'Why don't you grab the deckchair next to her,' said William. 'Give you the chance to find out what she's been up to recently – no good, I predict.'

'Do you ever stop thinking like a policeman?' Beth sighed.

'Not while she's sitting there like a praying mantis, because I can't believe she's come to watch the cricket.'

'The cricketers, perhaps,' said Beth, when she spotted Paul chatting to Christina.

'And that's never going to happen,' said William. He looked around the ground until his eyes settled on Ross and Jackie, who were sitting next to each other, deep in conversation.

• • •

'Whose idea was this?' asked Jackie as she looked around the ground to see that almost every deckchair had been taken, while others sat on the grass.

'Choirboy's of course,' said Ross. 'He felt there was a schism between the Royalty Protection officers and uniformed branch.'

'Not helped by the fact that a Royalty Protection officer can remain working for their principal for many years, while officers protecting cabinet ministers usually have a shelf life of about three or four years, less than the average football manager.'

'That's why the Super thought a cricket match might break down some of the barriers,' said Ross.

'Who's that walking out onto the middle of the pitch with William?' asked Jackie, shielding her eyes from the after-noon sun.

'Chief Inspector Colin Brooks. He was on the PM's security detail until the Hawk transferred him to head up Royalty Protection in place of Milner.'

'He can only be an improvement on that man.'

'He may be doing Milner's old job, but that's where the similarities end. Brooks is an old-fashioned copper who thinks of himself as a small cog in a big wheel. Milner had begun to believe he was the wheel.' Ross frowned. 'Looks like we lost the toss.'

'How come an Irishman knows so much about cricket?'

'Don't forget I spent my youth at a boarding school in Belfast,' said Ross, 'before I was expelled.'

'What did you do to deserve that?' asked Jackie as the two captains walked off the pitch together, chatting amicably.

'I broke the sixth commandment for the first time.'

'Who was the lucky girl?'

'My housemaster's wife. If the truth be known, it was she who seduced me, but they couldn't expel her, so I had to go,' said Ross as William walked across to join them.

'We're fielding,' he said. 'You'll be opening the bowling, Ross, so you'd better get warmed up.'

Ross stood up to find someone pulling at his trouser leg.

'Can I have an ice cream?' asked Jojo.

'Please,' prompted Ross.

'Can I have an ice cream, please?'

Ross took a pound coin out of his pocket and handed it to her. 'Make sure Artemisia and Peter get one as well.'

'Yes, Daddy,' said Jojo as she ran away.

'Wrapped around her little finger may well be a cliché,' said Jackie, 'but it sure applies to you.'

'Guilty as charged,' said Ross, watching as Jojo, holding up the coin in triumph, joined Artemisia and Peter, who had been waiting for her by the ice cream van.

Jackie smiled. 'Thank heavens she's got Beth to keep her feet planted firmly on the ground.'

'Right again. Truth is, I couldn't have taken on my present job without her support system.'

'Where are you taking Jojo for her summer holiday?' asked Jackie.

'Belfast. We're going to spend a week with her grandmother. If she can survive that, I'll sign her up for the SAS.'

'And what about the other woman in your life?'

'I'm going on holiday with her as soon as I get back, but I confess I'm not looking forward to it.'

'Why not?' asked Jackie, looking surprised. 'Half the world would like to go on holiday with Princess Diana.'

'I don't much care for her present . . .' he hesitated for a moment ' . . . paramour. A playboy, who enjoys basking in her reflected limelight.'

'Have you ever told her how you feel about him?'

'It's not my position to do so,' said Ross, sounding unusually formal. 'Although I'm not very good at hiding my feelings,' he admitted as William reappeared and tossed him the cherry. 'Right, Super,' he said. 'This is one lot I won't be protecting. I plan to send them straight back to the pavilion as quickly as possible.'

'Not too quickly,' whispered William. 'Remember our long-term plan.'

• • •

Beth's father, Arthur Rainsford, and Sir Julian were seated in the pavilion waiting for the first over to be bowled. They had, over the years, become close friends, and Sir Julian didn't make friends easily. They both wore smart blue blazers, Sir Julian's double-breasted with Lincoln's Inn brass buttons – even at play he was at work – white shirts and MCC ties, as if it were the opening day of a test match at Lord's, rather than a hastily arranged fixture between two branches of the police force.

'Who's opening the bowling?' asked Arthur as he focused his binoculars on a tall man who was shining the ball on his trousers.

'DI Ross Hogan,' replied Sir Julian. 'He's got a foot in both camps as he's currently the Princess of Wales's protection officer, which is useful because it means William had someone on the inside from the start.'

'Not an easy job at the moment,' said Arthur, without further comment.

'I think you'll find that Ross will be up to the challenge. He enjoys flirting with danger.'

'Beth tells me that's not the only thing he enjoys flirting with,' said Arthur as they watched Ross measuring out his run up while William set the field. 'You must be very proud of William. The youngest Superintendent in the force.'

'Nelson was a vice admiral by the age of forty-three, I had to remind him,' said Sir Julian. 'And Eisenhower was only a colonel when America entered the Second World War, but just two years later he was the supreme Allied commander in Europe.'

'So where will William end up?'

'He certainly won't be President of the United States,' said Sir Julian, glancing across at his daughter-in-law. 'How's Beth coping after being treated so appallingly by Sloane?'

'She seems fine, as far as I can tell,' said Arthur. 'She and Christina Faulkner are up to something, but I don't know what.'

'I hope Beth knows what she's doing. Mrs Faulkner isn't someone I'd want to rely on.'

'Good shot, sir!' shouted Arthur as the ball raced towards the boundary rope. 'The ministers have got off to a good start.'

'On a more serious note, Arthur,' said Sir Julian, 'now the children are at school, I think we'll have to top up their trust fund.'

'Fine by me. Ross Hogan has more than played his part since Jojo joined the fold.'

'Yes, that arrangement has worked out well, especially now Beth has been able to spend more time with the children since she resigned.'

'Well bowled, sir,' said Arthur as one of the opening batsmen's middle stump was uprooted and the fielders ran over to congratulate the bowler.

• • •

'I have a feeling,' said Christina, nodding to the old gentlemen, 'that those two are talking about us. Do they know we're partners?'

'Certainly not,' said Beth. 'And I don't intend to tell them until we've made our first hundred thousand.'

'I bet Julian finds out long before then,' said Christina as she opened a half bottle of champagne and poured two glasses. 'Any recent coups?'

'We made a couple of thousand profit when I sold the Brabazon Brabazon to the Chris Beetles Gallery in Mayfair.'

'*Chapeau*,' said Christina, raising her glass. 'So, what's next on your hit list?'

'Have you heard of the Newlyn School?'

'Can't say I have,' admitted Christina.

'A group of artists who worked in Cornwall at the end of the last century, and are just coming back into fashion. I've got my eye on a painting by Albert Chevallier Tayler that's coming up for sale at Cheffins in Cambridge. If I can pick it up for around three thousand, it would be a bit of a coup,' said Beth as Ross leapt in the air and cried, 'Howzat!'

A man in a long white coat pondered for a moment before raising a forefinger high in the air to indicate the fall of the second wicket.

'William's side seem to be doing quite well,' said Christina. 'Not that I have the slightest idea what I'm talking about.'

'That's never worried you in the past,' teased Beth as the batsman who'd scored a half-century left the field to cries of 'Well played, sir,' 'Bravo,' and 'Fine innings!'

'I hadn't realized,' Beth went on, 'that all the contacts and knowledge I've acquired over the past ten years could be turned into a profit. What's more, I'm more relaxed and have more spare time to spend with the children.'

'What's that called?' asked Christina as a ball soared high over the boundary rope and the crowd cheered loudly.

'It's a six,' said Beth. 'They happen quite regularly when William puts himself on to bowl. The truth is, I've made more in the last three months than a police superintendent earns in a year.'

'Don't tell William,' said Christina.

Beth decided this wasn't the time to tell Christina that she told her husband everything. 'Time for tea,' was all she said. 'And don't even think of stealing the sandwiches,' she added as they joined William, the two teams and their guests in the tea tent, although she feared Christina was more likely to try and steal one of the younger players.

'Are you winning?' Beth asked when William offered her a cucumber sandwich.

'No idea. You often can't tell who's going to win until the last ball of the day, which is part of the game's charm.'

'You should be able to knock off the hundred and sixty-three needed to win the match,' said the commander as he poured himself a cup of tea.

'It's a fairly challenging score,' said William. 'We'll need to bat well.'

'It would have been a lot less challenging if you hadn't put yourself on to bowl,' said Beth.

'I remain confident,' said William, ignoring the jest, 'that's assuming Paul gets his usual fifty.' He looked across the tent to see his opening batsman chatting to Christina.

'You'd better go and rescue the poor fellow,' said Beth when she spotted Paul being woven into her web, 'or he might never reach the crease.'

William strolled across to join Paul, who couldn't take his eyes off the forbidden fruit. 'Get your pads on, Paul, you're opening the batting.'

'But I usually bat four or five, skipper,' he protested.

'Not today you don't. You and Ross will be opening.'

Paul reluctantly left them to go and pad up. 'See you later?' said Christina.

'Much later, I hope,' murmured William.

'Whatever do you mean, William?' asked Christina, unable to hide a smirk.

'I need my best batsman to keep his eye on the ball, not on you. If you want to help, try and pick up that chap over there,' he said, pointing to a large, beer-bellied man scoffing a cream cake.

'Why him?'

'He's their opening bowler. Known as the dirty demon, so do your worst,' he said, before walking off.

'Not my type,' said Christina as she watched Paul putting on his pads.

• • •

Lamont stood in line at the visitors' shop. When he reached the front, he selected two KitKats and a carton of fresh orange juice. He handed over the two-pound voucher he'd obtained in exchange for cash at the reception desk before he entered the jail.

At the appointed hour, he joined a large group of wives, children and assorted criminals who were being escorted to the visitors' room, and received a plastic disc with the number 18 on it, indicating the table he'd been allocated.

He sat down in the blue chair, and waited, and waited, and waited. Nothing moves quickly in prison, unless there's a riot.

Eventually, prisoner 0249 appeared and sat down in the red seat opposite him.

'Before you speak,' said Lamont, 'just checking that you know half the officers watching us from the gallery are there with the single purpose of checking to see if anything passes between visitors and the prisoners. Drugs, knives, and I remember on one occasion even a gun, when the visitor ended up with an even longer sentence than the prisoner he was visiting.'

'And the other half?' said Miles.

'Far more dangerous,' said Lamont as Miles tore the wrapper off his KitKat and continued to listen. 'Trained lip-readers. They've helped solve several crimes even before they were committed just from the information they picked up during visits. You'll have to play the part of a ventriloquist unless you want our conversation to be repeated word for word to Commander Hawksby.'

'I've been wondering how to get a message to Hawksby,' said Miles, barely moving his lips. He glanced up at the gallery and quickly spotted the officer who'd been allocated his table, before looking across to the other side where he saw his opposite number. He intended to make sure they spent a wasted hour.

'I asked to see you because I know you do the occasional job for Booth Watson,' said Miles, quickly discovering that Bs were a problem.

'I do,' said Lamont. Two words that could be said without moving your lips.

'How much does he pay you?'

'Twenty pounds an hour,' said Lamont.

'He can't even tell me the truth about that,' said Miles. 'From now on, you'll be paid double. But under no circumstances is he to find out you're also working for me. Is that understood?'

'Understood,' said Lamont firmly. Another word that could be pronounced without moving your lips.

'I hope so, Lamont, because otherwise it will be the last job you do for me,' he paused, 'or anyone else for that matter.'

Lamont looked convinced.

'I want you to find out if BW . . .' Miles's lips hardly moved for the next ten minutes, while Lamont nodded several times.

'If you need to get in touch with me,' Faulkner said finally, 'you can phone the prison any afternoon at five past four.'

Lamont tried to hide his surprise.

'I've got a cooperative guard who'll be manning the switchboard at that time, and will be expecting your call. Just say the word "library" and he'll put you straight through. But don't stay on the line any longer than necessary.'

'Understood.'

'Be warned, if BW discovers you're working for both sides, he'll drop you and, more important, realize he's been sussed. If that happens, you'll have lost both your paymasters.'

Lamont got the message.

A loud buzzer sounded, the warning that in five minutes the prisoners would have to return to their cells.

Miles gulped down his orange juice and pocketed the second KitKat before he said, 'If you carry out the job successfully, Bruce' – the first time he'd ever called him by his first name – 'you can spend the rest of your days drinking piña coladas in Mallorca. If you fail, you could end up sharing a cell with me.'

Miles rose from his place and without another word got up and walked slowly across the room towards the waiting guards, but not before he'd glanced up at his lip-reader in the gallery, met his eye and said distinctly, 'I need to see Superintendent Warwick urgently.'

He turned to the other side and repeated the same message.

• • •

'I realize you have other things on your mind at the moment,' said the Hawk when William joined him at the tea urn, 'but I've just had an urgent call from Belmarsh that we will we need to discuss after stumps.'

'Of course, sir, but first I have to score a half-century if we're going to win the match.'

'Superintendents don't call me sir when they're off duty,' said the Hawk with a wry smile.

'That's just not going to happen, sir,' was William's immediate response.

'By the way, if Chief Inspector Brooks runs Royalty Protection as well as he's captaining his side today, that will at least solve one of our problems,' said the Hawk as an umpire stepped out onto the ground and loudly rang a bell to alert the players that the game would begin again in five minutes.

'Good luck, chaps,' the Hawk shouted as Ross and Paul made their way out to the middle.

Ross took guard. 'Middle and leg,' he said to the umpire.

'If you'll excuse me, sir,' said William, 'I've got an even more important match to attend.' He turned his back on Ross and Paul to watch a game of tip and run that was taking place by the side of the pavilion. Peter was facing up to some fairly hostile bowling.

'Howzat!' shouted the bowler when he hit Peter on the shins.

'Out!' cried another boy, and Peter burst into tears, bringing Beth quickly to his rescue, but Peter just as quickly pushed her aside.

William smiled at his son, until he heard the sound of leather on timber and a cheer coming from behind him. Turning around, he saw Paul, head bowed, walking dejectedly back to the pavilion, having failed to score.

Paul ignored the murmurs of 'Bad luck, old chap,' and 'Unlucky,' both of which he knew were untrue. He just hadn't been concentrating. After unbuckling his pads he grabbed a sandwich and went in search of an empty deckchair.

• • •

'Who's that sitting next to Paul?' asked Arthur.

Sir Julian glanced to his right. 'Rebecca Pankhurst. She's a member of William's inner team, and has just been promoted to Detective Sergeant.'

'That can't be an easy name to inherit.'

'William tells me she's every bit as formidable as her campaigning ancestor, and that she regularly outshines the rest of the team, himself included.'

'I'm an idiot,' said Paul.

'That can hardly be described as classified information,' teased Rebecca.

'I was determined to get fifty today,' he said, 'impress the boss and put us in with a good chance of winning.'

'Perhaps you should have spent more time in the nets and less time chatting up Christina Faulkner.'

'Touché. Though I think I'm in with a chance.'

'With her, even the umpires are in with a chance,' said Rebecca disdainfully. Paul looked even more hopeful. 'I hear you spent last week with the Prime Minister's personal protection officers,' she added, wanting to change the subject.

'Yes. Now that Colin Brooks has moved into Buckingham Gate to head up Royalty Protection, the Super asked me to keep an eye on the new guy who's taken his place.'

'Any good?'

'He was doing well until a passing car backfired when the PM was on a Saturday morning stroll around her constituency. Her two protection officers grabbed the Iron Lady, almost threw her into the back of her car and took off.'

'But isn't that standard procedure if a PO thinks his principal might be in any kind of danger?'

'Yes, but they left Denis Thatcher stranded on the pavement.'

Rebecca burst out laughing.

'I apologized to him, and he told me not to worry, as it wasn't the first time it had happened, and he suspected it wouldn't be the last. Damn,' said Paul as another wicket fell. 'It's not looking too good for us now. The Super's the next man in, and as he was a sprinter in his youth he'll probably run out Ross, who's our only hope. Close your eyes and pray.'

'Like you did when you were at the crease?'

Paul slumped back down in his deckchair, and looked to his left to see Christina smiling at him.

• • •

'You can forget about Paul,' said Beth, following Christina's gaze. 'He's strictly off-limits.'

'Why? He looks rather dishy.'

'He may well be, but while you're likely to be a star witness at your ex-husband's trial, he won't risk being seen with you unless another officer is present.'

'Do I get to choose the other officer?' said Christina as Ross raised his bat high in the air to acknowledge the crowd's applause for his half century.

'I thought you already had a boyfriend.'

'My latest is fast approaching his sell by date.' Christina sighed. 'So you'll have to find someone else to distract me until the trial is over.'

'How do you fancy Hans Holbein?'

'Can't say I've come across him.'

'That's hardly surprising, as he's been dead for over four hundred years. In any case, he's out of your league, otherwise I might have introduced you to him earlier.'

'Am I missing something?'

'Not unless you've got twelve million to spare, because I've recently been offered a Holbein portrait of Henry VIII. To be more accurate, the Fitzmolean was offered it, but as the envelope was marked private and confidential, my old secretary sent the letter on to me.'

'I'm intrigued,' said Christina, putting down her champagne.

'The letter was from a Mr Rosen, a Dutch gentleman who lives in Amsterdam. The irony is that the person he should have approached is Miles, who I know doesn't have a Holbein in his collection, but does have twelve million pounds.'

'Have you come across this Mr Rosen before?'

'No, but what makes the painting unusual is that there's a handwritten letter from Holbein himself attached to the back of the oak panel it was painted on. It's addressed to a Dr Rosen, who was apparently his doctor at the time of his death. So I think we can assume that the seller has inherited the painting and is having to part with it.'

'Having to?'

'Death, divorce or debt. One of that unholy trinity is usually the reason a painting of such importance comes on the market.'

'And is twelve million a fair price?' Christina asked casually.

'It could fetch as much as fifteen on the open market. But Mr Rosen may not want the world to know he's having to part with a family heirloom, so he won't be offering it to Christie's or Sotheby's. Not that it matters, because I've already sent his letter back to the Fitzmolean. The acquisitions committee will spend hours discussing how they can possibly raise the money to acquire the picture, before coming to the conclusion that they can't. They may even get in touch with you to see if you'll donate.'

'Not a hope after the way they treated you,' said Christina

as she turned and once again looked in Paul's direction, but her mind was preoccupied with something she enjoyed even more than sex: money.

• • •

'William's done well to hold up his end,' said Sir Julian, 'while leaving Ross to keep the scoreboard ticking over.'

'It's still going to be a close-run thing,' said Arthur as he checked the scoreboard. 'We need another thirty-three runs with only five overs left.'

'Then these two need to still be around at the close of play if we're to have any chance of winning,' said Sir Julian, just as William hit the ball high into the air. Everyone in the ground followed its trajectory as a fielder sprinted in from the boundary, dived full-length and caught the ball in one hand, before tumbling to the ground.

'The commentator's curse,' said Arthur ruefully as William raised his bat in acknowledgement of the fine catch before leaving the pitch. One part of the script he couldn't have planned any better. He returned to the pavilion to generous applause, took off his pads and rejoined the commander.

'It might have been better if you'd stayed out there for a couple more overs,' said the Hawk. 'You've left your lot still needing another thirteen runs to score with only a couple of overs left.'

'You wanted a word with me, sir,' said William.

'I did. Miles Faulkner has been in touch.'

William quickly switched back into his other world. 'By that, I presume you mean Booth Watson.'

'No, that's the strange thing,' said the Hawk. 'When Faulkner was returning to his cell following a visitor's meeting this

233

afternoon, he looked up at the gallery and gave a clear message to one of our lip-readers.'

'What was the message?'

'"I need to see Superintendent Warwick urgently."'

'He's got a nerve.'

'Agreed,' said the Hawk. 'But if you refuse to see him, and it turns out he has information that could prevent a serious crime, it would only give Booth Watson even more ammunition to regale the jury with when his case comes to court.'

'But if he's pleading guilty,' said William, 'there won't be a trial.'

'Unless he's decided to change his plea and wants to make a deal.'

'Who was visiting him at the time?' was William's next question.

'Lamont.'

'Then why didn't Faulkner get *him* to pass on the message?'

'I've asked myself that question a dozen times, and have come to the conclusion Faulkner simply doesn't trust him.'

'Well, at least that's something we can agree on,' said William. 'But why would Faulkner have agreed to see him in the first place?'

'All the lip-readers could come up with,' said the Hawk, 'was art collection, Lee, bank manager and Booth Watson.'

'I have a feeling Rebecca will enjoy working out the thread that links those particular words,' said William. 'But it still doesn't explain why Faulkner didn't go through the usual channels and ask Booth Watson to deliver the message, if it's that urgent.'

'Perhaps he no longer trusts him either.'

'You could be right,' said William. 'I've never understood

why Miles Faulkner, of all people, caved in so easily and agreed to only a couple of years being knocked off his sentence, when he had so much ammunition to fire at us.'

'Only Booth Watson knows the answer to that,' said the Hawk. 'And sometimes his right hand doesn't know what his left hand is up to.'

'Remembering the fuss Faulkner kicked up when we got him back from Spain,' said William. 'I've been waiting for Booth Watson to throw a damn sight more than the kitchen sink at us.'

'Which suggests to me,' said the Hawk, 'that what Faulkner wants to discuss so urgently has nothing to do with his trial. Frankly there's only one way we're going to find out what it is.'

William looked out onto the pitch, and tried to concentrate on two problems at once.

'If you do decide to see him,' continued the commander, 'take someone with you, so they can record every word he says, because I still wouldn't trust that man one inch.'

'And despite that, you still think it's a risk worth taking?'

'I don't think we've been left with a lot of choice, Super-intendent,' said the Hawk as a spectator drifted within earshot. 'It's going down to the wire,' he added, stating the obvious.

William glanced at the scoreboard, as he tried to concentrate on the game. The opposition captain was tossing the ball to the fast bowler who had removed Paul in the first over.

'Eight runs to get off the last over,' mused the Hawk. 'That shouldn't be a problem with Ross at the crease.'

They both switched their attention to what was happening in the middle, where the bowler, with a venomous look on his face, was charging in to deliver the first ball of the final over.

Ross leant back and hit an attempted yorker through the covers for two, but didn't set off for what would have been a comfortable third, as he wanted to retain the strike. He blocked the next two deliveries, leaving the royals still needing six runs off the last three balls.

'Shouldn't be too difficult,' declared the Hawk confidently.

William didn't offer an opinion.

The next ball was overpitched, and Ross swept it to the boundary, leaving just two runs required from the last two balls of the match. The bowler furiously polished the ball on his red-stained flannels, before charging in once again and delivering a bouncer that flew over Ross's shoulder, leaving him needing to score two runs off the final delivery.

A silence descended on the ground as the bowler polished the ball for the last time before once again advancing menacingly towards the wicket. A well-disguised slower ball seemed to take Ross by surprise. He stepped forward and was beaten by the flight, turned and desperately slid his foot back into the crease just as the wicket-keeper, who had been given a signal alerting him to the bowler's intention, had come up to the stumps, whipped off the bails and shouted at the top of his voice, 'Howzat!'

Everyone in the ground turned to stare as the square leg umpire considered his decision. After an agonizing few moments' deliberation, he raised a forefinger high in the air, which was greeted with cries of delight from the Royalty Protection team and their supporters, who immediately began jumping up and down and hugging each other to celebrate their victory by a single run.

'Unlike Hogan to lose his composure at such a critical moment,' remarked the Hawk as Ross departed from the field of battle, head bowed.

'He didn't,' said William quietly. 'He was simply carrying out orders.'

The commander stared at William for some time before saying, 'I do believe, Superintendent, that you're every bit as devious as your distinguished father.'

'That's the greatest compliment you've ever paid me, sir,' responded William, before strolling out onto the field. 'Well played, Colin,' he said as he shook hands with his opposite number. 'A well-deserved victory.'

'Every bit as devious as your father,' the commander repeated as he looked across at Sir Julian, who was quietly applauding.

CHAPTER 25

'How nice to see you again, Mrs Faulkner,' said Johnny van Haeften as Christina strolled into his gallery on Duke Street.

Christina was impressed that van Haeften remembered her, as she'd only met him on a couple of occasions when she'd attended packed gallery openings with Miles.

'Can you tell me anything about a missing Hans Holbein portrait of Henry VIII?' she asked, coming straight to the point.

'Hans Holbein the Younger,' said van Haeften, 'painted the King on three occasions. The earliest is on display at the Walker Gallery in Liverpool. The next was sadly destroyed in a fire in 1698. The third is in private hands, and hasn't been seen by the public since it was last exhibited at the old Staatsgalerie in Stuttgart in 1873.'

'If it were to come on the market, how much would you expect it to fetch?' asked Christina, sounding like a second-hand car dealer.

'It's difficult to make an accurate estimate for a picture of such historic importance, but certainly twelve million, and possibly fifteen in the present overheated market. Your husband, as you will know, Mrs Faulkner, has been looking for a Holbein for some years.'

She didn't know, but was delighted to hear it.

'He once told me he considered it a gaping hole in his Renaissance collection that he intended to fill if one ever came on the market.'

'How interesting,' said Christina, glancing at her watch. 'Forgive me, I have a lunch appointment. Must dash.'

As she turned to leave, van Haeften said, 'Do give your husband my best wishes when you next see him.'

'I most certainly will,' said Christina, adding under her breath, 'when I next see him.'

She slipped out of the gallery and headed for the Ritz. She didn't notice the man standing in a doorway on St James's Street, even though she walked straight past him.

• • •

'How are you, Constable?' enquired the prison governor.

'I'm well, thank you, sir,' said William, ignoring the tongue-in-cheek demotion.

'Any chance of you calling me Richard, after all these years?'

'None whatsoever, sir.'

'I'm not surprised, but then you were old school when you were still in short trousers.'

Rebecca laughed, then looked embarrassed.

'And who are you?' the governor asked, peering down at her.

'Detective Sergeant Pankhurst, sir.'

'You needn't worry about her,' said William. 'She's even older school.'

239

'Glad to hear it. But you ought to know your distinguished ancestor spent a few weeks here. Before my time, of course.'

'Only just,' whispered William to Rebecca.

'The last time we met,' continued the governor, 'you wanted to know about a young woman who was visiting her father at Pentonville, when I was then deputy governor, if I remember correctly.'

'You have a good memory,' said William, joining in the game. Rebecca looked puzzled.

'The young lady's father, a Mr Rainsford, was on remand while facing a charge of murder, and your brilliant father got him off. It must have been one of his easier cases, as even his fellow inmates knew he wasn't guilty.'

'It didn't feel that way at the time,' said William.

'Correct me if I'm wrong, but didn't you end up marrying the young lady in question?'

'I did indeed, sir. We have two children – well, three, in a way. A pair of twins, Artemisia and Peter, and—'

'Josephine Junior,' said the governor, 'Ross Hogan's daughter. A man I greatly admire, who, as you know, spent some time in Pentonville working undercover, which made it possible for you to close down the Rashidi drugs empire. I believe Hogan also came into contact with Miles Faulkner around that time, when he was first working in the prison library. Don't tell Faulkner, but I'm glad to have him back, as the library has never been more efficiently run.'

'It was good of you to arrange a meeting with Faulkner at such short notice,' said William.

'Jack Hawksby called me this morning, so I'm fully briefed. I'll take you to the library by the "off-limits" route. That way, there'll be less chance of any of the other inmates spotting you and the rumour mill grinding into action.'

Without another word, the governor led them out of his office and down a long, bleak corridor into a barren yard, surrounded on all sides by concrete walls topped with razor wire. They crossed the yard to an isolated brick building with a sign reading 'LIBRARY' on its door. The governor marched in, followed by William and Rebecca.

When William saw Miles, he was taken by surprise. A blue and white striped open-neck shirt, faded jeans and trainers had replaced the hand-tailored suit, silk tie and black highly polished leather shoes William had become accustomed to seeing him wearing. He'd also put on a few pounds.

Miles put down the book he was reading, stood up and said, 'Good morning, governor.'

'Good morning, Faulkner. But be warned, it won't be a good one for you if you cause my old friend, Superintendent Warwick, any trouble. If you do, I'll be looking for a new librarian. Is that clear?'

'Crystal, governor.'

'Good. Then I'll leave you two to get on with it, whatever it is you're getting on with,' he said, before departing.

'Please have a seat, Superintendent,' said Miles. 'I've just made a pot of tea, if either of you would care to join me. Not exactly silver service, but it is Earl Grey.'

'No, thank you,' said William as he and Rebecca sat down in the only two comfortable chairs. 'DS Pankhurst is here as an observer, and will take verbatim notes of everything that is said, in case you should—'

'I'm well aware of the rules of this particular game,' interrupted Miles as Rebecca opened her notebook and began writing. 'I cannot talk about my case, or anything associated with it, if I recall the governor's words. Should I break that agreement, I will, as the governor has just pointed out, not only lose my job, but will also be charged with wasting police time.'

Rebecca went on writing, but William didn't comment.

'I've been in here for just over nine months,' said Miles, perching himself on a stool in front of them, 'so it won't surprise you to learn that I've built up a network that has made it possible for me to know more about what's going on in this prison than your friend the governor.'

Rebecca turned a page of her notebook.

'What I'm about to tell you is therefore based on fact, not supposition.' Miles paused while he took a sip of tea. 'One of my inner team, a prisoner called Tareq Omar, works as a cleaner on the first-floor landing of A block, where Mansour Khalifah is currently housed.'

William grimaced when Khalifah's name was mentioned, but still said nothing.

'A nasty piece of shit that I'd happily flush down the nearest toilet,' said Faulkner. 'Excuse my language, miss.'

Something Rebecca didn't write down.

'I've been keeping a close eye on Khalifah ever since he arrived, which hasn't been easy as he's not exactly the sociable type. He has his own network of followers, known as the True Believers, who take care of his every need. His only reading material is the *Financial Times* and *Playboy*, and he hasn't applied for a library card.'

William continued to listen.

'However,' Miles went on, 'Tareq Omar is not a True Believer, as Mansour Khalifah was responsible for the death of his brother, which is why I had him switched to that wing as a cleaner. Over the past few months, he's ingratiated himself with Khalifah by supplying him with porn magazines, and a particular brand of dates he craves, which can only be purchased from Harrods. Recently, Omar has become more trusted, and is occasionally allowed to guard Khalifah's cell while he's praying. However, it's still taken him some time to come up with anything interesting.'

Miles climbed off his stool, walked across to the counter and extracted a brown file from the shelf below. There was nothing written on the cover. He sat back down and took out a glossy brochure which he handed to William.

William studied the four pages back and front, but still didn't speak as he waited for an explanation.

'As you can see, Superintendent, it's a booking form for this year's Promenade concerts at the Royal Albert Hall. Omar found it in Khalifah's wastepaper bin when he was cleaning his room. He checks its contents every morning, but this was the first time he'd found anything he thought might interest me.'

'You've underlined one particular date,' said William, turning to the final page of the brochure.

'Not me. It was already underlined when Omar handed it over.'

'Was he able to supply any other information?' asked William.

'Snippets of conversations he'd overheard on his rounds suggest Khalifah is planning something big for the Last Night of the Proms. He also caught the words, "Land of Hope"—'

'—"And Glory",' said William. 'But planting a bomb in the Albert Hall would be nigh on impossible. The whole building is checked by sniffer dogs and specialist search officers on the morning of every concert.'

'Which is why Omar is convinced Khalifah is planning to use a suicide bomber to carry out the job. Someone who's already been planted in this country, and is just waiting for the order to move. But I still didn't consider that was enough to interest you, Superintendent, until a few days ago when I had a stroke of luck – the kind on which we both have to rely from time to time.'

William leant forward.

'A well-known scalper sold a most unlikely punter a single ticket for the Last Night of the Proms, for which he paid way over the top. He didn't give it much thought at the time, until later when it began to nag at him.'

'Then why didn't he contact the police?' asked William.

'Scalpers don't advertise, Superintendent, and when they spot a policeman, they have a tendency to make themselves scarce.'

'I don't suppose he got the punter's name?'

'Scalpers only deal in cash, and don't ask questions,' Miles replied. 'But he described the man as young, short, thin, and of Middle Eastern extraction. What puzzled the scalper, and later made him suspicious, was that the man hardly spoke a word of English, and kept calling it the Last Night of *Poms*. He clearly isn't planning to place a garland of flowers around the bust of Sir Henry Wood.'

'So, we're down to a shortlist of about a hundred thousand,' said William.

'But I know you have a unit at Scotland Yard whose sole purpose is to keep an eye on anyone with terrorist connections. And let's face it, Superintendent, you now have one big advantage. You know exactly when and where he's planning to carry out the bombing.'

'Possibly,' said William as he placed the brochure in an inside pocket. 'If your information turns out to be accurate, you can be assured I'll personally inform Mr Booth Watson of the valuable role you played in preventing a serious terrorist attack, and recommend he raises the matter with your trial judge before he passes sentence.'

'That's the last thing I want you to do,' said Miles, once again taking William by surprise. 'But if my information turns out to be kosher, the next person I'll want to see won't be Booth Watson but your father, as I have something even bigger to offer him.'

William could not come up with a suitable reply. 'I can't make any promises, but I will pass your message on to him,' he said eventually as Rebecca continued to write down every word. 'Is there anything else you want to tell me before we leave?'

'No, but you can be sure I'll be watching the Last Night of the Proms on the television in my cell, Superintendent. I can never resist joining in the chorus of "Land of Hope and Glory".'

It was now William's turn to take Faulkner by surprise. 'What was the book you were reading when we came in?'

'*Beware of Pity* by Stefan Zweig. Are you familiar with his work?'

'Can't say I am,' said William.

'Then I can recommend him. When you're stuck in here all day,' said Miles, looking around the crowded shelves, 'you read a lot. Usually a chapter is more than enough for me, but that was until I came across Zweig, who can transport me out of this place for hours at a time. It's about the only good thing that's happened to me since you dragged me back from Spain.'

'Unless it turns out that you've foiled a terrorist attack, and saved countless innocent lives,' suggested William as Rebecca closed her notebook.

'Before you leave, Superintendent, may I be allowed to give you one piece of advice?'

Rebecca quickly reopened her notebook and took out her pen.

'Please tell your wife not to trust Christina under any circumstances.'

William had at last found something on which he and Miles Faulkner could agree, but Rebecca closed her notebook and they both left without offering an opinion. Once the door was closed behind them, he turned to Rebecca and said, 'How much of that did you believe?'

'Every word. Not least because there's nothing in it for him to set you up. And if his intel turns out to be reliable, the judge would have no choice but to take it into consideration when he passes sentence. What I can't be sure about is whether Mansour Khalifah or Tareq Omar – or both of them working in tandem – are setting Faulkner up.'

'There's only one way we're going to find out,' said William as they walked back across the yard. 'One thing's for sure, we can't ignore the threat. The first thing I'll have to do when we get back to the Yard is brief the Hawk.'

'Did Faulkner have anything worthwhile to say?' were the governor's first words when they returned to his office. 'Or was it a complete waste of your time?'

'I can't be sure,' said William, 'but for the moment I'm willing to give him the benefit of the doubt.'

'Pity. I was looking forward to putting him in solitary with only bread and water on the menu.'

'Not yet, governor, because if his information turns out to be reliable, we might well be returning again in the near future.'

'So be it. Goodbye, Superintendent. And remember to give

my best wishes to your commander, as I won't be seeing him on Saturday. We'll be sitting on opposite sides of the ground – that's assuming the idiot still supports Arsenal.'

'I'll pass on your best wishes, sir.'

'Ten points if you remember which team I support, Constable.'

'Tottenham Hotspur.'

'Not bad, Superintendent. And you?'

'Chelsea, sir.'

'I will allow vagabonds, scoundrels and even perverts to enter my prison, but not Chelsea supporters. By the way, do you have any idea who Faulkner supports?'

'Himself,' replied William.

• • •

When William got back home that evening, he found James Buchanan had arrived from the States and was sitting in the kitchen with Beth and the children, having supper.

James leapt up, shook hands with William and said, 'Good to see you.'

'You too,' said William as he sat down. 'No doubt the children have been entertaining you.'

'They sure have. I've been learning all about Artemisia's new best friend – Princess Diana.'

'The long or the short version?' asked William.

'I was about half-way through when you walked in,' said Artemisia, 'and was just about to tell James . . .'

'James didn't come to London to talk about Princess Diana.'

'Then why did he come to London?' Artemisia asked.

'Behave yourself,' said Beth. 'Try to remember James is our guest, and don't speak with your mouth full.'

247

'It's quite simple really,' said James. 'I came to seek your mother's advice on a delicate matter.'

'Must be about art,' said Artemisia, 'and not crime.'

'A little bit of both,' admitted James.

'Do you still own one of the biggest shipping lines in the world?' asked Peter.

'Peter!' said William, sounding exasperated.

'I was only asking.'

'No, I don't,' said James, smiling. 'My father is chairman of the Buchanan Shipping Line, but I'm still at Harvard, and when I graduate, I plan to join the FBI.'

'What's the FBI?' piped up Jojo, speaking for the first time.

'The Federal Bureau of Investigation.'

'Who do they investigate?' asked Artemisia as Sarah walked into the room.

'It's past your bedtime, children,' she announced firmly, which elicited a groan from Artemisia, before she asked, 'Can you read, James?'

'I think you'll find it's still a requirement if you hope to get into Harvard,' said James.

'Then you can read to us once you've told Mum why you've really come to London.'

'Out!' said William firmly.

James stifled a laugh. After several good nights and Artemisia giving her father a half-hearted kiss, the children were ushered out of the kitchen by Sarah.

Once the door was closed, Beth said, 'Artemisia was right about one thing, I can't wait to find out why you wanted to see me.'

'And not me,' said William, trying to sound offended.

James finished his coffee and waited for a moment as he gathered his thoughts.

'You'll no doubt remember my late grandfather, Hamish Buchanan, who founded the shipping line, and who, to say the least, led an unpredictable and complicated life. But it's only recently I've discovered just how unpredictable and complicated.'

Beth sat back and listened.

'I've recently become aware,' continued James, 'that my grandfather was a bigamist.' He paused for a moment to allow them to take in the revelation. William spilt his coffee, while Beth tried to remain composed. 'It turns out that not only did he have a wife in New York, my grandmother, but another one in London, who none of my family knew about.'

Several questions flashed through William's mind, but he remained silent. He had a feeling most of them were about to be answered.

'My grandmother, God bless her, still remains unaware of the double life Grandfather led, and my father wishes it to remain that way.'

'Understandably,' said William. 'But how did you find out?'

'I would never have found out if I hadn't received a letter from a solicitor in London who represented the late Mrs Isla Buchanan, informing me that she'd died and left everything to me in her will.'

'Didn't she have any children of her own?' asked Beth.

'That was my first question. But her solicitor assured me there were no other relations who had any claim on the estate.'

'Then I suspect she was doing no more than carrying out your grandfather's wishes,' said William. 'After all, it was well-known you were his favourite grandson.'

'So where do I fit into this unlikely triangle?' asked Beth.

'The bulk of her estate,' continued James, 'consists of a house in Onslow Square, which I've already put on the market.

However, it turns out that Isla also shared my grandfather's passion for Scottish art, and they collected works by Sir Henry Raeburn, Samuel Peploe, Allan Ramsay and someone called Charles Rennie Mackintosh.'

'Never utter those three words to a Scotsman without bowing your head. He's become part of Glaswegian folklore.'

James lowered his head and said, 'However, if I'm to comply with my father's wishes, I must dispose of the entire collection without drawing attention to its provenance.'

'You don't want to hold on to any of them?' asked Beth in disbelief.

'It's not a risk my father is willing to take. So I was wondering what you would advise me to do in the circumstances.'

'I'd live with them for the rest of my life,' said Beth, with considerable feeling. 'But if you have to sell them, you certainly can't risk putting them up for auction. The *provenance* would be listed in the catalogue for all to see.'

'So what's the alternative?' asked James.

'You'll have to sell them privately, and I'm afraid that could take some time.'

'Would you be willing to visit the house and take a look at the collection for me?'

'Of course I will. I'll go tomorrow and start making an inventory of the works and let you know how much I think they're worth.'

'I couldn't ask for more,' said James. 'But I fear I must now leave you.'

Beth raised an eyebrow.

'I have to go and prove to Artemisia that I can read.'

• • •

It had taken Christina only one visit to Gerald Sloane with the suggestion that she might be willing to reinstate her annual donation to the Fitzmolean for him to reveal everything she needed to know.

'Your visit couldn't have come at a more opportune time,' he purred.

'Why?' asked Christina, innocently.

After she had gleaned all the information she needed to know about the Holbein, she took a leaf out of Beth's book and thought carefully about what she would say to Mr Rosen when she phoned him. It was some time before her call was answered.

'Thomas Rosen,' said a refined voice, with a slight accent.

'Mr Rosen, my name is Christina Faulkner, and I understand from my good friend, Beth Warwick, that you have a picture for sale that I might be interested in.'

'Are you calling on behalf of the Fitzmolean, Mrs Faulkner?'

'Yes, I am. However, they wish the approach to remain confidential for the time being.'

'I understand,' said Rosen. 'Like you, we wouldn't want the sale to become public knowledge.'

'You can be assured of my discretion,' said Christina, who certainly didn't want Sloane or Miles to find out what she was up to.

'That being the case, Mrs Faulkner, I would be only too happy for you to visit me in Amsterdam where you could view the painting.'

'As well as the artist's handwritten note that's attached to the back of the panel?'

'You are well-informed, Mrs Faulkner, which doesn't surprise me. So if you'd be kind enough to make the journey to Amsterdam at your convenience, I'll have my chauffeur pick you up in the airport and drive you to my home.'

CHAPTER 26

No one recognized the officer seated next to the Hawk, but they were all aware of his reputation.

Assistant Commissioner Harry Holbrooke was the officer in charge of Counter Terrorism, and rarely seen in public. If you passed him in the street, you wouldn't have given him a second look, and would not have considered it plausible that he was the man the IRA most feared.

He couldn't have been more than five foot eight, weighing around 145 pounds, a featherweight when he entered the boxing ring, a heavyweight when it came to knock-outs.

'I'd like to begin,' he said in a broad Yorkshire accent that he made no attempt to soften for his southern colleagues, 'by asking Superintendent Warwick to give us a detailed report of his meeting with Miles Faulkner, and his opinion of the source's credibility.'

They all listened intently to William's account of what had taken place when he and DS Pankhurst had visited the prisoner in Belmarsh. Rebecca read out the occasional verbatim contribution from her notebook. When William had finished, he waited to hear Holbrooke's assessment.

'Let me say from the outset,' he began, 'that your principal informant can hardly be described as A1. As a source – which is graded from A, always reliable, to E, untested – Faulkner's a D at best, unreliable. For reputation – which is ranked from 1, known to be honest without reservation, to 5, suspected to be false – he scrapes in with a 4, cannot be trusted. So, your man is not only a D4 but currently serving a prison sentence for fraud and deception.

'In normal circumstances,' continued Holbrooke, 'information provided by such a source would be handled by a junior officer in SO13, and would be highly unlikely to reach my desk. However, I concede this cannot be described as "normal circumstances", and Faulkner has two things going for him. One, his undoubted intelligence, and two, what would be in it for him to invent such a cock and bull story? Let me now throw this open for discussion, commander,' Holbrooke said, looking towards the other end of the table. 'I'd like you to play devil's advocate on this occasion while your team try to convince me that I should make this a priority, because at present it sounds like a waste of my time.' The Hawk nodded. 'Then let's begin with you, Superintendent.'

'I agree with your assessment of the source's reputation,' said William. 'D4 at best. But I still believe we can't afford to take the threat lightly.'

'We've never had to deal with a suicide bomber in England,' interjected the Hawk. 'This would be a first.'

'True,' said Holbrooke, 'but the French faced a similar problem at Orly airport a few years ago, and were caught napping. Never forget it's our duty to try and be one step ahead of modern criminals, not playing catch-up all the time.

253

Some of us can remember when the public were appalled if they saw a uniformed officer carrying a handgun, which they now take for granted. So, let's assume the worst and go from there. What's the security like at the Albert Hall?'

'Bog standard,' said Paul, 'other than for the evening of the Festival of Remembrance in November, which the Queen and other members of the Royal Family always attend. But when it comes to the Proms, they barely check your ticket before you take your seat, they don't search handbags, and the prom-enaders are a law unto themselves.'

'Promenaders?' queried Holbrooke.

'During the Proms season,' chipped in Rebecca, 'the six hundred seats in the stalls are removed to accommodate eight hundred ticket holders, known as promenaders, who stand throughout the entire performance. The bookings manager describes them as eccentric at best and bonkers at worst. Jeans and scruffy T-shirts are the norm, and more than a few of them come with backpacks, and think nothing of eating a three-course meal while downing several cans of beer during the perfor-mance. Some of them have their established places directly in front of the stage, and woe betide anyone who dares to occupy someone else's long-held territory. Even when the management decided to double the price of a ticket, in the hope of raising the tone, the same people turned up the following year, and carried out the same rituals. They're fanatics. It seems that nothing will keep them away from their annual obsession.'

'Until,' said Holbrooke, 'a suicide bomber who has some-thing considerably more lethal than a sandwich in his backpack blows them to kingdom come, which will then define the Proms for the next hundred years. With that in mind, I've already put out an all-ports alert, and advised MI5 and MI6 to keep a particular lookout for any recent arrivals from Libya,

254

and to keep an even closer eye on known sleeper cells. SO13 are reviewing anyone of Middle Eastern origin who's on the security services watchlist, while GCHQ are also stepping up their surveillance. What more can you tell me about the Albert Hall? For starters, how many seats does it have?'

'Nearly five and a half thousand,' said Jackie, 'spread over five levels.'

'Entrances and exits?'

'Twelve,' said Paul. 'But number one is only ever used if a member of the Royal Family is attending a performance.'

'We're going to need every one of those doors covered on the night,' said Holbrooke, 'and however much it annoys the promenaders, their backpacks will have to be searched before they enter the auditorium. I will also have over a hundred high-vis Counter Terrorism officers circulating the perimeter of the building from first light, and nearly as many in plain-clothes. If anyone approaching the venue is wearing a backpack and looks even vaguely suspicious, they'll be stopped and searched, and, if necessary, detained for questioning. They can complain later.'

'Wouldn't it be easier just to cancel the concert?' suggested Jackie.

'That would only provide the terrorists with the oxygen of publicity, to quote Margaret Thatcher. And where would it end? Wimbledon, the Chelsea Flower Show, the FA Cup final? Never forget, we are like goalkeepers, we can make a hundred brilliant saves, but the only shot people remember is the one that gets past us. It's our job to protect the public without them ever finding out what we're up to.'

'Is it possible that Faulkner's setting us up, and this is no more than an elaborate revenge plot to keep us well occupied before his trial?' asked the Hawk, playing devil's advocate.

'Possible, but unlikely,' replied Holbrooke. 'But if he is, I'll lock him up in a place no one knows about, and throw away the key, because he's taking up far too much of my valuable time and resources when I should be concentrating on the IRA.'

'How do you make the decision—' began Paul.

'Over a hundred cases cross my desk every week,' said Holbrooke. 'Most can be dismissed out of hand, like the letter we received from a woman in Surbiton informing me that the Queen will be coming to tea on Friday, and asking when I would be sending in the sniffer dogs to check her house.'

'How sad,' said William. 'How do you respond?'

'That particular woman writes to me three or four times a year. Her husband, an ex-copper who won the Military Cross, was gassed in the Second World War, so she's been a widow for fifty years. One of my retired officers who looks like the Duke of Edinburgh has tea with her once a year.'

They all burst out laughing.

'But this case is no laughing matter, and we've only got a couple of weeks before the conductor lifts his baton. So we must do everything in our power to stop a potential catastrophe. Don't for one moment imagine any of you will be getting much sleep for the next fourteen days. You can start by cancelling any social engagements you may have,' said Holbrooke, looking around the table, 'unless it's to attend your own funeral.'

• • •

Mr Rosen was as good as his word, and when Christina stepped into the arrivals hall at Schiphol airport she immediately spotted a man holding up a card with 'FAULKNER' printed on it.

She sat in the back of a BMW going over her script one more time, not even noticing as she was driven across a wide canal with colourful barges passing below her. A few minutes later, the car drew up outside a magnificent seventeenth-century townhouse. The driver leapt out and opened the back door.

Christina stepped onto a cobbled street, to be greeted by an elderly gentleman wearing a herringbone tweed three-piece suit with a crimson silk handkerchief in his breast pocket. He was leaning heavily on an elegant briar walking stick with a silver handle. She was relieved she'd selected a conservative grey suit for the occasion, with a skirt that fell well below the knee.

'Welcome to my home, Mrs Faulkner,' said Rosen as he leant forward to kiss her hand. 'I do hope you had an uneventful journey.'

'I did, Mr Rosen,' Christina replied. 'And thank you for sending your driver.'

Her host walked so slowly that Christina had plenty of time to admire the fine antique furniture and a cabinet of Meissen porcelain that suggested faded, inherited wealth. Rosen stood aside to allow her to enter the drawing room, where a tray of coffee and a plate of stroopwafels had been laid out on a small oval table.

Rosen waited for her to sit down before he settled in a well-worn high-backed leather chair. He had placed her so the first thing she would see once she'd sat down was a small, exquisite portrait of Henry VIII hanging on the wall directly opposite her. Not to her taste, but she wasn't in any doubt that Miles would covet it.

Christina half listened to the old man as he reminisced about visiting London just after the war, while a maid served them coffee. Sensing he might feel uneasy about discussing money with a stranger, she came to his rescue.

'Mrs Warwick tells me you're hoping to get twelve million for the painting,' she said.

The old man looked slightly embarrassed, but eventually managed, 'That was the figure my father suggested to me not long before he died.'

'I don't want to waste your time, Mr Rosen, but I must tell you that the Fitzmolean does not have twelve million pounds in its acquisition fund.'

The old man looked relieved, and even managed a weak smile.

'However,' Christina continued, 'I do have ten million in cash lodged in a safe-deposit box with my bank in London. Should that be sufficient, I can assure you that the portrait will end up on the walls of the Fitzmolean.' A sentence she'd rehearsed in the mirror that morning.

The old man took so long to respond that she wondered if he had fallen asleep. Finally he almost whispered, 'I will have to consult my two sons, as they are the main beneficiaries of my will. I do hope you understand.'

'Of course,' said Christina.

'I will write to you once I know their decision.'

'Do take your time, Mr Rosen. I'm in no hurry.'

'Will you stay for lunch, Mrs Faulkner? It would give me the opportunity to show you the rest of my grandfather's collection.'

'That's very kind of you, Mr Rosen, but I have to get back to London in time for the Last Night of the Proms.'

'What a treat,' he said. 'Always such a traditional occasion for you British. I only wish I could join you.' He paused, brushed a crumb from his waistcoat and asked, 'Is there anything else you want to know about the portrait before you leave?'

'I would like to see the handwritten note Holbein wrote to his doctor.'

'Yes, of course,' said the old man. He raised himself slowly from his chair, walked unsteadily across to the picture and lifted it gently off the wall as if it were an old friend, before turning it over so Christina could study the letter attached to the back of the panel. After looking at it for some time, she was none the wiser.

'Allow me to translate it for you,' he said, 'though in truth I've known it by heart since I was a child.'

> April 15th, 1542
>
> Dear Dr Rosen,
> You have taken care of me for so many years, and have never once complained, even when your fees were not always honoured on time.
> Perhaps you would accept this portrait of Henry VIII of England as an inadequate gift to show my appreciation for your skill and expertise. I hope that you and your family will enjoy the painting for many years to come.
> I remain your humble servant,
> Hans Holbein.

'Holbein died just a year later, at the age of forty-six,' said the old man, 'and, to this day, the painting has never left this house. Should you wish to authenticate the letter, there is a copy in the archives of the Kunstmuseum. They were also unable to match the asking price, as the gallery has just undergone an expensive refurbishment, which is why I offered the painting to the Fitzmolean.'

'Where I assure you it will be given pride of place, should your sons agree to accept my offer,' said Christina as the old man hung the picture back on the wall. He looked happy to see it returned to its rightful place.

Rosen led his guest slowly out of the room and back to the front door, where he remained standing on the top step until the car was out of sight. He then returned to his study and made a phone call to his elder son.

• • •

'I've made what I consider to be a realistic valuation of the late Mrs Buchanan's Scottish collection,' said Beth, 'and I can tell you she had a good eye.'

James didn't interrupt.

'And in answer to your question as to how much I expect they could fetch: around £1.2 to £1.4 million on the open market. However, it might take some time to dispose of all of them, remembering you don't want any of the sales to become public.'

'Then I'll need someone to take them off my hands. So how would you feel if I offered you the collection for a million?'

'That's a fair price,' said Beth. 'How would you feel if I could only pay in cash?'

'Fine by me,' said James, 'as long as I'm not breaking the law.'

'I must warn you,' butted in William, 'the cash would be coming from a criminal.'

'Christina is not a criminal,' said Beth. 'In fact, she's my friend and partner, though I admit the money originally came from her husband, who's currently in jail.'

'Miles Faulkner?' said James. 'No, thank you. That would be jumping out of one fire and into another.'

'Without an extinguisher,' offered William.

'You're a lot of help,' said Beth, punching him on the arm. 'Just remember where trusting that woman has got you in the past.'

Beth remained silent for some time before she said, 'I may have a solution that would solve both our problems.'

James looked hopeful.

'I have a client in Edinburgh who for tax reasons might be willing to exchange a Warhol of Marilyn Monroe for your Scottish collection.'

'But I don't even like Warhol,' protested James.

'In which case you can put Marilyn up for auction in New York, where I'm confident she will fetch more than a million, and, even better, it could never be traced back to your grandfather.'

'Then how will you make a profit?' asked James.

'I'm confident enough to take ten per cent of everything you make at auction over a million.'

'Make it twenty per cent,' said James.

'That's very generous of you,' said William.

'Not really. Because if I don't make a million for the Warhol that Beth's so confident about, twenty per cent of nothing is nothing. If she's willing to take the risk, then so am I.'

CHAPTER 27

'I THOUGHT THE GOLD COMMANDER usually remained back at base while Silver ran the operation on the ground with Bronze to assist him?' said William.

'Then you thought wrong,' said Holbrooke, looking around to take in everything that was happening. He could see over a hundred highly trained officers surrounding the concert hall, all of them wearing high-vis jackets over their uniforms, to warn anyone who hadn't come to join in the chorus of 'Land of Hope and Glory' to stay away. Holbrooke clearly believed prevention was better than cure. 'Did your search officers come up with anything half interesting when they combed the building earlier this morning?'

'They went over every inch of the hall from the roof to the basement, sir,' said William, 'but all they found was an empty box of Swan Vesta matches that the overnight cleaners must have missed. I went up on the roof myself and walked around the glass dome, and didn't spot anything suspicious. But the dogs have just moved in and are checking the auditorium row by row, from the stalls to the gods.'

'Then he can't have entered the building yet. Several possible suspects were seen heading towards London this morning, coming from Manchester, Birmingham and Bradford, not all of them by direct routes. They could of course be decoys, but if any of them come within a mile of the hall, they'll be apprehended, taken in for questioning, and not released until later – much later. What time do the doors open to the public?'

'Six o'clock,' said William, glancing up at the roof of the Royal College of Art, where he could see half a dozen snipers sweeping the crowd with binoculars. 'The conductor, Sir John Pritchard, will walk onto the stage at seven thirty, by which time four of my team will be mingling with the promenaders.'

'Along with ten of my operatives,' said Holbrooke as he checked the traffic lights on the corner of Exhibition Road, which he had control over. William's gaze settled on the Albert Memorial, a hundred yards away in Kensington Gardens. On its steps a young couple were embracing, but he knew they weren't lovers, as one was keeping a watchful eye on the park, while the other focused on the road in front of the main entrance to the Albert Hall. William had to admire how calm Holbrooke appeared to be, while he himself remained uncomfortably on edge, all too aware that a couple of hundred operatives were out there on his recommendation and, even worse, on information supplied by a man he didn't trust.

By the time the sun began to dip behind the French Ambassador's residence, a steady stream of excited concert-goers were making their way towards the hall in anticipation of the evening's entertainment ahead.

'I'll leave you now, sir, and join my team inside,' said William.

'Make sure you're the last person to leave the building,' said the Gold Commander.

William liked the way Holbrooke ran things, leaving nothing to chance. He crossed the road and entered the hall as if he were an ordinary concert-goer, watching carefully as the punter's tickets were checked and then double-checked, creating a long line of disgruntled promenaders. Even after they'd escaped and made their way into the auditorium, they were then checked for a third time. One ticket holder protested when his backpack was emptied onto a table manned by a vigilant plainclothes police officer, and became even more heated when told he could pick it up from the cloakroom after the performance was over.

'Bloody police state,' he proclaimed at the top of his voice, before heading off to join his mates in the arena.

William made his way slowly around the wide corridor that circled the auditorium, before going inside to join the boisterous revellers. Some of them had already been there for over an hour, and would be the last to depart, long after the musicians had finally left the stage. He prayed they would depart singing.

He quickly spotted Paul and Jackie, then finally Rebecca, but they didn't acknowledge him. He nearly missed Ross, who was dressed in a scruffy T-shirt and torn jeans, blending in with the promenaders as if he were one of them. In theory it was his night off, but William knew nothing would have stopped him being there, even if he hadn't been invited.

His team were already settled in their positions at the four points of the compass, from which they were able to scan the crowd as they searched for a lone figure who looked out of his comfort zone.

William checked the tiers above him, where dozens of plainclothes officers – he could spot a copper at a hundred paces – were checking tickets, directing people to their seats and selling programmes, while at the same time looking for that one elusive individual who might have a cocktail of explosives secreted beneath a bulky shirt, jumper or jacket. The Gold Commander had warned his team that their quarry might have already attended several other prom concerts during the past month to get the lie of the land and reduce the risk of obvious 'signpost' warnings.

'Never forget,' Holbrooke had reminded them, 'we're dealing with a person who's been indoctrinated, and is willing to sacrifice his life for a cause he believes in.'

As each minute passed, the frenzy of expectation grew louder and louder. Eventually the orchestra made its way on stage, greeted by loud cheers, followed by a special ovation for the first violinist, who took a bow. Finally, when it seemed they could bear it no longer, the audience erupted as Sir John Pritchard made his entrance, stopping to bow several times before mounting the podium and turning his back on them. William scanned the crowd, but couldn't spot anyone who wasn't joining in the applause. At one level he was relieved, but at the same time, if he'd been set up, he was going to make sure Faulkner's sentence was doubled.

Sir John raised his baton and waited for total silence before he allowed the orchestra to strike up. The attentive audience were enraptured from the first note, and seemed to know every demiquaver of every concerto, as well as every overture that cascaded down from the stage. William ignored what was happening on the stage as he continued to scan the auditorium. His gaze settled for a moment on a woman seated in the front row of one of the loggia boxes in the second tier. Beside her sat a young man he'd seen at the Frans Hals opening a few weeks earlier.

Several times during the next two hours, William wished

Beth was standing by his side enjoying Rossini, Brahms and Benjamin Britten. He promised himself he would bring Beth next year – if it wasn't cancelled in memory of . . . But he didn't allow his attention to waver for a moment, although he found it difficult not to join in when all those around him began lustily singing 'See the Conquering Hero Come', followed by yet more rapturous applause.

Sir John waited for the tumult to die down before he raised his baton once again, to allow mezzo-soprano Sarah Walker to render the opening bars of 'Rule Britannia', and the audience to become the largest chorus on earth. Then the moment came, the moment they had all been waiting for, the moment William had been dreading. He prayed Faulkner was wrong.

The conductor turned around, faced the audience and raised his baton, inviting more than five thousand untrained voices to become his raucous choir. As they delivered the opening line of 'Land of Hope and Glory', William could spot only four people who weren't joining in.

The music reached its climactic conclusion and the audience cheered wildly, demanding an encore. Sir John turned to face them and bowed, smiling briefly before he marched off the stage, but to no one's surprise he returned a few moments later to an even louder reception, if that were possible. A hush descended as he raised his baton for the last time.

William waited for the final gasp of 'Britons never never never shall be slaves' and was breathing a sigh of relief when he heard what sounded like an explosion in the distance, muffled by the sound of crashing cymbals and the roars of delight as the orchestra rose to receive a ten-minute standing ovation.

William immediately charged towards the nearest exit and

out onto the pavement to find Rebecca was a yard ahead of him, with Jackie following close behind.

He could hear a siren in the distance, and turned to see the flashing lights of an ambulance speeding towards him. The Gold Commander stood in the middle of the road, hands on hips, eyes scanning in every direction.

William ran across the road as a second ambulance skidded to a halt a few yards from him. The back door was thrown open and two green-clad paramedics jumped out and were directed by a group of armed officers, who had seemingly materialized from nowhere, towards the Albert Memorial. William chased after them through a cloud of smoke to the far side of the park.

William could only watch as a motionless body was lifted gently off the ground and laid on a stretcher. He recognized the victim as the man who'd been embracing his fellow officer on the steps of the Albert Memorial earlier that evening.

The young man was carried gently back towards the waiting ambulance, and moments later its doors closed before it sped away, the traffic lights still green. Holbrooke had already arranged for every traffic light between the Albert Hall and the Brompton Hospital to remain green. He even knew the name of the doctor who would be waiting for his patient. The Gold Commander left nothing to chance.

A few minutes later the revellers began streaming out of the Albert Hall to make their way home, entirely oblivious to what had just happened a couple of hundred yards away.

They couldn't have failed to notice an unusually large police presence, with an ambulance, back doors open, parked on the opposite side of the road. Some stopped and stared, while others hurried on.

'A lucky escape,' said a voice, and William turned to see Holbrooke standing beside him.

'Will the young officer be all right?' were William's first words, as the ambulance reached the traffic lights, sirens blaring, lights flashing.

'They don't know yet. Just be thankful he's still alive.'

A few yards away a young woman, the other half of the embracing couple, was sitting on the ground, head in hands, weeping. Rebecca was kneeling by her side trying to comfort her.

'Thank God he didn't get inside the Hall,' said William.

'He got far too close for my liking,' said Gold as the boisterous crowd continued to hail taxis, climb on buses or head for the nearest tube station, many of them still singing. 'I never thought he'd find it possible to get past so many of my officers. He was finally spotted by the young Sergeant who'd been sitting on the steps of the memorial for more than eight hours. He challenged him, but the suicide bomber turned around and started to run away, while my man chased after him without any thought for his own safety. He'd nearly caught up with the terrorist when he blew himself up.' He paused as the ambulance turned right into Exhibition Road and disappeared out of sight. 'Fortunately, his colleague was far enough away when the bomb went off to avoid injury. What you won't know is that they were engaged.'

William wondered if either of them would be serving in the Met in a year's time. One injured physically, the other mentally. Another siren brought him back to the real world.

'So it looks as if Faulkner's status has moved from D4 to A1,' he said.

'Which only creates more problems.' Holbrooke paused. 'For both of us.'

'Like what?'

'Believe me, Warwick, Mansour Khalifah will want revenge. He'll consider this,' he said, waving a hand across the scene, 'a further humiliation, and will now be looking for an even bigger target. As you're the only contact we have with Faulkner, I'm going to tell you exactly what I want you to do.'

CHAPTER 28

CHRISTINA ARRIVED AT THE BANK well in time for her
meeting with Mr Rosen. She had spoken to the deputy director
of the Kunstmuseum in Basel, who'd confirmed the wording
of Holbein's letter to Dr Rosen, and that according to the
museum's records the painting was still owned by the Rosen
family, who lived in Amsterdam.

Mr Rosen was punctual, but looked worn out. After greeting
Christina he introduced his sons, Cornelius and Sander. One
was carrying a wooden casket adorned with a family crest,
while his brother had brought two large suitcases which
Christina assumed were empty.

'I'm exhausted,' Rosen said. 'But then, it has been some
time since I last travelled by plane, and even a short flight is
no longer a pleasant experience. Not as unpleasant, however,
as having to part with a treasured family heirloom.'

Christina looked suitably sympathetic, but her eyes rarely
left the little wooden box Cornelius was still clutching.

'Nevertheless,' continued Rosen, 'after considerable soul-
searching, we decided if you were able to confirm that the

270

painting will become part of the Fitzmolean's collection, we would reluctantly accept your offer.'

'I give you my word,' said Christina. A sentiment she delivered with complete conviction.

Rosen bowed, and she couldn't help reflecting on what an old-fashioned gentleman he was. His word was clearly his bond. Whereas his sons looked as if they were much more interested in the money.

Christina headed for the lift, and when they reached the basement they were met by a security guard who guided them along a well-lit corridor, stopping only when a floor-to-ceiling reinforced door blocked their progress. After entering an eight-digit code on the keypad, a code Christina had been assured was changed every morning, he pulled open the heavy door and stood aside to allow them to enter a room that held many secrets only the keyholders were privy to.

The walls were lined with safe-deposit boxes. The security guard checked the small red numbers, selected one and pulled it out as if it were a body in a morgue, then placed it on the table in the centre of the room. Producing a large set of keys from his pocket, he chose one and opened the first of two locks, before stepping back and saying, 'I'll leave you now, Mrs Faulkner. Please, take your time.'

'Thank you,' said Christina. She didn't move until the heavy door had been closed behind him; she then opened her handbag and took out the second key to open the client's lock. Rather enjoying herself, she lingered before lifting the box's lid, to reveal ten thousand neatly wrapped cellophane packets each containing twenty crisp fifty-pound notes.

Mr Rosen's sons stepped forward and after one look began to transfer the money from the deposit box into their suitcases, while their father sat silently behind them on the only chair.

Christina walked up to the table, unclipped the locks of the wooden casket and raised the lid. Henry VIII was staring directly at her, as he'd done with so many beautiful women in his day. But she rejected his advances until she had lifted the portrait from its bed of red satin and carried it nearer to the light so she could check the letter attached to the back. Once she recognized Holbein's hand, she felt reassured.

She placed the picture carefully back in its box, and closed the lid. The two young men were still filling their suitcases when she bade Mr Rosen farewell, before jabbing the green button on the wall by the door.

The old man rose unsteadily from his chair and bowed as the door opened and Christina quickly departed.

'They will be here for a few more minutes,' she said to the waiting security guard. 'I'll see myself out.'

'As you wish, madam,' he replied, before he pushed the heavy door back into place.

Christina took the lift to the ground floor and left the bank, tightly clutching onto the small wooden casket. She crossed James's Street, and hurried off in the direction of the Van Haeften gallery, a few blocks away. Once again, she failed to notice a man standing in the entrance of Lobb's, watching her walk past. He didn't bother to follow her, but then he knew where she was going.

The moment he saw the wooden casket, Johnny van Haeften recognized the family crest on the lid. He could feel his excitement mounting as Christina placed it on the table in the centre of the gallery. She flicked open the clasps and lifted the lid to reveal Henry VIII in all his pomp and glory.

'May I?' van Haeften asked, his fingers trembling.

Christina nodded, and he gently lifted the painting out of its red satin resting place. He studied Henry for some time before turning him over and reading the letter attached to the back.

'I think you said twelve million, possibly fifteen,' said Christina, 'if I remember correctly.'

'I did indeed,' replied van Haeften.

. . .

The man waited a few minutes before crossing the road and entering the bank, where he hung around in the lobby looking as if he were waiting for someone, which indeed he was. He didn't have to wait long before the lift doors opened and three men appeared, one of them pulling two large suitcases. They walked straight past him without saying a word, and left the cases by his side, before walking out of the bank and going their separate ways.

He gripped the handles of the cases and began pulling them towards the door, surprised by how heavy they were. Once out on the pavement, he hailed a taxi, hoisted the cases into the back and pulled the door shut. Safer than an armoured car, he'd decided, because that would only attract attention and require a lot of form-filling.

'Where to, guv'nor?' asked the cabbie.

'The Mayfair Trust Bank on Park Lane,' said Lamont. He would have given the address of his bank in Hammersmith if he'd thought he could get away with it. But he was well aware that other eyes would be watching him, and if he didn't deliver the money straight back to where it had originally come from, it would be the last cab journey he'd ever take.

. . .

Van Haeften studied the painting closely for some time before he said, 'Fifteen million would have been a fair price, had it been the original.'

Christina stared at him. 'But I saw it in Mr Rosen's home in Amsterdam only a week ago,' she eventually managed, her voice rising with every word.

'I'm sure you did,' said van Haeften calmly. 'And the casket, the oak panel and the frame are all contemporary, as is the painting. But sadly, it isn't by Holbein.'

'But the letter on the back,' she protested, 'proves it's the original. If you read it, you'll see that I'm right.'

'I fear not, Mrs Faulkner.'

'Read it!' she demanded.

Van Haeften didn't protest, knowing only too well that although the client was not always right, one should never contradict them.

April 15th, 1542

Dear Dr Rosen,

You have taken care of me for so many years, and have never once complained, even when your fees were not always honoured on time.

Perhaps you would accept this portrait of Henry VIII of England, painted by one of my most promising pupils, as an inadequate gift to show my appreciation for your skill and expertise over the years. I hope you and your family will enjoy the painting for many years to come.

I remain your humble servant,

Hans Holbein.

Christina was speechless.

'What would you like me to do with the picture, Mrs Faulkner?' van Haeften eventually asked.

'I don't give a damn what you do with it!' Christina yelled as she turned and ran out of the gallery. She didn't stop running until she reached St James's, where she crossed the road – narrowly avoiding being run over by a black cab – and pushed open the door into the bank. She charged up to the reception desk.

'Those three men I was with,' she snapped at the receptionist, still out of breath.

'They've just left, Mrs Faulkner.'

'Do you know where they went?'

'No, but they left their two suitcases with another man I did recognize, and I saw him get into a taxi.'

Christina didn't need to ask for a description of the fourth man.

• • •

'I know you'll all be glad to hear that the young Sergeant who challenged the bomber is no longer in a critical condition,' began Holbrooke. 'The medics think he'll make a good recovery, although he may lose the sight in his left eye.'

William couldn't explain why his first thought was of the angry promenader who'd complained about living in a police state after having his backpack searched.

'And his fiancée?' asked Jackie quietly.

'She handed in her resignation this morning. There was nothing I could do to dissuade her. It's one of the biggest problems we face in Counter Terrorism.'

'There's nothing in the morning papers about the incident,'

said William. 'Should I assume you slammed a D-notice on Fleet Street?'

'Only just in time,' said Holbrooke. 'The *Mail*'s front page was about to go to press. Their crime correspondent had put two and two together, and although he made about six, it was too close to the truth for comfort.'

'So can my team stand down and get back to their day jobs?' asked the Hawk.

'For the time being, yes. But don't be surprised if Khalifah has something else planned for us in the not-too-distant future, which, as I've already warned Superintendent Warwick, could be even more devastating.'

'Any ideas?'

Rebecca opened a file that she'd been working on overnight. 'In a few weeks' time, England are playing Sweden at a World Cup qualifier. Sixty thousand people will be at Wembley where the security is fairly lax. Then there's the Ryder Cup—'

'No,' said William, 'they won't wait that long.'

'The Edinburgh Festival?' said Rebecca. 'It wouldn't be too difficult to hide someone among the half a million young people who invade that city during August. And there's the final test match against Australia at the Oval. Sold out.'

'We don't have the authority to cover Edinburgh,' admitted the Hawk. 'They could plant six suicide bombers along the Royal Mile and we'd be none the wiser.'

'Don't worry,' said Holbrooke. 'I'll put a full team on to it immediately, and leave you to get on with policing London. I want you to know how grateful I am for the role you played, and not just on the night.' He gave William a nod as he rose from his place at the other end of the table. 'It's been a privilege to work with your team. But for now, you can all get back to protecting the Royal Family.' He smiled at Rebecca as he left and added, 'If you're ever looking for a real job, DS Pankhurst, you know where to find me.'

'Nail her to the ground,' said the Hawk as the head of Counter Terrorism left the room.

'Why didn't he offer me a job?' said Paul.

'If he had,' said William, 'we would have reluctantly had to let you go.'

'Right, the rest of you can bugger off,' said the Hawk after the laughter had died down. 'I need to have a word with Superintendent Warwick.' He waited until the door had closed before saying, 'I'm afraid you're going to have to visit Faulkner again. And this time, he'll be expecting more than an olive branch.'

'I'll fix an appointment with the governor, and report back to you.'

'By the way, why didn't Ross join us this morning?' asked the Hawk.

'He's taken Jojo on holiday. He won't be back for a fortnight, when he will resume his duties with the Princess.'

'Not dressed the way he was last night, I hope.'

'He's a chameleon, sir. He can blend into any background, whether it be a palace or a brothel. Do you need to see him?'

'Yes, but it can wait until he gets back. We've had a complaint from a promenader. It seems Ross kneed him in the groin during the final verse of "Land of Hope and Glory", and ruined the evening for him.'

'I don't believe it,' said William.

'You're getting better at lying, William,' said the Hawk. 'But you're still not very good at it.'

• • •

Lamont dialled the number at five minutes past four. The call was answered after four rings, without any acknowledgement. All he said was, 'Library,' and a few seconds later he heard a second ringing tone.

'Yes?' said a voice after another four rings.

'The money has been returned to your bank in Mayfair,' he said without introducing himself. 'I put it in your deposit box with the other twelve million, then returned the key to the head of security.'

'Expenses?'

'All covered, including the portrait of Henry VIII which is now on display at the Van Haeften gallery, listed as by a follower of Hans Holbein, with an asking price of five thousand.'

'Buy it, and have van Haeften send it to Mrs Warwick as a gift.'

'From you?' he asked.

'No. An admirer.'

'And the house in Amsterdam?'

'The keys have been returned to the agent.'

'And the actors?'

'Have all been paid well above Equity rates. I thought the old man gave a magnificent performance, every bit as accomplished as his John of Gaunt at the Old Vic a few years ago. His two sons may only have had walk-on parts, but they were also totally convincing.'

Miles was well satisfied. Christina had once again underestimated him and his knowledge of how the art market worked. But he would still have to remain wide awake, because she would exact revenge given the slightest opportunity, and she had one advantage. He was still locked up, while she was on the outside.

He assumed Lamont was still on the other end of the line. 'If you check your personal account tomorrow,' said Miles, 'you'll find the agreed sum has already been deposited. But don't even think about retiring yet, Lamont, because I've got an even bigger assignment for you. I'll be in touch.'

CHAPTER 29

'I'M GOING TO RECOMMEND TO the CPS that another two years is knocked off your sentence,' said William, who had taken Faulkner by surprise by returning to see him in prison so quickly. Holbrooke had made it clear there wasn't a moment to spare.

Rebecca began writing.

'That means I'd be out of here by Christmas,' said Faulkner with an undisguised smirk.

'I'm not sure how you work that out,' said William, unable to hide his surprise. 'Neither of us can be sure how many years the judge will add to your present sentence when you appear before him at the Old Bailey in a few weeks' time.'

'Clearly you are unaware of the deal I've made with your father. He's already agreed that if I plead guilty to the latest charges, the CPS will recommend a suspended sentence.'

William wanted to laugh out loud, but could see he wasn't joking.

'So if you get me two more years off my present sentence, that would bring it down to four, and if you then deduct the time I've already served, and my tariff is halved for good behaviour, I should, as I said, be out by Christmas.'

William couldn't believe what he was hearing. 'What makes you think the CPS would be willing to drop all the charges against you? If historic precedence is anything to go by, absconding from prison usually leads to the original sentence being doubled, which means you'll be lucky to be released before the end of the century.'

'But as I've explained, I've made a deal with the CPS, which you seem to be unaware of. I suggest you have a word with your father.'

Rebecca kept writing.

'Why would my father agree to drop the charges against you when it's an open-and-shut case?'

'In exchange for me not raising the subject of you and DI Hogan breaking into my home in Spain, stealing a Frans Hals, then bringing me back to England in my own plane, against my will.'

'Do you have anything in writing to prove you made this deal?' asked William.

'I most certainly do,' said Miles. He strolled across to the library counter, opened a drawer and, after searching through some papers, found what he was looking for. He handed the document across to William, who took his time reading it before passing it to Rebecca.

'As you can see, Mr Faulkner, my father hasn't signed this agreement.'

Miles noted that Warwick had addressed him as 'Mr' for the first time since he'd been in prison.

'Yes, he has. That's only a copy. BW has shown me the original and, I assure you, your father's signature was on the last page.'

William said nothing, but one look at Miles made him realize he just might be telling the truth. 'I'll make some enquiries and come back to you,' he eventually managed.

'Meanwhile,' continued Faulkner, 'I've got a maniac living on my wing, who must have his suspicions as to who made it possible for "Rule Britannia" to reach the second verse.'

'Mansour Khalifah was placed in solitary confinement earlier this morning,' William reassured him, 'and his small clique of followers have all been moved to different prisons. You're in no immediate danger.'

'And that's all the reward I get,' Faulkner paused, 'for saving how many lives?'

Fair point, William wanted to say, but satisfied himself with, 'I'll come back tomorrow, Mr Faulkner, by which time I'll have spoken to my father and Commander Hawksby.'

'What about BW? Don't forget he's got the original document signed by your father.'

'That's assuming you're telling the truth.'

'Was I telling you the truth about what Khalifah had planned for the Last Night of the Proms? Because if I wasn't, why was Tareq Omar found hanging from the railing outside my cell this morning?'

• • •

The front doorbell rang, and Beth wondered who it could possibly be at that time in the morning. The children were at school, it was Sarah's day off, and she wasn't expecting anyone.

She closed her Cheffins catalogue, walked out into the hall and opened the front door to find Christina standing on the doorstep, head bowed.

'What's the matter?' asked Beth. She knew only too well what the matter was, and had been wondering when Christina would finally turn up and admit it. Without another word, she took her through to the study. She didn't offer her a coffee.

Christina stood silently for a few moments, looking up at the portrait above Beth's desk, before bursting into tears. 'How did you get hold of that?' she managed between sobs.

'Johnny van Haeften sold it for five thousand pounds to one of his regular customers who asked for it to be delivered to me. No prizes for guessing who that customer was.'

'I'd always intended to split the profit with you,' said Christina, with a Girl Guide look on her face.

'That's the last thing you intended to do,' said Beth, no longer able to hide her anger.

'I've lost every penny because of my stupidity,' Christina admitted as she collapsed into the nearest chair. 'But then I should have realized Miles would use his knowledge of the art world to get the better of me.'

'And his knowledge of your ravenous appetite for money.'

Christina didn't attempt to defend herself.

'However, you haven't quite lost every penny,' said Beth, 'because van Haeften asked me to give you the five thousand

283

pounds. Just a pity you couldn't read Dutch, something I expect Miles considered a risk worth taking.'

Christina looked as if she were trying to summon up the courage to say something, before finally blurting out, 'I'm so sorry, Beth, but five thousand won't be enough. I need the hundred thousand back that I invested in your company,' she eventually managed, unable to look Beth in the face.

Beth sat down at her desk and wrote out a cheque for £127,000.

'Why so much?' asked Christina after Beth had handed it over.

'It includes the profit we made on the recent sale of a Warhol in New York, when we were still partners.'

'But that would mean you won't be able to carry on with your business?'

'I'll get by,' said Beth, 'although there are one or two opportunities I'll be sorry to miss out on. By the way, Christina,' she added, taking the portrait of Henry VIII off the wall. 'Don't leave without your latest boyfriend.'

'I never want to see the damn man again,' replied Christina, spitting out the words. 'I deserve the same fate as Anne Boleyn.'

'I think that's what Miles had in mind. But if you don't want Henry, I'll leave him on the wall to remind me in future only to take advice from friends I can trust.'

'Will you ever forgive me?'

Beth didn't reply as she put Henry back on the wall.

'Who can blame you?' Christina eventually managed.

'I'll never forget your generosity and support when I most needed it,' said Beth. 'But that doesn't mean I could ever trust you again.'

Beth turned to face Christina and was once again taken by

surprise when she tore the cheque in half and handed it back to her.

'If I can't be your friend, at least I can be your partner.'

• • •

'It wouldn't stand up in court,' said Sir Julian, after he'd read the pleading in judgment a second time.

'Why not?' asked William.

'The document hasn't been signed, so all Booth Watson would have to say is that it was the initial proposal his client had insisted on, although he'd made it clear to him at the time it had little or no chance of succeeding, with which any judge would concur. BW would go on to claim that Faulkner later accepted his advice and signed the most recent agreement in the presence of a senior prison officer, which stated that if he pleaded guilty his sentence would be reduced by two years, which is in line with the CPS's recommended policy in such cases. I can hear Booth Watson saying that he finally convinced his client that a sentence reduction of two years was the best he could hope for given the circumstances.'

'In which case, Faulkner wouldn't hesitate to tell the court what Booth Watson had been up to behind his back.'

'Who are they more likely to believe?' asked Sir Julian. 'A man currently serving a sentence for fraud and absconding from prison, or one of the leading counsels at the bar?'

'But if Booth Watson was found to have misrepresented his client, he'd have so much to lose.'

'But so much to gain if he pulled it off,' said Sir Julian. 'Think about it, my boy. BW isn't far off retirement, and he knows where all the bodies are buried, including one of the finest art collections in private hands. So if Faulkner were to end up spending the next fourteen years in prison, he could live a life of luxury during that time. BW might not even be around to face the music by the time Faulkner is finally released. And you can't kill a dead man.'

William thought about his father's words for some time before saying, 'Could you make an application to see the judge in chambers and express your concerns?'

'I could. But I can assure you he won't change his mind about the length of the sentence, unless I have some fresh evidence to present.'

'There's something else you ought to know about,' said William.

• • •

'Is that your signature?' asked William, turning to the last page of the agreement.

'Yes, it is,' said Faulkner. 'And although you have no reason to believe me, Superintendent, I can assure you it's the first time I've ever seen this document.'

'I do believe you,' said William, to Miles's surprise. 'And perhaps more importantly, so does my father.'

'So what's he going to do about it?'

'He's already made an appointment to see the trial judge, when I suspect he'll be the first Prosecuting Counsel ever to plead clemency on behalf of a defendant.'

'Perhaps he'll manage to get another couple of years off my sentence, so I end up only serving six? Big deal!'

'My father intends to make it clear to the judge,' William continued, ignoring the riposte, 'that the information you supplied about the planned suicide attack at the Albert Hall unquestionably saved countless lives.'

'If that's all you have to offer,' said Miles, 'I may as well plead not guilty, and take you down with me.'

'My father will also leave the judge in no doubt about the consequences of your changing your plea to not guilty, not only for DI Hogan and myself, but for the reputation of the Metropolitan Police Service.'

'That should get me another couple of years off my sentence. So now I'm down to four, while you'll no doubt be promoted to Chief Superintendent, for the role you played in saving those countless lives.'

'I think you may be pleasantly surprised,' said William. 'But you're going to have to trust me, and plead guilty if we're to fool BW.'

'How could I possibly turn down such a tempting offer?' said Miles. 'Especially as I'll still be stuck in here with no more than a fifty-fifty chance of even making it to the trial alive. Even you can't keep Mansour Khalifah locked in solitary for ever.'

'As a demonstration of good faith,' said William, 'the police will not put up any objection should you apply to be moved to an open prison. But—'

'With you, Superintendent, there's always a but. I can't wait to hear what it is this time.'

'Should you attempt to escape again, I'll come after you with every resource at the Met's disposal, and when DI Hogan and I eventually catch up with you – and believe me we will – we wouldn't bother with the niceties of extradition treaties. This time my father won't be asking for another eight years to be added to your sentence, but demanding life imprisonment. I have a feeling the judge will agree with him, whatever Booth Watson comes up with in mitigation.'

Miles didn't speak for some time before he eventually said, 'I'll accept your deal, Superintendent, as long as you can assure me that you've also got BW in your sights, now you're fully aware of what he's up to.'

'It can only be a matter of time before he's disbarred,' said William, with considerable feeling. 'Because let's face it, that man's his own worst enemy.'

'Not while I'm alive, he isn't,' said Miles.

• • •

When Faulkner reached the front of the queue at the canteen servery, he took his time selecting a glass of milk, two fried eggs, some baked beans and a slice of toast that wasn't burnt. He carried the laden tray slowly back to his table, but just as he was about to sit down, he stumbled and dropped the tray. The plate smashed into several pieces, and his breakfast was scattered over the stone floor.

A dozen prisoners came rushing to his aid.

'No, thank you,' said Faulkner, when one of them offered to get him a second helping. 'I'm not feeling too well. I think I'll visit the infirmary and pick up some paracetamol.'

He left the canteen, satisfied that over a hundred inmates and several officers had witnessed the incident, and headed for the prison hospital, which would be open for business in a few minutes. On the way he passed at least a couple of dozen other prisoners going to breakfast. Most stood aside to give him room, but at least another dozen noticed he was heading for the infirmary.

There was already a long queue of prisoners in the waiting

room. They fell silent as Miles made his way to the front, where he greeted Matron warmly.

'Good morning, Miles,' she replied to one of the few inmates she ever addressed by his first name. 'What seems to be the problem?'

'A dizzy spell, matron. And a slight headache. I wonder if I could trouble you for a couple of paracetamol?'

'Of course. I'd also suggest that you lie down for a couple of hours until you feel better. I'll give you a chit excusing you from work today.'

'Thank you, matron. I think I'll take your advice.'

She handed him two paracetamol, a glass of water and a slip of paper. After he had swallowed the pills and pocketed the chit, he gave her another warm smile, before making his way back past the long line of inmates and out of the surgery to carry out the second part of his plan. At least another twenty prisoners had overheard their conversation and, more importantly, Matron's sage advice.

Once he was outside, he glanced at his watch. Still thirty minutes before he could make his move. He headed back towards C block rather than in the direction of the library, where his deputy already knew he wouldn't be reporting for work that morning. If anyone should ask, he'd tell them Miles was resting in his cell on Matron's advice.

On reaching his block, he reported to the duty officer, explained why he would not be going to work, and showed him the chit Matron had given him.

'I'll make sure no one disturbs you, Mr Faulkner,' said the young officer. 'I hope you feel better tomorrow.' Miles was pleased to see him make a note of the time in his logbook.

Miles made his way slowly up to the second floor before

walking to his room at the far end of the corridor, known as the penthouse suite. Once inside, he closed the door and took his time changing into his gym kit, before pulling on his prison-issue jeans and a thick grey sweater. He paused to look out of the window, and reflected on the events of the past month. Warwick had been as good as his word: within days of their meeting, he'd been transferred to Ford open prison, where he'd quickly established with both the officers and his fellow inmates that if they needed a bob or two for any small luxuries that were normally difficult to obtain, he was a man who understood about supply and demand.

Miles had the only room in the block that overlooked the South Downs. He'd acquired it after its previous occupant found £50 in his canteen account. Another £50 ensured that the chief librarian was happy to become his deputy and do most of the donkey work, while he read the morning papers and made or received the occasional phone call – another privilege for which cooperative guards were suitably rewarded.

It was during a call from Lamont earlier in the week that he discovered Booth Watson had visited his bank twice in the past month and, even more worrying, had moved his treasured art collection from CFAS in Nine Elms to a warehouse on an industrial estate near Gatwick airport. Ever since Miles's meeting with Mai Ling, he had known it could only be a matter of time before . . .

By the time Lamont next phoned, Miles had a plan in place and explained in detail the role he would be expected to play. It would be another week before he could put his plan into action. After Warwick's warning, he was only too aware of the risk he would be taking.

Miles stared intently out of the window, watching, waiting.

He knew it wouldn't be long before the local Hare and Hounds cross-country club appeared on their morning run, the Hares striding out in front, followed by the Hounds trying to catch up with them, and finally came the also-rans, bringing up the rear.

When the first runner appeared on the horizon, Miles slipped out of his room and checked up and down the corridor before locking his door. A wing cleaner who was standing guard at the top of the staircase gave him the thumbs up. Miles made his way down the stairs to the ground floor, pushed open the fire escape door and jogged across to a clump of trees a few yards outside the prison grounds. He stripped off his sweater and jeans, hid them under a bramble bush he'd selected the week before, and waited for the also-rans to make an appearance. He knew he had to choose his moment carefully, because the seventy yards between the prison boundary and the path was the most likely time when one of the guards could spot him.

As the next group of runners came into view, he jogged across the dangerous 'no man's land' and fell in behind them while making no attempt to catch them up. He hoped to be nothing more than another dot on the landscape.

The group turned left when they reached the main road, while Miles turned right. After a couple of hundred yards he spotted a blue Volvo parked in a layby, its engine running.

He opened the back door, slid inside and lay flat on the back seat as the car sped off. He didn't move until the prison was out of sight.

'Good morning, sir,' said Lamont, without looking around.

'Morning, Bruce,' Miles replied, sitting up and pulling a freshly ironed white shirt over his gym vest. 'Is everything ready?'

'They're all waiting for you. Time is our only problem,' he added as he pressed his foot down on the accelerator.

'Don't break the speed limit,' Miles warned him as he slipped off his shorts and pulled on a pair of grey flannel trousers. 'Don't forget, if we're stopped by the police, I won't be the only person going back to prison.'

CHAPTER 30

MR AND MRS SMITH WERE the last passengers to board the aircraft. But few of their fellow travellers were fooled as they took their places in the back row, leaving four unoccupied seats in front of them.

She had told Ross she wanted to remain anonymous – 'melt into the crowd' were her exact words. But by wearing dark Gucci shades, a Chanel silk scarf and Louboutin high heels on a package holiday flight to Mallorca, she couldn't have made herself more conspicuous. Ross had advised her against the whole idea, but she wouldn't listen. It didn't help him to relax when he spotted the snapper he'd recently thrown out of Chalabi's home, sitting just a couple of rows in front of them. He wasn't in any doubt that Jamil Chalabi must have told him which flight she'd be on.

When the plane landed at Palma de Mallorca, the other passengers remained in their seats. A hundred pairs of eyes stared out of the cabin windows as she disembarked from the rear exit. If anyone hadn't realized she was on board, they certainly knew now. A Rolls-Royce was waiting for them at the bottom of the aircraft steps, two small Union Jacks fluttering on the front wings. Now the whole of Spain knew HRH the Princess of Wales was in town.

Ross took his place in the front seat, and glanced in the wing mirror to see his other problem hurrying down the aircraft steps. At least they would have an hour's start on him. Once they'd sailed off into the sunset, he'd be none the wiser. Or had he already been told where the sun would set?

Motorcycle outriders escorted them through the airport's private exit and on towards Palma, only stopping when they reached the port where *Lowlander*, Jamil's private yacht, awaited them. Unusually, Diana didn't address a single word to Ross during the journey, well aware he didn't approve of her going on this holiday with Chalabi, after what had happened when she'd spent the weekend at his country home. Ross still hadn't told her his side of the story.

The only concession he'd managed was to make sure Lady Victoria was also invited on the trip.

Ross had come to accept that the Princess was even more of a handful than Jojo, another young woman whose slightest whim he obeyed without question.

The car finally came to a halt beside the largest yacht in the harbour. Diana had leapt out before Ross even had a chance to open the back door. She ran up the gangway, where a man wearing a gold braided peaked cap was standing on the deck waiting to greet her.

As she threw her arms around him, Ross checked for photographers, and was relieved to find no sign of any. Her host introduced HRH to the captain, who saluted her before the senior steward accompanied the couple to the recently renamed 'royal suite' on a lower deck.

'Any hope of getting out of here as quickly as possible?' Ross asked after he'd introduced himself to the captain.

'I'm afraid not, Inspector. We won't be sailing until after dinner.'

'Of course,' said Ross. 'Giving the snapper more than enough time to catch up with us,' he muttered under his breath. He smiled for the first time when Victoria emerged from below deck wearing a light yellow summer frock and white sandals. She was obviously determined to enjoy the holiday.

'I'm your tour guide, Inspector,' she teased, before showing him around the yacht, which she described as a vulgar floating gin palace. Ross checked every inch of the vessel from the engine room to the crew's quarters to the galley, where the chef was preparing dinner, and finally the helicopter pad perched high on the aft deck. Everything except the royal suite, which was locked from the inside.

Once Victoria had completed the tour, Ross began to think this just might turn out to be an enjoyable fortnight after all. But when they emerged back on deck he caught sight of the rogue photographer, standing on the dockside, taking pictures of everything in sight as he waited for the Princess to appear. He didn't need to be back in Fleet Street; one particular picture desk would be waiting for his exclusive.

When Diana came up on deck a couple of hours later she was barefoot, wearing a white T-shirt and shorts, her high heels abandoned. She looked more relaxed and content than Ross had seen her for a long time. But he couldn't help wondering how the Prince of Wales would react when his private secretary placed the papers on his breakfast table in the morning.

The Princess and Jamil sat down for dinner just as the sun began to set, but the photographer had already left by then, as he needed to catch the first edition before the presses began to roll.

Ross didn't relax until he heard the engines turn over, followed by an order piped down from the bridge to the engine room, 'Slow ahead.' They eased away from the dockside and set course for a secluded bay where, the captain had assured him, no one would ever find them. Ross was pretty sure there was one person who would.

Ross was the last to go below deck, but not before he'd double-checked that all that could be seen in any direction was a calm sea with no other vessel in sight.

He walked quietly past the royal suite, no light coming from under the door, before retiring to his cabin on the same deck. Something he'd insisted on. He showered and climbed into bed, sinking down into the fresh crisp cotton sheets, his head resting on a feather pillow. If it hadn't been for the quiet murmur of the engines, and the gentle movement of the boat, he wouldn't even have known they were at sea.

'Don't get used to it,' the Hawk had warned him, 'or you'll lose your edge.' The last thing he did before switching off his bedside light was to look out of the port window to confirm one more time that no one was following them. No one was.

• • •

Lamont turned off the main road and followed a signpost pointing to a large storage facility near Gatwick.

Miles, now dressed in a dark grey suit, white shirt, highly polished black shoes and a striped tie, had completed the transformation from escaped prisoner to respectable businessman. He checked the bulging wallet in his inside pocket.

It would be empty by the time he climbed into bed that night. But which bed would he be climbing into?

Lamont parked on the far side of a large removal van, so they could remain out of sight of prying eyes. He then made his way across to the nearest building and disappeared inside.

He reappeared a moment later and indicated with a nod that it was safe for Miles to join him. Inside, a squat heavily built man wearing brown overalls, an open-necked shirt and a baseball cap was standing in front of a large reinforced door with two large padlocks.

'Reg,' said Lamont, 'this is Mr Booth Watson, who I told you would be coming to collect his paintings in person.'

'I'll need to see some ID.'

Miles took out his wallet and handed over £500 in cash, which quickly disappeared into a deep pocket. Identity established.

'Sign here,' said Reg, producing a transport authority form. 'Then my lads can get started on the loading.'

After Miles had squiggled an indistinguishable signature on the dotted line, Reg touched his cap and announced, 'We'll see you in Lambeth in a couple of hours' time, Mr Booth Watson, when . . .'

'You'll get the other five hundred, as promised,' said Miles. 'But not until the paintings are safely back in their old home.'

'Fair enough,' said Reg as he turned to unlock the security door.

Lamont and Miles returned to the car. Once Lamont was back behind the wheel, he checked his watch and said, 'We're going to have to get a move on if you're hoping to be on time for your next meeting.'

Miles gave him a curt nod, but didn't say anything other than to repeat, 'Don't break the speed limit.'

Lamont stuck to the inside lane as they headed towards London, all the time keeping an eye out for any police patrol cars. He didn't want to draw up beside one at a traffic light and risk one of them being recognized. He moved into the centre lane as they continued on towards Hyde Park Corner. Although Lamont had driven the course the day before, he hadn't been able to find a parking meter near the bank, and this wasn't a day for leaving the get-away car on a double yellow line. He circled the bank and eventually found a meter about a hundred yards from the bank's main entrance. A calculated risk.

Lamont fed the meter with enough coins to allow them a couple of hours, the maximum on offer; every minute of which they would need. As he began to walk towards the bank, Miles slipped out of the car and followed in his wake. They avoided the reception desk and joined a group of other grey suits who were stepping into a lift. Lamont pressed the button marked 5 and the door slid closed. It was clear to Miles that Lamont, like the experienced ex-policeman he was, had done his homework, to reduce the risk of surprises as far as possible. But Miles knew there would always be something he hadn't anticipated.

When the lift door opened on the fifth floor, Lamont was the first out. He walked briskly down the corridor and knocked on a frosted glass door that announced 'Mr Nigel Cotterill, Area Manager'. He didn't wait for a response, although they were a few minutes early for their appointment. They might need those few minutes later.

If Mr Cotterill was surprised to see his erstwhile client, he didn't show it, as he'd already had two meetings with Lamont and knew exactly what was expected of him.

Miles took a seat on the other side of the manager's desk, while Lamont stood a pace behind him. Their roles reversed.

'As Mr Lamont will already have told you,' said Miles, 'I require a new safe-deposit box, for which I will be the only keyholder.'

Cotterill nodded, opened a file on his desk, took out several documents and placed them neatly in front of one of the bank's most important customers. Miles read each one carefully before penning his real signature on the bottom line.

'What about my other request?' he asked as he screwed the cap back on his fountain pen.

'We are currently holding twenty-six million pounds in your name following the sale of your fifty-one per cent holding in Marcel and Neffe. But as you will be aware, the money is lodged in a client account so that Mr Booth Watson can withdraw funds on your behalf when required, or to cover his fees and expenses as your legal representative.'

'How much has he taken out while I've been . . . since I last saw you?'

Cotterill glanced at the debit column. 'Two hundred and forty-one thousand, seven hundred pounds,' he said.

Miles didn't comment, except to say firmly, 'While I'm moving the contents of my old safe-deposit box to the new one, make sure that the full balance in the joint account is transferred to my private account, from which I will be the only person authorized to make withdrawals.'

'I'll have all the necessary forms ready for you to sign by the time you return,' said Cotterill. 'Meanwhile, I'll ask our head of security to accompany you to the lower ground floor, and open the strongroom for you. The number of your new box is 178.' He handed over a key, picked up the phone on his desk and dialled security.

CHAPTER 31

'Lot number twenty-one, the Max Ernst,' said the auctioneer. 'I have an opening bid of seven thousand pounds. Eight thousand,' he announced after turning his attention to the other side of the room. 'Do I see nine thousand?' he asked, to be greeted with a nod. 'Ten thousand?' he suggested to the former bidder, but received no response. He brought the hammer down with a thud, 'Sold, for nine thousand pounds.'

'So how much profit did we make on that one?' asked Christina.

'I originally paid eight thousand for it,' said Beth, 'but after Christie's have deducted the seller's premium, we'll be lucky to break even.'

'How unlike you.'

'Everybody loses sometime. The trick is not to make a habit of it.'

'Are you thinking of buying anything else today?'

'There's a Graham Sutherland watercolour of Coventry

Cathedral that I'm interested in. Lot twenty-seven. But on this occasion, I'll be representing a client.'

'Why don't they bid for themselves?'

'Whenever this particular client attends an auction, she gets carried away. So she tells me her upper limit and then I bid on her behalf.'

'How much do you charge for your services?'

'Five per cent of the hammer price.'

'Lot twenty-seven,' proclaimed the auctioneer. 'The Graham Sutherland. I have an opening bid of six thousand pounds. Do I see seven?'

Beth raised her paddle high in the air. 'Thank you, madam. Eight thousand?' He received an immediate response from a telephone bidder. 'Do I see nine?' Once again, Beth raised her paddle.

'Ten thousand?' asked the auctioneer, and back came her rival. 'Eleven thousand?' He smiled hopefully at Beth, who shook her head, as it was above her agreed limit. 'Sold, for ten thousand pounds,' declared the auctioneer as he wrote down the paddle number of the phone bidder.

Beth's heart was still thumping, and she wondered how many years it would be before it didn't do so whenever she was bidding. She hoped it never would.

'That won't pay for lunch,' said Christina. 'Are we going to be given another chance of getting our money back?'

'Possibly. But Lot thirty-four is the only one I'm still interested in.'

Christina flicked through the pages of her catalogue until she came to a painting of a woman lying in a field of corn, by Andrew Wyeth. 'I like it,' she whispered.

'Did I hear you correctly?' asked Beth.

'You did. It reminds me of a Pissarro Miles now has after

I foolishly parted with my half of his collection. If he hadn't stolen all my money,' she said wistfully, 'I'd buy the Wyeth and start my own collection.'

Words Beth thought she'd never hear, but then Christina never failed to surprise her.

'Why are you so keen on this particular painting?' Christina asked.

'Wyeth's an American artist, and has a devoted following in the States, particularly in Pennsylvania, where he was born. If I can get hold of it, I'll put it back on the market with Freeman's, the leading auction house in the state.'

'Cunning,' said Christina. 'Unless of course there are any Americans sitting in the room.'

'We're about to find out,' said Beth as the auctioneer announced, 'Lot thirty-four, the Andrew Wyeth. What am I bid?'

'Will you—'

'Shush!' said Beth.

'I'm looking for an opening bid of five thousand pounds. Five thousand?' he repeated, several times.

'Why aren't you bidding?' asked Christina.

'Shush,' repeated Beth.

'Do I see four thousand?' he asked, trying not to sound desperate. Just when it looked as if he would have to call the lot in, Beth slowly raised her paddle. Her heart was at it again, and it only started to return to normal when the auctioneer's hammer eventually came down and he said, 'Sold, for four thousand pounds to the lady seated on the aisle.' Beth raised her paddle a second time so that the auctioneer could record her paddle number on his sales sheet.

'That's it for today,' said Beth, getting up from her place. As she and Christina were making their way out of the sales

302

room, a man rushed past them and grabbed her seat. 'A good morning's work,' declared Beth, before walking across to the sales counter and writing out a cheque for £4,400.

'So if you sell it for anything over four thousand four hundred, we'll make a profit,' said Christina as they stepped out onto Bond Street.

'I wish,' said Beth. 'We first have to cover the packing costs, shipping and insurance, not to mention the American auction-eer's seller's premium. Five thousand would be nearer the mark before we can even start thinking about a profit.'

They had only walked a few more yards when they heard a voice behind them shouting, 'Mrs Warwick?'

Beth turned to see the man who had seemed in such a hurry when he'd passed them in the aisle. He came to a halt, and caught his breath before saying in a broad American accent, 'I got held up at a board meeting. I'd intended to bid for the Wyeth, and wondered, if you're a dealer, would you consider selling it to me? I'd be willing to pay five thousand.'

Beth shook her head.

'Six thousand?'

Beth waited long enough for him to say seven, and was just about to accept his offer when Christina said firmly, 'No, thank you,' and began to walk away. He immediately left Beth and chased after Christina. 'Eight?' he said.

'I wouldn't sell it for ten thousand,' said Christina. 'It will fit in so well with my collection.'

'Eleven,' said the American, still breathing heavily.

'Thirteen,' said Christina, finally coming to a halt.

'Twelve,' he countered.

'Twelve thousand four hundred, and it's yours.'

The American took out his cheque book and asked, 'Who do I make it out to?'

'Mrs Beth Warwick,' said Christina, without hesitation.

He wrote out the cheque and handed it to Christina before bowing low and leaving them with a smile on his face.

'So now we've made a profit of eight thousand,' said Christina.

'You're a witch,' said Beth.

'Of course I am, but then I was taught by the head of the coven.'

'Miles isn't that bad.'

'I wasn't referring to Miles,' said Christina, smiling at her friend.

• • •

It took Faulkner and Lamont just over an hour to transfer the cash from one large safe-deposit box to another. After he'd checked the final amount, Miles realized Booth Watson must have helped himself to another £126,000 along the way, clearly having made several more visits to the bank during the last few weeks, accompanied by his Gladstone bag. Miles now knew the real reason BW wanted him to plead guilty; it would give his lawyer more than enough time to remove every last penny both from his business account and safe-deposit boxes before he was finally released.

As Lamont returned the empty box to its place, Miles extracted a fifty-pound note from his wallet and dropped it inside. 'Wouldn't want BW to go away empty-handed, would we?'

Lamont's thin smile turned into a broad grin when Miles took ten thousand pounds from the full safe-deposit box and handed it to him.

'I'll deposit another ten thousand in your account tomorrow, as long as I'm in bed before lights out.'

Miles locked the box, put the key in his pocket and pressed the green button by the reinforced door, which immediately sprang open. He stepped out into the corridor, barely acknowledging the security guard as he headed back towards the lift. When the door slid open, Miles stepped inside and hit the number 5 button with a vengeance. Lamont joined him just in time.

They returned to the manager's office on the fifth floor, to find all the necessary paperwork had been completed, and all Miles had to do was add his signature. He double-checked all three documents, and once he'd signed them, he handed his pen to Lamont and invited him to witness his signature. Miles knew this would ensure Lamont kept his mouth shut if he didn't want to end up sharing the same cell as the beneficiary.

'When you next see my esteemed lawyer,' Miles said as he handed back the old key to Cotterill, 'be sure to give him my best wishes.'

'And if he should ask—'

'Simply tell him I gave ex-superintendent Lamont my power of attorney while I was away.'

Once Miles and Lamont had returned to the ground floor, they left the bank without a backward glance and headed straight for the car. Lamont cursed as he removed a parking ticket from the windscreen.

'Make sure you pay it,' said Miles. 'It's always the little mistakes that catch you out.' Before Lamont could comment, he added, 'Let's get moving. We still have one more important job to do.'

• • •

'The Connaught Hotel. How may I help you?'

'Please put me through to Mr Lee's apartment.'

'May I ask who's calling?'

'Booth Watson.'

'I'll put you through, Mr Watson.'

BW didn't bother to correct her as he waited to be connected.

'Good afternoon, Mr Booth Watson,' said a familiar voice. 'I trust you're well.'

'Yes, thank you, Mr Lee. And you?'

'I am indeed,' said Lee, who considered that having dealt with the English niceties of small talk, he was now entitled to move on. 'Have you had an opportunity to discuss my offer with your client?'

'I most certainly have,' said Booth Watson. 'To my surprise, Mr Faulkner is willing to accept your offer of one hundred million dollars for his collection, and has asked me to handle all the details.'

'I'm delighted to hear that, Mr Booth Watson. So how would you like to proceed?'

'If you tell me where you want the pictures delivered, I'll organize the packing and insurance, and have them transported to Hong Kong.'

'Jardine Matheson have a large warehouse facility in Kowloon where the paintings can be stored. Once I've inspected them, I'll transfer the money to your account the following day.'

'That sounds most satisfactory, Mr Lee. I'll be back in touch once the paintings have been shipped so we can complete the transaction.'

'I look forward to seeing you in Hong Kong, Mr Booth Watson. Please pass on my best wishes to your client.'

'I most certainly will,' said Booth Watson.

'What did you make of that?' asked Mai Ling, after her father had put the phone down.

'He certainly hasn't taken advice from his client as he claimed. Faulkner would never part with his collection for a hundred million dollars, even if he was on death row. No, Mr Booth Watson allowed just enough time to pass before he called me back to tell me something he'd already planned even before he'd met me.'

'Do you think the pictures will ever turn up in Hong Kong?'

'Not a hope,' said Mr Lee. 'In fact, when Mr Booth Watson next visits his storage facility at Gatwick, I have a feeling he'll find the cupboard is bare.'

'But if you hadn't agreed to me visiting Mr Faulkner at Belmarsh, Father, you could have got hold of his entire collection for one hundred million.'

'If I'm going to make an enemy, my child, I would rather it was Booth Watson than Miles Faulkner.'

• • •

Ross walked onto the bridge and joined the captain.

'Can I borrow your binoculars for a moment, skipper?' he asked.

'Be my guest, Inspector.'

Ross turned back and scanned the beach about half a mile away. It didn't take him long to spot a lone figure lying flat on his stomach, his long-lens camera focused on two swimmers splashing around by the side of the yacht, who appeared blissfully unaware of his presence.

Like a fisherman, the photographer would wait patiently for Diana to return to the yacht and embrace her lover. He knew it was only a matter of time before he landed the picture he wanted. An embrace would be worth several thousand pounds, a kiss – not on the cheek – twenty-five thousand. How Ross despised him.

'I'm going to have a word with Mr Chalabi,' said Ross.

'Rather you than me,' said the captain. Ross left the bridge and made his way down to the main deck, where he found Chalabi lying on a lounger, a pair of dark glasses shielding his eyes from the midday sun. An abandoned paperback had fallen by his side while he snoozed.

'I'm sorry to bother you, Mr Chalabi,' he said.

Chalabi slowly came to, removed his glasses and looked up at the intruder.

'I thought you would want to know that there's a photographer on the beach taking pictures of the Princess and Lady Victoria swimming.'

'Perhaps I should join them,' he said, glancing over the side and not bothering to suppress a grin.

'It might be wiser, sir,' suggested Ross, 'if we were to move to a more secluded spot, where he won't bother you.'

'He's not bothering me. And as you can see, the Princess is clearly enjoying herself, so why don't we leave her in peace?'

'But that's the point, sir. She's not being left in peace.'

'That's for me to decide, Inspector, not you, and this time you won't be able to stop him.'

Ross clenched a fist.

'I may have to tolerate you being on my yacht, but you'd do well to remember you're nothing more than a butler with a gun.'

• • •

As the Volvo pulled into the parking lot beside a warehouse in Lambeth, Miles was relieved to see the removal van had already arrived, and half a dozen appropriately clad men were unloading its contents. However, he still had to hang around for another hour, and sign even more forms, before the last painting was safely deposited in its rack and the doors to his collection's new abode had been double-locked.

Another £500 changed hands before the storage manager was willing to hand over two large keys, which would allow Miles to enter his own private code and ensure that no one else could remove the paintings without his knowledge.

Once Miles had pocketed the keys, he joined the storage manager who was dividing the spoils among his crew, and said, 'If anyone should ask—'

'My boys never saw nothin'. Nice to have done business with you, Mr . . .' he hesitated, 'Booth Watson.'

Miles joined Lamont in the car, its engine already turning over. 'We're going to have to get a move on,' he said as he took off his jacket and checked his watch, 'if we're going to be back in under two hours and eleven minutes.'

Lamont took off, but the rush-hour traffic prevented him reaching the motorway for another forty-two minutes.

'To hell with the speed limit,' said Miles, finally giving in.

Although the speedometer rarely dipped below 90 mph, Lamont only managed to reach the layby near the prison with seventeen minutes to spare.

Miles, who had already changed back into his gym kit and trainers in the car, jumped out and set off at a pace that barely raised a sweat. Gone were the days when he could run a mile in under five minutes. By the time he reached the copse just outside the prison grounds, he was exhausted. He quickly retrieved his jeans and sweater from under the bramble bush and hurriedly pulled them on. He checked carefully in every direction before venturing out into no man's land, relieved to find some friendly clouds were masking a full moon that would have alerted a patrolling officer to a moving figure on the wrong side of the demarcation zone.

An anxious cleaner was waiting for him by the fire escape door, and quickly pushed up the bar to let him in. Miles wearily climbed the stone steps to the second floor, and when he was only a few yards from his room, the lights went out. He fumbled with several keys before he managed to find the right one to open the door. When the lock finally turned, he almost fell inside.

Before he had time to undress, he heard the night officer advancing along the corridor on his round to check that every prisoner was safely tucked up after lights out.

Miles slipped into bed, pulled the blanket up to his neck and closed his eyes.

There was a gentle tap at the door. The duty officer looked inside and flashed his torch over the bed. 'Hope you're feeling better, Mr Faulkner,' he said, before quickly switching off the torch.

'A lot better, thank you, officer.' Miles waited for the door to close before he got back out of bed, took off his clothes and hid four keys under his pillow, before falling asleep.

• • •

Superintendent Warwick and DS Adaja sat in an unmarked car in a layby a hundred yards from the prison.

'Are we going to give him a wake-up call?' asked Paul when the lights in C block went out.

'No. We owe him one,' replied William. 'But if he hadn't come back, I would have happily arrested him.'

'And if he tries it on again?'

'He won't need to. But I'd love to see Booth Watson's face next time he turns up at the bank.'

CHAPTER 32

TWO RIGID INFLATABLE BOATS DRIFTED into the bay. They were only doing two knots, so their engines wouldn't be heard on a still, windless night as they headed towards the stationary yacht silhouetted in the moonlight. Nasreen Hassan, sitting in the bow of the lead boat, raised her binoculars and focused on the only light coming from *Lowlander*.

A man sitting on the bridge of the yacht was playing a game of chess against himself to while away the long hours on anchor watch. So powerful were her binoculars that she could see him make his next move: queen to knight four.

Her next move had been planned some weeks ago. Once they knew the dates the target would be going on holiday with her boyfriend, they had begun preparations for their unheralded arrival.

They already knew the yacht Chalabi had hired was anchored in Palma, Mallorca. A small bribe to the assistant harbour-master was all it took to find out when it would be leaving port. They were even in possession of an architect's plan of the yacht. They had spent the past two days secreted in a small inlet further up the coast, putting the finishing touches to their plans.

Hassan checked her watch – 03.17 – confident that the only person on board still awake would be the young man on the bridge. Rook to bishop's four. He removed a knight from the board.

She looked back to check on the tiny flotilla and her nine-man team, each one chosen for their particular area of expertise. Sitting around her in the lead boat were five hired killers, none of whom was on his first mission. They all wore black from head to foot, and their faces were smeared with burnt cork so they wouldn't be spotted in the moonlight. Each one of them could go thirty-six hours without sleep – not that this part of the operation should take them more than a few minutes. It was disappearing without trace that would take time – and time, or the lack of it, was their only enemy.

Slung loosely over Hassan's shoulder was a Dragunov sniper rifle that she kept at her side even in bed. She had made her name killing a British soldier in Libya with a single bullet, from six hundred yards away. The other five carried Kalashnikovs, purchased on the open market. One of them had his cocked, the first round in the chamber. He only expected to fire one bullet.

The second boat was piloted by a 'for hire' captain with twenty years' experience of serving various cartels as a drug runner, and his number two, who'd spent more time in jail than on the high seas. Behind them sat the engineer, whose pale, lined complexion suggested years of heaving and sweating deep in the bowels of ships. The final member of the team was a doctor who'd been struck off, although for what Hassan had in mind, they would have been better off with an undertaker.

Every pair of eyes on the two inflatables was fixed on the yacht. The man who'd been chosen to eliminate the chess player would be the first on board, while Hassan and the other four men from the lead boat went below to where the Princess and Chalabi's other guests would be dreaming; dreams that were about to turn into a nightmare.

Hassan felt her mouth go dry, as it always did before an attack. Their beloved leader had selected her to lead this audacious coup, promising her that if she succeeded, not only would the British be humiliated in the eyes of the world, but her name would become part of the nation's folklore and inspire many other young women to join their cause. The irony was that she'd been born in Wakefield and recruited while she was at university. Like many converts, Hassan had become more passionate about and dedicated to the cause than any of the hired mercenaries seated around her, who were interested only in how much they would be paid.

When they were within a couple of hundred yards of the target, they slowed down to make sure the low murmur of their engines didn't alert the chess player on the bridge. Hassan smiled at the thought that one of the attractions of this particular vessel, as the charter agent had helpfully pointed out, was that even a child returning from a swim could clamber aboard without needing assistance.

With a hundred yards to go, they cut the engines altogether and allowed the two inflatables to drift up to the stern of the yacht, so that nine gatecrashers could join the party.

When the lead dinghy touched the edge of the landing deck, the chosen assassin was the first on board. He moved swiftly across the lower deck and up the short flight of steps to the bridge. The chess player looked up after playing his last move and a single bullet entered his forehead. Before he could make a sound, he collapsed onto the ground in a heap beside the wheel. Without a word passing between them, the new captain and his first mate took over.

Hassan was half-way down the spiral staircase that led to the guest quarters when Ross was woken by the shot. He was immediately alert, although for a moment he couldn't be sure if it had just been part of his dream. He leapt out of bed, rushed across to the cabin door, and opened it, to be met by the barrel of a Kalashnikov rifle aimed between his eyes.

As two of the gunmen dragged Ross out into the corridor, he instinctively looked in the direction of the Princess's cabin. The door opened, and out stepped Jamil Chalabi wearing a khaki uniform and carrying a gun. He leant forward and kissed Hassan on both cheeks before saying, 'You couldn't have done a more professional job, my sister. The cause will be forever in your debt.'

'Can I kill him?' she asked, looking at Ross.

'No,' said Chalabi firmly. 'I have other plans for him.' Hassan looked disappointed. 'For now, we stick to our original plan. Start by searching all the cabins. Look for weapons of any kind – guns, knives and, equally important, phones. After that, lock them all up. Put those two in the same cabin,' he said, nodding towards Ross and Victoria. 'I'm going to need my own room and I have a feeling the Princess won't be welcoming me back into her arms.'

'What should we do with these four?' Hassan asked, waving her weapon at the captain, the engineer, the steward and the chef, who'd been dragged out of their beds.

'You can kill them,' said Chalabi as if it were a compensation. 'That way we won't be outnumbered, and it will also make the Inspector think twice should he have any ideas about playing the hero.'

One of the thugs thrust a knee into Ross's groin, who bent double before toppling backwards into Victoria's cabin. The door slammed and he heard a key turn in the lock. Moments later, four shots rang out. Victoria instinctively clung onto Ross. She was trembling, but when she spoke, her voice was defiant.

'I never trusted that man. Given half a chance, I'll happily kill him.' Ross hadn't thought it possible he could still be surprised.

Chalabi left two of his men on guard in the corridor while he went back up on deck, where he found blood splattered everywhere. His favourite colour.

He was about to give the order to raise the anchor when he saw a flash coming from the beach. He grabbed a set of binoculars, and in the moonlight could just make out a lone figure holding a long-lens camera resting on a tripod.

'Damn, I'd forgotten about him,' said Chalabi. 'But as he no longer serves any purpose . . .' He didn't need to finish the sentence. Hassan, who was standing by his side, raised her rifle, rested it on the ship's railing and lined up her target through the nightscope. He was four hundred and fifty-eight yards away. She nestled the butt of the rifle firmly into her shoulder, and took a deep breath before gently squeezing the trigger. She was prepared to fire a second shot if there was any further sign of movement on the beach. There wasn't.

'Let's get going,' Chalabi shouted up to the bridge. He knew the *Lowlander* could only manage twenty knots flat out, so there wasn't a moment to waste if they were going to make it to the safety of their homeland, where the world would learn about the daring coup, and be left with no choice but to agree to their demands.

• • •

The phone was ringing on William's side of the bed. He grabbed it in the hope it wouldn't wake Beth. She groaned and turned over.

'Good morning, Warwick,' said a voice he thought he'd heard the last of.

'Good morning, Assistant Commissioner,' he replied, hoping he sounded wide awake.

'The body of a paparazzi photographer has been found by a local fisherman on an isolated beach off the coast of Mallorca.'

William's mind raced, as he tried to work out why this could possibly be of any importance to him, at five o'clock in the morning.

'The local police,' continued Holbrooke, 'found a camera by his side and have sent us the images he'd taken. That's all you need to know for now, except that a COBRA meeting will be taking place in Whitehall in an hour's time, and your presence is required.'

Why me, William wondered.

'We think it's possible Mansour Khalifah may be involved,' came back the answer to his unspoken question.

Involved in what, William would have asked, if he hadn't been cut off. He leapt out of bed and headed for the bathroom.

'Who was that?' asked a half-awake Beth, but he'd already closed the door.

• • •

Everyone stood as Mrs Thatcher entered the Cabinet Office Briefing Room just a corridor away from Number 10, with none of the usual prying eyes wondering why such a powerful group had been assembled at six o'clock in the morning.

She took her place at the centre of the long table and looked around at a score of the nation's top decision-makers, who'd all emerged from their warm beds at a moment's notice. Behind them sat a plethora of civil servants, who would ensure their masters' orders were carried out when they returned to their Whitehall warrens once the meeting was over.

'Assistant Commissioner,' the Prime Minister began, looking across to the other side of the table, 'perhaps you can bring us all up to date.'

'The situation is frankly fluid, Prime Minister,' replied Holbrooke, 'while our intelligence agencies are continuing to gather the latest information, as I speak. All we know for certain is that an armed group of terrorists, possibly funded by Colonel Gaddafi, boarded and captured a yacht off the coast of Mallorca, on which the Princess of Wales is a guest. Its current whereabouts are unknown.'

'I thought she and the Prince of Wales were on holiday at Highgrove,' commented the Prime Minister as she looked at a map that had been placed on the centre of the table.

'As does the rest of the outside world,' said Holbrooke, 'and I'd like to keep it that way.' He touched a button on his console, and a photograph of *Lowlander*, with two inflatable dinghies floating from its stern, filled a large screen that dominated the wall at the far end of the room.

'How did you get hold of that?' asked the Cabinet Secretary, who was seated on the PM's left.

'A paparazzi photographer was on the beach at the time the raid took place, and the Spanish police were able to retrieve his camera.'

'That was a lucky break,' suggested the Cabinet Secretary.

'Not for him,' said Holbrooke. 'He ended up with a bullet through his forehead.'

'What was he doing there at that time of night?' asked the Prime Minister.

'He would have been working for one of the tabloids and must have been aware the Princess was on board the yacht. Luckily for us,' continued Holbrooke, 'he'd already taken several photographs before he was murdered. His body was found by a local fisherman. The Spanish police also dug up a .54mm bullet which was embedded in the sand near his camera. The type favoured by trained assassins.'

Several voices began speaking at once, until the Prime Minister waved a dismissive hand and nodded at Holbrooke.

'We had no way of knowing who killed the photographer,' continued Holbrooke, 'until we received the pictures he'd taken last night.'

The image of the yacht on the screen was replaced by a young white woman's face.

'Who's she?' asked the Prime Minister.

'Ruth Cairns,' said the head of MI6. 'She was born in Wakefield, and studied politics at Manchester University. But she dropped out, and disappeared for almost a decade, until recently, when she came to our attention following a signals intercept. She now goes by the name of Nasreen Hassan, and has become one of Gaddafi's most trusted lieutenants.' A short video showing a woman beheading an American serviceman in front of a cheering mob left them all in no doubt what they were up against.

'Cairns appears to be in charge of the operation,' said Holbrooke.

'How many terrorists were involved in the attack?' asked the Foreign Secretary, speaking for the first time.

'There were only a couple of RIBs involved, so there can't have been more than a dozen at most,' replied Holbrooke. 'We think we've identified five of them who have records with our intelligence agencies.'

A succession of mugshots appeared on the screen, as Holbrooke briefed the COBRA meeting on who the suspects were, and the roles they were likely to have played in the operation. The next photograph to appear on screen was of two men dressed in black, standing on the bridge of the yacht. 'We think this has to be their captain and his number two, because they bear no resemblance to the five officers who sailed the yacht out of Mallorca on Friday evening.'

'Should we assume that the crew of the yacht are all dead?' asked the Prime Minister.

'Probably. Hassan doesn't believe in taking prisoners, especially when an unmarked grave is so conveniently on hand. But I'm confident the Princess is still alive, otherwise they've lost their bargaining power.'

'Bargaining suggests money or an exchange for something else,' suggested the Prime Minister. 'In your view, Assistant Commissioner, which is it?'

'Not something else, ma'am, someone else. Hassan wouldn't be interested in money,' Holbrooke assured them, 'otherwise it would have been Jamil Chalabi, the Princess's latest . . . companion, they were after, and not the Princess.'

'What makes you so sure of that?' asked the Cabinet Secretary.

'Chalabi is the son of a wealthy businessman from Dubai,' came in Commander Hawksby. 'He's a regular in the gossip columns, usually described as a multi-millionaire playboy or serial party-goer. According to Inspector Ross Hogan, the Princess's personal protection officer, he's not shy about letting anyone, including the press, know about his relationship with her.'

'If you don't think it's money they're after in exchange for the Princess,' asked the Cabinet Secretary, 'what else could it possibly be?'

'We're currently holding Gaddafi's right-hand man, Mansour Khalifah, in Belmarsh prison,' said Hawksby. 'So I don't think we need to look much further than Thamesmead.'

'You will recall, Prime Minister,' chipped in the Attorney General, 'that I sanctioned Khalifah's arrest a few months ago when he landed at Heathrow on the way to Moscow.'

'We're in no doubt,' added the Home Secretary, 'that Khalifah was behind the Lockerbie bombing, and more recently the failed attempt to blow up the Albert Hall during the Last Night of the Proms. Don't be surprised if Gaddafi has put him in charge of any negotiations.'

'We don't negotiate with terrorists,' said the Prime Minister, as if addressing a public meeting. But on this occasion, no one around the table believed her.

Several people began talking at once, but were silenced when the Prime Minister turned her attention to the Chief of the Defence Staff. 'So, what do you recommend we do next, Admiral?'

'I've got a Nimrod flying above the immediate area, with a second one on its way. *Lowlander* can't have covered more than a hundred miles since it was taken over, so I'm confident it shouldn't be too long before we locate it.'

'Where do you think they're heading?' asked the Cabinet Secretary, looking back down at the map.

'They won't want to hang about in Spanish waters,' said the First Sea Lord. 'My bet is they're heading for Tripoli,' a finger moving across the map, 'in the hope that they can reach Libyan territorial waters before we are given the chance to mount a full scale retaliation.'

'How much time do we have?' asked the Cabinet Secretary.

'If they maintain a speed of around eighteen knots, it will take them about forty-eight hours to reach the safety of their own territorial waters.'

'If they make it,' said the Foreign Secretary, who was seated opposite the Prime Minister, 'we have no more sanctions to threaten Libya with, so we're not exactly in a strong bargaining position.'

'A very weak one,' said the Prime Minister, folding her arms. 'So, what can we hope to achieve during the next forty-eight hours to make sure that doesn't arise?'

'I've got a crack SBS squadron trained in Maritime Counter Terrorism who are currently carrying out exercises on the Clyde near Faslane,' chipped in the Director of Special Forces. 'I've already issued an order that they should return to their base in Dorset soonest, where I'll be joining them later today.'

'Are any of our ships currently in the area?' asked the Cabinet Secretary, who leant across the table and dipped a finger in the middle of the Mediterranean.

'The aircraft carrier HMS *Cornwall* was anchored off the coast of Malta,' said the First Sea Lord, 'but is already heading towards the area at speed. They should catch up with them in about eighteen hours. We also have a submarine undertaking minor repairs in Gibraltar, which will be ready to get under way later this morning and should join up with the *Cornwall* some time tomorrow afternoon.'

'I presume,' said the Prime Minister, 'you've chosen a crack commander to head up this operation?'

'Yes,' said the First Sea Lord. 'He's the best. Because for something this big we certainly don't need a fimfop.'

'A fimfop?' queried the Cabinet Secretary.

'Fun In the Mess, Fool Operationally. I can assure you that Captain Davenport is not a man Khalifah will want to meet.'

'Under what conditions is Khalifah being held at this moment?' asked the Prime Minister, looking around the table, not sure who would be able to answer her question.

'He's currently locked up in the solitary confinement wing of Belmarsh prison,' said William. 'He has no way of contacting anyone on the outside, but I think we can assume he's well aware of what's going on.'

Everyone around the table turned and looked at William.

'Throwing away the key would seem an appropriate response given the circumstances,' said the Home Secretary.

'I only wish it was that easy,' said the Prime Minister. 'But for now, I suggest we all get to work and try to look as if it's business as usual. I don't have to remind you that it's impera-tive the press don't get hold of the story.'

'And if they do?' asked the PM's Press Secretary.

'I'll slap a D-notice on every printing press in Fleet Street,' said the Attorney General, without hesitation.

'What if a foreign source finds out the Princess has been kidnapped?' was the Press Secretary's second question. 'You can't slap anything on them.'

'If that were to happen, Bernard, prepare a statement for me,' said the Prime Minister, just as the door burst open and her private secretary came rushing into the room and handed the PM a note. She opened it and read the short message out loud. 'A Nimrod has located *Lowlander*, and you're right, Admiral,' she said, looking up at the First Sea Lord. 'They're heading east-south-east at around seventeen knots.'

'So it has to be Tripoli,' said the Foreign Secretary.

'Which means we've got,' said the Prime Minister, checking

her watch, 'about forty-seven hours before I have no choice but to accept a call from Colonel Gaddafi and negotiate from a very weak position.' She looked around the table. 'That's something I want to avoid,' she said firmly. 'Whatever the cost.'

CHAPTER 33

WHEN THE SBS DIVE SUPERVISOR got the call from the ops commander at Faslane, he steadied his boat and loaded a diver recall device before dropping it into the water. It sank below the waves, exploding moments later to alert the divers of M Squadron to return to the surface immediately. Within seconds, a dozen rubber-clad bodies appeared above the waves and began racing each other to the safety boat. They didn't need to be told it was an emergency, because they could see two faster vessels heading at speed towards them.

The order was simple. Return to the base at Coulport, get out of your dive kit and be ready to board a helicopter in twenty minutes. Anyone not on the helipad by then will be left behind. 'Left behind' were the only two words the ops commander repeated.

By the time the last of M Squadron reached the helipad at Coulport, the blades of the third helicopter were already rotating, waiting to lift off and, like the other two, be on their way back to SBS headquarters in Poole. No one missed the flight.

· · ·

'Are they terrorists or pirates?' asked Victoria, trying not to show how anxious she felt.

'Terrorists,' said Ross, without hesitation. 'Let's just hope the pirates are already working out how to rescue us.'

'Is it money they're after?' asked Victoria. 'Because if it is, surely all they'll have to do is negotiate the amount with the government?'

'I don't think this lot are interested in money.'

'What else could they possibly want?'

'Mansour Khalifah. The Libyan terrorist behind the Lockerbie bombing, who's currently locked up in Belmarsh. He's Colonel Gaddafi's right-hand man, and as we're currently heading south-east, I guess our next port of call is likely to be Tripoli.'

'As you hardly slept a wink last night, Inspector, do you have a plan to get us out of here?' Victoria said as she walked out and looked across at Diana's balcony, but there was no sign of her.

Ross joined her on the balcony, looked around, and announced, 'I didn't get one of these,' not wanting her to dwell on the one subject that was preoccupying both of them.

'Understandably, Inspector,' she replied, giving him a hint of a smile, 'but then it's not often I'm forced to spend the night with one of the below-stairs staff. Do you have any other reason to believe it might be Libya we're heading for?' she added, not letting him off the hook.

'When we were out in the corridor last night, I heard one of Chalabi's henchmen say "the Colonel", and then he raised a fist in triumph. But wherever we're headed, my first priority is to protect the Princess.'

'That won't be easy. In any case, we're probably in more danger than she is.'

'What makes you say that?'

'If you're right about them wanting Khalifah in exchange for the Princess, their only hope of getting him released will be to make sure they don't sacrifice their queen. Though they may be quite happy to remove a few pawns from the board, even the odd castle, which would account for those four shots we heard last night. It might also help the politicians in Whitehall to make up their minds. That's assuming your pirates fail to turn up on time.'

'You'd have made a good detective,' said Ross. 'So, what do you think their next move is likely to be?'

'We won't find that out until whoever Chalabi is planning to contact in London wakes up, which might not be for another hour or more. So, what should we do until then?'

'We could always go back to bed,' teased Ross, trying to keep her mind off what he feared she was really thinking about.

'I must confess,' said Victoria, 'I had considered several scenarios in which that might happen, but being forced to spend the night with you by a group of terrorists who needed a spare room wasn't high on the list. Frankly, I think you should be more concerned about the latest woman in your life,' she said, pointing in the direction of the upper deck. 'And with all your experience of the opposite sex, Inspector, I'd be fascinated to know what you make of her?'

'She's clearly ruthless and efficient. The whole operation was well planned, so she'll know exactly what her next move is. But one thing she might not have anticipated is that there was a paparazzi photographer on the beach when they took over the yacht last night, and he had one thing in common with me,' said Ross. 'He never let the Princess out of his sight.'

'So the morning papers might already have the story on their front pages.'

'Not if he's dead. I heard a single shot fired last night from a high-powered rifle, not from the gun that killed the other five,' said Ross as he peered up at the sky through the porthole.

'What are you looking for?' asked Victoria.

'I'm not looking, I'm listening. Once they realize back in London that the Princess has been kidnapped, there'll be a Nimrod somewhere up there trying to locate exactly where we are.'

'But won't the terrorists see it, and be alerted?'

'The pilot will make sure he stays high enough to be out of sight. And believe me, they're well capable of pinpointing a dolphin from twenty miles away, let alone a seventy-metre yacht.'

'Even if they do find us, what can they hope to do?'

'Every government agency will move into top gear, but it'll be the SBS who mount the rescue operation. Their biggest problem will be that they'll only have a limited window before we reach Libyan territorial waters.'

'Not exactly where the Princess had in mind to spend her summer holiday.'

'I'm bound to say, Victoria, you seem remarkably calm, given the circumstances,' though Ross noted a slight biting of the lip that rather expressed her true feelings.

'My family have faced worst in the past. My great-great grandfather lost a leg at the siege of Mafeking,' she said. 'My grandfather was killed on the beaches of Dunkirk, while my father foolishly invested the family fortune in Lloyd's of London and is now on what they describe as their "hardship list", so I expect my inheritance has gone down the drain and I'll end up having to do what the females of my clan have done so often in the past – marry for money. If you want to know the truth, I'm absolutely terrified. But as my grandmother used to tell my mother when the bombs were dropping on London, "Keep calm. Carry on, and always remember to put your knife and fork down between mouthfuls."'

Ross could only admire the way this woman reacted under pressure, but didn't tell her they had only experienced the first skirmish. Victoria went across to the desk in the corner of her cabin, on which there was a large pile of unopened letters addressed to the Princess. She picked up the top envelope and, using a silver letter opener, slit it open with practised efficiency.

'From one of her many admirers?' asked Ross.

'Yes, but this is just a small sample of what HRH gets every day. One of my tasks is to see they're all answered, even the ones that aren't too flattering. I brought a batch of them with me, so I could answer them when I've got nothing better to do.'

'How does she react to the unflattering ones?'

'She never sees them,' confessed Victoria. 'I always pick a few from devoted fans for her to read over breakfast, although I don't suppose I'll get the chance today.'

'Do you think the public would go on supporting her if it became known that she'd been on holiday with her lover and not the Prince?'

'Most of them, yes,' said Victoria. 'For the worshippers, she can do no wrong.'

Ross swung around when the door burst open and two of Chalabi's thugs charged into the room. They grabbed Ross by his arms, dragged him out into the corridor, and locked the door behind them. Alone in the cabin, Victoria burst into tears; her stiff upper lip having finally wobbled.

Ross was frogmarched up the stairs with the barrel of a rifle jabbed painfully in his back, before being shoved out onto the top deck, where Chalabi and Hassan were waiting for him. The morning sun blazed down on them, unaware they were no longer on holiday.

'The time has come, Inspector Hogan, for us to move on to phase two of my plan.'

Ross suddenly realized why they hadn't killed him.

'Every telephone call you've made from your cabin during this voyage has been monitored, Inspector. So, for the moment, and I stress for the moment, you're more use to me alive than dead. I want you to get in touch with Superintendent Warwick, as he appears to be the officer in charge of Royalty Protection.' Ross said nothing. 'You're going to get him on the line right now, so I can spell out in detail what I expect in return for not killing the next Queen of England.'

• • •

Once again, they all stood when Mrs Thatcher entered the room.

'Brigadier,' said the Prime Minister, before she'd sat down.

'An SBS team of highly trained operatives have been fully briefed on their mission, which has been given the operational code name "Overboard", and are already on their way to the Mediterranean,' said the Director of Special Forces. 'I flew down to Poole following yesterday's meeting and briefed the SBS with our latest information. We had an outline plan in place by the time I boarded the plane back to RAF Northolt just after midnight.'

'But won't it take days for even the most experienced operatives to be able to mount such a demanding operation?' asked the Cabinet Secretary.

'Not in fact, Sir Robin,' said the brigadier. 'The SBS spend every waking hour preparing for such a possibility, and can't wait to be tested by real terrorists, rather than volunteers acting the part.'

'But how can they possibly hope to board a fast-moving vessel, in the middle of an ocean, whose crew will be looking out for any sign of danger?' asked the Prime Minister.

'It depends on which direction they're looking when our lads turn up,' said the brigadier. 'But you can be assured they've worked on several variations of this theme countless times and are more than ready for the challenge.'

'Are you able to share any details with us at this point,' asked the Defence Secretary, 'or is it still too early?'

A map of the Mediterranean appeared on the screen at the far end of the room, with three large crosses marked in mid-ocean. The brigadier stood and walked across, a laser pointer in one hand.

'This is what's known in the trade as a three-pronged attack. To begin with, two dozen of HMS *Cornwall*'s most experienced men will mount a diversionary sortie from the east.' A pinpoint of light focused on one of the crosses. 'Once we've caught the terrorists' attention, twenty members of the SBS team, under the command of Captain Mike Davenport, will close in on the yacht from the west, six of them on two of the *Cornwall*'s helicopters' – the light settled briefly on a second cross – 'from where the men will fast-rope down onto the deck and neutralize the terrorists. The remaining fourteen SBS men will approach from the north-west in three high-speed RIBs' – the third cross was highlighted, completing a triangle that surrounded *Lowlander*. 'The crucial element of the plan is timing. All three parts of the triangle have to come together at exactly the right moment. None of them can afford to be even a few seconds adrift.'

'So where are the three parts of the triangle at this moment?' asked the Cabinet Secretary.

'Twenty-four of the ship's company, who will form a diversionary group, are currently being briefed on the vital role they'll play if this operation is to have any chance of success. The elite M Squadron should be' – he checked his watch – 'arriving at RAF Lyneham in the next thirty minutes in two trucks carrying all the equipment they'll need, including the three RIBs. Once everything is loaded on board the two C-130s, they'll take off at 1500 hours, earlier if possible. The SBS team should make contact with the *Cornwall* just after half past six in the evening, local time. I'd give you more details if I could, but the whole operation is very fluid and may well be subject to last-minute changes.'

'How do you propose getting thirty men off a C-130 and onto the *Cornwall*?' asked the Cabinet Secretary, looking at the map. 'There doesn't seem to be a runway within five hundred miles.'

'They'll parachute into the sea along with their RIBs,' explained the brigadier. 'For these men, that's as easy as jumping into a swimming pool is for you or me. Meanwhile, one of our latest submarines, the *Ursula*, is closing in on the yacht. In fact, they should already have made radar contact with them by now,' he added, a pinpoint of light indicating a position well to the south of the third corner of the triangle.

'What role does a submarine play in this operation?' asked the Foreign Secretary.

A long silence followed, before the Defence Secretary admitted, 'It's there as a last resort, Prime Minister.'

'A last resort for what?' demanded the PM.

'Should we fail to take the yacht.'

'And if that were to happen?' pressed the Cabinet Secretary.

An even longer silence followed before the Defence Secretary admitted, 'HMS *Ursula* would blow the yacht out of the water. But not before we're certain they've killed the Princess and, even then, not without your authority, Prime Minister,' he added as a phone began to ring from the far end of the table. William looked suitably embarrassed and was about to turn it off, when he saw whose name was flashing up on the screen.

William stood up, leant across and pushed his Motorola into the middle of the table, while placing a finger to his lips. A room full of men who were used to giving orders fell silent as William pressed the speaker button, so everyone could follow the conversation.

'Good morning, sir,' said a voice with a slight Irish lilt, that William recognized immediately. 'It's DI Hogan.'

He couldn't remember when Ross had last called him 'sir'.

'As you know, Inspector,' said William playing along, 'regulations require that in a situation like this you have to answer four security questions in order to prove your identity.'

'Understood,' said Ross, well aware William would be analysing every word he said.

'How many officers are under my command at Buckingham Gate?'

'Ten,' said Ross.

'How long does it take on average for an ambulance to reach a traffic accident in London?'

'About eighteen to twenty minutes,' responded Ross.

William wrote down the numbers 'ten', 'eighteen' and 'twenty', before asking his next question. 'What was the first car you owned after leaving school?'

'I wanted a Porsche, but had to settle for a second-hand MG, that only had a thousand miles on the clock.'

William added 'one thousand' to his list.

'What was your mother's maiden name?'

'O'Reilly. I had six brothers and four sisters. Our mother ruled us with a rod of iron.' William wrote down the numbers 'six' and 'four'.

'Thank you, Inspector Hogan. You can now tell me your reason for calling.'

'As you may know, Bill, the yacht on which my principal is sailing has been taken over' – he avoided saying, by a gang of terrorists – 'and their leader who is now in charge of the vessel wishes to speak to you.'

Everyone in the room expected the next voice they heard to be Nasreen Hassan. That was to be the first of several surprises.

'Good morning, Superintendent. My name is Jamil Chalabi, and let me assure you I have complete control of this vessel. Let me also make it clear from the outset, if you fail to carry out my orders to the letter, I will not hesitate to make your adulterous Princess walk the plank. That may sound overly dramatic, but I have a feeling the event would be peak viewing on every television channel around the world.'

A young secretary seated behind the Prime Minister fainted, and two of her colleagues helped her out of the room. Everyone around the table remained transfixed by the conversation.

'Your silence suggests that I've caught your attention,' said Chalabi. 'So I'll now tell you what will happen next if you hope to see your precious Princess again. First, you will release my leader, Mansour Khalifah, from solitary confinement in Belmarsh and have him transferred to the prison hospital, where I will be calling him in an hour's time. Is that simple enough for you to follow, Superintendent?'

'Yes, it is,' said William, refusing to rise. 'But you have to realize that releasing Mr Khalifah will be a decision for the

Assistant Commissioner of the Metropolitan Police, not for me. And I have no idea where the AC is at the moment.' William glanced across the table at Holbrooke, who gave him a curt nod.

'You have one hour, no more. And I suspect he's sitting in the room with you, so when I phone again, just be sure he's ready to take my call. Should you attempt to double-cross me, the first person to die – well, let me be more accurate, the sixth – will be your colleague, Inspector Hogan, who is listening to this conversation. His will be a special death, which I've given some considerable thought. I've always wanted to know how long someone can survive in the sea without a life jacket. Less than a few hours, would be my bet.' The line went dead.

'I thought you told us that Chalabi was meant to be a society playboy,' snapped the Prime Minister, 'not a ruthless terrorist.'

'There's been nothing until this moment to suggest otherwise,' said Commander Hawksby, coming to William's aid. 'However, I must confess that in the course of his duties as the Princess's personal protection officer, Inspector Hogan has warned me on more than one occasion that Chalabi shouldn't be underestimated, and that he was convinced, and I quote,' he said, looking down at his briefing notes, '"That he's not quite as naïve as he would have us believe."'

'That's for sure,' said the Prime Minister, 'because he's certainly made fools of you lot, and—'

'Was there anything else you learnt from the conversation with Hogan, Superintendent?' asked the Cabinet Secretary, butting in before the PM said something she might later regret.

'His answers to the security questions were actually a way of passing on vital information without arousing Chalabi's suspicions. DI Hogan mentioned the number ten when I asked how many officers I have under my command at Buckingham

Gate. The correct answer is fourteen, so we can assume that ten is the number of terrorists involved in the raid, plus Chalabi, making eleven.'

'So how long does it take on average for an ambulance to reach a traffic accident in London?' asked the Cabinet Secretary.

'About seven to eight minutes,' replied William. 'So I suspect eighteen to twenty knots is the speed the *Lowlander* is currently travelling.'

'And is currently about a thousand miles away from its destination,' suggested the First Sea Lord.

'Clever,' said the Cabinet Secretary. 'But what about the six brothers and four sisters?'

'I also know that Inspector Hogan was an only child,' said William, 'so I suspect the six brothers are active terrorists, while the four sisters are non-combatants. And rod of iron is slang for a Dragunov sniper rifle, which was presumably responsible for the death of the photographer on the beach.'

'And Bill didn't sit easily with the rest of the conversation,' suggested the Cabinet Secretary. 'I have a feeling you're a William, and Inspector Hogan would normally call you "sir".'

'It's an agreed code to let me know that everything he's said can be relied on, and is not being forced out of him at the point of a gun, or worse.'

The First Sea Lord gave William a respectful nod, before saying, 'We have less than an hour before we find out what Chalabi's next demands will be, by which time the SBS transport plane should be on its way to HMS *Cornwall*. You're going to have to buy me some time, Superintendent, because my lads will need total darkness before they attempt to board that yacht, and sunset isn't for another five hours.'

'No pressure,' whispered the Hawk, without any suggestion of irony.

'As I mentioned before,' said the Prime Minister, 'we never negotiate with terrorists. But that needn't stop us coming up with any excuse to keep them talking until the SBS are ready to play their part. With that in mind, Superintendent, if I might give you a word of advice: be sure your phone is fully charged.'

CHAPTER 34

'THANK GOD YOU'RE STILL ALIVE,' were Victoria's first words after the cabin door had been opened and Ross thrown back inside.

'Well, at least for another hour,' said Ross, trying to make light of it.

'What makes you say that?' she asked, anxiously clinging to him.

'I'll tell you later,' he said, although he had no intention of repeating what he'd overheard of the conversation between Chalabi and William. 'Right now, I need to speak to the Princess.'

'She's sitting on the balcony of her cabin, and she's still on the same page of her paperback as she was an hour ago.'

Victoria followed Ross out onto her adjoining balcony, to see the Princess, head down, looking fragile and lost, her usual shy smile replaced by a look of intense foreboding. When she saw the two of them, she leapt up and ran across to their side of the balcony.

'I owe you an apology,' were her first words. Ross didn't comment. 'You never left me in any doubt how you felt about him,' said Diana. 'If only I hadn't ignored your undisguised loathing of the man.'

'You weren't the only one who was fooled, ma'am. But for now, we have to concentrate on the present. So, if I tell either of you to do something, anything, don't even think about questioning me. Is that understood?'

They both nodded obediently, before Diana said, 'I'm just thankful you're still alive.'

'I think you mean surprised, ma'am,' said Ross, once again trying to lighten the mood.

'Did you learn anything from him?' Diana asked, pointing to the upper deck, but no longer able to mention his name.

Ross chose his words carefully. 'Yes, ma'am. He's been in contact with London, who were already aware of the situation, and are now trying to strike a deal to get you released.'

'What kind of deal?' asked Victoria.

'For now, ma'am, I want you to change into your swimsuit and sit on the balcony as if you were still on holiday,' said Ross, making no attempt to answer Victoria's question.

'What about Victoria?' demanded Diana, a little defiance returning.

'My only responsibility is to protect you, ma'am.'

'And Victoria,' said Diana firmly.

'If possible,' said Ross. 'But first I'm going to brief you on what I think is likely to happen during the next few hours, so that at least you'll be prepared.' He avoided saying for the worst, and lowered his voice. 'Have you heard of the SBS?'

'Yes,' said Diana, 'they held a dinner in my honour last year.'

'I don't think that's what they'll be holding in your honour this year,' said Ross.

The governor was pacing up and down outside the prison gates when William's car screeched to a halt. The Home Secretary's phone call had left him in no doubt about what was expected of him.

They didn't bother with any pleasantries. As soon as they'd shaken hands, he led William quickly through the open gate, a senior officer already on the move several yards ahead of them. He unlocked each of the double gates on the way, so their progress to the solitary confinement wing was uninterrupted.

Eventually they descended a narrow stone staircase that led to an underground passageway, where the light bulbs were thirty watts at most, and several of them needed replacing. They came to a halt by a solid metal door, outside which two guards had been posted. William flicked back the shutter to see a man he barely recognized hunched in a corner on a thin, urine-stained mattress in the far corner of the cell.

The duty officer unlocked the heavy door, pulled it open and stood aside to allow the governor and William to enter a space barely six feet square.

Khalifah stared defiantly up at them, but didn't say a word. The two guards lifted him from the mattress and led him slowly out of his windowless dark cell, and back along the passageway until they reached a spiral staircase, which they almost had to carry him up. Their painfully slow journey ended at the hospital wing, where the matron was waiting by a small empty cubicle, clearly expecting them. Khalifah collapsed onto the bed, as two men dressed in white coats appeared and began to carry out a thorough examination.

Khalifah still didn't speak while they prodded and probed,

and it was some time before the older doctor offered an opinion. 'He'll need to eat something substantial and take in lots of fluid before you even think about moving him again. But if I had to guess, I'd say this isn't the first time he's been in solitary, because he's in a lot better shape than I'd expected.'

'Can I ask him some questions?' asked William.

'Go ahead,' said the doctor.

William walked over to the side of the bed and looked down at Khalifah. 'Do you speak English?' he asked, articulating each word slowly.

'I would hope so,' came the reply. 'I was educated at the London School of Economics, one of your cultural outreach programmes that you British are so proud of, although I confess I didn't register under my present name.'

'How much do you know about why I need to speak to you?' asked William.

'As I have been taken out of solitary and am having a hospital check-up, I can only assume that my brothers,' he paused, 'and one particularly formidable sister, have successfully taken over the yacht which the Princess of Wales couldn't resist – or was it Jamil she couldn't resist? He frankly fooled every one of you, including the Princess's devoted lapdog, Inspector Hogan, so even you must realize this isn't going to end like the Albert Hall fiasco. If you ever want to see your future Queen sitting on her throne, Chalabi is about to tell you exactly what you'll have to do to make that possible.'

William remained calm, aware that losing his temper wouldn't achieve anything. 'We're expecting Chalabi to call at any minute, and you'll be allowed to speak to him. But not before Inspector Hogan has confirmed that the Princess is still alive.'

'That's assuming the Inspector is still alive,' said Khalifah, 'because if I know that lot, they will already be drawing lots to decide who will have the pleasure of killing him.'

William didn't react, but he feared the governor might not be able to restrain himself for much longer.

'I also need a bath and my own clothes,' said Khalifah. 'I don't intend to return to my country looking like a fugitive.'

The governor nodded reluctantly, and as he did, the phone by Khalifah's bed began to ring. William grabbed it and said, 'Warwick speaking.'

The next voice he heard may have been coming from under the Mediterranean sun, but it was as cold as an arctic blizzard. 'Good morning, Superintendent. Can I presume that my leader is no longer in solitary confinement, and is ready to take my call?'

'Not until I've spoken to Inspector Hogan,' said William, not sure what he would do if Chalabi refused. A long silence followed.

'It's Hogan, sir,' said the next voice on the line.

'Can you confirm that Her Royal Highness is still alive and well?' asked William.

'I can, Bill.'

'And Lady Victoria?'

'Shit-scared, to quote her,' said Ross. 'They're both outside on the balcony, sitting in the sun.'

'Satisfied, Superintendent?' asked Chalabi, after he'd snatched back the phone.

'Yes,' said William, who'd picked up two vital pieces of information that he would pass on to the Assistant Commissioner at the first opportunity.

'Then put me through to my leader immediately, or you'll have spoken to your friend Hogan for the last time.'

William reluctantly handed the phone to Khalifah, and although he couldn't understand a word of the conversation that followed, the name Diana occurred several times. After a few minutes Khalifah passed the phone back to William.

'Now listen carefully, Superintendent,' said Chalabi, 'because I'm going to say this once and once only. In a couple of hours' time, I will be phoning you again, and by then you will have arranged for a car to take His Excellency Mansour Khalifah to Heathrow, where he will board his private jet ready to take off for Libya. Do I make myself clear?'

'Two hours may not be enough time to find a car and get him to the airport,' protested William.

'Come, come,' said Chalabi. 'If you can't, I will have to execute one of my prisoners on the hour every hour. I'm sure Lady Victoria, like her ancestors before her, will set a good example. It shouldn't be difficult for you to work out who will follow her, if you make one false move.'

'But . . .' began William.

'There will be no buts, Superintendent. That is if you're hoping to see the Princess alive again. As you now have only one hour and fifty-eight minutes, I won't waste any more of your precious time.'

William had his next sentence prepared, only to find he'd already been cut off. Khalifah, who appeared to have made a remarkable recovery, gave him a condescending smile.

'I won't hold you up, dear boy,' said Khalifah in an exaggerated public-school accent, 'unless the governor wants to hang about and kiss my arse . . .'

The governor took a pace forward, but William threw out an arm, blocked his path and quietly led him out into the corridor, accompanied by a regal wave of the hand from Khalifah.

'I'd be happy to serve a life sentence for killing that man,' muttered the governor as the door slammed behind them.

'Let's hope it doesn't come to that,' said William.

The governor paused for a moment before saying, 'I owe you an apology, William, because I can't begin to imagine what else you know, and can't share with me,' he said as the younger of the two doctors came out of the hospital wing and joined them in the corridor.

'I told him I needed to take a leak,' said the young doctor, 'so this will have to be quick.'

'I don't think you know Dr Harrison, governor,' said William. 'We were on the same track team at London University, although he was a long-distance man.'

'Where I studied Middle Eastern languages, not medicine,' confessed Harrison as he shook hands with the governor. 'So I'm a PhD, not an MD.'

'What did Khalifah have to say for himself?' asked William, not wanting to waste any more time.

'I could only hear his side of the conversation,' said Harrison, 'but he made it clear that DI Hogan should be thrown over-board the moment his plane had taken off from Heathrow, and that once the yacht reaches Libyan territorial waters, someone called Victoria will suffer the same fate.'

'And the Princess?' asked William.

'They have no intention of letting her go, even if Mansour Khalifah is released.'

'Then what else do they have planned?' asked the governor.

Harrison hesitated.

'Get on with it, man,' said the governor.

'She'll be paraded through the streets of Tripoli on the way to Martyrs' Square, where she'll be beheaded. They've even chosen the person who will carry out the execution.'

'Nasreen Hassan, no doubt,' said William as he checked his watch. 'Which means I've now only got one hour and forty-nine minutes before . . .'

• • •

The C-130 carrying the elite SBS team flew over HMS *Cornwall* just after six thirty p.m., to be greeted by three flashes from a signal lamp. The pilot swung around and circled the vessel. The *Cornwall's* captain watched from the bridge as the rear door of the C-130 slowly opened, and three rigid inflatable boats appeared and parachuted slowly down to the sea. The plane circled the *Cornwall* once again, before returning to discharge its remaining human cargo.

The first to make the jump was Captain Mike Davenport, not a man who liked bringing up the rear. Once his parachute had opened, the rest of his men followed in quick succession, dropping into the waves just as the brigadier had predicted, as easily as children jumping into a swimming pool.

The moment they hit the water, they discarded their parachutes and swam to the nearest boat. Once they had all clambered aboard they headed for the *Cornwall*.

Davenport nipped up the rope ladder that was hanging over the ship's side. He stepped onto the deck to be greeted by an ensign before being escorted to the bridge, where the captain was waiting for him. They spent the next hour going over his plan in great detail, including the role those selected for the advance party would need to perform if the outcome was to be a success.

After the briefing, Davenport joined his men and ordered them to rest, not their favourite occupation. But as he reminded them, waiting is always the worst part of any mission, so they should try to get some sleep, as they couldn't begin Operation 'Overboard' until the sun had disappeared below the horizon. He was well aware that none of them would have a moment's sleep, himself included.

• • •

William phoned Holbrooke from the governor's office, to be told he was at Number 10 briefing the Prime Minister with the news that the SBS team were now all aboard the *Cornwall*, waiting impatiently for the sun to set. Something even the Prime Minister had no control over.

William's next call was put through to Holbrooke in the PM's office, when he spelt out in great detail not only what Chalabi expected him to do, but also that Diana was definitely alive and well and, equally important, was on her balcony on the starboard side.

'How can you be sure their cabins are on the starboard side?' demanded Holbrooke.

'There's no way Lady Victoria would ever use the term "shit-scared", even if she felt it.' William went on to warn the Assistant Commissioner what Khalifah had in mind for the Princess when they reached Libya, even if they did go along with his demands. 'He'll be calling back in forty-one minutes,' said William, checking his watch, 'when he'll be expecting me to confirm that Khalifah is on his way to Heathrow. If he isn't, I'm in no doubt he'll carry out his threat to kill Ross or Victoria, or both.'

'I'm sure you're right,' said Holbrooke, 'because, like us, he'll be working to a strict timetable. I'll tell you exactly what I want you to say when he phones back, but never forget that your first priority is to buy me as much time as possible. The SBS can't make a move until after sunset, 20.43 local time, which isn't' – he checked his watch – 'for another two hours and nineteen minutes.'

William listened carefully as Holbrooke spelt out in detail the message he expected him to deliver to Chalabi, because he knew he wasn't a man who repeated himself.

'The First Sea Lord's on line one,' said an urgent-sounding voice in the background.

'I'll be with him in a moment,' said Holbrooke. 'Your single purpose, Warwick, is to buy me time,' were the last words William heard before the line went dead.

William made four separate calls during the next thirty minutes. The first was to the Hawk at the Yard, who assured him that three cars would be waiting outside the prison to take him and Khalifah to Heathrow, well before the hour was up. Almost as if command had changed hands. He next called Paul, followed by Rebecca and, finally, Danny, to brief them on the roles they would play during the next two hours.

He barely had enough time to get back to the hospital wing, making it with only minutes to spare. He hardly recognized Khalifah, who was now dressed in a thawb and keffiyeh, and looking more like an Arab potentate than someone who'd just emerged from solitary.

'You're only just in time to prevent the next execution,' said Khalifah as William rushed into the room. 'I presume you have a car on standby, because I know Chalabi is looking for any excuse to sacrifice Inspector Hogan, who for some inexplicable reason seems to irritate him.'

The phone rang. William didn't need to ask who it was on the other end of the line.

'I presume you've spoken to Holbrooke and arranged everything?' was Chalabi's opening statement.

'Yes. A car will be outside the prison in a few minutes' time ready to take Khalifah—'

'His Excellency Mansour Khalifah,' corrected Chalabi. 'Yours isn't the only royal family.'

'—Khalifah to Heathrow,' said William.

'Where I assume his private jet will be waiting to fly him back to his homeland.'

'That's not going to be quite so easy,' said William defiantly. 'The plane hasn't been serviced for over three months and, although the engineers are working flat out, it could be some time before the airport authorities will allow it to take off. Unless, of course, you're willing to risk your leader's life?' he added, taking a calculated risk.

For the first time, Chalabi didn't respond immediately.

William took advantage of the silence. 'Once the safety regulations have been carried out, the plane will be refuelled. But we still face the problem of finding a crew who are willing to fly him to Libya. It's not what one might call a destination of choice.'

'Stop bluffing, Warwick,' said Chalabi. 'I'll call again in an hour's time, when I expect . . .'

'I'll need at least four hours before I can be sure everything's in place.'

'I'll give you two, not a minute more. Should His Excellency fail to pick up the phone when I call his private plane in exactly two hours' time, the executions will begin. I'll even allow you to listen to Lady Victoria's final words before she joins Inspector Hogan in the deep.'

The line went dead. William had bought Holbrooke an extra hour, but would it be enough?

CHAPTER 35

IT WAS STILL BROAD DAYLIGHT when six officers and two dozen hand-picked ratings cast off from the *Cornwall* in six boats, an hour before the main party were due to depart. Captain Davenport had emphasized during his final briefing that although theirs was a secondary role, it was no less vital if Operation Overboard were to succeed.

An SBS party of fourteen would set off in their RIBs an hour later, and the last to leave would be Davenport and six of his most seasoned operatives in the two helicopters. They would have to time their departure to the minute if they were to take advantage of their most powerful weapon – surprise.

• • •

Three unmarked, identical cars stood in line outside the prison gates. Mansour Khalifah sat in the back of the second car. William was in the front passenger seat of the lead vehicle. Beside him, Danny was waiting impatiently for the order to move. They had to be there in an hour and fifty-one minutes, when Chalabi would call the phone on Khalifah's jet and expect it to be answered by his master.

Remembering Holbrooke's words – 'Your single purpose, Warwick, is to buy me time' – William didn't want to get there any earlier than necessary, but couldn't risk being late.

'What's the longest it's ever taken you to get to Heathrow?' he asked Danny.

'I once took an hour and a half, guv, but only because there was an accident on the motorway.'

'Accident or no accident, if you can break that record, I'll double your overtime.'

'It's getting close to rush hour,' said Danny innocently, 'so we're bound to be held up. And I'll let you into a little secret. The slowest lane out of London before you reach the motorway is always the centre lane, unless you're approaching a round-about, when it's the outside lane.'

A man who normally thought nothing of taking corners at seventy, ignoring red lights or mounting a pavement during a chase, eased the gear lever into first and made his way into the centre lane. He slowed down as he approached the first traffic light and, when it turned amber, he gently touched the brakes. The black cortège made its way towards Heathrow at a funereal pace.

• • •

Three RIBs bobbed up and down in the water, waiting for the command to GO.

Davenport checked his watch once again, well aware that sending them off even a minute too early or too late could endanger the whole operation.

At last he slowly raised an arm in the air, as if he were a steward at the start of the university boat race. He waited until he had the attention of all three boat leaders before he brought it firmly down to indicate the off.

The three RIBs began to plough through the waves. The crews of two of them would attempt to board the yacht on the starboard side, seconds after the first helicopter appeared above its stern. The men on the third would have to wait, as they had the most demanding assignment of all, which was why they'd named their skipper 'The Royal Gillie'.

• • •

When Danny finally reached the airport an hour and forty-two minutes later, he took his time locating Khalifah's plane, despite it being surrounded by a dozen police cars, their lights flashing, with DS Adaja standing on the tarmac, clearly in command, which should have given him a clue.

Once they'd come to a halt, Khalifah remained in the back of his car until the door was opened for him. He stepped out onto the tarmac and said, 'You couldn't have taken much longer, Superintendent. For Lady Victoria's sake, let's hope Chalabi hasn't already tried to get in touch with me.'

William knew he still had nine minutes left before Chalabi was due to call, and didn't comment. He accompanied Khalifah across the runway to his waiting jet. He remained at the bottom of the steps while Khalifah entered the plane, feeling helpless as the door slammed in his face.

Khalifah sank into the large comfortable leather seat and checked his watch. They had used up almost every minute of their two hours.

'When will we be taking off?' he asked the stewardess as she poured him a glass of water.

'They're just finishing refuelling, sir, so it shouldn't be too much longer,' she said as the phone in his armrest began to ring.

• • •

The moment the three RIBs were out of sight, Captain Davenport turned and strode towards the helicopter deck, where the two pilots were carrying out their final checks before take-off. His men were pacing up and down like nervous boxers who, having put the gloves on, couldn't wait to climb into the ring.

Davenport had already been informed that HMS *Ursula* was patrolling somewhere below the *Lowlander*, ready to release a torpedo and blow it out of the water if the mission failed. He tried not to think about it.

Davenport was the last man to climb aboard the lead helicopter, and would be the first out. Once he'd strapped himself into his seat, he waited for the second hand on his stopwatch to go twice more around the dial, before tapping the pilot firmly on the shoulder.

The rotor blades revolved faster and faster, until finally the first helicopter slowly lifted off the deck, producing a gush of wind and salt spray that had the maintenance staff shielding their eyes.

The second helicopter followed moments later, and although they would never be more than a hundred metres apart, once they reached the target area they would peel off and go their separate ways.

'Ten minutes,' said Davenport, breaking radio silence.

'Can you make that eleven, sir?' came back the response from the leader of the RIBs.

'Wilco.'

As they approached the yacht, the sky grew darker, until the sun finally disappeared below the horizon.

• • •

If the phone on the jet wasn't answered, Chalabi had already decided who would die first. If it was picked up and his leader confirmed that he was about to take off, and looking forward to a hero's welcome in Tripoli, then all that was left for him to do was carry out the 'end game'.

Hassan had been chosen to hack off an arm and a leg of the so-called protection officer before he was cast into the waves. She had promised Chalabi that the lady-in-waiting would live long enough to see her lover and join him in the water, so they could share their last few touching moments together. Hassan was looking forward to seeing which of them would drown first. Chalabi intended to make a video of their death throes, so he could enjoy pressing the replay button again and again. Once they were back in Libya, it would be repeated endlessly on Al Jamahiriya television, so the whole world could witness his achievement. A hero in his own country, a villain to the rest of the world. What more could a man ask for?

Khalifah picked up the phone on the fifty-ninth second of the fifty-ninth minute of the second hour, to hear the words, 'Allah be praised.'

'Allah be praised,' repeated Khalifah, and put the phone down, feeling exhilarated but exhausted. Exhaustion won, and he fell into a deep sleep as the plane took off and the twinkling lights of Heathrow disappeared behind him.

'Allah be praised,' repeated Chalabi as he withdrew a pistol from his holster. He was about to give the order for Inspector Hogan to be brought up on deck so he could personally carry out the execution, when he was distracted by gunfire coming from above. He dropped the phone, fell to his knees and stared up into the sky to see a helicopter hovering above the stern of the yacht. When he looked back down he could see an armada of small boats heading towards them at speed.

Hassan's men were returning fire, but Chalabi knew it could be only a matter of time before they were overwhelmed, leaving him with just one chance of saving his own skin. He turned his back on his colleagues and began crawling towards the spiral staircase that led down to the lower deck, only to see a second helicopter hovering above the yacht's bow. A thick rope was now dangling from the second helicopter, and a man was fast-roping down towards the deck, another following close behind. Chalabi had reached the bottom of the staircase before Davenport hit the ground running.

The moment he heard the first shot ring out, Ross leapt across from one balcony to the other to join the Princess and Victoria. The SBS men on the first of the RIBs had already fixed a ladder to the yacht's side and he and his men were clambering up onto the deck, almost as fast as their comrades in the helicopters were coming down, while the *Cornwall's* diversionary force had reached the stern of the yacht. Ross knew the battle that followed would be over in minutes. But not for Jamil Chalabi, who was charging down the long corridor towards the royal suite.

As Chalabi burst through the door, Ross scooped the Princess in his arms, dashed out onto the balcony and threw her overboard. Within seconds, the third RIB was by her side and the

Royal Gillie leant over and dragged her unceremoniously out of the water. Once he'd seen her clamber on board, Ross grabbed a pistol he'd secreted under the balcony railing before running back into the suite. He threw himself to the floor and fired three times at Chalabi, who didn't move, making him an easy target. Instead of the explosion of gunfire Ross had anticipated, all he heard was three clicks. A self-satisfied smile appeared on Chalabi's face.

'You underestimated me once again, Detective Inspector,' he said as he slowly raised his gun, looked him in the eyes and took aim. He was about to fire when a hand grabbed his ponytail, causing him to topple back and fire a shot into the ceiling.

He was recovering his balance when he felt something sharp pierce the side of his neck. A silver letter opener slit his throat from ear to ear with practised efficiency. He collapsed onto the floor, blood spurting from every vessel in his neck. Chalabi lay at Victoria's feet, staring up at the lady-in-waiting.

'You underestimated me,' said Victoria, giving him a warm smile as he gasped his last breath.

Moments later, Captain Davenport burst into the cabin. He stared down at Chalabi's lifeless body in disbelief before saying, 'Did you do that, miss?'

'Yes,' said Victoria calmly as she took a tissue out of its box, wiped the silver letter opener clean, and placed it back on the table next to a pile of unopened letters.

'Have you ever considered joining the SBS?' Davenport asked.

'Certainly not. The Girl Guides were quite enough.'

• • •

The stewardess let him sleep for an hour before she woke him. 'We're just about to land, sir,' she said. 'I hope you had a comfortable flight.'

Mansour Khalifah didn't comment, as his mind was on greater things.

She gently lowered his armrest and helped him on with his seatbelt. He sat motionless, deep in thought as he went over the speech he'd prepared during those long days in solitary confinement. He even practised a wave to the crowd as the plane touched down and bounced along the runway. He wondered if the Colonel himself might be waiting on the runway to greet him.

After the plane had come to a halt, the stewardess opened the cabin door and stood to one side. Khalifah rose from his seat, straightened his long white thawb, adjusted his keffiyeh, and began to walk slowly down the aisle.

The captain came out of the cockpit, saluted and said, 'Welcome home, sir.'

A look of triumph appeared on Khalifah's face as he stepped through the doorway to face the flashbulbs and the cheers of the waiting crowd. He raised a hand in acknowledgement – but there were no flashbulbs and no one was cheering. He looked down and it certainly wasn't Colonel Gaddafi standing at the bottom of the steps waiting to greet him.

He quickly turned back towards the cabin, only for a high-heeled shoe to be planted firmly in the middle of his chest. Rebecca smiled as Khalifah toppled backwards down the steps and into the arms of the head of Royalty Protection.

Danny drove him back to Belmarsh in record time. The governor was waiting at the gates to welcome them.

• • •

Captain Davenport was disappointed that one of his men had been wounded during the skirmish – which was how he described the twelve-minute battle to the Prime Minister. Later that evening, the injury had been sustained by a young corporal who had been shot in the foot by a bullet that had inexplicably come from the deck below.

The eleven terrorists had already been buried at sea, as if the incident had never taken place. Victoria's nanny would have advised her, had the subject ever arisen, 'Least said, soonest mended.'

The *Lowlander* was all 'shipshape and Bristol fashion' by the time she sailed back to Mallorca, where Davenport handed the keys back to the charter company. Twenty men, who certainly hadn't been on board when she sailed out of that picturesque bay a few days earlier, made their way back to London on separate flights, before taking the train to SBS headquarters at Poole, to prepare for their next skirmish.

• • •

Ross was helicoptered to HMS *Cornwall* at first light the following morning, only to be told when he arrived on board that the Princess and Lady Victoria were having breakfast in the officers' mess with the captain.

When four bells rang out, the ship's company assembled on deck in full dress uniform to welcome their royal visitor. The Princess spent the rest of the morning being shown around the carrier, while thanking the crew for the vital job they were doing for Queen and country. After lunch with the ship's full complement of officers, she was helicoptered to Valetta, from where she would take a flight to Scotland.

The cheers and throwing of caps into the air that

357

accompanied her departure rather suggested that this myth would become legend, as the SBS were nowhere to be seen, and HMS *Cornwall* wouldn't be returning to Portsmouth for another couple of months.

Ross accompanied the Princess and Victoria on the flight to Balmoral, where his royal charge was due to attend the Highland Games the following day.

Ross was hoping to have a few moments alone with Victoria, but the opportunity didn't arise, because royal protocol dictated that he slept in the bothy on the Balmoral estate, while she remained in the castle. Lying in bed on his own only reminded him how close he and Victoria had become, the only woman he'd taken any interest in since the death of his wife. Perhaps the time had come to tell her how he felt. He fell asleep.

· · ·

The following morning, Victoria joined the Royal Family for breakfast in the dining room, while Ross went downstairs to the steward's quarters where he enjoyed the same breakfast with the household staff.

As he sat down to a bowl of piping hot porridge sprinkled with salt and honey, he glanced at the headline in the *Daily Telegraph* before it was ironed by the butler and taken upstairs on a silver tray. '*The Princess of Wales interrupts her holiday in Scotland to pay a surprise visit to HMS* Cornwall.'

Victoria had once told him that Lord Deedes, a former editor of the *Telegraph* and a privy councillor, could always be relied on when offered a front page 'exclusive' for the paper's first edition, confident it would make the second edition in every other paper, along with the grateful thanks of the royal household.

Only the *Daily Mail* stuck with its original banner headline reporting that its star royal photographer had mysteriously disappeared while on holiday in Mallorca. But as he wasn't their photographer, no other paper bothered to follow up the story. The Palace already had the words 'conspiracy theory' ready in case it got out of hand.

· · ·

Ross sat in the front seat of the Jaguar as the Princess and Victoria were driven to the Highland Games later that morning.

Once they'd arrived, he stood at the back of the royal box while Prince Charles and the Princess were driven around the track in an open Land Rover, returning the waves of an adoring crowd.

Ross enjoyed watching the Highland dancers as they performed the 'Dashing White Sergeant' reel, accompanied by the bagpipers of the band of the Scots Guards. He marvelled at the strength of the huge, brawny brutes who were trying to toss the caber, and at the six rather more lithe athletes who took part in the hundred yards dash, as they came sprinting down the grass track; the winner reaching the tape in under ten seconds. From time to time, Victoria glanced back and gave him a warm smile.

Ross was delighted when during tea Victoria broke away from the royal party to join him at the back of the box. He was about to ask her when she would be returning to London when one of the guests, dressed in a smart Lovat jacket and a kilt of blue and green tartan, strolled across to join them.

Ross had checked the guest list and the accompanying

photographs over breakfast, so he knew the gentleman was Sir Hamish McTaggart, chairman of Aberdeen Oil, one of Scotland's largest energy companies.

'Hamish,' Victoria said as he joined them, 'this is Inspector Ross Hogan, who's the Princess's personal protection officer.'

'Good to meet you, Hogan,' said McTaggart as they shook hands.

'Hamish,' said Victoria, linking arms with him, 'is my fiancé.'

It was some time before Ross managed, 'Congratulations.'

'Thank you, Inspector,' said McTaggart. 'Will you be spending the rest of the weekend with us?'

'No, sir. I return to London this evening, when one of my Scottish colleagues will take over.'

'That's a pity,' said McTaggart. 'You'll miss the highlight of the games. The tug of war between the Scots and a visiting team from England.'

'I think I already know who's won that battle,' said the visitor from England.

CHAPTER 36

'WHENEVER YOU'RE DRESSED UP LIKE a matinée idol,' said Beth, 'you're either off to court or seeing your father.'

'Both,' said William as she straightened his tie.

'Who's in the dock?'

'Miles Faulkner. He's about to find out how many more years he's going to have to spend in jail.'

'I know your team run a book on the outcome of any trial they're involved in. So when do you think he'll be released – 2003? 2004? 2005?'

'That will depend on how he pleads.'

'But even if he pleads guilty,' said Beth, 'he escaped from custody, faked his own death and went on the run. Surely the judge will have to take that into consideration.'

'True. But if the jury decide he was unlawfully abducted from his home in Spain, and taken to England against his will without an extradition order, it could be me who ends up in the dock.'

'I promise to visit you in jail,' said Beth. 'From time to time, as I'm rather busy at the moment.'

'It's no laughing matter,' said William. 'Booth Watson will also claim that I removed a valuable painting from Faulkner's house in Spain without his permission, brought it back to London and gave it to you.'

'Loaned it to me,' said Beth defiantly. 'I can prove I'd already agreed with Booth Watson to return it the day the Hals exhibition closes, which I did, meaning you only borrowed the painting and had every intention of returning it to its rightful owner.'

'But who is the rightful owner?' asked William.

'Christina. And she's already agreed that the Fitzmolean can add it to their permanent collection.'

'I suspect Booth Watson will dispute that,' said William, 'and claim that it belongs to his client.'

'Which at least proves you never intended to steal the portrait in the first place.'

'A nice point of law,' said William, 'as I'm sure my father would eloquently opine in my defence. But the judge might not agree with him, and you can be certain Booth Watson will keep reminding the jury, not to mention the press, that prosecuting counsel is my father, and perhaps the wrong man's in the dock.'

'That would be a pity,' said Beth, 'because I was looking forward to celebrating our wedding anniversary at Lucio's this evening and it might not be quite as easy to book a table at Belmarsh.'

• • •

'Where are you off to, my darling?' asked Sebastian as he helped Christina on with her coat.

'The theatre.'

'At nine o'clock in the morning?'

She laughed as Sebastian opened the front door of her apartment.

'The curtain rises at the Old Bailey at ten, but I'll be taking my seat in the stalls long before then.'

As they walked towards the lift, Christina added, 'The judge on this occasion will be played by Mr Justice Sedgwick, who will have to decide the fate of the lead actor, Mr Miles Faulkner. My ex may well be giving his farewell performance in front of an audience of twelve members of the public who hopefully, when the foreman is asked to deliver their verdict, will only utter one word.'

'But if Miles pleads guilty,' said Sebastian as they stepped into the lift, 'there'll be no need for a jury.'

'Not Miles's style,' replied Christina as they stepped out onto the ground floor. 'He'd rather go down all guns blazing than admit defeat. In fact, I have to confess I almost feel sorry for him.'

'I can't think why,' said Sebastian. 'After all, he tricked you out of your half of his art collection and then stole the ten million he paid you for it. Ten million that would have kept us in champagne and caviar for the rest of our lives.'

'Don't forget that Miles could be spending the rest of his life in a confined space with only bread and water to sustain him, while I'll still have the apartment and an income of two thousand alimony a week, as well as the occasional bonus from my partnership with Beth Warwick,' said Christina as they left the building and her chauffeur pulled up outside the front door. 'So you don't have anything to complain about.'

As the Mercedes moved off, she waved goodbye to Sebastian, having finally decided that he'd passed his sell-by date.

• • •

'Your usual, sir?' asked the head waiter as Booth Watson handed him back the menu.

'No. As I won't have time for lunch, I think I'll order the full English breakfast.'

The waiter gave him a slight bow.

Booth Watson settled back to read *The Times* as another waiter poured him a cup of steaming black coffee. His eyes settled on an article informing its readers that the Crown v Miles Faulkner would open in court number one at the Old Bailey that morning. He was pleased that Mr Justice Sedgwick had been chosen to preside over the case, as he was not a man who believed in clemency. Booth Watson was quietly confident that his client would be spending several more years in prison, which would look like a triumph for Sir Julian, as he himself would graciously acknowledge before telling his old rival that he'd decided enough was enough, and the time had come for him to take off his wig, hang up his gown and settle down in the country. He just wouldn't tell him which country.

Once his client had been safely shipped back to Belmarsh, Booth Watson would carry out his well-planned exit strategy. First, he would contact Art Removals Ltd and instruct them to go to Gatwick Storage, pack up Miles's art collection and ship it to Hong Kong. He would tell them he was in no particular hurry, as he had other matters to deal with before he left the country. Not least, he would need to make several visits to Miles's bank in Mayfair, as his Gladstone bag could only hold £100,000 at a time. So it would take a little time for him to remove the final ten million from the safe-deposit box. Perhaps he would have to take two Gladstone bags in future.

As Miles had stolen the money from his ex-wife, who in Booth Watson's opinion had more than enough to live on, he felt able to justify the transfer from one account to another, without losing any sleep. By the time he'd removed the last fifty-pound note, he would turn his attention to Miles's art collection – about to become *his* art collection – which should by then have been shipped to Kowloon, where Mr Lee would be free to inspect it at his leisure, before transferring a further hundred million dollars to another bank account that Booth Watson had recently opened.

Once the transaction had been completed, he would fly out to Hong Kong, before continuing a long, circuitous journey that would end up in Seattle. He'd already placed a large deposit on a magnificent penthouse apartment with a view over Puget Sound, and intended to complete the transaction once the judge had passed sentence.

Booth Watson had recently acquired a new identity, complete with a false passport, and had opened several bank accounts around the world. Amazing what Miles had taught him over the years.

'Take the prisoner down,' he mumbled as a plate of eggs, bacon, mushrooms and beans was placed in front of him.

BW picked up his knife and fork, ready for the attack.

•   •   •

Tulip put down his plastic fork.

'Will you be pleading guilty or not guilty?' he asked as Miles took a seat on the other side of the table.

Faulkner had been driven back to Belmarsh from HMP Ford to spend the night in London before his trial opened at the Old Bailey. The morning hadn't begun well, as he'd been told to join the end of the queue for breakfast, only to discover that his usual table was already occupied.

He thought about Tulip's question. 'I still haven't made up my mind. I can't decide who I distrust more, Booth Watson or Superintendent Warwick.'

'They're as bad as each other,' said Tulip, mopping up the remains of his baked beans with a slice of stale bread. 'So you'll just have to choose between the lesser of two evils.'

'You're a lot of help,' said Miles.

A warder he didn't recognize approached him, placed a hand firmly on his shoulder and said, 'Let's be havin' you, Faulkner. Wouldn't want to keep the judge waiting, would we?'

He pushed his untouched breakfast to one side, and wasn't surprised to see Tulip grab it. He made his way back to his cell, where he took his time dressing for the occasion: a smart navy blue suit that hadn't been worn for nearly a year, a freshly ironed shirt and an Old Harrovian tie that made him look more like a company director than a man who could be spending the next decade in jail.

He was checking his tie in the small steel mirror screwed to the wall when two guards marched into his cell, thrust his arms behind his back and handcuffed him. They clearly didn't know who he was. They led him down a green brick corridor, passing through several security gates before eventually emerging into a deserted courtyard and the cold light of day. The final gate to be opened would be a wooden one which led to the outside world.

'Look forward to seeing you this evening, Faulkner,' said one of the warders, unhelpfully, as they handed him over to three large policemen who looked as if they hoped he would try to escape.

They bundled the prisoner towards a waiting car, his feet hardly touching the ground, before they shoved him onto the back seat. A muscle-bound officer sat on either side of him, while the third took the front passenger seat. The doors automatically locked before the car set off, and two motorcycle outriders made sure there would be no unnecessary stops on the way to the Bailey. They weren't taking any chances this time.

Miles sat silently in the back seat throughout the journey, still contemplating how he would plead. He was no nearer to making a decision by the time the little motorcade drove through the prisoners' entrance to the Bailey and parked in the back yard.

Another three policemen were waiting to accompany him to a small, dimly lit cell in the basement, and there was no suggestion that his handcuffs would be removed. After they'd slammed the door behind him, he sat bolt upright on the end of the narrow bed, not wanting to lie down for fear of creasing his suit. The only reading matter was messages daubed on the wall by previous occupants: *The fuzz stitched me up*; *I'm innocent* . . . He'd had even more time to consider his plea when the heavy door finally opened, his handcuffs were removed, and he was led up a flight of stone steps into the dock.

He sat down on a rickety wooden chair flanked on either side by an armed guard as they all waited for the judge to make his entrance.

Booth Watson was sitting in his usual place on the counsels' bench, checking his opening remarks, while Sir Julian Warwick leant back, arms folded, consulting his junior. Miles glanced to his left and noticed Christina sitting alone at the back of the court, clearly hoping this would be the last time she would ever see him. All she lacked was a pair of knitting needles while she waited for the guillotine to drop.

He switched his attention to the other side of the court, where Commander Hawksby was sitting next to Superintendent Warwick. Miles thought Warwick looked nervous, no doubt wondering how he would plead. He wouldn't have to wait much longer to find out.

A clock struck the hour and, on the tenth chime, a door opened at the back of the court and Mr Justice Sedgwick appeared in a long red gown and a grey wig. Everyone in the court stood and bowed to His Lordship, a referee none of the players would have considered arguing with for fear of being sent off. He returned the compliment before placing a red folder on the bench in front of him, and taking his place in a high-backed leather chair. Once settled, he rearranged his gown and, looking down from on high, acknowledged first Sir Julian and then Mr Booth Watson, before nodding to the clerk of the court to confirm that proceedings could begin.

The clerk was dressed in a black gown, which gave him the air of a Victorian schoolmaster. He rose from his place and walked slowly across the court to carry out his most important duty of the day.

Coming to a halt in front of the dock, he said in a stentorian voice that echoed around the chamber, 'Will the prisoner please stand.'

Miles rose to his feet, but his legs were so shaky he had to grip the railing in front of him. Once he'd steadied himself, the clerk continued. 'Mr Miles Faulkner, you are charged with absconding from prison, illegally leaving the country under a false name, using a forged passport and faking your own death. How do you plead? Guilty, or not guilty?'

Everyone in the court was looking at the defendant, with

the exception of Booth Watson, who stared straight ahead of him. It was that single gesture that caused Miles to change his mind once again. He looked directly up at the judge and said, 'Guilty.'

Sir Julian thought he heard a sigh of relief coming from the other end of the bench, but it was drowned out by the uproar that followed, while several journalists rushed out of the court-room and headed for the nearest phone.

The judge waited for the clamour to die down before he opened the folder in front of him and considered the written statement he had completed only moments before entering the court. Earlier that morning he had been advised by the Director of Public Prosecutions that if the defendant pleaded not guilty, and the jury decided otherwise, he should follow the recommended procedure and double the defendant's previous sentence. That decision had now been taken out of his hands.

'I have given considerable thought to the sentence I am about to impose,' he began, looking directly at the accused.

Miles wondered if it was too late to change his plea, while Booth Watson allowed the hint of a smile to cross his lips.

'I have taken into consideration,' continued the judge, 'the facts that not only have you pleaded guilty, thus saving the court considerable time and expense, but even more impor-tantly, that after you escaped from prison you returned to England of your own free will, gave yourself up to the author-ities, and loaned a valuable painting to the Fitzmolean Museum, which I understand you have since agreed can be added to its permanent collection.'

Miles didn't react, while Booth Watson looked surprised. Christina simply smiled and nodded.

The judge paused and turned a page before proceeding. 'Recently, other matters have been brought to my attention that I was unaware of until I received a visit from the Attorney General. Following that meeting, I am persuaded there are substantial mitigating circumstances that will have some bearing on the length of your sentence. However, it would not be appropriate for me to mention those circumstances in open court. For that reason, I shall now invite the clerk to clear the court of anyone not directly involved in this case.'

It was some time before the jury, a few disgruntled members of the press, and those seated in the public gallery had all made their way reluctantly out of the court, some of them unable to hide their disappointment.

The judge did not speak again until the clerk had locked the door to court number one, and bowed to His Lordship to indicate that he could proceed with his judgment.

'I have also taken into consideration,' continued the judge, 'the commendable role you played in assisting the police in preventing a terrorist attack, which undoubtedly resulted in several lives being saved, while at the same time putting your own life in danger.

'Your precipitous actions also resulted in the police being able to prevent a further crime of national importance which could have caused considerable embarrassment for the government as well as the Metropolitan Police. Thanks to that intervention, the criminals involved are now in police custody. With that in mind, I will be imposing a sentence of eight more years' – Faulkner was about to protest until he heard the words – 'but, given the circumstances, that term will be suspended. However, should you be foolish enough to reoffend during that time, those eight years will be added to any further sentence, with no remission. Do I make myself clear?' the judge added, looking directly at the prisoner.

'Yes, m'Lud,' replied Faulkner, his legs suddenly steady.

The judge paused and turned another page of his red folder. 'The prison authorities have also brought to my attention your exemplary behaviour while in custody at Belmarsh, and more recently at Ford open prison, where you carried out the role of prison librarian.' William allowed himself a smile. 'Therefore, your original sentence will be halved, so you can expect to be released in three months' time.'

Christina leapt up from her place at the back of the court and headed for the exit, aware she had only a few weeks before Miles could seek revenge.

'I'm sorry, madam,' said the clerk, barring her path, 'but I am not permitted to unlock the door until His Lordship has completed his judgment.'

'Sir Julian,' said the judge, looking down at the prosecution counsel. 'I would fully understand if you felt it necessary to lodge an appeal against my judgment on behalf of the Crown.'

To the judge's surprise, Sir Julian rose slowly from his place, bowed, and said, 'I accept your judgment, m'Lud, without question.'

'I am grateful, Sir Julian,' said the judge, before turning his attention to an ashen-faced Booth Watson, who looked as if he did want to appeal against His Lordship's judgment, and would have done so had he not been counsel for the defence.

Booth Watson also accepted he only had a couple of months to remove the rest of his client's money from the safe-deposit boxes and have his art collection transported to Hong Kong before Miles was released. With that in mind, he turned and offered his client a congratulatory smile, accompanied by a thumbs up. After all, hadn't he promised Miles that if he pleaded guilty, he would be released by Christmas? Though he still had every intention of celebrating the new year in his recently acquired apartment in Seattle.

As the two guards led the prisoner out of the dock, he stared down at Booth Watson, gave him a warm smile and shook his head.

CHAPTER 37

'FOR YOU, MADAM,' SAID LUCIO, 'may I suggest the sole meunière, lightly fried in butter and served on a bed of portobello mushrooms, with just a hint of lemon sauce?'

'Sounds perfect,' said Beth as she handed back the menu.

'And perhaps to complement it, a glass of chilled Pouilly-Fumé?'

'An excellent choice.'

'How about me?' said William.

'For you, sir, fish and chips with mushy peas, and more than a hint of vinegar and tomato ketchup?'

'Served on a bed of—'

'The *News of the World*.'

'And complemented by?'

'A pint of warm beer.'

'Couldn't be better,' said William, looking pleased with himself.

'You have to understand Lucio, that he's a caveman,' said Beth, taking William's hand. 'His only virtue being that he's *my* caveman.'

Lucio uncorked a bottle of champagne, poured three glasses, raised his and said, 'Happy anniversary!' before placing the bottle back in an ice bucket and leaving them.

'Before I open my present,' said Beth, eyeing a small, neatly wrapped package on the table in front of her, 'I can't wait to hear how many years the judge added to Miles's sentence.'

'Zero,' replied William. 'In fact, he gave him a get-out-of-jail-free card.'

'What! How can that be possible?'

'Mitigating circumstances, was how the judge described it.'

'Such as?'

'You'll have to ask my father.'

'Who's even less likely to tell me than you.'

William drank his champagne without commenting.

'Booth Watson must have been overjoyed,' said Beth.

'You wouldn't have thought so, judging from the look on his face,' said William. 'In fact, when I saw him in the corridor afterwards, my father told me that, for a moment, he thought BW might even appeal against the sentence. But he must have thought better of it, because in the end, surprise surprise, he tried to take the credit for it.'

'Surely Miles didn't fall for that,' said Beth.

'No, he did not. In fact, I suspect Booth Watson has just lost his most lucrative source of income.'

'Don't underestimate that man,' said Beth. 'He's capable of switching sides faster than a weather vane in a high wind. He'd happily represent Christina without a second thought, and then it would be Miles who had to constantly look over his shoulder.'

'Where no doubt he'd find her accomplice lurking in the shadows,' declared William, then raised his glass and said, 'Happy anniversary, my darling.'

'Happy anniversary. I suppose we ought to raise a glass to Miles Faulkner.'

'Why?'

'Because if he'd pleaded not guilty, we might not be celebrating our anniversary this evening.'

'It must have been a close-run thing,' admitted William.

'Could it have anything to do with you leaping out of bed before the sun had risen to attend another COBRA meeting?' William took a sip of champagne. 'I don't even know what COBRA stands for,' admitted Beth, still pushing at a closed door.

'Cabinet Office Briefing Room,' replied William, without any further explanation.

'And the A?'

'Legend has it that a civil servant added the A as an afterthought, thinking it made the committee sound more important, while others suggest it's simply Committee Room A.'

After a long silence, Beth gave up and turned her attention back to the package in front of her.

'What could this possibly be?' she said as she began to unwrap it. 'A diamond necklace, perhaps?'

'I think you'll have to wait for our tenth anniversary before you can hope for that.'

'Pearls, rubies, or gold?'

'Thirty, forty, and fifty years,' teased William as she slowly removed the red wrapping paper before opening the box to reveal an eternity bracelet.

'How did you know this was exactly what I was hoping for?'

'Possibly because you've been unsubtly hinting about it for the past month,' said William, slipping it onto her wrist, clicking the clasps shut and using the tiny gold screwdriver to lock the bracelet into place.

'A life sentence,' sighed Beth, 'and no one to defend me.'

'I'm sure Booth Watson will be only too happy to represent you, as he's a bit short of clients at the moment.'

'I can't afford him,' said Beth, placing a forearm across her forehead and sighing. 'So sadly, caveman, I'm stuck with you.'

'Who gave you that?' William asked, when he spotted a Tank watch on her wrist that he'd never seen before. 'Do I have a rival?'

'Several. But the answer to your question, Superintendent, is Christina.'

'What a remarkably generous gift. I can assure you that her ex-husband didn't give me anything for fixing his early release.'

Beth raised an eyebrow, but William didn't oblige.

'As always with Christina,' said Beth, 'it's not quite as straightforward as it seems, because I remember her wearing the watch at the Frans Hals opening. But the crocodile strap looks new, and if I'm going to be offered hand-me-downs, who better than Christina to supply them?'

'Does that mean your joint enterprise is flourishing?'

'It certainly does, not least because I recently had a little coup with a Russell Flint watercolour.'

'Father or son?'

'Stop showing off,' said Beth. 'I was able to sell it on to a collector for a handsome return, and as Christina continues to reinvest her share of the profits, I've made her a fifty-fifty partner.'

'You're fast becoming a vulgar capitalist,' said William, after raising his glass once again.

'But for how much longer,' mused Beth, causing William to raise an eyebrow. She took a sip of champagne before answering his unasked question. 'I had a call from the chairman this morning, to let me know that Gerald Sloane has resigned as director.'

'Why would he do that?' William paused before adding, 'There has to be a reason.'

'If there is,' said Beth, 'they're keeping schtum about it.'

'How did you find out?'

'Christina found out when the chairman asked her if she would consider coming back on the board.'

'So she'll know the reason,' said William, then added, 'which means, so do you.'

'Let's just say that three of Sloane's secretaries handed in their notice during the brief time he was director, which the board may have considered to be one too many.'

'There has to be more to it than that.'

'You tell me what you know about Faulkner,' said Beth, 'and I'll tell you what I know about Sloane.'

William seemed to hesitate for a moment, and then thought better of it. 'Will you be applying for the job?,' he said, as if he hadn't heard the question. 'After all, they must realize you're the reason the Hals self-portrait is still hanging on the museum's wall.'

'I'm torn,' said Beth as she took another sip of champagne. 'If I were to become director of the Fitzmolean, it would mean a cut of around fifty per cent of my current income, and back to office hours, which means I'd see far less of the children. At the same time, I'd have to cope with the continual demands to raise funds to keep the museum afloat.'

'Then I'll have to be promoted to Chief Superintendent,' said William.

'Perhaps they won't even offer me the job,' said Beth wistfully.

'They won't make that mistake a second time.'

Lucio reappeared at their table and placed the sole meunière in front of Beth, then reluctantly dumped a portion of fish and chips on William's side of the table. Both of them looked content. The sommelier stepped forward and uncorked the Pouilly-Fumé, pouring a small amount in Beth's glass. She took a sip and smiled. He topped up her glass while Lucio placed a pint of beer in front of William.

Beth had just picked up her knife and fork, when William's mobile began to ring.

'You answer that at your peril, caveman,' said Beth.

William took his mobile from an inside pocket and was about to switch it off when he saw whose number it was flashing up on the screen. The rings continued while he thought about the consequences, but decided to take his life in his hands and pressed the phone to his ear.

'Good evening, sir,' he said. 'Can I assume you're calling to wish Beth and me a happy anniversary, as we're just about to begin our main course.'

'Happy anniversary,' said the Hawk and, without pausing, added, 'I've just had a call from Number . . .' William listened carefully to what the commander had to say, while Beth raised her fish knife high above her head.

'I'm on my way,' he said, switching off his phone and giving his wife an apologetic look.

'Can you think of one good reason why I shouldn't kill you?' she said, her fish knife inching towards his heart.

'No, I can't,' he admitted. 'But could I plead for a stay of execution until after I've seen the Prime Minister?'

Dear Reader,

I hope you have enjoyed William Warwick's latest adventure as much as I enjoyed writing it.

One of the pleasures I get over and above the writing is carrying out detailed research, which adds authenticity to the work. *Next in Line* was no exception. However, I had to take some liberties, not least with the timing of the Last Night of the Proms, and one or two readers might quibble about other, less important, inaccuracies. But before you put pen to paper, please remember, it's a work of fiction, and I just want you to enjoy the story.

Best wishes,
Jeffrey Archer

ACKNOWLEDGEMENTS

My thanks for their invaluable advice and research to:
Simon Bainbridge, Lee Bennet (Sgt Metropolitan Police Ret.),
George Burn, Paul Burrell RVM, Jonathan Caplan QC,
Kate Elton, Craig Hassall AM, Alison Prince,
Bob Sait (Detective Chief Superintendent Metropolitan
Police Ret.),
Ken Wharfe MVO and AW
Jim Beaton GC CVO

Special thanks to:
Detective Sergeant Michelle Roycroft (Ret.)
Chief Superintendent John Sutherland (Ret.)
and Brigadier (Ret.) R Copinger-Symes CBE, Royal Marines

If you've enjoyed
this book, make sure
you've read **all** the
William Warwick
books . . .

THE
WILLIAM WARWICK
NOVELS

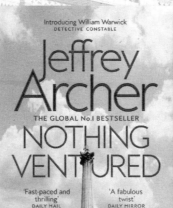

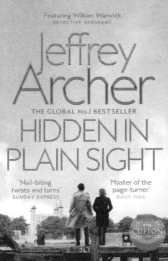

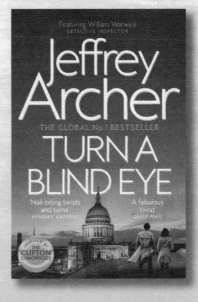

THE LATEST INSTALMENT IN THE SERIES

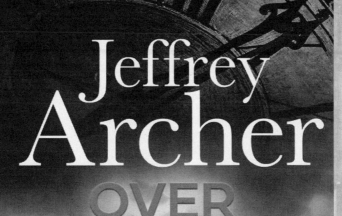

Jeffrey Archer

OVER MY DEAD BODY

'Nail-biting twists and turns'
Sunday Express

'Peerless master of the page-turner'
Daily Mail

REAL READERS LOVE JEFFREY ARCHER
275 MILLION COPIES SOLD

William Warwick
will return in
2023 . . .